SYD MOORE

Witch Hunt

AVON

AVON

A division of HarperCollins*Publishers*
77–85 Fulham Palace Road,
London W6 8JB

www.harpercollins.co.uk

A Paperback Original 2012

1

A catalogue record for this book is
available from the British Library

ISBN-13: 978-1-84756-269-2

Set in Minion by Palimpsest Book Production Limited,
Falkirk, Stirlingshire

Printed and bound in Great Britain by
Clays Ltd, St Ives plc

MIX
Paper from
responsible sources
FSC www.fsc.org **FSC C007454**

Acknowledgements

I must first acknowledge a direct reference to the master of the ghost story, M. R. James. The bone pipe that Felix finds in St Boltolph's bears a close resemblance to the object of evil which Professor Parkins stumbled across all those years ago, in 'Oh, Whistle, and I'll Come to You, My Lad', rated by many as the most terrifying ghost story of all time. For those of you whose whistles have been whet, so to speak, the story can be found in *Count Magnus and Other Ghost Stories*, published by Penguin Classics.

I am also indebted to Richard Deacon's book, *Mathew Hopkins: Witch Finder General*, which planted a seed of doubt concerning the circumstances of Hopkins' death. And to Peter Gant of Manningtree Museum who pointed me in the direction of Malcolm Gaskill's brilliant book, *Witchfinders: A Seventeenth-century English Tragedy*.

Thanks must go to the dedicated staff of Colchester Castle Museum for their help and untiring accommodation of some of my more bizarre requests, particularly the staff member who entered those grim prison cells and measured them for me. I am also grateful to Mark Curteis of Chelmsford Museum, who helped me make an educated guess as to the whereabouts of the gallows erected to execute those condemned in the 1645 trial. Emma Wardall was responsible for smuggling me into the cellars of the old Saracen's Head, where I was to view some strange cells in which, rumour has it, prisoners were kept prior to their trial.

I would like to take a moment to acknowledge my long suffering dad, Tony Moore, and his excellent chauffeuring service, without which I don't know how I could have got around Manningtree, Mistley and some of the more inaccessible points of north Essex (I promise this year I will learn to drive). And also Dave Cresswell for his companionable presence and his invaluable information on mental health procedures. Pat Watkins was also an exceedingly helpful driver and a robust springboard for many of my ideas. Thanks, Pat.

I also need to express gratitude to my sister, Josie, for her kindness and innately helpful nature. And for the long stretches we spent on bony knees laboriously plotting out Hopkins' hot spots in Essex and the witchcraft outbreaks in Massachusetts and Connecticut up to 1692 – a procedure that spanned weeks.

Sincere thanks also go out to: my editor, the lovely Caroline Hogg, who doggedly continues to work with me despite developing phobias about pinecones, cockleshells, Leigh Library Gardens, moths, plastic bags, scratching in attics and now Facebook. Thank you for your determined persistence and insight. To Keshini Naidoo for managing to copy-edit without making me cry (a skill indeed). To Juliet Mushens, fellow Essex Girl, agent extraordinaire and life coach. It is an on-going pleasure to be represented by a chick as glamorous and sassy as she is smart.

To the staff of Waterstones in Southend (especially Sasha James) and Leigh's Book Inn for their continued support. To Colin Sheehan who came up with the concept of turning Mercedes into Sadie, a thoroughly more palatable name for the protagonist of a spooky tale. And also to all my Facebook fans for their support, wisdom and frequently salient advice. To Frank McLoughlin for supplying me with the copy of Hopkins' burial registration. To my test readers Steph Stephenson and Jane Wilkes for their feedback and criticism. And to Kate 'Nobody seems to know what the hell is going on' Bradley for her enduring faith and flashes of brilliance. Thank you, my friend.

To Sean, Riley, Mum, Ernie, Pauline, Richard, Jess, Kit, Samuel, Steph Roche, Ian, Rachel L, Colette, Jude, Heidi, Jo, Hob, Rach, Caroline, Liz, Jo, Midge, Tammy and everyone that has taken the time to encourage me.

This book and its success belong to all of you.

For those who were prevented from telling their story.
And for Granddad York.

'Besides, when any Errour is committed
Whereby wee may Incurre or losse or shame,
That wee ourselves thereof may be acquitted
Wee are too ready to transferre the blame
Upon some Witch: That made us does the same.
It is the vulgar Plea that weake ones use
I was bewitch'd: I could nor will: nor chuse.
But my affection was not caus'd by Art:
The witch that wrought on mee was in my brest.'

Sir Francis Hubert
Quoted in *Witchcraft in Tudor and
Stuart England* by Alan MacFarlane

'The tools of conquest do not necessarily come with
bombs and explosions and fallout. There are weapons
that are simply thoughts, ideas, prejudices, to be found
only in the minds of men. For the record, prejudices
can kill and suspicion can destroy. A thoughtless, frightened search for a scapegoat has a fallout all its own for
the children yet unborn.'

Rod Serling, creator of *The Twilight Zone*
and civil rights activist

Prologue

They told me not to come.

He said 'Twill do no good. Nay more.' And he tried to touch my shoulder and bring me back into the court but I was too quick and ran pushing through the crowd. Some saw me and stepped aside, unwilling to be touched, as if they might catch my sin. Others shrieked.

I made off through the side lane.

And then I came here.

I have put on my cap and wrapped a shawl over too. So none may see me.

Though I see all.

And I see them: bound and tethered in a pen.

Like sheep.

Then there are the others, the eager spectators.

So many cluster before me, edging their way forward, craning to get a good view, that I can only catch glimpses through the space between my neighbours' shoulders. On their faces some have smiles. The girl beside me, only two or three years younger than I, licks her lips and stands up on her toes. Her father, in starched lace and black, pulls her back down and, with a stare, admonishes her excitement. But the woman beside him, whom

3

I saw at a stall selling nuts for the crowd, has a face full of glory. Her eyes are wide in anticipation. In her hands she has a knife and fingers it greedily. She will try to get some hair from the dead for keepsakes to sell on.

A hush falls over the crowd as the first is helped up to the scaffold. I can see from the way she stumbles it is Old Mother Clarke. Her ancient face is creased with lines of age and knots of confusion. Two of the men assisting the execution have taken an arm each to support her, for she cannot stand firm with but one leg. She staggers forward and clutches the man on her right to steady herself as the hangman puts the noose over her head.

A woman at the front of the crowd near the gallows hurls something rotten. It hits Mother Clarke on the chin and she looks about to throw some rebuke back but before she can open her mouth comes the push. Her wizened frame drops and cracks as the noose does its work. Quickly. Thank God. And she is turned off.

Next it is Anne Leech. Younger than Mother Clarke, she wrestles with the hangman as much as she can with her hands and feet bound. There is little way to fight. But she will not go without one. One of the throng of eager spectators, a man with a red beard and broad shoulders, goads her and calls 'Witch. You will go to the Devil now.' Anne always had more spirit than others and she spits at him and calls out a curse. The crowd starts to move, excited by the show, laughing as the hangman roughly slips over the noose. But Anne is angry and wild. She begins to bring down a curse on the hangman, but cannot finish: a shove from behind stops her words. But it does not stop her life and she twists and turns on the end of the line like a fish from the brook. The hangman speaks to the man at his side and points to the cross beam. The rope is coming apart. He calls for a ladder but not in time for the rope to unravel and Anne falls with it to the ground, catching the side of the scaffold as she goes down.

The crowd surges forward to watch. She is picked up and shown. To their delight they see she has dashed out an eye and is carried back up to the third noose and hanged once more. A deep red drip from her face darkens her dress yet still the twitching goes on. A girl at the front runs forward to pull on her legs but she is stopped by the broad-shouldered man.

Above Anne the hangman and his men throw up another rope. Elizabeth Clarke is being taken down. I cannot see where they take her corpse.

And there is another witch now on the platform. I do not know her name. She has soiled herself with fear. It is hot and her face is greasy with sweat. As she is brought to Elizabeth's noose she falls down in a fainting fit and is dragged over to the side. The hangman calls for a pitcher of water to rouse her. She must be awake to see her end.

And then she is there on the scaffold. Her long black locks move gently as she turns to the noose. I gasp as I see her watch Anne's feet jerking without rhythm to her side. But she says nothing. She is solemn. Silent. Unhearing of the jeers of the crowd come to witness her end. But I see her eyes searching over the faces.

For a moment I think perhaps our eyes meet and I see in them a movement, a quick darting, a widening of the whites. Does she see me? I raise up my face and move back my shawl, bolder now, unconcerned about what the spectators may do if they recognise me. My confidence is short-lived: I pull back suddenly and flinch as the noose comes down over her slender white neck. Her mouth opens and I think she is about to speak but I cannot be sure because she has been pushed from the stool. The noose has strung tight. Her neck snaps to an unnatural angle, the feet kick out and then are still.

And I fall to my knees and am sick across the cobbles.

Oh God have mercy, what have I done?

What have I done?

Chapter One

11th October, 2012

It was the night that I bumped into Joe. So I guess, you could say that it wasn't ALL bad. I mean, it was terrible. There was no getting away from it: painful, gut-churning and all the rest. But at least something *good* came from it.

And when I say I bumped into Joe I mean exactly that. Literally. I was drunk, but in my defence I had had a seriously bad day. Anyway, there I was, coming down from the high giddy arc of a – even if I do say so myself – quite magnificent thrashing pirouette.

I *know*. At my age: thirty-three going on fifteen. Ridiculous.

Though to be fair, I had checked with the fount of all knowledge, Maggie Haines, beforehand.

'Am I too old to slam in the moshpit?' I had been swaying even then. Maggie, my dear friend, sometimes boss and celebrated editor of arts magazine, *Mercurial*, had peered at me and wriggled her button nose. Her face had a distinctly kittenish appearance, which was thoroughly misleading. The pretty feline exterior concealed a steely determination and unsettling intelligence that had notched up two degrees and an MA and which had far more in common with panthers than domestic cats. I knew Maggie would give it to me straight – no messing. She was sober and had a grim look about her. And she hadn't wanted us to go to the club at all. In fact she'd been dead set on getting me straight home; I think I must have already been in a right old state when we'd left the pub. We were on the way to the local cab rank just a couple of blocks down when I heard the music coming from the basement of a venue and decided we should all go in. She'd said no. In fact she'd said 'No way,' and tried to wrap me up in her embrace and physically carry me down the road. But Jules, Maggie's hubby, put a staying hand on her arm and said, 'Let her.' Then he'd turned to me and said, 'Just for a bit, Sadie, okay?'

This time, though, Maggie looked like she was coming back with a firm 'no', but Jules convinced her (I think he'd had a few drinks and was starting to liven up a bit himself).

'Look around you, Sadie,' he said in answer to my question, with a grin that was only half-formed. There was sympathy in it and hints of condescension, but I didn't care. I followed his lead and stole a wider glance at the club. Stifling and dimly lit, it was packed full of sweaty bodies in varying states of inebriation and spatial coordination. The outfit on stage was playing at full pelt and the throng of clubbers clustered at their feet were going for it.

'Go on then,' Jules said. 'But we'll go straight home afterwards. Pogo is de rigueur here. Don't worry about your age. It's a punk covers band. We're surrounded by middle-aged spread. That bloke down the front with the red mohican looks past sixty.'

He was right. The place was jammed with bald heads and beer bellies. Not a pretty sight. The majority of blokes

8

were in the full throes of midlife crisis, desperately trying to hold on to their proudly misspent youth. The band themselves would have averaged about fifty-five in a '*10 Years Younger'* age poll. Though if you went on energy levels alone, you'd put them in their early twenties. They were setting the crowd on fire.

Saying that, you can't go wrong with the Buzzcocks, can you?

So, once I'd been granted permission, I launched myself into the front of the crowd and for about three minutes and twenty seconds I was able to submerge myself in the thumped-up beat and drag my head away from the awful images reeling in my head. Ironically the only time my thoughts stilled that day were as my body whirled and whirled.

For that, I will always salute thee, Punk Rock.

So, what happened was this; the alcohol had interfered with my sense of perspective and, in addition, boosted my energy. The result was a grand overshooting of the moshpit. In fact, I think if Joe hadn't been there with his mates, I probably would have landed flat on my arse amongst the broken glass at the edge of the dance floor.

That would not have been a great look.

But he was.

A six-foot-something, human monolith, standing there, very upright, radiating principle and that good old-fashioned honesty of his. You could suss his confidence from the way he owned his space. He was firm. Unfazed. And, luckily, ready to cushion my fall. I remember the way he propped me back up and looked at me, and, because he was out of his usual context, I had a split second of objectivity. I took in the regulation cropped brown hair, the round wholesome eyes and not-so-designer stubble, casual t-shirt, jeans, trainers. He could have been a manual labourer: a carpenter or a builder. He had a pint in his hand and a cheeky grin on his face that gave him dimples. I remember thinking 'Not bad at all,' and then doing some hurried shoe shuffle on the floor to correct my balance and retrieve what shreds were left of my dignity. And then he said, 'Nice of you to drop in on me like this, Sadie.'

I recognised the voice and looked closer and said, 'Oh. Joe?'

And he laughed and said, 'One and the same.'

But after that, it's just fragments.

I must have talked to him and his mates for a bit till I returned to the dance floor, pulling Joe greedily and then taking him with me. I don't think he particularly wanted to dance. In fact, even though my perception was pretty clouded, I got the impression he was just going on bodyguard duty for me.

Then I rebounded back to Maggie and Jules and introduced him. I think they were saying that they wanted to go but I wanted to stay, and made some big dramatic thing of finding my drink and downing it in one. I bet that's what pushed me over the edge, because the next moment I was in the toilets revisiting the dignified spread that had been supplied earlier at the pub.

When I came back Maggie and Jules had got my coat and Joe had got his.

Maggie said, 'I dunno – he's offered to drive us home. How many has he had?'

I laughed and said, 'Not likely to have had any, Mags. He's a copper.' Then I got twisted up in my coat and Jules frowned.

I think Joe must have heard all that because he leant over and flashed his warrant card and said, 'It's all right, I'm not over the limit. She's off her head and needs to go.'

And I put my arm round his shoulders and said, 'But I haven't been cunting at all Drinkstable.' Then I hiccupped.

When I woke up in the back of Joe's car we were outside my flat. Maggie and Jules had already been dropped off. Joe brought me up the stairs of my small flat. I think he even carried me into my bedroom, laid me on the bed and took my shoes off. And that was over and above the call of duty to be sure.

I remember trying to kiss him. And that he pulled away and said, 'Not tonight, Sadie. I would but I can't.' Then he did that phone thing that people do with their hands – an L-shape like an old receiver – you call me or I'll call you.

I think he was sympathetic.

But when he closed the door I started bawling. And I carried on doing that till I passed out.

What a mess.

To be expected I suppose.

After all, it's not every day you bury your mum.

Chapter Two

Tuesday, 17th October

It began like a drip in a far off place. A vast echoing chamber. Or a faltering trickle into a dark yawning cave. First sibilance. Just off a hiss. Followed by a wheezy gasping sound. 'Ssss – rhey.'

Was it drawing closer or becoming louder? It was certainly getting clearer, wafting to me on an unfelt breeze. 'Sorr- rhey.' Puffed out in tones of torment. Fleshed out with a sob.

Falling on my ears, with a cold snatch of breath I got it. The single word. And it was on my lips. 'Sorry.'

Then I was sitting up in bed, awake. Fully alert. Despite the lightness of the cotton nightie sweat had pooled under my breasts. I was gulping down air as if I had only just reached the surface of some dark, subterranean lake. The bed sheet was twisted around my legs like a boa constrictor trying to eat me alive and my heart was banging like mad.

What *was* that?

Had I said that? Or was someone in the flat?

I strained to listen into its depths.

The hum of the fridge. The trees shushing in the breeze outside my window. The sound of roadworks further up the hill. A door slamming in the neighbour's flat. The deceleration of a train pulling into Chalkwell station.

But nothing else. No one in the flat.

It must have been me.

Well, I knew I had just articulated the word – said it out loud as I was coming into consciousness. But I had a notion that I was merely repeating someone else's plaintive cries.

Sorry.

It had happened several times since the funeral. Each time I had woken up from a nightmare I couldn't remember, with the absolute conviction I was not on my own.

But then, the mind has a funny way of dealing with grief.

And of course, I *was* sorry.

Terribly.

The guilt was almost unbearable.

I knew Mum had been trying to talk to me. That last time we were alone at the hospice. I'd walked in to find her sleeping, so had kissed her on her forehead. Her hair was spread like a black fan across her pillow. She had been a young mum, and if you looked past the lines the illness had carved on her face, with her perfect semi-circles of long dark lashes and her thick black hair, she was still as serene and beautiful as a Renaissance Madonna.

But she'd woken at my touch and when she realised it was me she'd made a big thing of trying to meet my eyes. At first I thought she said, 'Sadie – fit.' It was difficult to tell. Her speech was much impaired since the last stroke. She'd been left with paralysis on the left side of her face and was unable to move her left arm.

'You okay, Mum?'

She was frustrated. 'Ift.'

I said nothing, waiting for her to try another attempt.

She struggled up a bit. I reached behind her and helped her sit up onto the pillows, plumping them carefully as she rested her neck.

She took a breath and looked at me. Her mouth opened, tongue lolling to the front. 'Gift.'

'A gift?'

She nodded.

'Okay. Who for?'

She moved her good hand in my direction. 'You.'

'You have a gift for me?' I looked at the bedside table. Glass, hand cream, anglepoise lamp.

'No. Come.' She paused for breath. 'To . . . you.'

'I have a gift coming?'

She expelled a lungful of air and shuddered. I could see the frustration scratching across her face. 'Speak Dan.'

Dan was my mum's boyfriend of about twelve years. A nice chap with a heart of gold. But he'd gone AWOL a couple of days before and Mum was in a real state about it, naturally. The poor woman was totally incapacitated, unable to do anything to find out where he was.

Thing was, Mum and Dan had a lot of things in common. They were both educators; both furious campaigners for human rights; and they both loved me. But, and this was a big but, they had both experienced long periods of depression. Mum's strokes had been a result of high blood pressure, which, in turn, it was suggested, had been brought about by her often high state of anxiety. See, Mum didn't have bouts of sadness, she had episodes of deep clinical depression, some of which developed into psychosis and paranoia. Just like Dan. In fact, that's where they had met – in a private clinic. Therefore we were all concerned about his absence. I shook my head and said, 'We still can't find him, Mum. He's not at work. He must have had to go somewhere urgently.'

Mum did a shrugging sort of action with her good side and said, 'Sadie.' She made a move that looked like she was trying to shake her head, making an effort to form her lips and shape the words. Though her dark eyes were alert I couldn't understand her, so I took her good hand and placed a pencil in it. Mum's elegant fingers groped for the pad of paper that never left her side. It took her a while.

Her writing was getting worse. When she finished I tried to decipher what she'd written. I could make out a 'B' then an 'O' but the figure after it could have either been an 'X' or a 'K'.

I looked at Mum. 'Box?'

Mum's lips suckered in. She looked more fragile than ever. Then she let out a wail and started to judder, her head shaking back and forth. It was so frustrating for her.

With the functioning side of her face she tried to speak. 'Earme.' Working hard to take in a good breath of air, she swallowed and said, 'Portent.' She was really het up. I hated to see her like that but I just couldn't understand her meaning.

'Sorry, sorry.' I focused on the writing. Perhaps it wasn't an X but an O and a K? 'Book?'

She made a sound like the air going out of a balloon. I leant in and smiled at her. She was sweating and her hair was messed up. I pushed a couple of black strands away from her eyes. Despite everything, she still had only a dusting of grey.

Stiff creases divided her forehead. Her good hand was

clenched into a fist. She was working out how to say what she needed to tell me.

I cut in, trying to relieve her of the effort. 'Okay, the book. I know you don't like the idea but Mum . . .'

She made a strangled sort of sound, then slumped back into her pillows, giving up communicating. But her hand crept into mine. I squeezed it. Gently.

See, I finally got my book commissioned ten days previously. It wasn't life-changing but it was definitely a good deal. In between the various loops and curves of my volatile career as a freelance journalist, I had been writing a book on the Essex witches.

Mum always said she thought we were distantly related to one. And there was this song, an old Essex folk ballad, *The Weeping Willow*, which Mum thought was connected to an ancestor. And there was a game in the playground: the kids would form a circle around one blindfolded child, the 'witch', and then you'd all dance around. When the verse ended the blindfolded child would try to catch one of the circle dancers. Whoever they caught was out. I can't remember all of it but there are a couple of verses that stick:

> *They kicked them off and laid them down*
> *And put them in the cold hard ground*
> *The summer wind blew long and chill*
> *The Divil bade her do his will*
> *Pale and wild pale and wild*
> *The witch did down the child*
>
> *She picked her up and put her down*
> *The willow's leaves wrapped round and round*

Her evil cries filled the air
And so did end the bad affair
Pale and wild pale and wild
The witch did up end the child

I think it was the song that got me interested, even as a child. That, my mother's proud connection to it, and the fact that Essex had so many witches. There was folklore and myths about them everywhere I turned. And, if I'm honest, I did seek them out. I was always a bit of a spooky girl, fascinated by rather macabre stories and shrunken heads. My dad tried to get me interested in Roald Dahl, but to his great disappointment I quickly cast off *Charlie and the Chocolate Factory* in favour of *Tales of the Unexpected*. As I got older, I started delving into the witch hunts. It turned out to be rather sobering. In fact I soon became both horrified and hooked. The statistics were phenomenal: between 1580 to 1690 the combined total of indictments for witchcraft in Hertford, Kent, Surrey and Sussex was 222. In Essex alone over the same amount of time it was 492 – although recent studies put the number at 503. More than most other counties in the UK, by a long stretch. All those poor souls put to death by superstition. And did we know their names? No. We knew about the Witchfinders: James I, Matthew Hopkins, John Stearne. But if you were asked to name one of their many victims you'd be lost.

When I read about their stories I was revolted. They stayed with me. I just couldn't get them out of my head.

I'd been a freelance writer for several years and I guess a book is always floating somewhere in the back of your mind. But it seemed almost like the idea just sprang into my mind, fully formed, like it had been nestling in the shadows all the time. I spent some time on a synopsis and had pitched it to a fair few publishers. I knew Mum was proud of me – she had wanted to write herself and even considered going into publishing when she was a teenager. She once told me she did work experience but had been put off. She wouldn't say why. But she was pleased, I think, in that way that parents are, that I was doing what she had failed to. Anyway, the book was not met with the unbridled enthusiasm I had expected. In fact, I had had a series of rejection letters and was just about to go back to the drawing board, when I got a call from Emma of Portillion Books. She loved my sample chapter, and what she called my 'fresh new unstuffy voice'. The proposal, she said, had been presented in an acquisitions meeting and got a rapturous reception. Consequently, I had been given a contract.

I was elated.

But there was a fly in the ointment: Portillion Books were the literary part of the Robert Cutt empire. The owner of a fleet of fast food restaurants, a football club, a few social networking sites, several magazines and two new private academies in London, Cutt was a powerful tycoon and a generous donor to the Conservative Party. The current rumour was that he was hoping to be made a Lord with a view to fast-tracking to a cabinet position. Political commentators were speculating that the Department of Culture, Media and Sport had already reserved him a parking space.

In our house Cutt's name was a swear word. He wasn't known for his great pay and conditions and cracked, as in *broke*, most of the unions his workers had been affiliated to. Plus, he was generally a bit of a git. Ruthless, you know the sort – did well out of the banking crisis. You could see corruption all over his face whenever his mug was in the papers.

I came from a firmly socialist background. Mum, a History teacher, and Dad, with his background in trade unions, constantly railed against continued control and acquisition of British media till Dad departed when I was sixteen. Dan had been less vehement when he came on the scene in my early twenties, but only fractionally. Unsurprisingly, Cutt was our antichrist.

But I was desperate to get my book published and I kind of felt that I'd have to swallow down my righteous outrage to get the witches' stories out. It was a compromise, true, but I was prepared to make it. A whole chunk of me didn't like or approve of that, but I was weak. And okay, okay, if I'm honest, there was the ego thing going on. It was, I justified to myself, only the book wing of Cutt's empire, after all.

Mum, on the other hand . . . When I'd sprung it on her she'd had a mixed reaction. At first she was over the moon to hear I'd at long last got a book deal, but then, when I told her who it was with, her expression dimmed. She'd started trying to say something about jewellery. I don't know if she was making some point about wealth or something but whatever it was she'd got so distressed that the nurse, Sally, had to come in and sedate her. It was horrible. I didn't ever want to see that again.

So you can see why, on that particular day, when she was really not looking very well at all, I was trying really hard to sound upbeat and positive about it all.

'I'm due to meet Emma next week.' My voice sounded purposefully cheery. 'I'm so excited. I'll get the contract, then

19

as soon as I sign it they'll give me part of my advance. Isn't that great? I mean it's so tough being freelance. A lump sum will really help out. And it's my chance to get the stories of the witches out there. Maybe I can find our ancestral witch. And if we *are* related, then surely it's a kind of duty too?'

Mum was frowning and doing her best to say something, but I didn't want to hear what she had to say. I wanted her just to listen and be proud of me and to say it was okay.

And it wasn't only that which made me fill up every inch of breathing and conversation space in her room in the hospice that afternoon. No. At the back of my mind there was the notion that what she truly wanted to tell me was that she loved me and I couldn't let her. Don't get me wrong – we did tell each other quite often, but there was something in the atmosphere that afternoon that made me desperately not want to hear it. Almost as if I did then there would be finality in the words. For if she told me she loved me and I told her I loved her too everything would be harmonious, and she would be able to slip off away into the everworld, her work here done.

And I didn't want that. I wasn't ready to lose her just yet. So I didn't let her speak.

God, if only I had. I should have. I should have let her tell me.

She so wanted to. In fact, she was struggling with all her might to tell me.

And now, I know what it was, I am ashamed.

She was seriously worried – rightly so.

If I'd let her speak she would have told me the truth. Then maybe I would have been forewarned. And forewarned is, as they say, forearmed.

But I didn't, did I?

I gabbled on and on until the nurse came in and had to administer the drugs. And then Mum was tired. When I came back in, she had fallen asleep. So I went home.

And it was that night, as the moon sailed upwards, my mother, along with her unspoken words, finally let go.

But I couldn't.

And now I was haunted by my stupid stupid actions. Hearing the word 'sorry' in my dreams, waking up to unknown sobs.

I moved my legs off the bed and crept into the shower.

Unfortunately there are some stains that just won't wash away.

Chapter Three

I thought grief would be the worst thing.

Though Mum's health had been on a steep decline, and I more or less expected it, when death actually came it still shocked me.

During the first few days after she went, there had been pain. Then the sharpness of it eroded, and I was left with this sense of great guilt. Which was worse. Though this guilt *was* an energiser. It could have made me go round the bend it was so great. But I found a way of handling it – as soon as it came upon me in the mornings, I went into action, hoping that physical exertion might knock regret from its number one spot at the forefront of my mind. It kind of felt that if I didn't do that, then it would engulf me entirely. Then I could see myself just sitting in the flat, crying and crying on my own. I didn't want that. Mum wouldn't have wanted that. So I went with the extreme activity option.

That morning, after I had rinsed as much shame as I could out of my hair, I combed it out in front of the living room mirror. In my twenties I'd earned the nickname 'Lois Lane' amongst my friends and peers, partly because I shared a terrier-like commitment to my cub reporter's role on the local rag. It wasn't quite the *Daily Planet*, but I was proud of what I did and used to talk about it non-stop. But there was also a physical resemblance to the actress in the TV series of *Superman*, Teri Hatcher. We were both dark, had well-defined eyebrows and had short, sassy bobs. I didn't mind the comparison.

In the mirror today, a pale reflection stared back. I looked worse than I'd expected: my eyes, though grey, had a purple darkness about them – the surrounding skin was dry and blotchy and pink from bouts of unscheduled weeping. My hair, black like Mum's, was broken up with russet lowlights though there was a good inch of regrowth that needed attention. And I was thinner. Maybe half a stone less than I was two weeks ago. Most people wouldn't mind that, but it made me look gaunt: although Dad was unusually tall (six foot three), my slight frame had come from the maternal line.

Jeez. In the harsh daylight I looked like I could have been in a car crash. In fact, I thought, as I went into the bedroom and dried myself, that was far too generous. In this light, I could pass for a junkie who had been in a car crash. I made a mental note to buy some decent food, and get a haircut. Then I threw on my 'uniform': black jeans, black shirt, suit jacket (to lend it formality) and trainers (comfy).

Once dried and dressed I returned to the living room and got my laptop out. As I powered it up, I could hear scratching above me in the loft. It had been going on for a few days now. I needed to call out pest control; I added it to my list of things to do. It was probably rats but didn't help at all with my state of mind – it sounded like my conscience itching.

I had enough time to go through some emails before I

needed to set out for the offices of *Mercurial* for an appointment with Maggie.

I padded round my flat, cooking up a strong coffee and installing myself in the living room. Despite its modest dimensions, I did love the place. Tucked under the eaves of a 1970s purpose-built block, I had a smallish bedroom, bathroom and kitchen, and a very spacious living room that doubled as a dining room and study. It was sparsely furnished. I'd not taken much with me when I split up with Christopher, my last long-term boyfriend. Just the high quality stereo, a very comfy leather armchair and this gorgeous antique mirror he bought me from Camden Lock market. I knew the ornate rococo decoration and black stains on the bevelled plate were at odds with the modern minimal interiors he admired, so it was a kind of testament to his initial affection. He made no effort to keep it when we were divvying up our joint goods so I'd kept it in storage until I got this flat, then hung it in pride of place over the mantelpiece, where I gazed at it from my writing desk. This was an old glass dining table, which I had shoved towards the floor-to-ceiling windows that led out onto my balcony.

Our block had a particularly glorious vista – looking over the railway station to the beach, yacht club and tidal plains of the estuary. Chalkwell was a good location. I'd chosen it for its transport links to London. My relocation didn't happen overnight as I still had a lot of work in London and had to make the trip into town at least two or three times a week. But it was only a forty-five-minute journey from here and I'd always liked the place; mostly populated by elderly couples and families, it felt safe and as a newly single young woman, that was a primary concern. When I first saw the flat, it was the view that got me. Sunny mornings would see the front room filled with the unimpeded honey rays that crept up over Southend's pier (the longest pleasure pier in the world, don't you know). And, if you were lucky in the evenings you'd get a front seat view of Mother Nature's chosen sunset, framed lovingly by the tops of the oaks in the front garden.

That morning's clouds, however, were wearing the same dark grey shroud they had done since the funeral. It seemed everything had muted itself in respect.

I took a look at the incoming tide and sat down at the desk, ready to click on the internet icon.

The big life stuff, the events that change your life – the births, the deaths, the crises, always start in a small way, I've found, with a twinge or a rumble or blip. And that's more or less how this story began. In a very ordinary, mundane manner.

I ignored the strong pull of my guilt trip and went straight into email. There was a message from one of my local news contacts asking me if I could interview a couple about a fundraising effort. I replied that I could fit it in within the next two days, noted the address and then scrolled down past the offers of Viagra to an email from someone called Felix Knight at Portillion Publishing. The Felix guy was introducing himself ahead of tomorrow's meeting. My editor Emma, he explained, had been promoted into another division and he had been handed responsibility for my book. He was extremely excited about it, looking forward to meeting me and suggested that, after a formal introduction in the office, we have lunch at a nearby restaurant.

I liked the sound of Felix but, to be frank, I was happy

to work with anyone who was happy to work with me. I replied that that would be 'fantastic' and I was very much looking forward to meeting him too.

My next email was an old friend expressing condolences. I clicked on the link and went through to Facebook. Then I did the standard reply: 'Thank you. Yes, it's been crap, but I'm getting on with life.' I had to deal with it this way – if I went into detail I was worried that I'd unleash a torrent of real grief that might wash me away. I was about to shut down, when a message box popped up on the screen.

Unusually, it had no name attached. There was still the regular green dot in the top left-hand corner and the other function symbols across the toolbar. But no name. I looked down at the message.

'Are you there?' It read.

Of course I bloody am, I thought. But I simply wrote, 'Yes.' Then I waited, curious to see who it was.

Nothing happened for a few seconds then the words 'Where are you?' appeared.

What did that mean? Most of my Facebook friends knew I had moved out of the Smoke eighteen months ago.

A little irritated by the stupidity of the question, I chucked it back at the unknown messenger. 'Where are *you*?' and sat back to see the response.

There was a bit of a time delay. I glanced at my watch. I couldn't spend long on this joker as I should be getting my stuff together to leave fairly soon.

Then the words popped up on the screen, 'I can hear you but I can't see you.'

Mmm. Weird. I regarded the screen for a moment then retyped: 'Where are you?'

26

A breeze outside nudged the oak leaves against the window. They sounded like little metallic fingertips on the panes.

The reply came up: 'I do not know. Everything is dark here.'

Okay, this was getting creepy. What to do? Coming up with no good reply, I sat still and contemplated the screen.

My correspondent was typing. 'There is only blackness,' they wrote.

Then underneath that, 'I am scared.'

That stopped me.

Was this a joke? An inappropriate friend trying to freak me out? Some random viral marketing ploy? I tried to think of a way to respond without looking stupid if it *was* a prank. Though, at the back of my mind, I was wondering about what to do if it wasn't.

'Who are you?' I tapped out on the keys and hit enter.

'I'm sorry,' they replied.

I stopped and looked at it. Then I swallowed. The words had been on my lips just an hour ago.

Then another line of text: 'Hush.'

Hush? That was an odd choice of word.

Quickly, more text appeared. 'He may come back.'

Now cynicism was overruled by a more concerning impulse.

'Who might?' I wrote. 'Who might be coming back?'

The screen was still for a moment, then the words 'Oh God' tapped out on the screen.

Without letting my head intervene in my now more emotional response, I wrote 'Where are you? Are you okay?' But when I hit enter this time my screen died and turned to black.

I cursed and looked down at the on button. My battery had run out.

I hastily reached for the power cable and plugged it in. The computer took several frustrating seconds to reboot and when I returned to the site there was nothing there. No box. No evidence of our conversation. I scrolled down my list of online friends. There was no one I didn't recognise.

I could have left it alone, but a part of me felt responsible. After all, this hadn't been a chat room – it had been a dialogue with one other person. A private communication sent only to me. I was troubled but not yet scared. Just worried that I hadn't stepped up to my civic duty if indeed, this was a genuine message. Crap. This had to be the last thing I needed right now – more guilt.

I bit my lip then made a decision, pulled out my mobile and dialled the one person who I could possibly pass this on to. I was in no fit state to get involved with anyone else's business right now.

He answered pretty quickly. 'Hello, Sadie. How are you feeling?'

So thoughtful, always concerned about others. You could see why he'd entered the police force. He was a nice bloke. And he'd been a good friend. In fact, before I met Christopher, he'd been more than just a friend. I'd met Joe six years ago, whilst covering some high-ranking officer's retirement. It was lucky I had taken the job. I'd hooked it on impulse as Mum was on a bit of a low and I wanted to spend more time with her. As soon as I met him, there was an instant connection: we ended up drunkenly eating chips on the seafront and watching the moon set over Canvey Island. He had a really lovely smile (those dimples were just gorgeous) and a kooky sense of humour that chimed with mine. One thing had led to another and another. We were both due some time off so I didn't leave his flat for two days and nights. We followed it up with the usual sort of thing – trips to the cinema, dinner, a fabulous weekend break in the country. It was great. But I knew I had to go back to London, and somehow, despite the fact it wasn't that far away, I think I had it in my mind that it was only a holiday romance, something casual. Not that we ever discussed it, but he was four years younger than me. It doesn't seem much now, but at the time I was twenty-seven, and twenty-three seemed way too young to be serious. When he went off to Carlisle for training and Mum felt better I returned to my life in the metropolis. We texted each other a few times, but he backed off completely when I started seeing Christopher. Yet he still had a physical effect on me. I'd bumped into him a couple of times since I'd moved back and could never stop myself stealing furtive glances at his sinewy frame. Even now I had to do my best to sound together and competent, instead of breathy and slightly chaotic.

'Hi Joe, I'm okay.'

'Glad to hear it,' he said. 'You must have had a bad hangover after the other night.' I could tell he was smiling as he spoke. Voices sound more distinct when mouths are pulled wide. Then, remembering the specific occasion of my last major bender, he took his voice down a note and hastily added, 'Understandable of course.'

I took it in my stride. 'I'm okay, honestly. Thanks for, er, helping out. I'm sorry if I, er, embarrassed you . . .' Oh God, there was that image – me catching his lapel, pulling him down, slobbering all over him. I pushed the mortifying grope from my mind and concentrated on the present issue.

Joe was generous. 'Think nothing of it.' It was a full stop on the matter.

Gallant too. You absolute gem, I thought.

'Listen,' I said, changing the subject super quick. 'I've just had a weird thing happen.' And I explained about the messaging.

I hadn't expected him to laugh, but that's what he did. It left me feeling stupid and gauche.

'Someone's having you on, Sadie,' was his conclusion. 'You wouldn't believe the number of calls we get about this sort of stuff. Texts, emails. It's all part of new generation cyber-crime.'

Now I was cross, bordering on outraged. Not at him. At the unknown idiot who had virtually freaked me. 'Well, who would do that to me? Especially now. When, you know, I'm a little more fragile than . . .'

Joe's voice piped up, the perfect example of good victim support training, 'Don't take it personally. You're probably a random selection. There's some bored teenager chuckling away in his bedroom right now. In future, don't respond. If you don't engage them, they'll get bored and move on to something else.'

It seemed like sensible advice, so I agreed not to.

'Is there anything else I can do you for, Ms Asquith?' Was it me or was there a teensy bit of hope in his voice?

The question was open-ended, leaving it up to me to pick up the ball and run. I told him, 'Right this minute, no, just the dodgy internet business. But I'll call you soon. For a drink maybe?' He said that would be nice and I thanked him for his advice.

'Glad to be of service to the public, madam.' He was very jovial. 'Now take care of yourself and feel free to phone me if this sort of thing happens again.'

I told him I definitely would and hung up, a little thrill rippling through me.

Now I was fifteen minutes behind schedule.

I had stuff to get on with so slammed the laptop shut, got my things together then whizzed out the door.

The gloomy October morning had bled into a gloomy October afternoon. The light breeze had notched up into a strong south-easterly wind and was whipping rubbish into tiny twisters, screeching through the bare branches of the sycamores that bordered the wide Georgian avenues of Southend's conservation area. Everybody on the street was buttoned up, faces down, slanting diagonally into its oncoming draughts.

The offices of *Mercurial,* a quarterly arts magazine, were nestled between an ancient accountancy firm and a design agency. I liked working for them. They were cool: as a freelance writer who specialised in Essex affairs, kudos was rather thin on the ground, and the mag's cachet rubbed off on me.

It was now eighteen months that I'd been living in the borough of Southend. Initially, my move had been born out of an urge to be closer to Mum. Her health was going downhill and although Dan was around, I wanted to be there for her too. Then after I split up with Christopher, London quickly lost some of its shine and I accelerated the relocation.

It had been good for me. Though I kept my hand in with my old bosses in London, I had enjoyed rediscovering my old patch. Southend had grown and changed. Lots of things were going on and *Mercurial* reflected that. They were good to know – always had an ear to the ground – and I had actually grown very fond of the staff at the office. For a bunch of artistic individuals they were all pretty down to earth.

I'd known Maggie for nigh on twenty-five years, as we'd attended the same high school. Though you'd never believe it to look at her now, she was actually far more rebellious than I in our youth: we shared clothes; a couple of boyfriends and several cigarettes down the bottom of the sports field, promptly losing touch when we left school and went on to different universities. When our paths crossed again, a couple of years ago, she invited me for lunch and we soon ping-ponged into regular friends again.

I think it was on our third or fourth lunch date, as we knocked back a few glasses of plonk, that Maggie suggested I wrote a small piece for her mag. I leapt at the chance and once the shrewd editor – rather than the friend – worked out that I was as good as I said I was, she began feeding me more assignments.

Mags was what my dad would call a good egg: helping a lot over the past few months and especially kind when Mum died.

She was sucking on the end of a biro, squinting at a document several pages in length, in the small box room she called her office. The sash window was a couple of inches open. Still, the air was thick with the stink of cigarettes and Yves St Laurent's *Paris*.

'You'll have to get an air freshener. You must be getting through bottles of perfume,' I said as I sauntered in and threw my satchel on the floor. 'And it's against the law now, you know.'

Maggie's tangle of pillar-box red hair jerked up. She dropped the pen on the mound of paper. 'Shit, Sadie! Can't you knock before you come in?'

She looked funny like that – all indignant eyes and open mouth. 'Everyone else has to go outside for a fag,' I chastised her half-heartedly.

She shrugged, relaxing now and held her hands up in mock surrender. 'I'm giving up. Seriously. Did you know it's bad for you?'

I said I hadn't heard that.

'Just got really into this submission,' she was justifying herself. 'New writer. Very good. All about the internet: Facebook, Twitter, blah blah, Generation Z's youthful rebellion.'

I sauntered over to a filing cabinet that stood by the window. It was sprayed gold and decorated in what was probably a radical artwork but to my uninformed eye looked like bog-standard graffiti. It was very *Mercurial*. The gurgles from the coffee maker on top indicated it was ready to pour.

'Interesting spin,' I said and took two mugs from the shelf above. 'I think I just experienced some of that, myself.' Maggie didn't answer so I coughed and nodded at the coffee. 'I'm presuming this is for me? Mags, would you like one too?'

She grunted an affirmation and grudgingly gathered up the sheaf of paper, stapling the top right-hand corner and dumping it on an in-tray already several centimetres high.

'Might as well close that window too,' she shivered and pulled a fluffy purple cardigan tight over her shoulders. 'I thought it'd be warmer this week.'

I placed the mugs on her desk, and brought the window

33

down with more force than I intended resulting in a loud bang. Maggie tutted. I ignored her. 'They say it might turn nice for the weekend.'

Maggie cast her eyes through the windowpane at the fluttering leaves of the sycamores. A plastic bag whipped up from the street and caught a branch directly outside. 'If only the wind would drop.' She grimaced and came back to me. 'How are you going?'

I plucked out my standard response. 'Coping with it,' I told her.

She accepted that without further comment. 'Have you been to the house yet?'

She was referring to my mum's. 'I thought I'd wait until I saw Dan.'

Maggie's eyes narrowed. 'He's not turned up then?'

I shook my head. I was still livid that he hadn't been at the funeral. That was another reason why I let off so much steam that night at the club. But beyond the anger there was concern. Or perhaps it was the other way round?

Yesterday I'd nipped into Mum's hospice to fetch the last of her belongings and had seen one of the day shift nurses, Sally. Her husband, Michael, had once worked at Dan's school and Mum had known Sally socially prior to her last illness. Not well, but enough to pass the time of day. We had wondered if that might make it awkward but her familiar face reassured Mum. We'd had a chat and she, too, asked about Dan, reminding me that Mum had a key to his flat on her keychain and suggesting that I pop into his place to check it out. We'd phoned endlessly and I'd knocked on his door with no joy, trying to find him before Mum . . . well, before things came to a head.

'He'll need your support more than ever now,' Sally said. She was a homely woman, with an immense bosom, and an extraordinarily generous nature. I guess you have to be when you're in that job.

'I know,' I had said and promised to go there.

'And,' she said. 'Please do me a favour. I was talking to Doctor Jarvis about Dan going off like this. He said it'd be an idea to check his medication. Can you bring back a bottle, if there's a spare somewhere, and he'll have a look? Just to be sure.'

I had told her I would and was planning on swinging by his place after I'd finished up here at *Mercurial.*

'Oh dear,' Maggie was saying though her voice kept steady. 'Do you want to talk about it?'

I could be upfront with Maggie. 'No,' I said. 'I'm going to check his flat later. To be honest I'd rather talk work.'

'Okay. Well, let me know if you need anything, yeah?' Maggie straightened herself out and put on her professional head. The set of her jaw was firm and ready for business. 'Right,' she said. 'Fire.'

I tasted the coffee and removed my notebook from my bag. 'You mentioned another Essex Girls' piece?'

I'd been fascinated with our regional stereotype for a very long time. Firstly because, as a grey-eyed, raven-haired Essex chick, I adored the leggy, booby, blonde ideal. Surrounded by Barbies and Pippas from an early age I'd cottoned onto the fact that this was the generally accepted notion of beauty. I couldn't believe it when, as I made more excursions beyond the county's limits, I discovered it was considered vulgar and stupid and a lot lot worse. The realisation left me feeling cheated and rather annoyed.

Later, as I left the borough I'd lived in all my life to venture North for uni, I found that not only being a joke, mentioning my home county often resulted in humiliation and embarrassment. My surname, Asquith, which I thought sounded a little posh, however did little to temper the constant barrage of wisecracks that I faced, as an Essex Girl called Mercedes, and as a consequence I shortened it to Sadie. Most people called me by that name these days, apart from my dad who stubbornly stuck to my full moniker. Anyway, the whole Essex thing was as exasperating as it was formative and as a consequence of this battle I went on into journalism, 'to get my voice heard without shouting', as my mum used to put it.

Although I didn't relate the writing to my county or my gender I kept an edgy, working-class feel to my tirades. Luckily, people liked them and I was able to make a living from my rants.

Returning to my roots, Maggie indulged me and published a series of articles in which I challenged the negative connotations attached to the stereotype of the Essex Girl.

'Essex isn't like other counties. Its daughter isn't like those of Hertfordshire, Herefordshire or Surrey,' I had written. 'She isn't demure, self-effacing or seeking a husband. She's audacious, loud, drops her vowels and has fun. Like Essex itself, the Girl is unique. It's about time we showed some filial pride.'

Got a good reception, that one. Circulation went up. Maggie commissioned another one, and another, then another.

In an attempt to trace the etymology of Essex Girl my last feature harked back to the dark days of the witch hunts and examined whether there was a link between Essex's reputation as 'Witch County' and the genesis of Essex Girl. The two areas collided and, after further consideration, I concluded that there was and readers and commentators alike had not stopped filling up the web forum ever since.

Many comments spilt over into other sites, forums, newspapers and magazines. Positive or intensely outraged, Maggie didn't care how they reacted, just that they did. 'This is the kind of thing *Mercurial* needs. It's getting our name out there into a broader market. We need more, and I'll up your rate. Just give me something good and meaty,' she'd said on the phone a couple of weeks back.

So here I was, with something perhaps a little on the sketchy side, but definitely spicy.

Maggie took a tentative swig of her coffee then blew on it. 'Go on then – spill it. What you got for Mama?'

'Okay.' I flicked open my notepad and traced my notes to the relevant entry.

'I'm delving deeper into the witch hunts. You know this book deal? Well, I'm churning up a lot of good stuff. I think I can funnel some articles over to you.' I glanced up to catch a reaction. Maggie was nodding, her tongue licking her top lip, so I ploughed on.

'Why did Essex lose so many women to the witch hunts?'

Maggie snorted. 'Did we? It's a long time ago. Some people might say "so what?"'

I leant in to her. 'Yes, we did. Significantly more. It's the sheer volume that warrants attention.'

Maggie picked up the biro and took a drag on the end. 'You didn't go into that in your last article did you?'

I shook my head. 'No, it was more about the witches

themselves and the qualities they shared with the contemporary Essex Girl . . .'

Maggie cut in. 'Yep, yep. They "were poor, dumb and 'loose' as in not controlled by, or protected by men".' She was quoting my article. I got her point – she knew it back to front. 'So *why* exactly did it happen then? To the extent it did here? I assumed that Essex and its inhabitants already had a reputation for being thick, flat and uninteresting?'

I coughed. 'No, not at all. Up until the witch hunts, Essex was seen as the "English Goshen".'

'I last heard that word in Sunday School. Fertile land and Israelites. Now don't go all religious on me, Sadie. We're not the *Church Times*.'

I sighed. I hated having to explain things to her. She had such a high IQ and always made me feel like I was rambling. 'Goshen also means place of plenty. And that's a pretty fair description: Essex has an interesting geology. Sits at the southernmost point of the ice sheet that covered the rest of the island. Soil's full of mineral deposits brought down from up north via the glacier.'

Maggie pulled a face then converted it into a smile. 'Geology's a bit of a turn off for our readership . . .'

I held my hand up. 'Hang on. Let me get to the point – it was perfect for farming, for cattle, for livestock. It's surrounded by rivers and the North Sea for fishing. Until the 1600s it was seen as a pretty cool place to be. But after that it changes a bit.'

Maggie's eyes blinked. 'Because?'

I cleared my throat. 'Well, this is where I come in. I think a) because it was quite the revolutionary county in the Civil War. Backed parliament. Wanted reform. Was seen as the "radical" county. And b) because of the extent of the witch hunts.'

'Which were because?' She cocked her head to one side and sat back in her chair.

'Lots of things, I think. One was class aggression – you look at the European witch hunts and they had it in for all different types of people: aristocrats got burnt at the stake and their lands neatly confiscated by the Church. But in the Essex witch hunts the victims are mostly poor. At the same time you've got a mini Ice Age, crop failures, Civil War, a general breakdown of law and order. Indictments in Essex were already higher than elsewhere in the country. Then suddenly in 1644 the numbers spike dramatically. It was down to Matthew Hopkins, whose dick must have fallen off or something.'

Maggie raised an eyebrow. 'Language, darling.'

'Well, he's got serious issues with women. Killed more than any of the other Witchfinders put together. Decided to call himself the Witchfinder General and got rid of whole families of,' I lifted my fingers to draw imaginary quotation marks, '"witches" in his brief career from 1644 to 1647. Some sources suggest that he was from Lancashire, others from Essex or Suffolk. That he worked in shipping as a clerk and spent some time in Amsterdam learning his official trade, where he witnessed several witch trials.'

I looked up to catch her expression. 'And?' she said, eyebrows furrowed, not giving anything away.

'So he comes back and starts on Essex Girls in Manningtree. That's where he was based. There and Mistley. The Thorn Inn is where he had his headquarters.' I jerked my chair closer to the desk. 'Killed a good hundred more people than

Harold Shipman, who I might add, we can draw comparisons with – he also enjoyed murdering older women living on their own. But, like I said, it's thought that Hopkins killed more. Possibly making him the number one serial killer of all time. Conservative estimates look to about 350-odd victims. And,' I drew breath for emphasis, 'he was only twenty-six or twenty-seven when he snuffed it. That was in 1647. In 1692 you get the Salem witch hunts – and guess where they were?'

Maggie drummed her fingers on the desk. 'I'd put my money on Salem.'

'Okay. I didn't phrase that well. What county do you reckon Salem is in?'

'It's in Massachusetts, no?'

'Yes, that's the state though. Salem is in Essex County.'

'That, I didn't know,' said Maggie thoughtfully. 'You have my full attention. What are you thinking?'

'Not sure yet. I have to do some digging. I've got a tingling feeling going on. I think I could come up with something strong. Perhaps, and this is just a perhaps at the moment, it could be part of a bigger series – The Essex Girls' History of the World.'

Maggie's eyes brightened – pound signs were presumably whizzing through her brain. 'Now you're talking. What are you saying – six, twelve articles?'

'I don't know yet. Let me see what I can come up with.'

'I like it. I *really* like it. Sounds like you're talking ahead of the next deadline. Can you come up with this in three weeks?'

I'd already thought about that and shook my head. 'I'll definitely need longer.'

Her eyes dipped and hardened. 'You've got a current deadline. This is like an ongoing column. Readers will be expecting a piece in the next issue. Be a dear and sort something out for that please.'

I already had something up my sleeve. 'What about little-known Essex Girls of import . . . ?'

Maggie picked up my line. 'That go against the stereotype . . .'

I gave her a stony stare. 'All Essex Girls go against the stereotype . . .'

She ignored my comment. 'Yes, okay, you can have that. But I don't want you trotting out the regulars: Helen Mirren; Sally Gunnell . . . yada yada. There was a piece like that in the *Standard* just the other week.'

'I've got enough research to concoct a decent article pretty quickly. There's Anne Knight who campaigned against slavery and for women's suffrage . . .'

Maggie sniffed. 'Not too political though please, Sadie. We need an arts or culture steer.'

'Come on – she's a notable woman. A lesser-known notable . . .'

'Oh dear. I'm going off the idea. Who else have you got?'

'Okay,' I said, reaching mentally for someone a little more exciting. 'Maggie Smith?'

'Mmm.'

'Oh and also Mary Boleyn – the "other Boleyn Girl". You could run a nice pic of Scarlett beside it.'

'Was Mary from Essex?'

'Lived in Rochford for about ten years.'

'Born here?'

'Not exactly . . .'

41

'She'll do. Stick in a couple more like that and think pictures.'

She wrote something down in the book on her desk. 'Good, good,' she said to herself and bit the end of her pen with gusto.

'Then I can go into Hopkins?'

'Darling,' she said, replacing the pen and fixing me with one of her scary smiles. 'After that you can do whatever you like – as long as you hit your deadline and make it contentious. We need debate. Especially on the website. The bigger the better.'

'Great. Thank you.' I said it in earnest. 'I'm going to get something good out of it – got an instinct with this, believe me.'

Now she leant forwards. 'Very topical Essex is right now.'

'That, I know, dear Yoda.'

She grinned. 'Do you think you could explore your contacts and get some coverage in the nationals? If you come up with anything biggish?'

'I can't promise anything but it's always a possibility. I'm pretty sure there's an angle I could work out that could pull in the wider population. Hopkins has more than a regional fascination.'

Maggie's eyes were fixed on my face. 'Excellent. I want more than an "And Finally" on *Look East*. God knows we need to boost circulation.' She leant forwards and picked up her mug.

I mirrored her. The coffee was hot and delicious so I gulped it greedily, feeling the heat in my throat, then processing her last comment, I said, 'I thought you were doing great.'

Maggie sighed. 'We are, in terms of readership and profile. Best it's ever been. But our landlord's putting the rent up; the price of paper is going through the roof right now, and what with the recession or whatever this dire slump we're passing through is called, a lot of our regular advertisers have had to pull. A fair few have gone bust still owing us. Marketing is always the first thing to go when times are hard.'

I stared up and caught a sagging around her eyes. 'I had no idea.'

Maggie reached for a fag and projected her chair to the sash window. Lighting it, she pushed the bottom half up and craned her mouth to the opening.

'Please don't tell anyone, Sadie. I'm confiding in you as a friend, not an employee. I don't want it to get out to the others.' She blew a long sigh of smoke through the gap. 'We'll be lucky if we're still trading this time next year.'

'Ouch,' I said.

She faced me. Her regular kittenish expression disappeared. There was more of a hungry alley cat look going on there. 'Pull this "Essex Girls' History of the World" article off and I'll think about upping your rate to something bordering on decent and throw in your expenses.'

I sat back and looked her squarely in the face. 'That's a generous offer. Considering . . .'

'I said I'd *think* about it. You know me, always one for a get-out clause.' She laughed, and the kitten returned. 'Let's call it a calculated risk. I have faith in you.'

A strong blast of air came in through the crack, scattering several loose papers across the desk and blowing my notebook shut. I gathered them up, feeling a little less excited than I had been just moments before. 'Thank you for the vote of confidence. I'm not sure that I deserve it. Not yet.'

'Don't be so down on yourself.' She shot me another look and said more softly, 'You sure you're okay?'

It was an invitation to talk. But I didn't want to open those particular floodgates so I sniffed, swallowed down all self-doubt and wobbliness, and smiled as brightly as I could. 'Fine. Honest.'

'Right then,' her tone changed: she was wrapping up. Our transactions were like that. I'd got used to Maggie's looping behaviour that swung from utter professionalism to friendly concern then promptly back again. 'Can't stay here chatting about books and whatnot. You get going. Crack on with your witches. When do you think you can give me an idea of where you're going with your leads?'

I told her about two weeks should do it and stood up to go.

'Great,' she said as I made for the door. 'Oh, and Sadie. Call me if you need any help sorting Rosamund's house.'

I told her she'd be the first on my list and said goodbye.

She was second actually, but I appreciated the gesture.

Chapter Four

Okay, so the first on my list would be Dan. I wouldn't ever say that he was like a father to me: he came onto the scene when I was hitting my twenties. Although Dad had upped sticks and remarried by then, we stayed in touch, and he did his paternal duties to the best of his ability. There was no gaping hole there and I had no desire for another father figure. Thankfully Dan didn't attempt to patronise me by insinuating himself into my life. That's not to suggest there was conflict there – although we enjoyed a good debate, holding opposing views on many issues, it rarely strayed towards heat. We gradually learnt that we shared several traits: an unfashionable respect for the Beckhams, a crossover in early punk CD compilations, a distrust of online shopping and, of course, we both loved my mum, Rosamund.

I couldn't understand where he had disappeared off to?

It was so unlike him.

But I was going to sort it. I was determined. After I left *Mercurial* I drove over to Leigh.

Dan's flat was on the third floor of a large 1920s block with stunning views over the Thames Estuary to Kent and beyond. It wasn't massive: two large bedrooms, a contemporary kitchen/diner and a lounge with a balcony just big enough to squeeze on a round table and two small chairs, three at a push if I happened to pop in. The first time I visited I was impressed by the minimalist interior. Later I discovered his style was a product of divorce and OCD, rather than fashion statement.

Over the past few years he'd chosen his furniture carefully, with an eye on simple classic design, and as a consequence his flat had a groovy, contemporary vibe that was quite charming.

That afternoon though, I was surprised by what I found. Not that there was anything immediately concerning, well not anything I could put my finger on straight away. In the kitchen Dan's laptop sat on the work surface half open. It wasn't plugged in and the battery was flat. Next to it was a three-quarters full, stone-cold cup of coffee with a thick skin on the top.

It wasn't like Dan not to clean up after himself.

I crossed the kitchen and entered the lounge. The TV was on, volume way down low. Perhaps he had returned and gone out?

Maybe he was here? Asleep in his room? The bedroom came off a central hallway. As I pushed it open, I tentatively called out his name.

I felt intrusive entering his bedroom, but once I was assured no sounds of life came from within, I opened the door wide.

His bedroom was in a state of mild disarray. But I mean, *mild*. In my place it would be considered tidy; the duvet was jumbled up loosely in a mound at the end of the bed. Some of the drawers from the large mahogany chest had been pulled out and not pushed back in.

So, although it was more chaotic than Dan liked, it didn't resemble a robbery. The laptop was in full view and the plasma TV that hung on the wall hadn't been touched.

Perhaps he'd been searching for something. Or packed in a hurry.

But it just didn't feel right.

Like most recovering depressives, since Dan had learnt to control his moods, everything else under his rule was managed efficiently and tightly too. He was as likely to leave this mess as he was to miss an appointment with his doctor. Or with my mother, for that matter.

Could an old infirm relative have needed him? Family crisis? Then why not let Mum know?

Why not send a message at least? It was selfish not to.

Anger tightened my brow.

Remembering Sally's request, I stomped into the bathroom. A quick scan revealed an unusually tousled cabinet. At the back, on the bottom shelf, there were two bottles of Dan's regular medication. I stuck one in my bag and closed the bathroom door.

I felt odd leaving the place all messed up like that, so I nipped into the kitchen, closed the laptop, stowed it away under the sink and washed up the mug.

As I was locking up on the landing the neighbour's front door opened a few inches.

'Who's that?' The voice belonged to an old, well-spoken woman. Through the crack I could vaguely make out sleek white hair, and elegantly bespectacled blue eyes.

'I'm Sadie, Rosamund's daughter.'

The door trembled then opened to the length of the security chain.

The smell of grilling bacon wafted out into the hall.

Dan's neighbour squinted through the gap. 'Where's your mother?'

I gave her a taut explanation and the blue eyes softened a little. 'I'm sorry to hear that.'

'Thank you,' I said. Standard response.

The woman regarded me with what I assumed was pity, then she sniffed and lowered her head and said, 'I've heard things, you know.'

Most of us tend to gloss over non sequiturs like this but as a journalist, when people come out with lines like that, I'm always straight in there, probing. You usually find they're spoken in unguarded moments – when the conscious, or the conscience, is struggling with the subconscious mind, and not guarding the 'truth lobe'.

'What things? Do you know where Dan's gone, Mrs . . . Sorry, I don't know your name?'

I held out my hand and took a step towards her. It completely backfired. The woman took a step back and her door slammed shut.

I hung about for a couple of minutes, waiting to see if she was going to open it again, then shrugged mentally and put the neighbour's words down to old age or battiness and left.

As I crossed the ground floor foyer I passed a tall man in a black leather jacket with a remarkably expensive-looking tan, not the kind you get from living in the UK. Or out of a bottle for that matter. And, believe me, I'm from Essex – I *know*.

He smiled as if he knew me. That kind of reaction wasn't uncommon: Leigh was a small town, people tended to know of each other, even if they hadn't yet met. I nodded back.

As I approached the large glass doors at the front, the tall man skipped in front of me. He smiled again, this time revealing perfect white teeth and a pair of intense blue eyes, then he held open the door for me. 'Ladies first.' There was an accent there, though the exchange was too brief to pinpoint it.

'Thank you.' I stepped through it and continued over to my car expecting him to follow me out.

He didn't.

As I swung out of the car park I saw him behind the glass door.

I couldn't swear to it, as I was a fair distance away, but I think he was watching me.

Back at the hospice, I found Sally.

'I think it's all right to take them,' I told her and handed over the bottle. 'There was another one there of the same. I know Dan usually has a lot of spares in case he mislays the meds. He's not going to run out for a good while.'

Sally heaved a sigh. 'It's all been very stressful for poor Dan. You're managing to cope, Sadie. You're young and have friends and your dad. Dan's pretty much on his own and I think he might not be handling this too well.'

I had been so wrapped up in feeling sorry for myself and Mum that it hadn't occurred to me what Dan might be going through. Now I saw Sally could be right. I remembered a conversation I had once with him about his medication. He described the drugs as creating a 'semi-porous wall' which managed to keep out what he referred to as 'the dark'. 'Sometimes,' he told me, 'it's just not strong enough.'

'What do you do then?' I asked him.

'We go back to the doctors,' Mum interjected.

What with everything that had been going on lately, I doubted very much that Dan had thought about making an appointment.

'Oh God,' I said. 'I never thought of that. It's been a very difficult time. I've been completely self-obsessed.'

Sally's eyes crinkled into deep lines around the corners of her eyes and across the top of her cheeks.

'Don't beat yourself up about it, love. You've had your own cross to bear.' She smiled gently. You could tell she did that a hell of a lot. The pattern of lines was etched deeply into her face through years of usage.

She held the bottle up to inspect then said, 'Dan might have taken some time out to get his head straight. Then again, he well might have relapsed. If you're not acting rationally, then you don't think things through logically. Stress makes people react in different ways.'

'Yes,' I nodded. Now Sally was putting it like that, it did seem like the reasonable conclusion – Dan was probably taking a break. Perhaps he *was* running away. Maybe he was being cowardly. But perhaps that was necessary in order to preserve his own sanity. If I knew Dan, and I thought I did, whatever he was doing, he would have seen it as imperative.

Sally grunted at the pill bottle. 'Forty milligrams. Not sure about that. Doesn't look like a forty mil dose. Never mind,' she shook the bottle and popped it on the shelf behind her. 'I'll ask Doctor Jarvis to advise.'

With a sense of unease I said my goodbyes and hurried home.

Chapter Five

The landline answer phone was flashing when I finally got back to the flat. It was a message from my dad, checking in on me to see how I was going. Lots of people were doing that. I didn't phone many back. It was weird – although I wanted to be *able* to talk about it, I didn't *want* to talk about it. I guess I just needed to know I had the option.

However, I should return Dad's call at least.

I picked up the phone, hit ringback and got my stepmum, Janet, who informed me Dad was putting the kids to bed and would probably be another fifteen minutes. I said I'd call back in the morning and that, no, it wasn't urgent.

'You're still coming on Saturday though, aren't you?' Janet wanted to know.

Saturday, Saturday. What was on Saturday? I reached into my handbag and pulled out my diary. 'Wouldn't miss it for the world,' I told her, still unsure of what I'd committed to.

'Good, good. I know it's a fair way. Your dad will appreciate the effort.'

'Right. Of course,' I thumbed through to Saturday's entry – Uncle Roger's birthday. I groaned.

'Mercedes?' Like my father, Janet too had developed the annoying habit of calling me by my full name.

'Sorry, Janet. I had forgotten. I'm sure he wouldn't miss me if I didn't come.'

'Mercedes, honestly! Don't say that. Your dad certainly would. You know you're the apple of his eye.'

I managed to stifle a snort of contempt. This was pretty typical of lovely rosy Janet, but a blatant lie. Dad had always been a remote sort of parent, though not unloved or unloving. But the emotional and physical distance increased when he and Mum split and he moved out of our home back to his native Suffolk. I'm not being self-pitying when I say he never appeared particularly interested in me. True – he did the regular check-up and monthly phone call thing. And true – it didn't bother me one iota. But then my half-sisters, Lettice and Lucy, came along.

Janet was a homely and family orientated woman. A fair-haired big old farmer's wife type, who insisted that I got more involved with the family. When I did, I saw that Dad absolutely idolised his new daughters with an affection that was doting. It was different to the parenting style I'd known, for sure. But to be frank, I couldn't blame him: Lettice and Lucy were cool. Fourteen and eight years old respectively, and completely feral. Borderline punk. I liked their attitude.

I think a lot of their wildness came from living in the country; after he left, Dad bought a row of dilapidated cottages in the middle of nowhere. He did the first one up and moved into it whilst renovating the rest, then sold them on, retaining three of them to rent.

It was a canny move. Over the past couple of decades the

'middle of nowhere' had transformed into 'desirable rural location', affording him a very comfortable early retirement.

'Mercedes? Are you still there?' Janet's voice brought me into the present. Oh yeah, the birthday party.

I made a snuffling noise.

'Oh come on, love. Uncle Roger might not be around for much longer. His kidneys aren't looking good.'

Dad's rather morose older brother was a permanent downer at any festive occasion.

A small sniff conveyed my cynicism. 'He's been saying that for years.'

'Yes, well now it looks like he's right.' Janet made it sound like a final reflection, demanding of compassion.

I sighed audibly. She changed tack. 'It'd do you good to get away. And everybody's expecting you. The kids are looking forward to seeing you and you know how upset your Dad will be if you don't . . .'

'Okay, okay. I'll be there. I'll only stay for a couple of hours though.'

'That's perfect. Thank you. See you Sunday then. One p.m. Try to be prompt.'

I hung up.

It wasn't that I didn't like visiting Dad. It was just with everything going on at the moment . . .

Though I didn't want to think about any of that. Instead I decided to distract myself with some brain candy so I dumped myself on the sofa and flicked on the TV. Out of habit I surfed through to my preferred twenty-four-hour news channel.

There was some kind of kerfuffle outside County Hall. I couldn't get what was going on at first then, as the report built up the eyewitness accounts, I sussed that Robert Cutt had been visiting and got an egg in the face from a couple of bystanders protesting about media monopolies.

The mere image of him flashing up on the screen made my stomach tighten. Though he'd moved to England in his thirties, his white-blond hair accentuated a classic American face: fantastic cheekbones, wide jaw, good teeth and eyes that showed hyena-like cunning mixed with the blank dumbness of a circling shark. Sometimes in a certain light, it looked like there was nothing going on behind those startling peepers. Like the man had long said goodbye to his soul.

Yet none of this did anything to detract from the overall effect; even his most vociferous opponents had to admit that Robert Cutt was a very handsome devil indeed. Regrettably the well-groomed exterior and contrived panache concealed a business savvy that was ruthless and pretty unethical in its hunger for power.

I couldn't help thinking, as I watched the sixty-something politician brushing away the cameras, that despite the egging he looked rather pleased with himself. It was gross: there was something about the man that really creeped me out. It wasn't just the fact that, a few months ago, he'd been coaxed into revealing in a rather probing and frank interview that he believed that men were infinitely better adapted to leadership than the female of the species. Following on from that another documentary had revealed his friendship with TV evangelist, Pat Robertson.

I knew about Mr Robertson before I had ever heard of Cutt: a friend once bought me a joke present for my birthday. It was a mug that had one of Mr Robertson's quotes printed on it. It read: 'The feminist agenda is not about equal rights for women. It is about a socialist, anti-family political movement that encourages women to leave their husbands, kill their children, practise witchcraft, destroy capitalism and become lesbians.'

Bless his little cotton socks.

After that documentary Cutt did a fair bit of political manoeuvring to put a respectable distance between their camps. Even so, there were similarities; both advocated a stable family should have a mother and father (one of each sex). And there was an insidious suggestion that women should remain within the home, though it wasn't stated explicitly. Nor was it their conviction that human nature was ever nurtured. It was more about genetics and nature. But that was easy for him to say, coming as he did, from a line of pilgrim Baptists back in the good old US of A. Mr Cutt made a big deal of those roots and set himself up as something of a paragon of ancestral virtue.

God knows how he came to be a political contender in the UK.

And yet, it was none of that that had me reflexing into gag response when I saw his nauseatingly beautiful face. No. It was something about his eyes. The hard grey circles reminded me of someone.

I'd just never been able to put my finger on who.

I almost convulsed with repulsion as the screen showed him ushered by bodyguards into a black BMW: just before he got in, he waved a two-fingered victory sign at reporters.

The scene had dulled my mood, leaving me with a restlessness that I couldn't counter. I switched channels trying to find some comedy. Unfortunately the smarmy mogul had dampened me, so I cut my losses and retired to bed.

I was just sinking into a light slumber when I heard that noise again: a scratching followed by a creaking of sorts. When I strained my ears, I could tell it was right above me, in the loft.

I groaned and buried my head under the duvet, underlining my mental note to call pest control in the morning.

But it got louder.

I pulled the duvet down from my face and stared at the ceiling. 'Shut up,' I yelled at it.

Magically, the shuffling stopped.

Chapter Six

The offices of Portillion Publishing were on level six of the larger umbrella company's head office. The sleek glassy building had won several architectural awards for innovation and was set in the financial heart of London. I use the term 'heart' loosely: it was at the centre of the complex of roads and warrens that calls itself the City of London. I'd never felt comfortable about being in that place, with all those bankers. The lack of vegetation, the inhuman scale of the buildings, the overriding predominance of grey, the uniform of suits, the set pace of walking, all combined to give the impression that when you got off the train at Fenchurch Street, you entered a mechanised world set up purely to produce money. Don't get me wrong, I didn't have a problem with the individuals as such – some of my best friends worked in the City – but en masse, the whole set-up was overwhelming.

As I walked towards the river, I had the sense of being swallowed up or, perhaps, it was more like joining in. Whatever, I was almost relieved as I went through the revolving doors of Cutt's castle.

Portillion Publishing was originally situated in Mayfair, but when the mogul acquired it, the outfit was 'streamlined'. Accusations of asset stripping and general nastiness were flung around but faded once the concern was relocated to this nerve centre. It was enormous, shaped like a glimmering spire: a cathedral to Capitalism.

The offices came off an inner courtyard that had the full height of the thirty-five-storey structure. Large glass elevators reached skywards to the ceiling where a crystal pyramid capped the top. Chrome fittings and mirrored pillars amplified the light. The effect was dazzling.

A tall, willowy PA in a black designer suit collected me from the reception area. Her chic asymmetric bob and red lipstick were so impressive I felt immediately underdressed in my beloved vintage dress and boots. To cover up my nerves I tried to make small talk as we walked towards the lifts.

'This is a fantastic building,' I gestured upwards. 'So much light.'

Delphine, as she introduced herself, sniffed. 'Yes. It's a great place to work.' Her voice dragged with vague ennui.

'Is Cutt based here?' I asked, following the tap-tapping of her kitten heels across the marble floor.

'Mr Cutt's office is there,' she indicated a large tinted glass window that covered the whole of one side of the first floor.

'All of it?'

Delphine managed to crack a smile. 'It's an expansive concern.'

His office directly faced the entrance, security checks and reception. 'He gets a good view of everybody coming in and out that way, I suppose.'

'Oh, Mr Cutt is an extremely energetic man. Not one to drop the ball. Robert likes to keep his eye on things.'

'Quite literally,' I said and stitched on a chuckle. 'He can more or less see everyone from that vantage point.'

She didn't reply.

The short journey upwards was uncomfortable. We stood either side of the lift doors staring out of the glass sheets. Delphine didn't speak and I didn't bother to try any more conversation. She was one tough nut to crack, I thought silently, tension creeping along my shoulders as I contemplated the kind of fella this Felix Knight might be. His email had an old-fashioned jauntiness to it that had me picturing a white-haired man in his fifties, in a sort of geography teacher get-up – leather-elbowed tweed jacket and cords. But after the intimidating pillar of reserve that was his secretary, I was beginning to think he was probably more of a reptilian guy. To command authority over Delphine, he'd surely have to be older, wiser and far, far colder.

Both my visions were wrong. Felix Knight turned out to be a phenomenally friendly sort. My age, or possibly younger. He had fantastically clear skin that gave the impression he was fresh out of the shower. Despite an impeccable tailor, the rest of him was a little unkempt; his hair was a mass of carefree brown curly waves, week-old stubble was spread across a firm jaw. I wasn't surprised he hadn't shaved – you could cut yourself on those cheekbones. He had a very very wide smile that wrinkled up the sides of his eyes. Out of the context of the publishing house and out of that suit, he could easily have been an actor or an academic, or, because his build was tall and fairly broad across the shoulders, maybe a young farmer. There was a slap-happy aura about him that immediately put me at ease.

And he was rather attractive too.

We shook hands. His was a firm super-confident grip, his eyes incredibly sparkly.

'Do come in, Miss Asquith.' He pulled a chair out and helped me into it. Well-spoken but not intimidating, his body language communicated both bonhomie and impeccable manners. He thanked Delphine and asked her to fetch some coffee, 'if it is no trouble. Otherwise,' he said, 'I'll hit the canteen.' Delphine assented with a nod and so Felix slipped round to the other side of his desk and plopped into a high-backed chair. I saw him steal a glance that swept over me from the top of my head downwards, taking in bust size, hips, and legs. For a nanosecond he lost his self-possession, as if surprised by some aspect – I didn't know what. Was it the vintage dress? Knee-high boots? Leather jacket? Perhaps he'd expected me to rock up in a suit. Well, tough, I thought, that ain't ever gonna happen. Anyway, it was fleeting: Felix Knight mastered himself so quickly the blunder was barely perceptible.

'Well,' he said brightly. 'I'm so pleased to meet you at last.'

At last! He only introduced himself yesterday. But then again, the handover from Emma had probably occurred a couple of weeks ago. It was only I, the author, who had learned of Portillion's plans twenty-four hours ago.

I told him I too was pleased to make his acquaintance and made myself comfortable in a jazzy chrome and leather chair.

The offices of Portillion Publishing were kitted out with an array of gizmos and screens, all carefully selected to compliment the vast oak bookshelves displaying some of Portillion's top-selling authors.

'I'm sorry that Emma had to take off so quickly,' he said once hc was seated back behind his desk. I watched him casually cross his legs, his large right hand smoothing over a wrinkle of fabric around the kneecap. He coughed and smiled. 'These things tend to move rapidly once decided. However let me assure you I am very impressed by your proposal and can't wait to read the first instalment.' I liked the way his tongue lingered over the 'r's in a breathy maybe Irish, though more likely American style. Unlike other media types I'd encountered who aped the linguistic idiosyncrasies of the Super Power to evoke a cool cosmopolitan image, Felix's accent sounded genuine. I guessed he was well travelled.

'That's great, thanks, Mr Knight.' I nodded vigorously to match his level of enthusiasm.

He swung his chair and placed his hands on the desk. 'Oh please,' he said, lowering eyes and voice simultaneously. 'It's Felix.'

Bloody hell – was he flirting? No. Couldn't be. Not on a first date. I noted my Freudian slip and corrected 'date' to 'meeting'. It must just be that old public school charm offensive.

'And actually, my friends call me Sadie,' I said, and squeezed in a little self-conscious grin.

He stroked the skin behind his jaw and regarded me with a grin. 'So, formalities over – how have you been, Sadie?'

It threw me a little. Was this publishing getting-to-know you-speak? Or had he heard about my recent loss?

'Well,' I squigged myself forwards onto the edge of my seat, so that I could sit up straight and suck in my stomach. 'I'm very pleased about the publishing deal. It's come at a good time. You sec, my mother passed away a couple of weeks ago . . .'

'Oh I'm sorry,' he said and assumed a concerned bearing; eyes down, head cocked to one side. I'd seen it before. It's what people did. Felix went a step further and clasped his hands, his eyebrows pointed towards his nose. It was a sincere expression. 'Was it sudden or . . . ?'

'She'd been ill. But well, you're never prepared for it, are you, no matter how expected?'

He glanced away and back again quickly. 'Condolences to you and your family. That can't have been easy . . .'

'Thank you, I said and moved on. I wasn't comfortable with this. I didn't want to start my new career with negativity. 'So, as you see, I'm ready to get on with the book right away.'

'And I am certainly not going to stop you,' he said, and his face began to shine again. 'Shall we clear up the formalities and head off for a bite to eat? I don't know about you, but I'm famished.' He sat back and touched his stomach. It looked as hard as a board.

'Starving Marvin, as they say in *South Park*,' I said and immediately regretted the crass pop culture reference.

'Quite,' said Mr Knight. He reached for a document at the side of his desk. 'We're all quite enamoured of your colloquial style. You don't come across writing like that very often. Wondered if you'd speak like it too. So often you get authors who write in one way and speak in quite a different manner. But you seem to be the genuine article.'

What was that meant to mean? Genuinely working-class? Genuinely Essex? I didn't want to risk offence by asking for clarification so simply smiled. Felix did too – that wide gleaming grin (no overbite, white pearls verging on perfect), displaying zero visible dental work, evidence of good, strong, well-nourished stock.

He selected a pen and pushed the wad of papers towards me. 'Let's get your signature down here. Then we can release the funds.'

The restaurant was Spanish, full of little round tables. Across the walls hung strings of what I first thought were tacky plastic garlic bulbs and chillies, but then realised were the real McCoy.

After signing the contract Delphine popped in to let us know our taxi had arrived and since arriving at the restaurant our conversation had spun away from work into taste in food. It was only after we'd knocked back our first glass of wine that we got down to nitty-gritty book talk.

I explained that I'd already written an introduction about the factors that led up to the witch hunts, then, developing my original proposition, outlined the fact I was planning on setting the work out in three sections: the hunts up to 1644; the Hopkins campaign of terror; and then the decline of prosecutions up to the last known arrest of Helen Duncan, aka 'Hellish Nell', who went down for witchcraft in 1944, if you can believe that. Hers was an odd case. She was convicted of fraudulent 'spiritual' activity after one particularly informative séance in which she gave out classified information about military deaths. I had to include it. Felix was fascinated. Or at least, he gave the impression of being utterly absorbed; the eyes zoomed in on my face, his mouth set into a line. His expression was neutral, listening, but there was a shadow of a wrinkle across his forehead which betrayed intense concentration.

Enjoying the attention, I went on to explain I had pretty much sketched out the first section and was now focusing on Matthew Hopkins.

'I don't know a great deal about him other than what you've précised in your synopsis.' Felix leant forwards across the table expectantly then reached out and refilled my glass. 'Please do go on. You'll have to excuse my ignorance on the subject.'

As it was fresh in my mind, I took him through an overview of that particularly nasty witch hunter who had made such an impact on my county.

'What do you think his motive was? Power? Greed?' Felix asked as the tapas arrived on the table. I took a modest forkful of meatballs, but didn't start on them.

'Of course: they're your basic tools of capitalism at a time when that economic system was emerging.' I took a breath. The final cadence of my sentence made me sound way too preachy. I moderated my voice and glanced at Felix.

He didn't seem to mind and nodded me on, eyebrows higher, a smile twitching at the corners of his lips.

'I mean,' I went on, 'yes, he gained financially from the deaths. And, yes, I'm sure that that was certainly a motivating factor. In one town alone he made about £23 from the executions, which works out to about £3.5k today. Some sources reckon, he netted the equivalent of about £100,000 for a year spent witch hunting. Quite an incentive.'

Felix swirled his wine glass, sniffed it, and took another swig. 'Exceptional.' I wasn't sure if he was referring to the vintage or the witch hunter's income. 'But to kill in such quantities? To witness the last moments as the life was squeezed from them. And then to continue – he's got to have been mad, surely?' He tilted his face towards me, as if waiting for me to clear up that quandary.

'I know,' I said. 'I think he must have partly believed what he was doing. I mean, he *had* to believe in witchcraft and the Devil. Everyone did at that point in time. The country was one hundred per cent convinced not only of the existence of witchcraft but the idea that its practice could empower some people. Witchcraft was as real to them as, I dunno . . .' I searched around for a contemporary angle, '. . . electricity is to us.'

'That is a fact, however,' he said. 'Electricity *is* real.'

'Yes, but we can't see it. We see the results of manipulating or conducting it. We don't see "it". But we believe it.'

A slight droop of the eyelids told me the metaphor wasn't working, so I moved on. 'Well, anyway, my point is – he probably did believe that some of them were witches. I mean, in a few of the confessions you get the sense that some accused may have been convinced that they *had* caused their victim's misfortune: you go begging, someone refuses you charity, you curse them, then they die or fall ill. That sequence of events might have happened fairly regularly – the psychological stress that people underwent when they were "hexed" probably did have a pretty negative effect on their health. Your average seventeenth-century villager hadn't got a clue about strokes, heart attacks and fits. It was all the work of the Devil.'

'So, by contrast, he was doing God's work?' Felix offered. 'That's how he saw it?'

'Christ no,' I said quickly. 'Hopkins made stuff up to convict them. He fabricated stories and coached the accused so that they'd be convicted. I think he enjoyed it.'

'He was a serial killer then,' my editor spoke up once more. 'He got a kick from seeing the cases through from hearsay to execution. Or else why do it?' Felix shone his metallic eyes on me. 'Where did he stand with God? How did he reconcile what he was doing?'

I reflected for a moment. 'I don't know. The rubbish that he came up with in his book, *The Discovery of Witches*, reads like he was on the back foot, defending himself, like he knew he'd done wrong. Some of the justifications for starting his campaign are insane.'

'Like what?'

'Like seeing an imp transform from a greyhound with the head of an ox into a child of four who ran around without a head!'

'Ah, but you can't put yourself in the shoes of those in the past. All these apparitions and manifestations seemed very real to those who lived amongst them.'

I took another sip of my wine. It *was* exceptional.

Felix looked into the mid-distance. 'Wasn't there some suggestion that hallucinogens were part of the witch craze?' He returned to me.

'Plants with potentially hallucinogenic effects were used in ointments and medicines during that period. Deadly Nightshade, mace, nutmeg, even saffron, contain essential oils that can have that effect. But you're probably thinking of ergot fungi. It grows on grasses and cereals and can bring on hallucinations too. There was a book out in the seventies which suggested the Salem witch trials were due to young women eating ergot-infested rye.'

'What do you think about that?'

'Well, I'm no biologist but I imagine it's doubtful. You'd have to consume a lot of it. You know I once read an article that talked about the impact of tobacco and pipe smoking in the seventeenth century and suggested that Hopkins was a stoner. As, like most gentlemen of the time, he was often seen with a little white pipe.'

'Was he?'

'I've not found any evidence myself yet, but you never know.' I smiled. 'The problem is, any explanations of that type just sound like an excuse: "I'm sorry, Your Honour, but I was drunk/stoned/smashed." You know the kind of thing. That doesn't cut it with me. Not if you look at the detail.

'It's clear, when you actually sit down and read about the trials, that there are instances when you can see his victims were just repeating what he'd told them to say.'

Felix leant back. 'Give me an example.'

'Right,' I said, selecting an episode from my memory. I didn't then know how or why I found it so easy to recall facts and figures from these particular witch hunts. Ask me the balance of my current account and I'd be umming and ahing but Hopkins' crimes were burnt into my brain. 'Well, in the Huntingdonshire trials you start seeing "witches" cite names of imps that have already been used in the Essex trials: Blackman; Grizzell; Greedigut for instance. Quite distinctive. Some of the witches forgot what they were alleged to have said and were prompted by Hopkins at the trial.'

'Idiot,' Felix said quietly. I was really starting to like him. That full mouth was definitely quite passionate, I could tell.

'So he was greedy and power hungry without discipline or intellect,' he said eventually. 'It has to be handled firmly – power and money – if one is to succeed.' He took a hand and smoothed it back through his hair. A little lock fell down over his forehead.

'Well, you've obviously known power. I can't say I have.'

'No. I mean – look around you. Look at all the corruption

and greed – business, politics . . .' he sighed and took up his glass. 'It's a disgrace.'

'I'm hearing you,' I said.

He looked up into my face. 'I guess you are too,' he said and smiled appreciatively.

Of course, I thought. He can't come across many like-minded individuals being stuck working for Cutt. I would have felt sorry for him had another strong emotion not started to simmer within.

I swallowed and pushed around some food on my plate. 'I'm sure Hopkins was also a sadist,' I said, getting back on safe ground. 'But able to get away with it. Though now demanding of closer inspection, I believe.'

Felix joined my gaze and smiled.

'Which brings us neatly to our purpose,' he said. 'Essex is certainly full of surprising little gems.'

I popped an olive into my mouth and looked at the table again.

'Are you from Essex by the way, Sadie? I know you write about it, but an interest doesn't necessarily make one a native?'

'I am indeed lucky enough to have been born in that county, yes,' I ventured so far as to send him a wink.

'That's grand,' he said and pushed his plate into the centre of the table for the waiter. He folded his arms and regarded me. 'So do you go back a long way? Both parents?'

'Dad's originally from Suffolk, just north of the border.'

'And your mother?'

'Yes. Born and bred.'

'Grandparents?'

'One left on my dad's side.'

'And on your mother's?'

68

I paused. What was he fishing for? Enough credentials to validate my links to the county? 'I never met them. They died before I was born.'

'Oh, that's a shame.' Felix nodded, that sympathetic wrinkle sewn back across his forehead.

'Yes, well.' I refocused the conversation. 'Don't worry. You don't need old family connections to get the gen on Essex folk. We have a brilliant records office and don't forget, I *am* a journalist. My press card opens doors. As does my winning smile.' Cue cheesy grin.

Felix shifted then leant forwards, his eyes a little misty. Any remaining formality had vanished.

I glanced down at his hands. No wedding ring. He caught my gaze.

'So,' he said, cleared his throat and grinned. 'What's Manningtree like? Where Hopkins commenced his hunt? Is it very rural? I've never been.'

'Oh,' I said, a little shamefacedly. 'I haven't actually visited the place yet.'

Felix's eyes widened in mock horror. 'But the home of the beast himself! You must go. I say one can learn a lot about a man, or woman, from their home and surroundings. It might make interesting reading.'

He was right, of course. 'I'll stick it on my list of things to do,' I added. 'In fact I'll schedule it after Colchester. I'm planning to go there next week. That's where the witches were gaoled. Haven't been since I was a school kid.'

'Ah. Colchester. What day are you planning to visit?'

I shrugged. I liked to keep my diary flexible in case any local jobs came up.

'If you make it next Monday,' he was saying, 'I might just

be able to accompany you to the castle. I quite fancy the idea. One of my authors has moved down to that neck of the woods and she's due a conversation about her last edit. Could kill two birds with one stone? Visit said writer, and combine a short tour of the city with another from the Portillion fold.' His eyes arched expectantly. I saw, with a mild buzz of appreciation, that they glinted with splinters of quartz. For a second it looked like he was holding his breath.

'Of course,' I replied. 'But remember – I haven't been for a long time. I won't be a very good guide I'm afraid.'

Felix wagged his hand playfully. 'Then we shall be on an equal footing. And you can bring me a progress report on the book. Are you happy with your timescale?'

He wanted the first draft submitted within five months. A little bit of a push, but as I had the research and structural outline already, I thought I could make it. Plus the money would come in very handy indeed. 'Yes. That's fine.'

'Excellent. Then shall we drink to the deadline?'

'We shall,' I said and raised my glass.

It's a funny old phrase – the deadline. Comes from the American Civil War. Refers to a line drawn around prisoners. If they crossed it, they'd be shot.

Obviously it never struck me then, but on first meetings, why drink to a finishing point? Why not to a profitable association or ongoing success?

But Felix had elected to drink to the deadline. The line of the dead.

His choice was to be uncannily prophetic.

Chapter Seven

On the train home I realised I was a little tipsier than expected. Felix was such a genial host, and never let my glass go empty, so I had no idea how much I'd drunk. Now I was feeling rather drowsy and there was nothing for it but a little nap. I woke up to the sound of my mobile bleeping. A text from Maggie: it was the birthday of *Mercurial*'s art director, Felicity, and they were celebrating in Leigh Old Town. I was welcome to join them. Her mis-spellings suggested they'd been there a while, which suited me quite nicely. I made a mental note to get off the train a stop earlier.

The next call set my heart racing. It was from Sally. When I looked at the screen and saw the name of the hospice flash up I went into a reflexive panic. Then I remembered that the worst had happened and instantly my spirits, that had been so giddily high after lunch, plummeted back to the abyss of reality.

'Hi Sadie. How are you going?' Sally's voice still conjured up sympathy and cups of tea.

I told her I was getting on.

She murmured heartening phrases about Mum wanting

me to do exactly that, and not to dwell on things, then she asked me straight out. 'Have you seen Dan yet?'

I told her that there was still no word on his whereabouts. 'Oh dear,' she said.

I asked what the matter was.

She seemed reluctant to tell me, but then I heard the sound of an inner door shutting and her voice reduced to a whisper. 'Don't repeat this. Promise?'

I swore I wouldn't.

'Doctor Jarvis looked at Dan's medication yesterday. He's rather concerned. It seemed that although the prescriptive label on the bottle was accurate the tablets inside were like nothing he'd seen for that drug before. He's sent a couple off to the lab for analysis. But,' said Sally, 'if there's been some kind of a mix-up, then it means that Dan may have unwittingly stopped taking his medication.'

'Shit,' I said, for want of anything better to express my alarm. 'Which means?'

'Possible onset of depression, psychosis, delusion . . . the list goes on. The main thing is he needs to see a doctor, pronto. Have you *any* idea where he is?'

I shook my head. 'No, not at all. I tried everywhere I could think of before Mum . . .'

Sally huffed out a sigh. 'Michael managed to speak to his department. They still haven't seen him. All they've had is some message that he's taken leave to sort out a personal matter. Any ideas?'

'No,' I said, though this news was somewhat positive. There'd been forethought at least. He hadn't suddenly gone off the rails. 'So, what can we do? For Dan? Should we call the police?'

'I don't think it's a good idea to get them involved. Keep an eye out. If you see him or hear from him, tell him about the mix-up and get him to his doctor's at once. He'll understand the urgency.'

I thanked her and told her to phone me if she had any more news. She gave her word.

After all that I was a bit wired and completely forgot to get off at Leigh. Instead I disembarked at Chalkwell station, popped into the flat, changed my boots and swapped my dress for jeans and t-shirt.

Afternoon had become early evening. Though we were at the late onset of autumn it was not yet cold and I decided to stroll down to the Old Town via the cinder path, hoping the fresh ionised air would cleanse my aura of its Dan-centred worries.

It was a lovely walk, running the length of the shoreline from Chalkwell station to Leigh Beach. Peaceful too. Above me an aeroplane, flying its passengers to warmer climes, chalked its stubby vapour trail across the fading pinky-blue sky. On the horizon Kent warped in a cloudy mist. Twenty metres out in the estuary a solitary seagull arced high above a moored yacht, flapping its wings without cawing. Closer to land an old guy worked his way up the tidemark, swinging a metal detector back and forth in time to the slow lulling rhythm of the waves.

The evening sun hung low over the chimneys of Canvey Island. There was no wind that evening and everything felt very still.

I dawdled past the Wilton, a former navy warship, now used as a clubhouse by the Essex Yacht Club. The gentle tinkling of glasses and faint chat of the members drifted up across the water. It was an uplifting sound, full of conviviality and good humour, and for a moment I had the feeling that there was a change on its way.

Of course, at the time I assumed it would be for the better.

When I reached the corner of the beach that met Bell Wharf, I paused for a moment to take in the view. A fishing boat was returning from a day out in the North Sea. A man on the front deck wearing plastic orange waterproofs waved at someone out on the wharf.

'Psst!'

I continued watching the boat chug along the creek, leaving a widening trail of froth.

'Psst!' Same voice. Behind me.

Assuming it was directed at someone else passing by, I didn't move.

Then it went, 'Psst. You there.'

I swivelled around, darting glances over the road and up into the Leigh Yacht Club. There was a shelter by the old railway station, now the LYC bar. In the dusky twilight I could only vaguely make out a darkness in the centre of the bench. I took a few steps forwards to get a better view but the interior was filled by murky shadows. Light from one of the street lamps threw a dim glow on what looked like the creases of a greyish stained skirt that dropped down to the floor. In the midst of its folds was a bony walking stick. Two wrinkled hands clasped the top. I saw the nails were dirty and gritty, the skin papery. The gnarled old fingers were tensed, their large white bony knuckles shining through the skin like phosphorous peach stones.

'Hello?' I couldn't penetrate the gloom obscuring her face. 'Do I . . . ?'

She started, hands fastening tighter on the stick. 'No further. You'll not want to see.'

The smell that was coming from the poor dear was grotesque. She couldn't have bathed for a month. I took her advice and stood where I was.

'Oh, tell her mercy.' She was whining, her voice touching a chord of emotion: pity. I hated to see old people like this.

'Are you okay?' I said feebly and held a hand towards her. I heard a gasp. Then she snapped, 'You can see. See.' It was more of a command but it made no sense – she'd just asked me not to get any closer. Not that I was going to. How could I see, then? I sighed inwardly, realising the old dear was undoubtedly demented and most likely disorientated into the bargain. Maybe she'd wandered out of a residential home. There were a few up on the hill. Mind you, with that stench they can't have been taking care of her at all well. More probably she came from a cottage in the Old Town.

'Where do you live?' I asked gently. 'Is it nearby?'

She spat and banged her stick on the floor. 'End it, mercy.'

Charming, I thought. The jangle of keys on metal attracted my attention. Aha, it was the coastguard locking up his hut for the night. Perfect. I couldn't be so heartless as to abandon the poor love; if she stayed here any later she'd be swamped with teenagers and roving drunks. However, if I alerted the coastguard I would certainly be doing my civic duty . . .

'Excuse me!' I called out as I ran across the cobbles, waving my arms. He uprighted himself and smiled, but when I explained about the woman, he glanced at his watch and grimaced.

'She's just over here.' I pointed to the shelter.

He screwed up his face. 'Can't see nothing,' he said doubtfully.

'No, I know,' I told him, holding my arm out in a kind of 'You first' gesture. 'It's dark in there. She's sitting in the middle of the bench. Someone should get her home. The kids will be out soon.'

He was obviously well aware of that.

We fell into step and crossed the road. As we approached the shelter my eyes flicked over the darker black line of the bench. It was uninterrupted.

A couple of feet from it the coastguard stopped. 'Gone,' he said and gestured to the empty space.

'No. Can't . . .' I stammered and took another step into the darkness, running my hand up the cold wooden bench where she had been sitting. He was right. There was no one here. But that was impossible. The distance from the shelter to the coastguards was nothing. Twenty feet. Maybe less. I had only been away a matter of seconds. 'There's no way someone as frail as her could have disappeared so quickly,' I told him.

He got a torch out of his rucksack and shone it round the shelter. 'No one here, love.' Now he was getting irritated. I was wasting his drinking time. And mine.

I stepped back and looked up to the path that ran along the beach. A couple were walking their dog. No one else was about. I looked left, up the high street of the Old Town. A couple of smokers clustered outside the Mayflower pub. A van reversed into the car park. Other than that, there was not a soul to be seen.

'Maybe it was kids mucking around?' he said when he could see I wasn't buggering off. 'We're coming up to Halloween, unfortunately. They all get overexcited these days, don't they? Dressing up like the Americans. Someone could have put on a costume to spook you or summat.'

'No,' I said firmly, putting my hands on my hips. 'She was real enough.'

'Well, she's gone,' he said, throwing his torch upright and catching it with the same hand. The gesture indicated he was finishing up, thank you very much. 'I'll inform the police. They can keep their eyes out.'

'Okay,' I said and nodded unsteadily. It made no sense. She'd made no sense.

But I was a practical girl, not given to fancy. I selected the 'Case Unsolved File' in my brain and slotted it in there.

Okay, I admit I was unnerved. But up ahead was a place that sold medicine that sorted out that particular ailment. I bid goodbye to the coastguard and marched onto the street, my pace unusually feisty.

The *Mercurial* crew were sitting outside the Billet on a couple of trestle tables they had inelegantly wedged together. Half-empty foam punnets of cockles and prawns were interspersed across the table, along with several glasses. Most of them were just off empty so my arrival and inevitable offer of drinks produced an uproarious response and a multitude of orders. Maggie clumsily extricated herself from the squash of buttocks on the wooden bench and followed me into the pub to help carry the order.

While we were waiting to be served I filled her in on my afternoon, omitting my recent experience with the old dear. I didn't want to appear like a nut. I had a thing about that, you understand – what with Mum and everything. So I concentrated my narrative on the comely Felix.

'Great. He sounds interesting,' she said, steadying herself on the bar. 'You're doing well, Sadie.'

I smiled at my reflection in the mirror behind the optics. 'I think so too.'

'Was he posh then? Portillion Publishing sounds it.'

'Not really. Pretty down to earth. Wealthy.'

'Do you think you can work with him?'

'Well, obviously it's not going to be like working with you, but I have to say – the pay's a hell of a lot better. And, actually, there's a few things I think I'd quite like to do with Mr Knight.'

Maggie's eyebrows moved up her forehead. 'Oh, like that is it?'

'He's very charming.'

'What does he look like?'

'Tall, good body. Has a bit of an Irish look about him.' I thought back to that broad smile.

Maggie took in my face and punched my arm lightly. 'Good for you, girl. You could do with a bit of luck.'

'Well,' I hesitated. 'Just saying – he's nice.'

She looked pleased and wagged a teasing finger at me. 'Just don't let the Man from Del Monte distract you from my deadlines though. I want my Hopkins article. Make it nice and juicy please.'

Minutes later I emerged with a tray of wine and glasses, whilst Mags followed, spilling a dozen millilitres of beer from the two pints she was carrying.

The group were in fine spirits. Even Felicity, or Flick as she was usually referred to, their quiet, conservative art director was gabbling away at top speed to Lola, the part-time PR girl. I used to think Flick rather stuck up. She never made eye contact and spoke very little, taking in everything from underneath her dark, wispy hair. One night, at the launch of a significant issue, she confided to being painfully shy and hiding it with 'attitude'. I liked her after that.

Next to Flick, sat Rik, the sixty-something part-time ad exec who managed the advertising to supplement his pension and keep him golfing, and Françoise, the young speccy editorial assistant-cum-generally-put-upon-dogsbody. Rik was in the middle of telling a joke to Maggie's husband, Jules, and her mini-me teenage-rebel daughter, Willow. I hoped he'd carry on but once he clocked me and Mags he insisted on starting all over again. The last navy streaks were disappearing from the sky as he began. It was black by the time he got to the punch line.

I can't remember what the joke was about but I have a distinct recollection of laughing till I cried.

Which was good, as there was a hell of a darkness on its way.

Chapter Eight

I didn't stay long at the pub. Usually I don't work after I've had a drink but tonight, the excitement from my meeting with Felix was carrying me through.

I spread out my file of notes. I wanted to go back over the first section of the book to check that I'd got everything I wanted in there.

There was a hell of a lot to cover. The first few trials were pretty small fry, the convicted, either being fined or pardoned. Most of their crimes centred round causing livestock to fall ill, or in several pitiable cases, children. But then there was the Hatfield Peverel outbreak, with Agnes Waterhouse the first person to be put to death as a witch. Her daughter was also accused but turned witness against her mother and was found not guilty. Agnes allegedly confessed to being a witch. Her primary crime was owning a cat, who she talked to often. Its name was Sathan. Not the most sensible choice for an old woman living on her own in sixteenth-century rural Essex.

The hanging of Agnes Waterhouse set a precedent, and soon more and more women were executed. Mostly for 'bewitching' people to death. In 1582 in St Osyth fourteen were indicted. Of these, ten were found guilty. Ursula Kempe was accused by her eight-year-old son, whose testimony led to her execution and Elizabeth Bennet's. In 1921 two female skeletons were found in a St Osyth man's back garden. They had been pinned into the ground with stakes and iron spikes had been driven through their elbows, wrists and ankles. They were thought to be the remains of the two women and were bought by collectors in the nineties, for exhibition in their private collections. Imagine that – your remains bought and sold, then put on display for the rich to gawp at. I couldn't imagine the women rested in much peace.

Then there was the sad case of Avice Cony. She and her sister and mother, Joan, were all charged with causing a number of people to die. Avice's son was made to give evidence against her in the trial and, consequently, praised by the judge. Though he was only ten, his testimony sealed their fate. They were all found guilty. Joan Cuny, Joan Upney and Joan Prentice were executed within two hours of sentencing. Avice declared she was pregnant and was examined. After her claim was validated she was thrown into gaol until she gave birth. Then she was hanged the next day.

It was a shocking story, but one that was repeated time and time again. I noticed that I'd left the date off that last trial and, rather than sift through reams of notes, googled it. 1589. I wrote it in my notebook to insert in a minute.

When I replaced my hands on the keyboard an unwelcome sight greeted me: a private messaging box. Facebook had opened itself.

'I'm sorry,' the words in the rectangle read.

I picked up my biro and tapped it on the side of the table. Again, there was no name to note at the top of the box.

'Little git,' I thought.

'Are you there?' Same question as before.

I knew Joe had told me not to reply but part of me wanted to find out more details so I could trap the teenage tinker. Before my weakling impulse control was able to kick in I saw myself write, 'How old are you?'

There was a pause, then, 'You know. 15.'

A teenager in his bedroom. Joe was right. But this prankster was obviously rather thick too. He shouldn't have responded. Now I had some info about him.

Would he be foolish enough to reveal more?

I tried it. 'Where are you?'

Another pause. Then, 'You know.'

The temptation to respond was overwhelming. Perhaps I could draw him out and hand over the details to Joe. 'I don't,' I wrote.

Would he bite?

I waited for a moment then it came up: 'I'm right here with you.'

A trail of goosebumps crept down my spine.

Hadn't seen that coming.

I took my cursor to the 'x' and shut messenger down, silently cursing myself for playing right into his sweaty hormonal hands.

Still, I had to admit, it was a little unnerving. I pushed back from the table and went to look out the large front windows. There were no houses opposite, only the meandering curve of the grassy hill; the brownish silhouette of the station bathed in the orange half-light of the street lamps. I directed my gaze to the west. From this angle I could just about see a foot or two beyond the periphery of several balconies. To my left, the house next door bulged out. The

82

upstairs windows were dark. I knew the old couple who lived there, Mr and Mrs Frenten. They were in their eighties and totally benign. I couldn't see them trying to freak me out like this.

I turned back and, from my vantage point by the window, surveyed the room. The table was about four foot away. My laptop was turned into the room, so that when I worked I could take eye-breaks on the view.

There was a thin side window that looked over the flats to the west, but it was further back into the room and so narrow no one could see in. Even so, I had a good look out of it. The view was limited. Directly opposite, a frosted window was fogged up with condensation. A small round opening beside it billowed out steam. Someone was having a late shower.

There was no one who could see me at my computer.

Okay, well, I guessed it was the right time for a break. I got up and went into the kitchen. It was too late for proper coffee so I fixed myself a nice steaming instant and returned to the living room.

I stopped halfway across the room.

It was there again on the screen.

I sucked in some air and walked tentatively to the computer.

'I'm sorry,' it read.

Nope. Not having it. I scrolled down and disabled my internet connection. Bugger off.

Then I plonked down my coffee and returned to work. Where was I? Oh yes, 1589. I flipped into Word and inserted the date at the beginning of the paragraph.

The message box appeared on the screen. 'I'm frightened.'

Quickly I checked my connection. The line was flat. I should be uncontactable.

'I can feel him here.' The words tripped across the box. 'I can smell him.'

I didn't want to answer it but that familiar sense of pity, alarm, was returning.

I tapped out 'Who?'

'The Devil.'

Right, too much. I slapped my laptop closed. Shit. My hands had a shake to them.

Now what? I stood up and took my cup to the mirror above my old seventies fireplace. My eyes were wide. A tight line fixed across my forehead like an arrow.

Screw it. I went to the table and picked up my phone.

Was I being stupid?

Probably.

He was slower to answer than before. 'Evening.'

My voice was higher than usual, full of restless energy. 'Hi Joe. I'm sorry to disturb you. I hope it's not inconvenient, it's just that, you know what I was talking about the other day? Well, it's happened again. But,' I faltered. 'It's more threatening now. They said that they're here with me. And I took my laptop offline but the messaging continued . . .' I was speeding through the explanation like a lunatic.

'Hang on. Slow down. You're on speakerphone. I can't hear you.'

I waited a minute then took him through the details, describing the specifics of disconnecting from the internet.

'That can't happen, Sadie.'

'I know.'

The connection cracked and buzzed. A horn blared down the line. He was driving.

'Look, I'm busy tonight but I can pop round tomorrow afternoon and you can show me. How does that sound?'

I nodded then realised he couldn't see me. 'Yes please. I'll be home by about three. Thank you.'

'In the meantime, get off your computer and have an early night or something. You sound tired.'

I was. I suddenly *so* was. I said goodbye and took his advice.

It took a while to get my head down, what with the scratching up above, but once I was gone, I was well gone.

Chapter Nine

Impossible pain racked my abdomen. Coming and going in waves. Blackness all around me. Wind howling. Wet mud. It was coming again. The pain burnt through me like a flame forcing a scream from my lips: 'No!'

I couldn't stand it. The spasms were beyond anything I had known before, racking me, taking me, unloosing a howl that came from the depths of my soul.

'Oh God. Mother. No.'

I woke myself up screaming it.

Another nightmare I couldn't remember, only the lingering sting of agony.

My hair was plastered against my forehead, nightdress twisted up around me. I pulled it down and saw my hand left a red trail.

Lifting the duvet gingerly I found myself drenched in blood. What? I wasn't due on for another two weeks. Though I suppose everything had gone a bit haywire after Mum. I hadn't been eating and I hadn't been sleeping so well.

It was earlier than I normally got up which was lucky as I had time to bundle my sheets into the washing machine and jump into the shower. Though I couldn't dawdle: my interview was in North Essex.

I popped a couple of ibuprofen and downed a bitter coffee then dragged my sorry arse out of the flat and into the car, submerging my nightmare in music.

Beryl Bennett was one of those women whose age is hard to determine. She had the manner and wrinkles of a septuagenarian but the sleek brown hair of someone much younger. Her make-up, too, was quite contemporary – subtle beige eyes and a hint of bronzer under the cheekbones. Essex women always take care of themselves. Still, readers liked to know how old people were so I'd have to ask. That'd be tough on her, I thought as she put the kettle on. Though what with one thing and another, I never did find that out.

I knew this wasn't going to need a lot of effort – it was just a puff piece for the *Essex Advertiser* on Beryl's and her son, David's, fundraising efforts for a children's leukaemia charity.

I liked these little jobs. Back when I was doing news, up in the Smoke, it was so much harder; the questions more intrusive, the scenes more distressing. Down here in the suburbs and countryside, I found it quite refreshing that they filled up pages with news and events that, however mundane they might appear, actually testified to human compassion and community spirit.

David Bennett sat opposite me at the kitchen table. He was in his late forties. A thickset man with thinning grey hair and a brown jersey pulled over the beginnings of a good beer belly. There was something in the way he moved about the semi-detached house and interacted with his mother that made me feel sure he'd never left home. When I pulled the wooden chair back to take a seat it made a squeaky noise. David made a naff joke about farting and cracked up. He had the kind of unashamed chortle that sounded well practised in the art of laughing alone. Beryl appeared to have given up being embarrassed years ago. Much as she obviously loved her son, she made no attempt to hide an outstanding ability to filter out his crap gags and howlers. Selective deafness, I think they call it.

'Be a dear,' she called to David. 'Fetch out the biscuits.' He instantly obeyed Mrs Bennett and went to one of the units in the corner, producing a lurid floral biscuit tin, the like of which I hadn't seen since the seventies.

The kitchen was decorated similarly; a pretty room, with poppy-patterned curtains that hugged a large window to some cutesy rear garden, complete with plastic flamingos. David plonked the tin on the table. 'Garibaldi, Miss Asquith? Or perhaps a baldy Gari?' He laughed alone.

I smiled politely. 'Lovely, thanks,' and took a biscuit. 'Please call me Sadie.'

'Lady Sadie?' he asked.

'Just Sadie,' I told him.

'Maybe Sadie.'

I said nothing.

The corners of his mouth drooped when he saw I wasn't picking up the ball with this one. 'So,' he said, changing the subject. 'I'm afraid we haven't got the big cheque any more. Is that okay? Your photographer came on Monday and took some photos of us holding it.'

I shook my head. 'No, that's fine. We don't need it. This

is just for me to ask a few questions for the piece. Make sure I've got all the facts right.'

'Well, we appreciate you coming down, dear,' said Beryl, setting out a tin tray with cups and saucers. 'I know John is grateful.'

'Right,' I said and took my notepad out of my bag. 'So that's John who?'

David leant forwards as he spoke. 'John Adamms. Two "m"s.' He watched me write them down.

'And how does John fit into this?'

'He's Polly's dad,' Beryl called out as she opened the fridge and took out the milk.

'I see. And Polly is the little girl that died?'

'That's right,' said David. 'We were all very moved. That's why we decided to raise some money.'

Beryl brought the tray over to the table and lifted the cups, milk jug and teapot onto the lace doily in the centre. 'Tragedy. Life is full of it. Milk and sugar?'

'Just milk please. And so how do you know the Adamms?'

Beryl heaved herself into a chair. Her thin, wrinkled hands passed me a cup of tea then nudged David's towards him. 'They've been part of our group for a while now.'

'And what group is that?'

'The Hebbledon Spiritualists.'

'Oh,' I said and looked up. No one had mentioned anything about nut bags. I'd assumed it would be your usual sponsored walks and coffee mornings. No wonder the staff writers had farmed it out.

Beryl noticed my reaction and grinned. 'We're not screw-balls, you know. Quite your everyday sort of people. We have accountants in our group, PAs, bus drivers. Bob's a fireman.'

'And we have a Postman Pat.' David grinned.

Beryl smiled at him with the sad acceptance of parental disappointment.

I made a note about the Spiritualist group. 'So how did you raise the money? It was a fair bit wasn't it – a thousand pounds?'

David replaced his teacup into the saucer and leant towards me. '£1050,' he said and watched me write it down again. 'It *was* £1031.75. I made it up with my own money. People like nice round figures.' He looked at my notepad. I didn't write it down.

'Wow,' I said to Beryl. 'Not bad.'

Mrs Bennett tested her tea with her tongue. 'We're getting more of the general public coming along to meetings now than ever before. But believe it or not, there are still a fair few people out there who have some odd notions about Spiritualism.'

No kidding, I thought. 'Really?' I said. 'In this day and age . . .'

'Yes, I know.' Beryl made a tutting noise with her tongue and rolled her eyes. 'So, we thought, well, why don't we do some open evenings? Get local people in so they could see we were just ordinary people – doing our stuff to help others out. And of course we wanted to raise money for Polly's charity.'

'Mum's a medium,' David said. 'Very talented too.'

'I do my best,' said Beryl, a proud little grin appearing on her lips.

'Right,' I said. 'Is that what you did then? Er, medium nights? What do you call them?'

Beryl opened her hands and spread them across the table. 'Evenings of clairvoyance,' she said in a singsong voice. 'Yes, we put on quite a few and also ran a series of taster afternoons.'

I wrote that down in my notepad. 'Which were what?'

'I call them old skool,' said David and laughed.

'He means they're old-fashioned,' Beryl said gently. 'There's a few of us that have practical skills – reading the tea leaves; auras; dream interpretation, that sort of thing. A young lady, Tanith, from the neighbouring village is one of them Witchens.'

David leant in to correct his mother. 'She's a Wiccan.'

'She does a lovely tarot, don't she, David?'

Bennett Junior nodded. 'Very accurate.'

'So we got together and ran about ten of those. One a month. With volunteers selling tea and cake. And we hosted evenings. All the funds came through suggested donations.'

'And you raised that much?' I asked, doing a rough calculation in my head.

'Some of the recently bereaved can be very grateful when they make contact with loved ones on the other side. It helps, you know.'

I wrote that down in my notepad and then flipped it shut so I could take a gulp of tea. 'So, do *you* have practical skills, David?' I turned slightly to him. He was on my left side facing the door.

'Numerology,' he said brightly. 'Numbers. And astrology.'

'Right,' I said, searching for the right word to express limp engagement. 'Interesting.' It sounded so disingenuous I asked Beryl quickly, 'And what about you, Mum? Do you have more skills? Other than clairvoyance of course?'

Beryl nestled into her chair and beamed. 'Palms. Chiromancy, I like to call it. Always been able to do it. Even before I had the calling to clairvoyance. It's just something I've grown up with.' She chuckled. 'I can see in your face that you'd like to have a go.'

'Oh.' She wasn't that great a clairvoyant – I hadn't thought about it. But the idea had a certain appeal. 'What, now?'

'Won't take a moment, love.' She patted the chair to her side. 'Come and take a seat.'

I placed my teacup next to my notebook and swapped chairs. Beryl put her cup down and rubbed her hands. 'They're a bit cold, so 'scuse me.' Then she picked up my right hand. 'David, love, could you fetch my specs. They're beside the cooker.' David scurried over and came back with a small brown case. Beryl popped the glasses over her nose. She examined the skin of my palm and stroked a couple of fingers, then peered down at the left side of my hand.

After a minute she cleared her throat. The smile that hung upon her chocolate lips faded. 'Were you very ill when you were young, dear?'

She looked over the tops of her glasses at my expression.

'No,' I said, blankly. 'Not that I'm aware of.'

Beryl touched her throat then reached out and picked up the cup of tea. She swallowed hard and returned to my hand.

David was also scrutinising it, drawn in by the attention his mum was giving.

She pummelled the flesh beneath my little finger and grimaced.

'What is it?' I asked, trying to grin.

'Mmm,' she said slowly and pushed the glasses back up her nose. 'Sorry to ask this, but you're not adopted are you?'

I laughed. 'Definitely not.'

David stood up and gazed over his mother's shoulder at my palm.

'I don't think it's coming through well today, love.' Beryl's voice had risen.

'Blimey,' said David. 'That's a short one.'

'What is?' I asked too quickly.

Beryl sent him a warning look but he didn't catch it.

He leant forwards and swayed on the balls of his feet. 'By my reckoning . . .' he started to say.

'David!' Beryl nudged him sharply in the ribs.

David's brain didn't connect with his mouth in time. 'By my reckoning,' he said in mock horror, 'you're already dead!'

He laughed heartily.

I didn't.

I had become very cold.

Beryl sucked her teeth in annoyance. 'David, sit down. Now don't you go scaring people like that. Honestly,' she said wearily. The bags under her eyes had darkened into swollen crescents of lilac. At that moment she did look *very* old indeed. 'Typical man. No tact. Just like his dad.' She sighed and pushed my hand away. 'I'm sorry, love,' she said, sitting back into her chair. 'Can't do any more. I'm not feeling too good.'

'Oh dear,' I said, returning to my previous seat. 'Sorry. I hope it wasn't anything that I . . .'

She didn't reply to me. Instead she addressed the next instruction to her son. 'Go fetch my pills please, love. They're on the bedside table nearest the door.'

David got to his feet immediately and dashed out the kitchen.

Beryl was now the colour of ashes. Her make-up seemed only to be resting on top of her skin; beneath the foundation little muscles were flicking and flexing, as if an electric current was running through them.

'Would you like a glass of water?' I asked gently.

She rasped a reply I couldn't understand. Then her eyes fixed on me. All the rigidity and animation seemed to leave her body at the same moment and she slumped back in the chair. For a second her neck went slack and rolled backwards.

I stood up, worried yet completely unsure of what to do. Something was happening to the poor woman but I couldn't tell what. I simply stood there and watched with growing alarm as Beryl's neck moved upwards and forwards, pulled by an invisible thread. Her head slowly followed. And what a strange sight that was – the luscious brown hair, obviously a wig, slipped off, revealing a thinning layer of feathery white tufts. When I saw her eyes I very nearly screamed. They had rolled round so that all that poked through the hooded lids were the bloodshot whites. And then the shaking started. Not a sideways motion but a juddering up and down, quick sharp micro-moves.

A horrible creak was coming from inside her mouth. Her jaw slackened and then fell open, making a grating noise, then slowly it appeared to unhinge and drop lower than I ever thought possible without splintering bone.

Despite Beryl's agonised movements I could do nothing but stare. A terrible paralysis had crept over me. I watched her kindly face disappear into a barely recognisable combination of features in seizure.

Her hands began to scratch at the table and the whites of

her eyes fixed on my face, as if something beyond them perceived me.

Beryl's frame jerked backwards, the upper half of her body shaking uncontrollably.

A gurgling came up from her throat. I could see she was struggling to breathe.

'Oh God,' I said, coming to my senses at last, and rushed round to Beryl's side. 'What can I do? Beryl? Mrs Bennett, are you okay?'

And then I heard it, coming up through her windpipe: a kind of wheeze; a low-pitched primal scream. Something like, 'Ashhhh bitten.' I couldn't be sure: the word was wrenched out of her, fuzzy with sibilance and choked with phlegm.

Beryl convulsed. Her hand flew to her neck. The body heaved. She coughed once, twice, then gagged. As her face surged forwards to the table, her lips opened wider yet.

I gasped with shock and repulsion as I observed a black moth fly out of her mouth.

'Shit.' I was jittering now, backing away from her.

The kitchen door was flung open just as Beryl's body lolled forwards and she collapsed onto the table.

'Jesus Christ,' I said to her son, pointing to his mother's prone form. 'I think she's having a fit.'

David rushed over and lifted his mother's sagging shoulders back onto the seat.

'Get some water,' he barked.

I tore over to the tap and brought back a beaker.

Beryl was coming round.

Her irises had returned to her eyes but there was a dizzy circling going on in them.

David took the water and held it to his mother's lips. 'Come on, Mum. Take them down.' With his fingers he popped a little yellow pill on her tongue.

'What happened?' I asked him, looking on anxiously at his mum. 'Is she going to be all right?'

'She'll be fine in a bit,' he said. 'Look, if you don't mind, I'd like to get her onto the sofa for a rest.'

'Yes of course,' I said and gestured to Beryl's arms. 'Shall I take this side?'

'No,' he snapped, knocking my hand away from his mother. 'Don't touch her. I've got everything under control.'

'Right,' I stammered, feeling disproportionately guilty.

'Please leave, Ms Asquith. You can see yourself out I presume?'

'Yes, of course,' I said and gathered up my things super quick. 'I've got everything that I need to put the article to bed. Thank you for your time.' David Bennett had already picked his mother up and carried her from the room.

I was opening the front door when I heard Beryl call out weakly. 'Take care, Ms Asquith. Be sure to.'

I murmured that I would and shut the door; though privately I reflected of the two of us it was probably she who should be more solicitous.

Chapter Ten

The tide was out. Mud filled up most of the view from my window. It had a dark sullen pallor to it, the colour of an angry toad. You could see a paler line of grey further out: the water slithering to Chalkwell. A light fuzz above it suggested it was bringing in a mist.

And there was something else out there in the air that occupied the space between me and the creeping sea. Something I couldn't yet make out but could feel – like a million unseen eyes watching me. Or perhaps they were just early stars?

It would be a cold night tonight.

I shivered and turned away from the gloom.

The mirror above my fireplace had a woman in it who looked slightly nuts; sad eyes, as grim as the dirty river. The pink skin underneath my lower lids had taken on a shade of damson plum. My bob had shaken free of any style and formed itself into something more brush-like. I peeled a strand away from my cheek. I needed a trim and several nights' sleep but for now hairpins, some good foundation and lipstick would have to do.

I was finishing off the repair job when Joc arrived. To be

honest, I was a little surprised to see him a) in uniform and b) accompanied by a female officer, who he introduced as Lesley.

I led them into the living room and offered them cups of tea. They refused. I saw that Joe, though quite bouncy as usual, had assumed a brusque air of efficiency. In fact he didn't waste any time and asked to see my computer straight away. 'I've filled in Lesley with the details,' he said.

Lesley nodded from the sofa. She was a short woman. Probably weighed about the same as Joe, and wasn't particularly forthcoming. She had the kind of face that made you feel sorry for her, like a bowl of rice pudding with two raisins in it. I imagined she was tolerating Joe's detour to my place as a favour.

I opened the laptop and began to type in my password. 'I did exactly what you suggested – closed the lid and left it. So everything should be here,' I told Joe.

He came over and leant his hands on the table, lowering his head to look at the screen. Our faces were only a couple of inches apart. I could feel his body heat and smell him. A quick glance reminded me that he looked fit in uniform. Always had. Looked pretty good out of it too.

I recalled meeting him at an old friend's thirtieth three years ago. He was with a large group of people and I think he had a girlfriend there too. But it was okay, his sunny demeanour wasn't dented by embarrassment. On the contrary, he looked genuinely pleased to see me and presented me to his friends as 'an exceptionally talented writer', or something along those lines. I followed him with the usual self-deprecation and he smiled at me, almost as if he were proud. When I met his eyes, later that night, while Christopher was off at the bar and his girlfriend was dancing, there was definitely a twinkle there, like he was letting me know that there was something for me whenever I was ready. There was no pushiness about it or any sense that he was demanding an acknowledgement. It was more like an open-ended and unspoken question that lingered in the air between the two of us; 'would you ever . . . ?' Nothing more.

Anyway there we were, by my desk. Joe met my gaze and smiled. I sucked in my abdomen and registered a small thrill.

He seemed oblivious to the effect he was currently having on me: his eyes swivelled over the living room to his partner on the sofa.

'Let's have a look.' This from Lesley. 'Dragged me all this way, might as well sort it out.' She plodded over to the chair next to me and heaved her large behind into it.

'What were you doing?' Her voice was gruff and fat.

I sniffed and sucked in her smell. She reeked of nights on the computer, microwave meals for one and two cats. 'I was working on Word – ah – here it is.' The document was there, cursor still flashing halfway down the third paragraph after the date 1589. 'And I'd just been on Google to check that date. I minimised the window.'

Lesley grunted. 'So you *were* online?'

I shook my head. 'Not for long. We had a conversation for about two minutes.'

Joe sighed and looked at me. 'I told you . . .'

'I know,' I said, justifying my folly. 'I just wanted to see if I could draw out some details. And I did – he said he was fifteen.'

Joe nodded in a kind of 'you silly sod' manner and turned

to the screen. His back was broader than I remembered. I wondered if it was still as lean.

'But then you closed the dialogue box, right?'

'Yep,' I told them both. Lesley's eyes reduced further into wriggly slits as she concentrated on the laptop. 'But then it popped up again. That's when I disabled the modem. Look.' The internet icon indicated it was disconnected. 'And still it came up.'

Lesley grunted. 'I suspect it was more of a time delay on your part. Or a misremembering.'

That sounded like an accusation. 'No, honestly. I distinctly remember it came up *after* I came off . . .'

'What did they say?' It was Joe now.

'He said "I'm sorry" . . . He's coming or I can feel him here. Something about smelling him. I asked "who?"'

Joe huffed out a sigh. 'You replied to them? Sadie, I told you not to. You're fuelling them. This is what people like that get off on.'

I was embarrassed now. He was right – it had been a foolish thing to do. But it was born out of concern. 'I was worried about him. In case he *was* in danger.'

'Don't do it again.' Lesley's weary condescension was leaking into Joe's voice. 'So, who did they say was coming?'

'The Devil,' I said simply.

Joe and Lesley exchanged a glance.

Joe nodded. 'And this is what scared you?'

'Yes,' I said. 'I know it sounds ridiculous now in the cold light of day, but last night, it really freaked me.'

Now it was Lesley who spoke, obviously wanting to wrap up her visit as quickly as possible and get on to a proper job. 'Okay, so if you minimise those windows, we should be able to see the dialogue box. That may give us some information we can use, should you continue to be stalked.'

Stalked – now that was an unpleasant word. I hadn't thought of myself as communicating with a stalker. It had connotations of hunting and predators that didn't seem to characterise these episodes. But anyway, I did as Lesley instructed and closed all the windows to reveal the pale blue wallpaper of my start-up screen. There was no dialogue box. 'That's odd,' I told them. 'I definitely didn't close it.'

Lesley shot Joe a sideways glance. 'You must have.'

'No I didn't. I just closed the lid.'

'Well, they don't shut themselves down.' She pulled the keyboard nearer. 'I'll bring up the history. Will probably be there.' Her tongue stuck out as her chunky fingers stomped over the keys.

I looked at Joe and smiled weakly. He returned it with such strength that I was briefly bowled over. His eyes twinkled and he winked. For a second my bones seemed to dissolve. I blew out and dropped my head trying to concentrate on Lesley's far less attractive behind.

'Well?' he asked her after a minute.

She brought her hands back onto her lap. 'Nothing. Google, as you said. Nothing else. The other stuff is dated from two days ago.'

I turned the laptop towards me and stared at the column. 'That can't be true. It's deleted itself. Is that possible?'

Lesley looked at her watch and levered herself onto her feet. She darted a nod at Joe. 'I'll wait in the car. Nice to meet you, Sadie,' she said, though it was plain it wasn't.

Straightening up I looked at Joe. He was still bent over the laptop, trying a couple of the keys, looking through the different menus. 'There's definitely nothing here,' he said at last and righted himself.

'I don't know what's happened.' It was truly perplexing.

Joe cocked his head to one side and smiled. Oh no – here came that look again, of gut-churning sympathy. 'It's been a hard time for you lately.' His eyes were going sort of dewy. 'Could you have closed the dialogue box down without realising?'

'What, and deleted that particular section of internet history too?' The irritation in my voice was in response to the pity he was showing, not the concern, but it all got jumbled together and my words came out more sarcastic than intended.

Joe kept his head to the side. 'Had you had a drink or three, Ms Asquith?'

'No!' It was a knee-jerk response that masked the truth. I corrected it. 'Yes. But I wasn't drunk, if that's what you mean. I had my wits about me.'

He nodded. 'Okay. Well, try and work offline . . .'

'I *was* working offline,' I cut in then shut up. It was point-less – he didn't believe me.

His lips formed a line. 'Right, well I can't leave Lesley downstairs . . .'

I stood up, put my hands on hips, sighed then showed him to my door.

He turned around on the outside landing and said, 'Call me if it happens again and you want to talk. Okay?'

I nodded. He took a step down the stairs and looked back. 'In fact, call me if you want to talk at all – I have good shoulders that are pretty water-resistant, should you want to cry on them.' He made it sound like a jaunty joke but I was out of kilter with his mood now. I made my eyes unnaturally wide so that they would hide the glare that was behind them. Joe didn't deserve to be the butt of my anger.

'In fact we could do it over dinner if you fancy? Next week?' His voice was hopeful, on his face hung a tentative grin, his eyes flitting to and from my own weird wired look.

I forced out a grin of my own. 'That'd be nice.' The look he gave me was tinged with a blush.

'Great,' he said and vaulted down the stairs with the controlled grace of someone used to training their body. 'I'll be waiting.'

I closed the door with a silent 'Oh well,' and went into the living room. I would give Joe a call at some point but not imminently. I had a date with Felix on Monday and a stack of work to get through. It was important that I pleased my new editor, wasn't it?

Chapter Eleven

Despite Lesley's glum reassurance, I couldn't bring myself to work at home that afternoon. Instead, I popped my computer into a bag and walked up the hill to Leigh Broadway. There was a nice café on Elm Road that did a great coffee and had Wi-Fi.

I ordered an Indonesian-Brazilian blend, positioned myself in the corner with my back to the counter and got stuck in to my piece on the Bennetts.

It had been a creepy experience and I have to say, I was glad to be writing it up somewhere comfy and cosy: the café had once been a vintage clothes shop and retained a pre-loved feel.

I blocked out the Dusty Springfield soundtrack and poor Beryl Bennett's fit and concentrated on the fundraising, pulling out my notebook to check the odd fact here and there.

Once I'd polished it and mailed the piece off to the news editor, I trotted out some prose for Maggie, that filler Essex Girls article we'd talked about. I mentioned Mary Boleyn, Anne Knight, one of the first campaigners for women's suffrage, Ruth Pitter, Kathy Kirby, the first female poet awarded the Queen's Gold Medal for Poetry, Ruth Rendell. I stuck in a reference to Jilly Cooper (yes, she's an Essex Girl), played around with the structure then posted it to the subeditor. Once I was sure it had gone I disconnected my modem and focused my mind on my book and that bad bastard, the Witchfinder General.

Over the course of his ultra-short career, which began in 1644 and ended with his death in 1647, Matthew Hopkins was responsible for the condemnations and executions of around 230 alleged witches. At least, those are the ones that left a paper trail. God knows how many more were done in by the angry mob. The notion of villagers with pitchforks and torches has become a parody of violent herd behaviour, but that's what it was actually like back then. And these mobs, well, they kept no record of who they strung up. Others were dispensed with in local kangaroo-type courts that also left no evidence behind, whilst who knows how many more didn't make it through the torture to those courts. A lot of the 'witches' were old and frail and when you're past your prime, there is only so much stabbing and 'testing' your body can take.

Most experts reckon the total figure was probably fifty per cent more than the 230 recorded. But that's a conservative estimate. And if you thought about the fact that it was all carried out over thirty-odd months – that's a hell of a lot of people in a very short time.

According to a pamphlet written by the Witchfinder, in which he referred to himself in the third person (obviously more than slightly deranged), it all started because '*there was a horrible sect of Witches living in the Towne where he lived, a towne in Essex called Manningtree, with diverse other* adjacent Witches of other towns, who every six weeks in the night (being always on the Friday night) had their meeting close to his house, and had their solemn sacrifices there offered to the Devil.'

'So let's get this right,' I wrote, continuing my chapter. 'You've got a bunch of boisterous women, meeting up on a Friday night, making lots of noise and swearing a bit. Surely that's a seventeenth-century girls' night out? Or in. Depending on which way you look at it. And of course they were talking about sacrifices. What woman doesn't?'

The problem for those particular Essex Girls was that Puritan-mania had taken over England. It was a bit like Beatlemania, with all the hysteria and none of the fun. Puritans viewed revelry as so sinful that in 1644 the government enforced a ban on celebrating Christmas and made it a compulsory day of fasting.

'Party on Puritan dudes,' I wrote, then deleted it. That was too colloquial. My sarcasm was genuine though. I mean, really, what a time to live? Poor sods. Even having a few drinks could get you into trouble. Though most people overlooked it.

Not Hopkins though. He went on to add that these women, this coven, sent a bear to kill him.

'Mmm,' I thought and regarded the screen. I should stick that part of his account in the book. It certainly illustrated his capacity to stretch the truth. Or indicated Hopkins was taking a trip to Nutsville.

I wriggled my shoulders and sat back from the table, then I flicked through his book to the bit that I should transcribe.

'*They 'peached one another thereabouts that joined together in the like damnable practice, that in our Hundred in Essex,*

29 were condemned at once 4 brought 25 miles to be hanged, where the Discoverer lives.' I could see him in my mind, clad in the big boots he was depicted wearing in contemporary engravings; the hat incongruously like a witch's hat; the puny build; the sweaty white skin. I typed on, repulsion rising. *'For sending the Devill like a Beare to kill him.'*

I stared at the lower blank half of the Word document, and my eyes lost focus for a second and seemed to fill up with whiteness. The solidity of the screen was dissolving into a cloud-like substance.

It was bizarre but just when I was about to look away and blink, I seemed to see shapes in the mist – a flat stretch of earth; Essex sky everywhere. No trees, just stubby brown grass below. In the whiteout above – a dark dot. Tiny, like a winged insect or a black moth. Getting bigger.

The vista opened itself up, drawing me in. Although I could see it, I was not 'in' it. It was an odd sensation – like I was eavesdropping on someone else's daydream. But I went with it, tapping the keys of my laptop with haste, trying to capture what was unfolding in my head. This could be good.

'He stood up looking into the clouds, watching it coming down. Whatever it was,' I wrote. 'It was large now, more than nine feet high. Then, a few feet away, just as its claws touched the tops of the grass shoots, it metamorphosed before my eyes into a giant bear rising up on his two hind legs. Its eyes glowed red and it screamed, high and shrill, like a pig having its throat cut.'

Euch. Where had that come from? I had never witnessed an animal's slaughter. Well, the simile was certainly evocative.

I stopped typing and read back.

'"Before my eyes"?' I murmured to myself and changed 'my' to 'his'.

I'd almost entirely filled up that page. It was good, strong. But there was no place for it in my chapter. It was the stories of the witches I wanted to bring out. The real tragedy and horror of that time. Not this; this was fiction. His fiction. I cut and pasted it onto a document entitled 'Weird Bits'.

Then I moved on to the witches. Poor, unfortunate women living on the outskirts of society. They were epitomised by Hopkins' first victim, Elizabeth Clarke. She was a one-legged octogenarian, and when arrested the old dear was strip-searched by the witch hunters looking for the Devil's Mark. This was a place on the body where the witch's 'imps' (familiars and demon spirits given to her by Satan) came and sucked. Sometimes the mark was a deformity. Mostly it was as commonplace as a birthmark, a scar, flea-bite, spot or blemish. When it had been located, Hopkins and his Witchfinders would then 'test' the spot, the theory being that as this 'teat' nourished non-human imps, it was also inhuman and would not bleed.

The witch would be pricked all over with a 'witchpricker' – a knife with a retractable blade that discreetly went back into the handle when required. Witnesses would then watch with horror as the witch screamed and bled from her wounds yet did not react when her 'Devil's Mark' was pierced (and these monsters, Hopkins and his sidekick John Stearne, usually found these marks in the 'privvy parts'). The absence of pain would confirm the witch's guilt. If she continued to protest her innocence she would be 'swum'. Right thumb tied to left toe, she would be hurled into a body of water. If she floated, she would be declared a witch. If she drowned her name would be cleared.

I think they call that Sod's Law.

Seventeenth-century law, doing its best to seem 'fair', insisted that for a conviction the witch should also *volunteer* a confession.

I'm not sure any of Hopkins' victims *volunteered* their confessions freely. To ensure that they did 'fess up' to something, anything, the Witchfinder deprived them of food, water, sleep and 'walked' the accused up and down rooms for days on end. This had most inventing fantastical stories just to bring a halt to their torment. At other times the 'witch' was tied cross-legged to a stool for twenty-four hours, denied food, water or access to the toilet. During this time they were constantly watched, and if any insect or animal of any kind entered the room these were deemed to be the witch's familiars or imps and her guilt was proven. Like the 'walking' exercise he employed, the cramping, degradation, humiliation and pain that this inflicted on (mostly) old women had them confessing to all sorts, just to be untied. Though of course there were some who came up with the goods pretty quickly. I looked at a few of those confessions and thought almost straight away – dementia. But Hopkins would still 'prick' them.

Utter bastard.

On March the 4th, 1645, after applying these methods to the women accused, Hopkins sent Elizabeth Clarke, Anne Leech, Helen Clarke, Anne West and her daughter Rebecca to a preliminary court charged with witchcraft. They were found guilty and thrown into gaol at Colchester Castle.

Delighted by this success, Hopkins and Stearne then set off to roam neighbouring villages, searching for more witches. They pulled in a huge haul; Margaret Moone got done in for spoiling someone's beer and Elizabeth Gooding for being refused a piece of cheese (talk about transference of guilt). One woman was accused because Hopkins saw two rats go into her home. These, he insisted were familiars. Another poor old dear was condemned when a watcher saw a 'fly' come into the room, damning evidence of her communication with demonic imps.

In each case Matthew Hopkins was the chief witness. Everyone believed what he had to say, what with him being a gentleman and rather well to do. So his testimony led to huge numbers of women being sent to the gallows.

He worked his way round Essex, fanning out in a kind of horseshoe shape from his headquarters at the Thorn Inn in Mistley. I'd mapped his 'hits' myself in red dots on a map that hung on the living room wall next to my rococo mirror.

Once he'd 'sorted out' Essex he crossed the northern border into Suffolk; the same horseshoe pattern characterising his movements. He was clearly developing what the police called a 'modus operandi'; first he would establish himself in a town, making the local inn his headquarters. From there he would gather intelligence about witchcraft in the area. Always, he would avoid larger towns. For it was there that more cultivated folk lived, and they were likely to have objected to, or at least been sceptical of, his methods.

In Suffolk the confessions started to allude to sex. Priscilla Collit, kept for three days and nights and only allowed an hour's sleep, confessed that she had carnal copulation with the Devil, borne him two children and sunk a couple of ships into the bargain. Others, old and unstable such as Anne Cricke, admitted that the Devil had use of her body, though admitted she was not sure if they had copulated. She had no idea what 'copulation' meant.

In Ipswich he managed to burn someone: Old Mother Lakeland was alleged to have killed her husband by poisoning. Though witchcraft was mixed up in the accusation, the murder of a male spouse was considered to be Petty Treason, which was punishable by burning at the stake. It is said Hopkins watched in the square that day as the flames licked round her and she was burned alive.

When he entered Huntingdon he came across a man who was not convinced of his methods. This was the Reverend John Gaule who had uncovered some terrible occurrences; such as one accused 'witch' who, having been searched and no marks on her found, was swum. When examined again afterwards the woman was found to have been bitten on the neck and all over her lower body. The sign of a predatory sadist.

Then there was the case of old Elizabeth Chandler. This one really upset me. The poor old love was so reviled and forlorn, she had no company at all, and to help her get through the misery of her existence she gave names to two sticks that she used – one, which she used to walk, the other, which she used to stir bowls of frumenty. I could almost picture her there, sitting with her stick between her skirts. But Hopkins insisted that these inanimate lumps of wood were imps and, as his word was the law, the lonely old woman was convicted and swung.

Thank God at that point the tide started to turn. News of some of the dodgier witch hunting methods was spreading into London and worrying some of the educated sections of society. Feeling increasingly insecure, Hopkins raced back home to Manningtree.

The fate of the Witchfinder was up for discussion. Some said that he was accused of being a witch himself and swum but drowned. Others say that he floated and so was duly executed by the mob. Good. I hope he was. Probably wasn't though. Most felt that he probably died of bog standard tuberculosis.

Such a short life, but so much damage.

And how typical of someone like that to die in the comfort of his own home. He should have been held to account for his crimes. There was no justice, I thought as I typed, 'Matthew Hopkins, the Witchfinder General, was buried in Mistley churchyard in August 1647.'

I sat back and drained the last of my coffee. It had started to rain. Everybody outside was covered up in hats and umbrellas. I cursed the fact that I had neither.

As my eyes returned to the laptop a charge of adrenalin ripped through my stomach. For there it was, back on the screen – the message box, the words flashing: 'He wasn't . . .'

I pushed back from the table, frozen into the pose of an alarmed cat – stiffened shoulders, taut limbs, staring hypnotised at the message.

The young woman sitting at the table in front turned round and asked if I was okay.

'Yes, thank you,' I rasped and she returned to her drink.

But I wasn't.

Inside, my head was thawing out of its sudden panicked freeze. How could the sender know what I'd been writing? Was someone watching me?

I looked around the coffee shop. There were only five tables. A couple in their sixties sat beside me reading the newspapers. The guy behind the counter was serving a customer with takeaway coffees.

I got up and went to the window. The rain had turned heavy and forced most people inside. There was a young guy smoking in the doorway of the deli opposite. I watched as he was joined by a woman. They walked off arm in arm towards the church.

I bit my lip and made towards to my table but one glance at the screen stopped me dead in my tracks.

The message box was full of script. I crept closer to read it:

'He wasn't He wasn't't'

What the hell . . . ?

I moved my cursor to the top of the Word document and saved what I'd written. Then, I slammed the lid shut and slumped into the chair.

What was this? What was going on? No one could see what I was doing, let alone read what I had written.

I swallowed down my trepidation and opened the lid again. My Word document was still there. I minimised the screen.

There were no messages.

Whoever was doing this had enough nous to make sure they were covering their tracks. But for what reason? To scare me? Or to make me look nuts and paranoid.

Nuts and paranoid. Now, there was a thing. It was a phrase I'd used before. To describe my mum. She'd had an episode about ten years ago when she was sure she was being followed, and contacted by 'beings'. In one of our long, hand-wringing sessions before she got sectioned, I'd lost patience with trying to follow her convoluted forays into reasoning and had told her to 'pack it in', that she was being 'nuts and paranoid'.

She was all right again in a month or so, but it took a while for us to rebuild our relationship. And after that I always sensed that she was holding stuff back from me, unwilling to fall into the trap that had got her banged up in the clinic.

And now, here I was, aping her behaviour.

But I wasn't mad. I wasn't making it up. I had seen it with my own eyes. That was no hallucination.

And I wasn't being paranoid. Someone *was* out there contacting me. Or frightening me. Both actually.

Rationally it had to be some remote hacker who had got into my computer system and planted some ghost in the machine that was able to monitor my computer.

The main thing to do was not to play into their hands again. To stay level-headed. What was it they said in the war? Keep Calm and Carry On.

I shut my laptop down properly and made a point of adding some hardcore debugging software to my shopping list.

I would sort this out, but for now, I was done in. I decided to call it a day and paid for my coffee.

Though for the first time, behind my forced rationale, a tiny but very real seed of fear had been planted in my hitherto cogent mind.

Chapter Twelve

There are things in the darkness with me, moving around: skittering claws on stone, scurrying in the straw and filth.

Why won't he let me go back to the others?

I promised to do what he desires.

Something crunches and stops outside the door.

A step. A breath, coming heavy from sick lungs.

A pause, then a scrape of metal on the old wooden door.

Another step. A shove, a scrape.

Please God, don't let him come upon me again. I cannot bear to feel his hot stink upon my face, his claw-like fingers on my breasts. And the cruel reek of the bone pipe he used on old Mother Clarke, to bleed her, find her mark.

I am so afear'd he will turn it on me. No, it cannot be. I cannot endure . . .

The door creaks open wide and I see his eyes, red, come inside.

'No more. No . . . Please.'

I was upright again. In bed. Another nightmare still had me in its grip.

This one stayed with me for a full minute before it started to recede into the impermeable darkness of my mind.

The room was black. It wasn't yet morning. Outside, the cloudy sky blotted out any starlight.

Beads of sweat trickled down my forehead. Fast noisy panting laboured my chest, drowning out other sounds. Though as they slowed I picked up another noise in the flat. A sort of cooing, like a pigeon trapped up the chimneybreast. Though it was louder than that – with more strength. I listened to it.

Was it sobbing?

Following me from the dream?

I tracked the direction of the sound out to the hallway.

What was it?

A wounded dog? I listened intently and prayed that there wouldn't be another sound.

But there was.

A yelp. It was definitely coming from my front room. The suggestion flashed across my brain that there was someone up my chimney.

No, that was impossible.

But the voice kept on sobbing.

I swivelled my legs over the side of the bed and considered the situation. Perhaps I should phone Joe? I was too worried now to give a toss about how I came across to others. I looked for my mobile on my bedside table. It was too dark to see anything and I didn't want to make any noise for fear of drawing the weeping thing's attention.

'No.' The word echoed through the living room into the corridor to me, sitting rigid on my bed.

Okay, that was real. That was human. There *was* someone in here.

I fumbled around for something heavy. Nothing came to hand but a stiletto shoe. It'd have to do.

Slowly I eased myself off the bed. Should I switch on the light or might that alert the intruder? No, darkness could be my cover. Stiletto in hand, I inched across the room. The black fog of night made it hard to navigate but soon I felt my bedroom door and opened it onto the small corridor between the living room, bedroom and kitchen.

The sobs were getting louder. More gut-wrenching. Like someone was becoming hysterical.

The living room door was the nearest to me. Silently I squeezed the handle and crept into the room.

At first everything appeared normal; the room was empty. But then my eyes cast over the far wall and stopped.

Something strange had happened to the mirror.

There was a glow, a sort of greenish luminosity, emanating from it.

I stared at it for a long moment, trying to take on board the unreal sight. My first thought was that it could be some kind of optical illusion caused by the glow of the streetlights outside, so I closed my eyes and changed position slightly.

When I opened them it was just as before.

Then the sob came again. From directly behind the mirror.

Curiosity briefly overcame terror and I stumbled forwards. Now I was in the middle of the room facing it.

Inside the mirror it was pitch black.

I couldn't see any kind of reflection.

Then came the voice, 'Who's there?'

I scanned the mirror. Nothing. Only a depth of jet black. Yet it seemed like the sobbing had come from within.

This is stupid, I told myself. I'm dreaming.

I took a Bambi step forwards and suddenly a face rushed up into view – ghostly white features with terrified coal eyes, surrounded by wild twisted hair.

I shrieked. She shrieked.

I jerked back and hurled my shoe at it. The mirror fractured on impact. Swiftly, I turned on my heel and dashed out of the living room back to the bedroom.

Did I imagine it or did I hear a voice say 'I'm sorry'?

I didn't know.

I was too strung out. Whimpering and crying, I hugged myself in the middle of the bed, pulling the duvet over my body, tense, waiting for the thing in the mirror to get me.

It never came.

Chapter Thirteen

I knew I couldn't keep this to myself any more. I had to share it; had to sound out what was going on with someone else. The hacker, well that was one thing. This, the thing in the mirror, was something else entirely. I just wasn't sure *what*.

I'd forced myself into the living room at some point in the early hours of the morning. The sun wasn't fully up but there was enough insipid grey lighting there to see, sure enough, fragments of mirror scattered across the carpet.

I did my best to clear them up by hand then got the vacuum out. By the time I'd wrapped the glass up in paper and stuck it in the bin, dawn had broken across the estuary, filling the room with tawny hues. It looked cosy, normal. And for about five minutes, I did sit down and wonder if I had been sleepwalking. Or perhaps the hacker had won his mind game and infiltrated my subconscious?

Though I was aware that the sobbing had been female, had got the distinct impression that the hacker was male. But that might just be my own prejudices converging. Anyway, my head was too wired for me to sort through it rationally, so I decided to pay a visit to someone who could.

She was sitting in the main office with Felicity when I walked through the door. There were only the two of them there. The place felt like it hadn't woken up properly yet. Maggie looked surprised to see me, but once she saw the expression on my face, she excused herself and showed me into her office, just off the main room.

I followed her in.

'You all right? You want a coffee?'

I told her yes please. 'I don't know if I'm all right though, Maggie.' Then I spilt it – from the first message, to the strange nightmares and then the woman in the mirror.

Maggie listened carefully as she pottered about the room, filling the machine with coffee beans, wiping a couple of mugs. For the most part she stood by the filing cabinet nodding her head in time with my speech, encouraging me on.

We were sitting either side of the desk when I finished.

She gulped down a lungful of air before she spoke. 'I don't want to sound trite, or like in any way I'm trivialising your experience . . .'

I cut in, 'Just say what you think.'

She put her mug carefully back onto the table, and clasped her hands together. 'You've been through a lot lately.'

I had a hunch that she was going to say something like that and a small, exasperated sigh escaped me.

She stopped then shrugged. 'You did say . . .'

'I know, I know,' I waved my hand at her. 'Go on.'

'People deal with grief in different ways. The messaging

for instance – you said the person on the other end was saying that they were sorry?'

'That was *one* of the things they said . . .'

'When someone dies, it's very common for those left behind to feel guilt of some measure – to feel you could have done more, seen them more often . . .'

'It's not like that,' I snapped. 'I'm not doing this to myself. I couldn't have sent those messages to myself. This is not some crazy *Fight Club* plot twist. This is real.'

'But, Sadie, listen to what you're saying. Joe's not found any evidence on your laptop. These things have been happening when you've been alone. When you've been tapping away at the computer in a semi-alert, semi-meditative state. Also, and I think this is pertinent, it's happened when you've been researching Hopkins. Do you think perhaps you are projecting some of *his* guilt? Perhaps as a distraction from your own?'

My face was screwed up into an expression of contempt. 'You're joking, right? Why on earth would I empathise with him?'

'I didn't use that word. I'm saying it might have a psychological root. All that horrid Hopkins research at a time when you've just lost your mother, for God's sake. Perhaps you've drifted into some dark place. It's a metaphor, but . . . It wouldn't be unusual for someone bereaved to do that. And, you know, you should make time to heal yourself. Maybe take a break? Go on holiday. Grab some sun? Let your mind have a rest.'

I collected my thoughts and reformed them so that I didn't come across as petulant. 'I don't think I'm imagining any of this. I think,' I lowered my voice, kept it firm and stable, 'whatever is happening is coming from an outside entity. I'm not sure who. I'm thinking this hacker has fixated on me. And he's clever about what he does. The fact I'm going through emotional upheaval is irrelevant.'

Maggie bit her tongue, then she said, 'Can you hear yourself, honey? Do you know how you sound? You are so very ready to dismiss the idea that some of this could be an externalisation of your current state of mind. It smacks of self-denial. In your heart, you know that. Give yourself a break. It doesn't mean you're going round the twist. It just means you're stressed out. And that, my dearest Sadie, is quite natural in your present circumstances.'

I frowned. She *was* starting to sound convincing – though I still didn't believe her. I couldn't be hallucinating the interaction with the hacker, could I? Or could I have absently switched off and let my hands doodle across the keyboard while my mind focused on other things?

It was uncomfortable but it was one answer. Maggie was right about Joe and Lesley not finding any evidence . . .

I put my head in my hands and propped my elbows on her desk. 'So the woman in the mirror, you think is . . . ?'

Maggie saw I was catching her drift and let the certainty of her conviction ease into her voice. 'You woke up from a nightmare, walked into the living room and looked in the mirror. There you saw a woman with a stricken white face and black hair. Someone who was screaming.'

I nodded.

'I think you may have been looking at yourself, sweetheart.'

'I wasn't. It didn't . . .' My voice cracked with new doubt. 'It looked like someone else . . .'

Maggie continued on: 'You were tired, half asleep, maybe

122

even still dreaming . . .' She tailed off and let me think on that a bit.

There was logic in it.

Argh. My conviction was wavering.

Crap.

Maybe it *had* been me who was crying. It didn't sound like that but it was plausible that the nightmare had disturbed me and that I had experienced the darkness of night, the acoustics of the flat, in some hypnogogic state, which had then got my imagination going into overdrive.

'Just get some sleep, some counselling and some new software,' she was saying. 'If you won't go for all three, make sure you get the last. I think it's fairly unlikely that you've been hacked in the way you've suggested but if there is someone interfering with your computer you should sort that out as a priority. Especially in your line of work. You don't want anyone nicking your ideas or corrupting your files, do you?'

'Nope. Most definitely not.' That was a good point.

'Make sure you're backing your work up, yeah?'

I nodded. 'Yes, definitely. I'm going to get a virus check too.'

My confusion over the mirror woman was beginning to ebb. Of course, I could have dreamed it; after all I was having lots of strange dreams. This was a new twist in the nightmares. I should monitor myself and if they got worse or more physical I'd start using the sleeping pills the doctor had prescribed when Mum . . . I still couldn't say it or think the word.

Maggie must have seen my expression, as her forehead wrinkled and she sent me a look of immense compassion.

Her red hair clouded round her face, brushing her shoulders and paisley pashmina. 'Okay?'

I nodded again, relaxed my brows and poked my forehead. 'Brain working again.'

She smiled sympathetically. 'Call me, whenever you want to talk. You know there are bereavement counsellors out there. I'm sure I can fix you up with someone I know.'

I got to my feet. 'I'm okay. I'm just, I dunno. Put it this way, when I'm on my own it all seems pretty real.'

'That's the point though, isn't it? Take it easy for a bit, Sadie,' she said and grinned. 'The article you filed yesterday was great by the way. I loved it. Keep positive. Think along those lines. Mind you, don't for one moment think you're getting an extension on that other piece we talked about. If that's what you're fishing for it ain't working . . .' She winked.

I tugged myself up from more contemplative depths to meet Maggie's banter. 'You gotta give me marks for originality,' I said. 'Most prevaricating writers would dish up something like writer's block or "other commitments". Not me – I go for full-blown psychotic meltdown.'

'Or tiredness,' she added and straightened herself up. 'Though I know you're really just here for the coffee.'

'Well, it sure ain't the company,' I said as I passed through the door.

She didn't answer but a pen whacked me on the back as I turned out of sight.

I navigated around the desks to the front door.

'Er, hi Sadie.'

It was Flick. She'd stuck her head above her monitor in a half-risen position and was looking kind of sheepish.

'Oh, hi Flick.'

She sat back into her chair, so I moved round the other side of her Mac to see her as she spoke.

'I'm really sorry, but I couldn't help overhearing.' She extricated a strand of dark hair from her mouth. 'The door wasn't closed.'

'Oh,' I said. Heat touched my cheeks. 'Sorry, it was meant to be a private conversation. I was just, er . . .'

She cut in. 'I know, but it was fascinating. When you were talking about that hacker. When you said you were in the coffee shop? Did you say something along the lines that you'd just written the details about where Hopkins was buried?'

I was looking at her from above. She was slender and petite. Just then her tiny frame seemed so fragile. 'That's right.'

'And you were freaked out because that meant that whoever had messaged you, could see you and what you were writing.'

'Yes,' I said. 'I thought it could be some virus or remote . . .'

'You're hooked on the idea that they're trying to spook you by implying that they can see you. What if it's not about that? What if it's more about the facts that you're writing? Could they be suggesting Hopkins wasn't buried there? What if it was *what* you had just written that was the trigger, not the fact it was *you* writing it, if you see what I mean?'

'You think the hacker is fixating on me because of my research?' I looked doubtful.

She shrugged and cocked her head to one side 'Forgive me for saying this, but you're taking a very ego-centric approach to this for someone who professes that it's not about them. If it's not your grief and it's not your work then what *is* it about? Your irresistible animal magnetism?'

My eyebrows were practically on the ceiling. The girl had balls – you had to give her that. But she'd gone too far. I was about to respond with unthinking indignation but she continued on. 'If it's not about you then surely it's about what you're writing. You've got a book deal. That means you've got a voice, right?' She looked up, beyond me, to the rafters, thinking through her words as she spoke. 'I'm not sure. It's just – is there any doubt about what happened to Matthew Hopkins? I mean, is it concrete?'

I gave up being offended, pulled in by the fact that, although it had flitted through my brain yesterday, Flick might be right. I had been way too focused on poor me. I mentally rummaged through my files. 'There is some hypothesis, but it's not regarded as kosher by academics and historians. Might be worth a squizz though, true.'

'Just a thought,' she said, as if her comment had been nothing more than a throwaway quip, and drank some water from a glass on her desk. 'You know there's this whole thing about automatic writing? Have you heard about it?'

I had a vague memory of some eighties documentary. 'Remind me please, Flick.'

'It's the state that you get into when you sort of lose your overriding conscious and let your subconscious come through. Or other people think, it's more like channelling, and actually what happens is that a spiritual source is in control.'

'Well, I don't think I went into a trance or anything.'

'No, I don't think you have to. I think it can happen in a waking state.'

126

'I don't know,' I said reflecting. 'It's all slightly strange. There's a lot to think . . .'

She sniffed and broke in, 'Could be your subconscious coming through, trying to communicate with you? To lead you?'

My frame slumped. 'Don't you start. I've just had a half-hour psychotherapy session with Maggie.'

Flick laughed and sat back. 'I don't really think that,' she said and smiled.

'You don't?'

'No.' She shook out her wispy black hair. 'I'm more likely to think it's a ghost.'

I examined her face to see if she was joking. Too hard to tell. 'A ghost? Why?'

She shrugged. 'Look at me – I'm a Goth. That kind of thinking comes with the territory. I love supernatural phenomena, don't you?' She peeked at me, scrutinising my reaction.

'Well, I like it when it's on the TV or in books or films. Not when it's happening to me.'

'I'd love it,' she smiled confidently.

There was no time to comment, as she was off again. 'The automatic writing thing is worth looking into. You could try it out. See if it happens when you're in control and have a go at bringing it on.'

I rubbed my chin. 'I don't really fancy that. It's too creepy. I'm hoping it's going to go away.'

'Okay,' she said and turned back to her computer. 'Do me a favour and let me know how you get on.'

'How I get on?'

'Yes,' she said, tapping at the keys. 'I'm interested.'

To be honest I was more than taken aback. This wasn't the shy, retiring wallflower I was used to. Still, I told her I would. Then I left.

I had software to buy and a present to pick up for Uncle Roger's party.

Chapter Fourteen

Despite Janet's pessimism my uncle was in fine form on Saturday. In fact, seated in a sturdy wooden chair in the shade of the gazebo holding court, he looked like he'd last long enough to see a telegram from the Queen. The weather was exceptionally warm that October weekend and the party had, in Great British fashion, transferred itself to the garden, in order that its pasty-faced revellers might soak up every last ray of autumn sunshine.

Lucy, my stepsister, who I had last glimpsed gallivanting naked in the tree house, was playing the violin whilst the assorted friends and family listened on in a semi-circle of picnic blankets and deck chairs. She had obviously got a little more self-conscious in the intervening three months and was dressed in a lemon skirt and matching blouse. Her rendition of *Happy Birthday to You* was slightly squeaky but very well received by the indulgent audience. Once the clapping had ceased I stepped into the garden and coughed to alert the company to my presence.

'Mercedes!' Dad creaked to his feet from a blanket just in front of Uncle Roger's chair. There was about eight years between them but whilst my dad looked sprightly for his age, Uncle Roger had an old-fashioned granddad-type look to him. Dad's hair was greying but still kept some of his youthful deep brown curl, and today he had on a cricket jumper and linen slacks. They were very last season but kind of right for the day it was turning out to be.

'At last!' Dad's mouth tucked up into the corners, suggesting a suppression of his usual characteristic irritation. 'We thought you would never come.'

I looked at my watch. 1.45 p.m. 'I'm only forty-five minutes late.'

Dad kissed me on the cheek. 'I did say one o'clock.'

'Oh, right. Sorry.'

'Never mind. How are you, dear? Are you coping? Have you managed to do the house yet?' He reached out and put his arm around my shoulders and gave me a quick squeeze. I wasn't used to his physical embrace. We never had that kind of relationship. Nonetheless I knew he was trying and smiled.

I shook my head. 'I haven't got round to it yet. Maybe next week. You got something you want me to look out for?'

Dad gave me another squeeze. 'Not at all. I thought you might want me to come with you? Help you go through your mother's things. It won't be a particularly pleasant experience.'

I was grateful for his concern but told him I'd be fine on my own.

'Righty ho. Well you know where I am if you need me. You do understand that don't you?'

'Of course,' I said and settled a play punch on his belly to mask my awkwardness.

'You all right?' he asked before releasing me.

'I'm getting on,' I told him. And I was. Since I had loaded the new firewall onto my laptop the Hackerman had ceased his mischief.

The nightmares hadn't stopped. But this was neither the time nor the place.

'Good. Glad to hear it. Now you go and say happy birthday to Uncle Roger. What can I get you to drink? We're all on champagne.'

'Thanks but I'm driving.'

'What?' His face fell. 'We've made you up a bed in the spare room. Your cousins aren't getting here till five. Come on, stay over. What have you got to run back for?'

I glanced at Janet who had come up to greet me. She had a 'please' look on her face.

Bugger. I would appear churlish now. 'I'll see how it goes,' I said, kissing Janet on the cheek.

'Hello love,' she greeted me. 'One glass of fizz won't hurt will it?' They were an ebullient couple and enjoyed life to the full. Though if you hung out with them for more than a day or so you did get the impression that alcohol was an integral component of 'fun'. But it was a good-natured thing.

'You two are terrible. All right, just one.'

They both smiled and Dad went off to fix me a drink while Janet guided me through the legs and glasses and plates to Roger's square of shade. 'We've been so lucky with the weather,' she said. 'I think this will be the last of it though. We thought we'd enjoy it before it disappears completely. Ah, here's the birthday boy.'

Uncle Roger was talking to a plump middle-aged woman with dyed frizzy burgundy hair. They looked an odd couple, sat there against the backdrop of purple agapanthus and

Michaelmas daisies; she, in her tasselled hippy skirt and bejewelled flats, he, with his neatly trimmed Captain Birdseye beard and dark tweed suit. He always looked immaculate did Uncle Roger.

Janet waited for a pause in their conversation before introducing me. 'This is Mercedes,' she said to the woman. 'Ted's eldest.'

The red-haired woman tried to stand up to greet me, but she was wedged into a rather small metal deck chair and it was causing a few problems. 'Oh,' I said, shaking my head. 'Please don't get up. You're comfortable there.'

She gave up and sent me a look of gratitude. She had pretty eyes highlighted with a matching dab of blue eye-shadow and a cheerful round face. 'It's lovely to meet you, Mercedes.' She held out her hand. Her cheeks looked like rosy Pippins. 'I've heard a lot about you. I'm a friend of Janet's, Amelia Whitting.'

I grasped her palm and shook it heartily. 'Please call me Sadie,' then turning to Uncle Roger said, 'Happy birthday,' and handed over my present. He took it and reached up crookedly to kiss me. I bent down quickly to offer my cheek so he didn't have to rise.

He smacked his lips on my chin and plopped back down, screwing his eyes up. 'Mercedes, that's a very short skirt you've got on.' There was more than a smidgen of disapproval in his eyes as he surveyed my ensemble. Both Dad and he had this superior than thou thing going on. But where Dad tried to hide it, Roger let his disregard run free. I'd chosen the dark linen dress because I knew it would be cool on the leather driving seat. Of course, I should have known Uncle Roger would have found something to censure. He always did.

Janet beat a hasty retreat, while Amelia cooed out something about me looking smart.

There were no free seats nearby so I squatted down by his feet.

'How are you then, Mercedes?' He was easing himself back into the comfy padding of the chair now, putting my package on the coffee table at his side. But I wasn't having any of that; I'd spent weeks researching his gift. Uncle Roger used to be a shop steward and, like Dad, a thoroughly committed trade union man – the socialist movement ran through their blood. Their father had taken part in the Jarrow March. Neither of them ever stopped banging on about it. I'd managed to track down a very mouldy reprint of the crusaders reaching the outskirts of London, had it restored and framed. It had cost a pretty penny and I didn't want it left on the table without him commenting on it. 'Aren't you going to open the present?'

Uncle Roger fingered the gift then withdrew. 'No, we're opening them when your cousins get here.'

'Oh,' I said, not trying to hide my disappointment. My uncle gave a familiar sigh.

Amelia took the cue and piped up. 'So Sadie, Janet and Ted tell me you're a journalist. What are you working on at the minute?'

I took a long gulp of my champagne and eyed my uncle, then I told them both about my meeting with the publisher.

At the end of it Amelia was practically jumping out of her seat. 'Oh that's fantastic.'

'Yes,' I said to Uncle Roger. 'Can you imagine? A publishing deal?'

Even he nodded at that, acknowledging it was a massive

coup although he'd never had any interest in writing. 'That sounds interesting, Mercedes. The witch hunts. It's a sad truth that we know more about the Witchfinder General than his victims. Obviously as a Suffolk man I'd like to point out that our county lost more souls to that nasty gentleman . . .'

'But,' Amelia interjected. 'Overall during the witch hysteria Essex lost far far more.' She eyed Uncle Roger for a response.

I was hoping we weren't getting into a 'we came off worse than you' standoff. The truth of the matter was that that argument camouflaged the real nature of the conflict – the rich and powerful versus the poor and beleaguered. Same as it ever was . . .

Thankfully Roger agreed. 'Yes, fair enough. What a horrid barbaric time. Mercedes, are you sure you want to go into all of this?'

I nodded my head vigorously. 'I'm Essex through and through. And I'm female. Why would I not want to delve into it? There was a great wrong done to our ancestors, and I'd like to have a go at bringing it into contemporary consciousness to make people think about it.'

Roger rubbed his beard. 'Do you not think, Mercedes, some things are better left undisturbed?'

Amelia glanced at me, sensing a clash coming on. Her look was a hush; I didn't obey it. I said 'No way. This is part of my heritage. It's part of who I am.'

'But what about what's going on *now*?' Roger fixed me with a determined stare. 'Surely there's more to be made from scout fetes and council corruption than digging up the past?'

I glared at him, thinking right, that's just what you'd like me to do isn't it? Just then Janet appeared with a bottle of champagne. 'Oh, empty here are we? Do let me top you up.'

In spite of my earlier decision re: the car, I let ⌐.
my glass and within seconds more guests had appe⌐
Roger got up to greet them and moved further down ⌐.⌐
garden.

Amelia however was still back in the dark days. 'Sadie, I'm
intrigued. I have an interest in this.'

I glanced at her skirt. I wanted to steer clear of any airy-
fairyness. 'Are you into that New Age stuff? That's not the
angle I'm taking.'

Amelia laughed. 'No, not at all. I may wear the uniform
but I'm not in the club, so to speak. I live in Manningtree,
that's all. Well, just outside. The local history is fascinating.
No one really speaks of Hopkins. Not any more – they've
been there and done that. But I'm not a native so I've found
all that side of the town history very interesting. I'm from
Launceston originally, in Cornwall. It's near Boscastle. Do
you know it?'

I shook my head. 'I recognise the name but I haven't been.'

Amelia grimaced. 'Got hit awfully badly by those floods
eight years back. You probably saw them on the news.' She
tutted. 'Terrible. But,' she clasped her hands over her knee,
'they've also got a Museum of Witchcraft. Wonderful.'

'That's interesting.' I was being genuine.

'I went back a couple of years ago and gave a lecture on
what I found out about the dastardly Master Hopkins. Did
the Women's Institute too.'

She caught me arching my eyebrows. 'The W.I.'s not all
jam and fairy cakes these days, you know. We're quite
progressive. Anyway, it went down well. All quite amateur
sleuthing though, I'm afraid.' She raised her own eyebrow
now to imply faux modesty.

'Really?' I asked. Now I was seeing Amelia with different eyes – as a possible source. 'So do you know much about Hopkins?'

She leant her shoulders into me. 'I know he wasn't born in Manningtree. Suffolk more likely. There's a will of a James Hopkins who was a minister of the parish of Wenham. Most people agree that was his father. Personally I'm not that interested in his birth. No, it's his end that interests me. There are stories that tell of him being lynched by a mob when he returned to Manningtree. Some think he went overseas.'

I could hear the West Country twang in her voice now.

'I've heard some of that before,' I said, thinking back to what Flick had said about my 'ghost in the machine', the unknown hand that had sent that missive to me – 'He wasn't he wasn't he wasn't'. Thing was, most people thought Hopkins was buried in Mistley and I said as much. 'I'm sure most of that's conjecture. Isn't the consensus that he died of tuberculosis? That's what his sidekick Stearne wrote, I believe.'

'Yes. All true,' she said with an enthusiastic nod. 'But you have to agree that it was a rather sudden disappearance. Tuberculosis is slow and creeping. And perhaps Stearne had thrown the towel in with Hopkins. The Witchfinder was involved somehow with Lady Jane Whorwood. Some thought that association was the end of him. She was a Royalist. Absolutely pro-Charles I; visited him in prison. They may have possibly even had an affair. She certainly helped him escape. Perhaps the Parliamentary Puritans who backed the witch hunts grew weary or suspicious of Hopkins' motives. Or perhaps, as you say, he just wasted away . . .'

I could tell she was saving the best for last so I asked, 'You don't reckon that happened then?'

Amelia beckoned me closer. 'I always wondered if he wasn't murdered,' she said, throwing her hands up in the air.

'Really? By whom?'

'I don't know exactly. But I have a half-formed theory.' She sat back and took a large swig of her champers. 'Who gains from Hopkins' sudden disappearance?'

I had a think but came up with too many suggestions to mention them all.

Jumping in quickly she answered herself and said, 'Men. That's who.' And gave me this hybrid look that married satisfaction and smugness with a sort of leer.

Then she leant forwards and touched my knee.

Crap, I thought. That's all I need – a predatory radical lesbian on my case. Just when I was loosening up and starting to enjoy myself. 'How so?' I countered in a tone that suggested scepticism.

'Well,' she leant back into her chair and cradled her champagne flute in both hands. I could see a lecture coming on.

'It was in the middle of the Civil War. And you know this was quite a time for women. A lot of them took advantage of the breakdown in law and order to come out of traditional female roles. A few women were involved in a peace movement, which tried to persuade men not to participate in the war. Women of all classes battered on doors pleading with people, attacked soldiers . . . Also, with half the male population off fighting, women had to take a practical and physical part in society. But then people got edgy. Firstly witches, whether real or not, challenged authority. So people were quite pleased to see them smacked down and neutered. But later the country realised that it was mostly women getting hanged, and mostly because women couldn't speak for themselves, attitudes started to change. Popular opinion turned.'

'Funny,' I said, listening to what she was saying and making parallels. 'When you put it like that – I know the whole Essex Girl stereotype started when women were really beginning to infiltrate the work place during the eighties; banking, engineering, the financial sector. The Essex Girl stereotype slapped them back down again by suggesting they were thick, lustful, passive sluts. Which is kind of what they'd rather they were.'

Amelia tossed back her hair. 'Wouldn't be surprised.'

'Hopkins sexed up the "witches" too. Before he came to the stage, it was just finger pointing and local feuds, but once he got his mitts into it the whole thing took on a vastly more lascivious aspect. It was all about women, and some men, letting imps suck them. Women would copulate with the Devil too. Lots of mentions of "carnal relations".'

Amelia's hair wobbled atop her head as she nodded. 'That's the thing. It was all spiralling out of control. If you believed that Hopkins was right then you had to concede that half of South England was in the orgiastic grip of Satan. People knew this wasn't so. Ergo, seventeenth-century rationalists finally speak out and the debate surrounding women's status kicks off. Only on the fringes but it's there. For the first time in history,' Amelia said cheerily and sat up in her seat, 'men could see that the women involved weren't witches. And also that they couldn't speak out for themselves. They had to have a brother, or cousin, or father or son to speak for them. Most of the women accused lived on their own. There was this huge discrimination. If you recognised this unfairness then you started to see the lack of gender balance: any sane-minded individual had to concede that things weren't right. Then, to prevent this spread of hysteria, the solution was perhaps that women should be granted some kind of status . . .'

'Okay? So?'

'The idea is growing. Something has got to change to stop the witch hunts. And then all at once Matthew Hopkins disappears. Overnight, everything goes cold.'

I reflected upon this for a moment. 'So what are you saying? That the momentum to give women more rights fell away because of the decrease in witch hunts?'

Amelia nodded. 'Yes. That took the wind out of the "feminists'" sails.' She threw me a meaningful glance. 'In lots of ways Hopkins stirred up a hornets' nest. Let's face it – we were only forty or fifty years off of The Enlightenment, when rationalism took to the fore.'

'So you're saying that he was eliminated? Murdered because he was indirectly challenging the status quo?'

She raised her glass to me. 'I'm giving you a steer.'

'Well, I haven't heard that conspiracy theory before.'

'Is it a conspiracy theory? He'd outlived his usefulness. He wouldn't be the first person to be silenced in the Civil War.' She raised her glass. 'The W.I. loved that angle, I can tell you. Anyway, take my number and visit me when you go to Manningtree. And you've got to stay at the Thorn Inn in Mistley. He's meant to haunt it, you know?'

'Hopkins?'

Amelia winked at me. 'Oh yes. Apparently he's been seen sitting on a chair in the attic and another one of the rooms.

They like to play it down but people talk. And we all love a good ghost story don't we?'

In the context of the previous few days it was the last thing I loved right now. But I was courteous in my response. 'Thank you,' I said. 'That's all *very* interesting.'

'Here,' she said, reaching into a bag at her feet. 'Call me if you decide to pop over.'

We exchanged numbers and were depositing phones back into handbags when Janet came over and the conversation dwindled to more domestic subjects.

At some point I was dragged off to play cricket with Lettice and Lucy who were in fine spirits and ran circles round me in my semi-inebriated state.

'Why is Aunty Mercedes wobbling?' I heard Lucy ask as I was getting a good innings in.

'Because she needs another drink,' said an older male voice. It was cousin Ian, grinning from the sidelines, a champagne flute in either hand. 'Here,' he said. 'Refreshments.'

Somehow it had got to five o'clock and almost immediately we were called into the living room to watch Uncle Roger open his presents. As it turned out he loved the photo. Bloody good job too, I thought. I would have done my nut if it had been passed over without comment.

There were a couple of speeches and numerous toasts and before I knew it I was going way way way over the legal limit and agreeing to stay.

When that had all settled down Ian and I went outside and sat on the swing chair. It was good to see him.

'Roger seems well,' I commented after we'd caught up on romantic attachments (his), careers (mine) and Mum's funeral. 'The way Janet was talking I thought he'd be at death's door.'

Ian shook his head. 'No, he's looking all right now, but his kidney is on the way out.'

'Really?' I kicked my feet up and pushed the swing back. 'So what's the prognosis?'

'Well, he's only got one left so I guess, traditionally, it would be a transplant . . .'

'So why doesn't he get one?'

Ian's face had a very solid look to it. He was always the very essence of calm benevolence. 'You can't buy them at the supermarket,' he said gently, as if breaking bad news to a child.

I was going to protest that people like Roger went on forever, but Dad was marching over the lawn towards us.

'Come on you two. Roger's leaving. Come and say goodbye.'

The swinging had made me feel a little sick anyway. So we got up and staggered into the house, through to the hallway where there was a queue of well-wishers bidding farewell. Roger was halfway out the front door, his face flushed, his eyes bright and watery. He was having a great day.

I was quite pissed by now and an unexpected wave of compassion flooded through me.

Ian and I pushed through to Uncle Roger. Ian shook his hand and I, filled to the brim with bonhomie and bubbles, threw my arms around him and slopped a kiss on his cheek. 'Uncle Roger, it's been great to see you. Happy birthday. And listen, I know you're poorly and I've thought about it and I would be happy to give you my kidney if you want it. No really. Yes.'

Roger took a little gasp of air. Then he broke into a broad

smile. 'Oh Mercedes, that is kind of you. But the photograph will do just fine.'

He leant forwards and stroked my cheek. It was an affectionate gesture but at the time I was full of drunken passion and determined to donate a vital organ.

'No,' I said tersely. 'I mean it.'

Roger sighed. Then he said rather quickly, 'You keep it. It wouldn't do any good.'

I smiled and said, 'Go on. You don't know till you've tried. Have it. It can be your Christmas present.'

He reached down and grabbed my hand. 'You don't know how much that means to me, Mercedes. Thank you. But we wouldn't be a match, my dear. Take it from me, I know.'

Dad had come up from behind, clearly embarrassed by the turn the conversation had taken.

He patted my shoulder and prised my arm from his brother's. 'Mercedes, your uncle is very tired. Stop bothering him. Ian, will you take her back into the party? She's had a bit too much –'

Ian gave my dad a wink and took my elbow.

As I was pulled away I told Uncle Roger, 'I mean it, Rog. I'd do it for you.'

Then I hiccupped.

Inebriation so detracts from serious intent.

But I meant it.

And so, I realise now, did he.

Chapter Fifteen

I'm not sure at what point I finally went to bed, but when I woke up I had a serious hangover. It was nine o'clock. Dad and Janet must have risen early but let me sleep on, because when I came down into the kitchen they were sitting round the table with Lettice and Lucy.

For a minute I watched them from the doorway. Dad was pouring Lucy a juice. Lettice must have just said something funny to Janet, because she was looking over smiling. If you didn't know better you would assume that they were the perfect family. Maybe they were. The thing is, I saw very clearly that morning that they were happy and self-contained.

They didn't need me.

They never had.

And I knew they would be just fine if I weren't there at all. Don't get me wrong, it wasn't that I was full of self-pity. I could see that they *worked*. Later I would remember the scene. It would clarify a hard decision I was going to have to make.

It wasn't long before Lucy spied me and called out my name. 'You were drunk last night,' she said, full of childish satisfaction.

'I was tired,' I told her, sloping into the kitchen and ruffling her hair. 'You are way too perceptive for your years, young lady.'

After many cups of coffee and a full English breakfast I finally extricated myself from the household and was on my way by eleven.

Halfway home I had to pull in for petrol. I was close to Manningtree and considered for a minute whether I should detour and scout the town. But at the back of my mind there was a notion that if I mentioned the visit to Felix, he might wish to accompany me – and that was far too tempting to jeopardise. I was seeing him tomorrow in Colchester. I might drop it into conversation.

Instead I filled up the car, bought some mineral water and a damp sandwich and was just about to leave the shop when a glance at the magazine shelf stopped me. A local journal was running a feature on witches. I took it to the till, was offered a bag, said I didn't need one and headed towards the exit, arms full – and promptly bashed into a large man clad in a black leather jacket. Everything spilled onto the floor.

The big guy dropped to his knees, full of yanky sounding apologies, and helped me scoop them up. It was only when I righted myself that I looked into his face. It was familiar, tanned. He smiled, revealing a set of immaculate white teeth. I couldn't place him.

'Sorry,' I said. 'It was my fault.' He didn't offer a verbal response, just nodded and looked away. I felt a little bit of an idiot knowing I probably reeked of last night's fizz so I quickly shuffled out to the car.

Depositing my goods on the back seat, I took out the mineral water. Still not fully compos mentis I opened it and released a fizzy shower of water all over the dash and driving seat. Bugger. I had cleaning stuff in the boot so hopped round and fetched it. As I slammed the boot I saw the man in the leather jacket get into a black BMW on the other side of the forecourt. He settled into his seat, pulled his seatbelt across his chest and then just watched me.

I smiled.

He smiled.

I turned away and dried the car, inwardly cringing, the clumsiest oaf in town.

Within minutes I was on my way again not thinking any more of the encounter, drawn in to the meditative hum of the road. The smooth Essex landscape opened up either side of me – flat green-brown squares of land, fringed with shady spinach-coloured thickets.

Beyond the sunshine autumn was clearly on her way, shading the hedgerows with her amber paint, fleecing the copses of their frayed leaves. The air outside smelt smoky and ripe; the earth was ready for harvest.

An uneventful hour later I pulled into my drive. My back had been aching a little so I stretched my arms up and rubbed my neck. I don't know what made me look but just as I was about to get out of the car I clocked a black BMW pulling in across the road.

No one got out. The side windows were tinted.

I adjusted my rear mirror to get a better view. Then, I shivered. I didn't know why at the time.

An older man in a light-coloured suit got out of the back. He had a trilby pulled over down over his ears so I couldn't see his face. He sauntered a couple of yards to the post box and posted something through the slot.

I thought it might have been the big man with the leather jacket, but was glad it wasn't. Silly of me to assume that. Let's face it, there were thousands of black BMWs on the road these days.

I locked my car, took my stuff up to the flat and got on with the rest of my day.

Before I went to bed I fixed myself another sandwich, tuned into the news channel and half-stifled a groan. Robert Cutt had been at it again. This time there were allegations of bribery; something to do with access to a list of potential mayoral candidates. Cutt was coming out of it all right though – there was a fall guy, Gerald Harp, some executive way way down in the Cutt hierarchy, testifying that Cutt had known nothing about the alleged misdemeanour. Yeah right.

Photos showed Harp was on the puny side: very fair with see-through eyelashes and matching hair. The last photo on the TV coverage had him in a geeky white blazer, at some sporting event.

After a few minutes of commentary outside the House of Commons they went to a shot of Cutt leaving a meeting. Reporters jostled with each other to get into a prime position. His bodyguards managed to whack a few out of the way, but one determined newshound got their mic right under his nose.

'Do you have any comment to make on this latest allegation, Mr Cutt?'

A bodyguard shoved the camera, which tilted to the floor, showing Cutt's strangely effeminate pale blue suede shoes. The reporter herself was undeterred. 'Mr Cutt, do you have anything to say about this revelation?' The camera was back up, trained on Cutt's face. He stopped and offered his good side to the camera. He didn't give a toss about the fall guy, you could tell. The operator clumsily zoomed in and Cutt's broad high-cheeked visage filled the screen: 'My family and I have always lived a moral and correct life. Despite these slurs, that will continue.' The light American accent still lingered in his voice.

'Amen,' said a bystander and a couple of nearby nutters applauded. Why? He wasn't an out and out Christian but he did have that American thing about brandishing his genealogy. The more he did it, the more popular he got.

God, he was smug.

He gave the camera one last devilish smile, then left the frame. The crew attempted to follow him but were hemmed in by men in suits.

Some of us could see what Cutt was doing – using every possible media opportunity to promote his wholesome credentials in order to get that power seat in the cabinet. That wholesome image was a well-thought-out strategy. Right on the money, if you forgive the pun. I could almost applaud its engineer: we were up to our ears in secular unrest right now – what with the riots, the Eurozone, the bankers, foreign mafia infiltrating our shores. Never before had a return to some kind of thinly couched Christian 'Back to Basics' ethic been so well received by the press. People wanted a quick fix and Cutt was positioning himself as the answer to it all.

It made me seethe.

Arrogant git.

Not all of his family could have lived a good life. There

must be someone somewhere who had been a bastard and spawned this crook.

'Well, let's just see about that, shall we,' I said to myself, ramming the last piece of sandwich into my mouth. I fetched my laptop, put his name into Google and sat back. The search brought up hundreds of hits.

A quick tour through the labyrinth led me to Cutt's own website where his family tree was displayed proudly for all to see.

It was true – though his parents were working-class people from Wyoming, their roots, through his father, went back to Jediah Curwen-Dunmow of Massachusetts who died in the late seventeenth century.

Curwen-Dunmow was, according to a mini biog, a fine upright elder. He fathered a son, Certain (who dropped the 'Curwen' and kept only 'Dunmow'), very late in life. Although Curwen-Dunmow himself had no certificates to substantiate a lineage before him, the line from Certain Dunmow to Robert Cutt was strong and unwavering. It stopped at his name. There was nothing else on the bottom of the screen, just his pompous flashing moniker.

He was right, then. No dirt there.

I sighed and pushed back my laptop. My fingertips were tingling. That usually meant something: my intellect often managed to converse with my body way before my conscious mind got wind of it. But mindful of the fact I was online, and wanting to avoid any communication with Hackerman, I closed down the PC and retired to bed. It was just gone ten o'clock but I had to get my beauty sleep.

I would be seeing Felix tomorrow. I wanted to look my best.

Chapter Sixteen

The weekend's good weather continued into Monday. In fact I might have almost described that day as glorious; I remember the sun being very bright and having a good go at warming the air around Colchester. Which made it not so bad when I got a call from Felix telling me he would be an hour late. His author needed to go over some contractual details and, although he was annoyed that this hadn't been flagged up earlier, there was really nothing else to be done but take her through the small print.

I didn't mind that much, instead taking the opportunity to have a wander through the narrow streets of the city centre. Colchester was a kooky kind of place; full of lanes and byways, Tudor homes converted into hairdressers, antique shops in modern shopping malls. I grabbed some lunch in a small café teeming with students fresh back from the summer break, bubbling with enthusiasm and new stories to tell.

With twenty minutes to kill I sauntered down to a place I'd passed near the car park where I'd deposited the car. St Boltoph's Priory was a towering ruin of arches and windows that, at some point, must have been spectacular.

In its centre a smattering of tombs and plaques peeped up between stubby brown grass and earth. Peacefully removed from the buzz of the main roads, a couple of late lunchers were sitting on the benches finishing their treats.

Making my way back up to the castle I nipped into the tourist shop opposite and bought a small handy guide to Colchester, which, the assistant assured me, contained a fair amount of history on the castle. On my way out I paused to check my reflection in the shop window. Not bad for a journo. I didn't look overdressed for the occasion; slim black jeans and a navy sparkly jumper teamed with a tailored jacket and black boots gave me a professional but louche kind of attitude. Well, that's what I thought until Felix marched up, a youthful energy to his gait. He bent down and stroked my cheek with his stubble and I felt his lips press against my face firmly. The breeze had picked up the ends of his hair and ruffled them about a bit. He pushed up his fringe and smiled.

There was something about Felix Knight that was really quite magnetic. I gave an approving nod to his out-of-office get-up: chinos, Converse, jacket – all immaculate and probably worth more than a month of my wages.

'Hello, esteemed author,' he said, stitching on that easy grin. 'You've got lipstick on your teeth.'

Luckily olive skin hides blushes.

Once I removed the offending cosmetic accident I returned my face to him and shrugged. He dispelled my embarrassment by immediately blustering out apologies for his tardiness, promising to take me for a drink or 'proper English tea' after we'd toured the castle. I, of course, assented.

'But first,' he said breezily, 'would you mind if I grabbed a quick bagel or something? I'm famished.'

'Sure,' I said. 'I passed a sandwich bar down the road, near St Botolph's. Looked okay.'

'St Botolph's?'

'It's an old church further down. Nice grounds.'

'Old?'

'Church looks maybe a couple of hundred years old but the ruins are much older.'

'Sounds great. I'll get a sandwich and buy us coffees and we can have a late alfresco lunch. Do you mind?'

'Not at all.' The air was still bright, the sun peeping intermittently from behind white clouds. And Felix's smile was warming. No, I didn't mind at all.

I waited outside 'George's Tuck to Go' while Felix got his sarnie (salt beef and dill), then we ambled down to the church and wandered around a bit before we hit on a nice bench beneath a tawny sycamore.

I brushed away the fallen leaves and we sat down.

'Who is St Botolph then?' Felix asked.

'Aha,' I said and took my guidebook out of my bag.

'You must have been a girl guide,' said Felix and sent me a roguish grin. 'Always prepared.'

I looked down at the book. 'I'm a writer. We're always pre-prepared.'

He opened his mouth wide as he bit on the sandwich. 'Uh?'

'Research,' I told him, conveniently overlooking the fact I had only bought the book half an hour since. 'If you fail to prepare, you prepare to fail.'

'Very wise,' he said through a mouthful of beef and wiped his mouth on a serviette.

I looked the place up quickly. 'Apparently no one knows

much about St Botolph. He was alleged to have founded a monastery around here, blah blah blah.' I skimmed the text. 'Patron saint of travel. Gave his name to Boston in Massachusetts.'

Felix started and looked up sharply. 'Are you joking?'

For a second his face took on a pinched shrewish look.

'No,' I said. 'That's what it says here. It's a bit of a stretch, I'll give you that – from St Botolph to Boston – but they have similarities: B, T and two "O"s.'

He shook his head, as if shaking out a thought. 'No, not that. The fact that he's the patron saint of travel and ended up going from here to Massachusetts.' He searched my face as his voice trailed off.

I must have looked completely blank because he nodded then simply said, 'Sorry. It doesn't matter. I thought you said something else.'

'Oh right.' I must have missed something but had no time to reflect as Felix had already moved on, turning his attention to the book on my lap.

'What's that?' He moved a fraction closer and pointed to a picture. There was a dribble of mayonnaise on his chin. I really wanted to lick it away, but managed to restrain myself and transferred my attention to the double-page spread.

There was a sketch of what the building may have looked like in its heyday: a Norman church, surrounded on its northern side by a chapter house, cloister, refectory and dormitories. It must have been quite an impressive sight pre-Reformation. Unfortunately most of the buildings were demolished by Henry VIII in the 1530s. 'The priory church,' I read aloud, 'served the community until the siege of Colchester in 1648. Says here, that the siege happened during

152

the Civil War. Well, in 1648. A year after Hopkins died.' That man was never far from my thoughts, crouching in the corners of my mind, waiting to rise up at any opportunity. 'The city,' I continued, 'was forced to open its doors to the Royalist army. When the Parliamentarians rocked up a siege ensued. Went on for eleven weeks, and ended with the surrender then execution of the Royalists' leaders. After the constant bombardment of the Parliamentarian cannons the city was pretty much in ruins. St Botolph's was particularly badly hit. It says here that local people are still turning up bullets and shrapnel in their walls and gardens.'

Felix nodded. The mayo had disappeared. He was wiping his hands on a paper serviette.

I cupped my coffee in my hand. Here was a curious paragraph, he'd enjoy this. 'During the siege messages were sent to the Parliamentarians by concealing letters in hollowed-out bones and throwing them over the city wall nearby.'

'They don't mean human bones?'

'Doesn't say,' I told him, glad that he was interested. 'But the place was a graveyard. There were enough around.'

I watched his eyes wander over the scattered shards of tombstones. His eyebrows were wrinkled and he had swapped his smile for a face-scrunch. I expect he was imagining the grave robbing. 'Pretty gross,' he said finally.

My own eyes had returned to the book. 'This is worse: "When Hythe Church was captured, its defenders were taken prisoner. Sir John Lucas's house was then attacked. Soldiers broke open the Lucas family tombs in the chapel, cut off the hair from the bodies and wore it in their hats."'

'Grosser,' Felix said and quivered with disgust. I laughed. Despite the reading matter I was feeling light and frivolous.

'At least they were dead. You can see why the witch hunters came and went without much dissent. The war brutalised people. I guess life at that time must have been absolute hell: soldiers running round seizing what little resources you had, killing, pillaging and raping. Loads of them. Two different sides. Blimey. And all this comes on top of crop failures, famine, zero law and order. You'd have to be totally focused on surviving and looking after your own. Who'd care about a few old women hanged here and there?'

Felix sniffed in the air and tossed his head back. The sunlight touched his crown, picking out golden threads. 'Puts it in context.' He sat up brightly and crushed the empty coffee cup in his hand. 'So, shall we sink into some more history? Is Ms Asquith ready?'

I nodded quickly and stood up. 'Here,' I said holding out my hand to him. 'Give me your rubbish. I'll put it in that bin over there.'

I honestly don't know why I did the next thing. I suppose it may have been eagerness to get out and on our way round the castle. Maybe I was showing off to Felix. Whatever, it all backfired.

A semi-circular flowerbed stretched between our bench and the bin. I should have nipped round along the pavement to it but instead I decided to skip over the actual bed. The soil was wetter than I anticipated and, once I'd popped the rubbish in, I spun around and felt my heel slip. Failing to correct my balance I tried to take another step forwards, but was suckered into the muddy part of the bed and fell head first onto the dirt. Fantastic, I thought kneeling there on my hands and knees. Good look.

Felix, being the gentleman he was, wasted no time in

coming to my aid. This time even my olive skin didn't manage to hide my flush.

He gallantly helped me to my feet and brushed me down, avoiding the smattering of mud on my arse. I was in full flow – apologising whilst focusing hard on scraping mud off my jeans, when I heard him say, 'Good Lord.'

He was crouching over the earth where I had fallen. 'What is *that*?' he said, and poked a cluster of soil.

There was a slick furrow of mud where my boot had slipped. On one side, under the crumbly mass of earth I'd dislodged, something thin, whitish in colour, protruded from the ground. I put my hands on my dirty knees and leant over to inspect it more closely.

It was a small object, no more than three or four inches long, perhaps a quarter of an inch wide, hollow, like a whistle or a pipe.

Felix put his hand out to touch it and looked as if he was about to pick it up when an awful feeling of apprehension came over me.

'Don't. Don't touch it,' I shouted.

He withdrew his hand sharply and looked up. 'Why? What is it?'

'Don't touch it.' I moderated my tone. 'I mean, you shouldn't touch it. I don't know what it is. But it might be –' the word on the tip of my tongue was 'evil'. Where had that come from? Bloody ridiculous notion. Thank God I stopped myself in time I thought, and quickly substituted my chosen word for something far less hysterical. 'Antique,' I said. 'Old.'

It was indeed ancient looking *and* fragile, but that wasn't my worry. There was something indescribably nasty about the thing. I was sure it was made out of bone and had a feeling that it had once been human. 'We should get someone official and tell them what we've found.'

'Is it a pipe?' Felix ignored my warning and stretched out his hand to prod it.

An image of the Witchfinder sucking on its end flashed in front of my eyes. Wasn't he meant to have smoked? I couldn't remember. I couldn't actually think clearly at all. In fact, I felt unaccountably wobbly.

A cloud briefly blocked out the sun, as the pipe flipped over to reveal a tiny row of characters on its underside.

'Wow.' Felix was fascinated. He picked it up. 'Ouch,' he hissed. 'That's sharp.' The smaller, narrow end of the pipe was jagged like a broken tooth. 'The damn thing cut me.' Felix held up his hand to show me, a drop of blood bubbling from a thin horizontal slit in his palm. He cursed and pulled his gaze back to the thing in his hand.

'Look, it's got writing on it.' His shirt cuff rubbed lightly against the pipe. The skinny red dribble of his blood smeared over the characters, the contrast lending them clarity. 'I think it's Latin. Quis.'

'That means "who".' My grammar school education had its uses.

Felix was peering closer. The letters were minuscule. 'Qui est iste qui venit.'

My Latin was worse than rusty, more like completely decayed. These days I could just about remember something about Caecilius in the atrium and that was it. But my head nodded almost without me being aware of it moving. 'Who is it who is coming.'

I don't know how I knew it but, there, I had said it.

Sometimes, I thought to myself, these skills, strengths or talents lie dormant until we need to use them.

I wasn't wrong.

'Strange,' Felix was saying as he got to his feet. I came to the same conclusion. 'Vicious yet intriguing, don't you think?'

'Put it down.' The sight of it in his fingers made me wince violently. It was an exaggerated reflex that went right through my body and down to the ground.

But he was rapt, spellbound, beyond caution now.

I noticed a vague nausea in my stomach. It started to strengthen, reaching out and up my throat as I watched Felix turn the thing over in his hand. Then, without any warning he lifted it to his lips.

Panic shot through me and I opened my mouth to yell at him to stop. I couldn't bear the thought of that thing touching his lips, entering his mouth, contaminating his body. But it was too late. A dreadful sound came out of the pipe – high-pitched, faint, and unearthly, like the last rattling breaths of a hundred sacrificed souls. Darkness and earth. Despair, death and sorrow.

A wave of revulsion swept over me. For a moment I thought I was going to vomit.

Felix felt something too, I was sure, for the pipe dropped from his fingers and rolled into the soil. He took a step backwards, shook his head and rubbed his chin. 'Did you hear that?' He swallowed.

I got myself together and nodded.

'Peculiar noise,' he said. 'Do you think maybe it was used in rituals? Ceremonies?' He laughed but it was hollow. For a minute we didn't speak, just stood there gazing at the thing which had produced that dreadful sound – white bone reddened by blood. A sacrifice. Or a summons.

It felt like the damage had been done.

I edged away from it. 'I suppose we might as well take it to the castle museum now. As we're going there.'

Felix shook a hanky out of his jacket and wrapped the pipe, popping it into his breast pocket for safekeeping. I didn't like the idea of it being so close to his heart. It was like it might infect him. He already looked a little peaky. I think the sound had shocked him.

'We should definitely let the castle experts deal with it,' I said.

'Sure thing,' he replied and smiled weakly. I tried to return his smile as we headed out of the priory but I couldn't muster much at all. A terrible feeling of doom had fallen across me. The sun receded behind a cloak of clouds and the daylight had grown dim. A stale mustiness pervaded the air.

Felix swallowed. 'Come on. It's exciting isn't it? Could be the greatest archaeological find of the decade.'

I glowered at the grey flagstones under my feet. I think somehow I knew that now he'd blown on the pipe nothing would be the same.

He called him, you see. And we both felt it. It was cursed. And his blood had whet its appetite.

It had broken the veil.

Though, of course, it didn't register at the time. It was just a weird thing that had unsettled me. *Another* weird thing.

We reached the castle and sauntered across the wooden bridge to the vaulted entrance. A young bloke at the till inspected the pipe and called a female colleague down from an office. They were both interested and asked us to come to the office. I gently declined, guilting Felix into accompanying the castle staff by pointing out that I'd already been delayed (by him) and really needed to get stuck into my research. Plus I didn't want to be near that revolting relic.

Felix didn't need much persuasion. In fact, as he told the staff how we came across it, his eyes kept darting back to the bone pipe. You could see he was quite taken by the thing.

I was more than happy to leave them to it.

I paid at the entrance then passed under the eyes of a stone sphinx depicted perching on the mangled remains of a human head, hands and bones, and then through into the museum proper.

Colchester Castle was a gloomy structure indeed. Mind you, the place had a huge legacy: once the capital of Roman Britain, many of the displays in the cabinets testified to its early importance. There were ancient vases and plates; some gorgeous necklaces, the like of which might have been replicated and displayed on several D-list celebrities of today; a replica chariot used by the warrior queen, Boudicca or Boadicea, as she was known in my childhood. I don't know when her name changed but I really preferred the original. Mum had too, telling me that nobody really knew how it was pronounced and I could say it whichever way I wanted. She liked the warrior queen but she thought her story wasn't all there. 'History,' she'd tell me, 'is a matter of who tells the tale and why.' I remembered her having a bit of a rant over Tacitus's account. 'He was writing years after the events but we take his words as gospel. It's us who allow time to reduce history to a half truth. It's only one person's perspective. You got to watch out for that, Sadie.' Well, I certainly was. I was here in Colchester Castle wasn't I? Getting my own perspective on the place. She'd be pleased about that – solid primary research.

I was looping through the Middle Ages section when Felix found me, lingering on an ornate hair clasp. Woven into its design was a cluster of butterflies and moths. One of them had been darkened by some kind of chemical technique to accentuate the pattern.

'The moth and the butterfly were Japanese symbols of the soul,' read the accompanying text. A vision of Beryl Bennett's mouth flashed up. But it was gone in the next instant when Felix began to speak.

He was full of the 'bone pipe', and told me how he had signed an 'entry form' and would be contacted once they'd identified it and had been able to assess its historical significance.

'*My* object,' he repeated, chin jutting out with pride. (God, he'd taken ownership of the thing.) 'That's what they called it. It will be returned to me. Unless of course, I want to donate it to the museum, if it's of any historical significance.'

'You shouldn't have it back,' I said. Another shudder went through me.

'Why ever not?' he asked. 'Could be old. Roman even. A little bit of our ancestors' empire. I don't see why anyone wouldn't want it.'

'Just makes me feel odd,' I told him, expecting him to disagree or make some joke, but he nodded.

'It's quite an odd sort of thing,' he said. 'Can't say I like it. But certain collectors may. Don't you think it's intriguing? If I sell it on, you can take a cut. If you hadn't fallen I never would have found it.'

It was generous of him but I declined. 'I don't want to have anything to do with it. It's yours.'

'Spoken like a historian of witches!' he said and winked one ironic eye.

'It's not that,' I said, but it was.

'Well, then I'll lay claim. If you don't mind. You don't, do you?' His voice was casual. I could see him in the reflection of the glass cabinet in front of me. He glanced at me from under a tuft of fringe, one hand thrust deep in his pocket, but the other reaching up nervously to scratch the back of his head. He wanted it. A lot.

'No, it's fine,' I told him.

'Fantastic,' he said with far too much zeal.

I didn't know how to respond so I just went, 'Mmm.' And he didn't come back with anything.

A dismal sort of anti-climax trickled down over us.

Felix shrugged and offered me his arm. I threaded mine through his and thus we continued to work our way through the sections. We both tried to be bright, with quips here and there, but there was a crookedness about us that we just couldn't shift. It felt like we were still carrying the bone pipe with us.

Despite Felix's wit and charming company I found myself becoming nervy. As we turned a corner into the Middle Ages I came face to face with a weary-looking dummy in the stocks and screamed to high heaven. Felix thought it was hilarious and insisted on taking a photo of me next to the display. I tried to laugh it off but my chortle was fake; tension in my shoulders had forced them so far up that they were touching the bottoms of my earrings.

We were nearing the prison.

The castle, I was fully aware, was where the accused witches were transported after they had been tortured and confessed. In fact, most of the building was used as a gaol during that period.

Certainly it was here that *he* conducted further interrogations and here that many of them perished before trial.

It wasn't difficult to see why.

The dungeons felt subterranean. I wasn't sure if they were, as there was virtually no natural light. An artificial yellow haze amplified the sinister atmosphere.

We stepped down into an antechamber, which formed the entrance to the cells. It was full of information boards about torture and crime, with some interactive pieces for kids, attempting on one hand to be educational and bright, and on the other to thrill and horrify with grimly salacious details.

On one side of the wall was a feature about the Witchfinder General and the women he had sent to this place. A paragraph mentioned young Rebecca West who was indicted in March 1645. Another sentence told of how, in their village, the Wests were thought of as 'saintly', pious and devoted to God. Rebecca was only fifteen at the time. The plaque detailed that on the 18th of April she was interrogated alone by Hopkins. One could only wonder what happened to her when the Witchfinder took her from the communal prison into some other godforsaken part of the gaol.

Whatever occurred, Hopkins managed to bring about a heart-breaking betrayal: Rebecca West turned on her own mother.

How awful for them both, I thought. To be suckered into that trumped-up charge. It was almost like becoming an accomplice to an act of mass murder. And for the daughter it was matricide.

Some writers speculated that Hopkins may have developed a relationship with Rebecca West – she was at the time only eight or nine years his junior and probably the prettiest of the witches. If there was a sexual element motivating his persecution of the women, I shuddered to think of what she must have gone through, all alone with the Witchfinder.

Separated from those she knew, locked up in some dark corner of the castle with that man, Rebecca confessed she had joined a satanic coven on her mother's insistence. But unlike so many of the witches' hallucinatory declarations, this wasn't an orgiastic witch group. No, Rebecca's testimony began in a fluffy, teenage manner – a whimsical fantasy in which she kissed and cuddled the witches' imps, which, funnily enough, appeared in the form of adorable kittens.

After she had pledged allegiance to the Devil, he popped up in the form of a little black dog and jumped playfully onto her lap. So, as most teenage girls would, Rebecca stroked and petted it.

Hopkins must have been so frustrated to hear of such an innocent encounter with the demonic. So on he went, drawing out more.

A fifteen-year-old pauper, isolated from her mother, questioned by a higher-ranking gentleman, frightened, alone, damned; either Rebecca's instinct for survival kicked in or perhaps she was tortured into confessing or Hopkins' authority induced her to please him. Whatever occurred in that interview, something changed in the girl and soon her tale took on a more sensational tone as the Witchfinder retold her confession: that night however the 'Divel' came to her in the form of a handsome young man and pledged to marry her. When asked by the worked-up inquisitor if she had had carnal copulation with the Devil, Rebecca admitted she had. He must have wet himself. It was just what he needed.

In her later trial Rebecca told the court, amidst heckles and jeers, that she was asked 'divers questions by a Gentleman that did speake severall times with her before and afterward (giving her godly and comfortable instructions) she affirmed that so soone as one of the said Witches was in prison, she was very desirous to confess all she knew, which accordingly she did'.

She, surely, could not have recovered from her treachery? It would have been too great a burden to bear. Like most of the women, no one knew what happened to her after the trial. Only that she was freed.

And her mother? One can only speculate what she felt. To see her daughter turn against her like that must have been more devastating than the torture she endured. Or perhaps she was prepared to sacrifice herself to see her daughter escape the noose?

I jotted down some of the details with a sigh.

The cell in which Rebecca and the witches had been held first was in front of me, through a low, arched doorway fastened with a heavy wooden door. It was wedged open with a block of wood. An iron grid was embedded at head height. I touched its metal and chilled. Part of the flaking wood detached itself and fluttered up past my face to one of the display lights. I retracted my hand immediately.

'You all right?' Felix had seen me shiver.

I looked again at the flake skittering about the light bulb. 'Just another moth. Creepy.'

'Where?' he said, following my sightline.

I pointed to where it had been but it had merged into the metallic support beneath the bulb.

I shrugged. 'Sorry, I'm a bit jumpy.'

'You're bound to feel sensitive, given your research.'

I smiled, gratefully, pleased that he was here and stepped over the threshold.

The whitewashed room was three metres square with a fireplace near the door. This was the gaoler's quarters.

In the corner opposite stood a small wooden cupboard. A man in his forties was explaining to his son that this was where they put you if you were too 'loud and naughty'. His son stared at it a moment then tugged on his dad's sleeve and asked to leave. I knew what he meant. It was nasty down here.

To the north and east side of the gaol were the cells: one for men, one for women. These were large windowless rooms, separated from the main room by a thick wooden wall. Like the door, they had metal grilles fastened across a small window. But for a slit high on a slanted wall, the grilles would have let in the only other light, and even that would have been the weak glow of the fireplace or the gaoler's candles. The atmosphere was morbid: the air stifled by dust and our appalled gasps.

A disembodied recording told us that the occupants, despite their forced incarceration, had to pay the gaoler a penny a day for their food and water or else simply go without.

Being here really brought it home. My heart heaved with compassion for those doomed wretches. Before the July Assize of 1645 there were over twenty-nine of them in here, old, infirm or poor. They would have been shackled to the wall. Never allowed out, not even to wash or piss or shit, rats slithering between their manacled limbs, biting and nibbling at those comatose or in brief fits of sleep. Or dead. Not to mention how they dealt with periods. The stench of it all must have been awful. It was a small wonder that only four died before they made it to trial. A lot of them were kept down here for nearly four months, until they were forced out into carts and transported to Chelmsford to stand in the dock, filthy and malnourished. The spectators would have been full of hate, the magistrates and clerics repulsed by the accused's ravaged and wasted appearance.

And the women? They must have at least been utterly bewildered. And so frightened. Perhaps knowing that the next step from the dock was to their death. What they must have gone through.

They all pleaded 'not guilty' but justice did not come for them.

'Hello?' Felix's voice broke through my thoughts.

I turned around to find him speaking into his mobile: 'Hang on,' he said then mouthed at me, 'Got to take this call.' He pointed upstairs. 'Back in a sec. That okay?'

Eek. I didn't really want to be left alone down here, but what could I do? Tell him I was a pussy and ask him to hold my hand?

Not my style. I squeezed out a bright grin.

Felix gave me a thumbs up and marched out of the gaol. I was alone.

There was, of course, nothing to worry about, I reassured myself. Thousands of tourists passed through these cells every year. Nothing untoward happened.

I straightened my shoulders and stepped over to inspect the other cell. It was only slightly wider than the first and smelled rank. Curious dark patches stained the lower half of the walls. 'Don't even go there,' I told myself firmly. In a place like this it was important for a reporter to keep their imagination under control.

The documentary soundtrack came to an end. The few school kids that had been squealing in the antechamber had gone now, having exhausted all the interactive buttons. But for the sound of my breathing, the silence was unbroken.

I peeped through one of the metal grilles at the cruel i nterior beyond. Dingy and damp. The cell was so small, barely four and a half metres square. I could imagine the moans and pleas falling on the merciless ears of the gaoler, who, I had read, liked to beat those that cried out too loudly. The corners were particularly dark. That's where they crawled to die.

I was beginning to feel a little claustrophobic, so decided to head for the exit. That was enough for now. I had a sense of what it was like to be here and a few extra details for my research. I could meet Felix upstairs.

I fumbled with my bag, opening the flap to replace my notebook.

A loud clattering bang echoed about the room.

Looking up I saw, in the entrance arch, the heavy wooden door had slammed shut, leaving me locked inside the gaol.

For a moment I stood still, hesitating. Perhaps I should phone upstairs to reception? One glance at my mobile told me there was no signal in here. Bugger.

So instead I took a wavering step towards the doorway then stopped: something rustled in the straw of the cell behind me.

Surely a mouse. This was a dungeon. In a castle. Of course they had mice. And rats probably too.

Nevertheless, the thin stretch of hairs on the back of my neck prickled to attention.

The unseen thing rustled again. Though this was less of a rustle as such – more like the lurching sound of something heavy dragged across the dungeon floor.

Although I didn't want to, I felt a compulsion to turn my head in its direction. So, slowly, feeling like I was trapped in some kind of surreal horror film, I moved my shoulders and body to face the sound. It was coming from the furthest corner of the cell, where the dying were chained.

I couldn't see through the grid, so took a step forward.

The rustling receded and stopped.

I stopped too. And strained my ears.

Nothing.

Twenty seconds passed as I held my breath and listened.

Nothing.

Whatever was there it had shuffled off into the gloom.

I was just about to go back again and try the door handle when I heard another noise. This time I froze.

At first I thought it was a hiccup, but it repeated itself; a high, faltering sound. Quiet but clear.

A sob.

A woman's sob.

To convey the fragility of the noise and the emotion it was steeped in, to describe it fully is impossible. All I can say is that it was like a whimper quivering with endless misery, the sound of utter dejection.

And it was coming from the corner of the cell.

The lower portion of my throat made a muffled squeaking noise, like the surprised yelp of a wounded dog.

'Get a grip, Mercedes, it's the recording. It's started again but with effects.' I said it out loud. My voice was reassuring: it was real, a product of cause and effect, the words vibrating on my vocal cords and then issuing into the air.

But then another voice reverberated through the cell. 'Are you there?'

I was fixed to the spot.

No, no, no. This wasn't happening. Not here. Not now. This wasn't real.

I was imagining it. It was some kind of aural projection.

Then it came again. 'I can hear you.' Fragile, young, female. 'I'm sorry.'

I clapped a hand over my mouth and for a moment the bang bang of my heart overwhelmed all other senses. I took a gulp of air through my fingers and was filled with an intolerable stink: sulphuric, stagnant, death-bringing.

But still the sobbing went on: 'Mercy.'

Then another voice cut through, louder. A kind of throaty gurgle. Far more horrible than the one before. Nasty, ill, wheezing.

My breath was coming in quick pants. Beads of sweat ran down the sides of my face.

Then the dark voice came again, harsh, full of bass and resonance: 'Leave us.'

As I recoiled from the awful sound a dark horrid sensation came up from my stomach. A tense, knotted emotion – displeasure, fear, repugnance, disgust, horror – all of that, all at once, rising up from my very soul like the spasm of an unflexed muscle or a memory, long-forgotten.

Something in the prison made a creaking sound and suddenly very real terror was upon me.

There was a footfall in the cell.

Fear spilled over and I thrust out my hand, ready to defend myself, reflexively rotating my head to the sound, tensing myself for a fight. Through the cell window I was just able to see a glimpse of something that looked like a stained sack moving against the far wall.

And then the lights went out.

Something screamed from within the gaol. It could have been me. I don't know. But it triggered a charge of chemicals that flooded my body, commanding my limbs now to flight. I raced over to where I hoped the door would be and met the cold, hard curve of the fireplace. My hands, shaking up to the elbow, felt along the wall, as I sidestepped, crablike, until I reached the wood of the door. My breathing was becoming fitful, the air harder to take down into my tense closed lungs, whilst all the time that awful scratching, lurching sound was getting closer and closer. Heart hammering right up against my ribs, trying also to escape its cage, I pounded on the wooden planks, a dreadful uncontrollable hysteria overtaking me.

'Help me. Let me out,' I howled through the grid.

I can't be sure as I recollect now, as at that point the light of consciousness was dimming, but I thought something touched me on the leg.

There was an icy blast on the back of my neck, and then nothing as I blacked out.

When I came round I was in the antechamber. Felix and one of the staff we'd seen earlier had me propped up against the wall. The attendant was holding a glass out and urged me to drink.

I squinted at them and straightened my body. My brain

was still wonky, thoughts random, scattered about by the overload and consequential shutdown.

What had happened there? The door had closed, then I'd heard a man's voice, then – what? I couldn't remember.

The officer held out a hanky. I took it and dabbed my face. I was still hot.

'I'm sorry about that, dear,' she said. Her face had a worried look, Health and Safety rules probably fleeting across her official brain. 'Must have given you a fright. Bloody kids, they do that all the time. Usually to each other, though.'

Felix was standing above me with his hands on his hips, his expression half bemused, half concerned, like he was struggling with which one to go with. 'I think you fainted. Do you usually faint?'

I shook my head, too confused to talk, glad to be out of the room, but not totally reassured. I could see the cells opposite. Danger still clung to the air around me.

I took a sip of water and nearly gagged. The dreadful sinister atmosphere of the place had seeped into my bones. I needed to get out of there. 'It was the voice. The man's voice. Horrible.'

The attendant tapped my shoulder and laughed, a full belly laugh, like she was properly amused. 'It's the soundtrack.'

No, it wasn't just the soundtrack. I had heard something move in there. Part of it was coming back to me. 'Then there was someone else in the cell. I heard them. They said "leave us".'

'That's just the information spiel.'

I grimaced at the memory. 'It was quite scary though. I think it's a bit too much for a public museum. Especially with kids around.'

The officer folded her arms and said to Felix, 'Well, we've never had any complaints before.' Then she looked at me sympathetically and loaded up a sort of 'come on – pull yourself together' smile. 'You've given yourself a fright. There's not much air in there,' she added.

'Then the lights went out,' I said to them, trying to reassemble the memories that were coming back.

The woman jerked her head at me but addressed Felix. 'Vivid imagination, your girlfriend's got, eh?'

Felix ignored her comment and knelt down. 'Sadie, the lights were on when we found you.'

'They never go off till we lock up at night,' confirmed the officer.

'Oh,' I said. 'They did go off. And there was someone in there. It was a shock.'

Despite my inner chaos, I think I must have looked blank, for the officer clucked her teeth and shifted, as if I'd conceded to her explanation. She slapped a big jolly grin on. 'Just imagine what it was like for those locked up, eh?'

'I can,' I said grimly and got to my feet. Though I couldn't make sense of it, I could see that my editor was beginning to look embarrassed.

'I need to get out of here,' I said.

'Good idea,' he said.

The woman apologised again and Felix took me by the arm and led me outside.

I have never been so grateful to be in the open air.

Chapter Seventeen

Felix insisted on buying me tea. 'You're going to have a full feast with me now. Women,' he said. 'Never eat enough.' Which was his reasoning for my 'turn'.

We were in a pub just a short way away from the castle. I had insisted on buying a packet of cigarettes and smoking one outside before entering. My hands were still unsteady, though my breathing had returned to normal. Felix had gone in to order the drinks so I had time to get some nicotine into my system and sort myself out.

The experience in the gaol had left me uncertain and insecure. Immediately after it happened I had been sure I had heard those cries and screams – not fainted and dreamt them as Felix was suggesting. But now I was wondering if I had misremembered the chronology of it all, as Lesley had suggested with the internet messaging. Did that mean the problem was with me?

When my brain unfroze in the antechamber we exited across the drawbridge and my mind dived into a mass of fleeting explanations. I had never been one for flights of fancy. Not until Mum died.

But I knew I was stressed – I had had a lot on my plate

lately. Perhaps my frazzled mind could have freaked, going into some kind of weirded-out double-flip. Like a version of déjà vu.

Or perhaps it was a dream? A hallucination? A trick of my subconscious. Had I tuned into the horrors that centred on this room? Picked up on them? Maybe even 'seen' a past event?

That sounded daft. There had to be another explanation. A logical, sound, scientific sequence of events that was as solid and authentic as Darwin's Theory of Evolution. Science, after all, was responsible for illuminating the strange 'religious' phenomena of the past: the Northern Lights, eclipses, shooting stars. Not to mention all the diabolism thought inherent in epilepsy, schizophrenia and the like.

As I stood outside the pub smoking I groped for objectivity. The fact that the door had shut on me was an undisputable truth. The rooms down there were airless and anyway, no gust of wind could have moved that heavy oak door; it was a good three inches thick and weighted down with metal bolts and locks.

The attendant was positive it had been kids messing around. There *had* been a bunch of schoolchildren in the museum that afternoon, but they'd not been more than ten or eleven years old. And there was no noise in the antechamber before it had happened. It seemed rather calculated and cruel. Was it just a prank or had I been selected? Had they been compelled to do it when they saw me in there? Could Hackerman have followed me in?

No, I couldn't give in to paranoia. I wasn't special. I had nothing to threaten anyone with, had I?

I flicked through my current pieces of work: the Bennetts'

piece had been filed earlier in the week. And I'd also mailed Maggie my interim piece on Essex Girls. Currently on my list was a write-up of a local artist-come-good, now exhibiting in the West End – that was positive. Who'd want to scupper that? A piece on town-planning and the fascism of architecture – but the local councils I had fingered weren't interested in what I wrote. I was small fry.

But then there was the Hacker.

I remembered again his last appearance when I'd written about Hopkins' burial. 'He wasn't he wasn't.' Could Hackerman be Hackergirl?

I'd heard both a female and male voice in the dungeon and I was sure there were other sounds.

Perhaps someone had been in there trying to freak me out? Though why bother with just one woman? Why not do it to a bunch of kids or adults?

There was no way I was about to entertain any notion that I might be hearing voices. At least not in my head. I recalled Mum's bad episode, coming home to find her on her knees in the living room, looking under rugs and chairs for listening devices. She had heard voices telling her she was being watched. That she knew too much.

It was heart-breaking. Her eyes were permanently swollen and red and she was so confused and miserable that she wasn't entirely sure what was real or imagined. It was an awful awful time. And as such, I'd made sure I was always pretty rational, veering towards scepticism. But, I liked to think, compassionate towards those who weren't as balanced.

So what I was thinking, as I stubbed my fag out on the metallic ashtray, was that maybe what I heard was something that played on long after the initial introduction had stopped, like a secret track on a CD that you only heard if you left it running for a while. A private joke added by the company that made the documentary.

It *had* been freaky though. I couldn't imagine kids enjoying that kind of thing, or schools approving of such a disturbing evocation of dungeon life. But at least the authorities knew about it now. I had insisted that the officer reported my experience to her manager. And that in the interests of the old and infirm they took some time to listen carefully to their CD. She'd agreed, finally.

That just left the lights. That one was fairly easy. They must have flickered just before they went out, casting strange shadows in the cells. Then, when they went off, I'd flipped over into terror, and had been both super-sensitive to and disorientated by the sounds and the atmosphere of the castle. Maybe my bag had fallen off my shoulder and touched my leg. It had a long strap and the main body of it hung at calf height when held in my hand.

And the lights themselves? Got to have been a short circuit. Or whoever had dislodged the wedge and shut the door had, in their haste, tripped a wire too.

It was possible.

It was, in fact, probable.

The problem was I didn't believe my own explanations. I wanted to. Desperately. But I didn't. As I trundled through the doorway into the warmth of the pub I was doing my damn best to internalise them. But, somewhere a little voice was telling me to be careful. To think about what Flick had said. Could it be?

As I sat down at the table beside Felix I told myself whatever it was, it was certainly unpleasant, and so gladly accepted

176

my editor's offer of a whisky despite the fact that I was going to drive home.

'Get this down you,' he pointed to the glasses on the table. 'I'm sorry about what happened.'

'You're not responsible for the incident, Felix,' I told him and lifted the glass to my lips. The whisky was rich and warming. I hadn't realised it up till now but I felt very cold. 'Must have been the tape.' There was a lack of conviction in my voice. 'It sounded like there were actually people in the cells moving and moaning. If it was the sound effects then I don't think they should continue to use it. It's too much.'

Felix nodded. 'They do that in some places don't they? When we went to the London Dungeon they had these guys who jumped out on you in the scary sections,' he said, shaking his head at the memory. 'That guillotine tableau. Euch. Totally over the top. Totally.'

I reflected for a moment. 'I should complain to the council.'

'Oh Sadie, don't blow it out of proportion.' He leant forwards to me. 'You've been doing lots of research on the subject – your imagination ran away with you. And you are a splendidly imaginative writer. It's what textures your language and observation. Don't lose it, use it. Perhaps filter some of the experience into your Hopkins chapters.' The quartz in his eyes glittered. 'I like the fact that you were scared. That the whole experience came to life for you. Incorporate it. Bring it to life for your readers.'

I thought about that. Perhaps there was something in what he said. Though I did have one reservation. 'Don't you think that people will, er, think I'm mad?'

He threw me a look of triumph. 'Isn't madness just a kind of genius?'

I blushed. Had my editor just alluded to genius? In reference to me? Wow. I leant into him. 'Okay, I'll be guided by you. It will certainly give it an edge.'

Felix fastened a smile on his face and poked my leg. 'Hey, you don't think it was ghosts do you?' There was a lulling pull in his eyes, a subtle undertone of flirtation.

I took a slug of my drink. 'I did a series of features a couple of years back for Halloween. Interviewed a paranormal society in the East End. Asked them all about ghosts and urban myths, that sort of stuff. One of them, the main investigator, told me he thought that ghosts were memories.'

'Memories? Sounds strange.' He leant in closer. 'Do tell more.'

'Okay,' I said, not entirely comfortable with outlining what could be construed as a particularly wacky theory. 'Though please bear in mind, that the views expressed here are not necessarily those of the speaker.'

He wrinkled his nose. 'Go *on!*'

'Okay, what he meant by memories is this – what we see as "ghosts" might be the visual projections of events that have occurred in certain places, perhaps projected by a number of different people, which somehow attach themselves to the physical place. If something sudden or extreme – violent – has happened there, it leaves a residue which some people pick up. Not everyone of course. But some can pick up on it. Or at least some have the latent ability to pick up on it, depending on how they are feeling and their emotional state at the time. Everyone has some spooky story to tell or knows someone who has "seen" something.'

Felix nodded, thinking the idea through. 'So you're saying

that you think what you heard and saw could be that? A memory of what happened?'

I squeaked out a disapproving snicker. 'I'm not saying anything of the sort, indeed. That was one of the paranormal society's explanations.'

'I'm sure our readers wouldn't mind a little bit of paranormal hypothesis.'

He grinned.

That was a turn-up for the books, so to speak. I always assumed with non-fiction you had to write just that. But I wanted to please him too. 'I'll certainly mention the prison and the gaol and try to evoke what it was like for the women in there.'

'Very glad to hear it,' Felix sniffed.

I breathed in and smelt the reassuring whiff of home-cooked sausages, something garlicky, beer and the smoke from the nearby fireplace. 'I hope the food comes soon. I'm starvin'.'

This time he gave me an open-mouthed smile, treating me to a good view of white teeth, set into that super-strong jaw.

'So,' he said and yawned, sinking back into his armchair. 'Is this a good time to ask you about how the writing's going?'

'Oh yes,' I said and brought the folder out of my bag. 'I've some notes and questions here.'

When we'd finished up, Felix paid the bill. I promised to send him a rough chapter by the end of the week. It wouldn't be a problem; I'd already started that section. And I wanted him to come back to me with feedback. Actually I just wanted more contact.

Outside on the pavement we stood a metre apart. I wondered for a brief second if he was going to snog me. He had a wild look in his eyes. But then again, maybe it was the flush of whisky. Whatever, he didn't make a move.

He did, however, offer to walk me back to my car, but I declined.

We kissed, a sort of business-like peck on the cheek, and went our separate ways.

Halfway down the street I had a quick squizz to see if he was watching me, but he wasn't. His determined figure strode swiftly up the hill and turned right out of view.

I was full of our meeting as I wandered down to the car park. Thinking about the look in Felix's eyes, the glimmer of triumph, his magnetic, almost bestial, leer that I had caught under the streetlights. On one hand, it felt as though he was reeling me in, sending little signals of seduction. Yet on the other hand, he was staying professional, pushing me away. Mind you, that thing with the pipe had dampened my ardour somewhat. Shame really as he was a pretty decent catch. An unusual man. Complex.

I would have thought on it more but as I approached the NCP an unwelcome dread began to prick at me.

It was dark now and, as I climbed the concrete stairway, one of the fluorescent lights spluttered, sending shadows crawling across the floor, setting my nerves on edge. Disorientated by the flashing light, a small black moth kamikazed off the fitting and straight into my face.

I brushed it off.

God, I hated car parks. They were meant to be safe, but at night, when you were on your own, they felt far from reassuring. And there was a cold similarity to the cells, which brought back that godawful incident.

I hurried up the steps and turned the corner too quickly, finding myself face to face with a bundle of rags. I steadied up. This present landing was darker than the rest. The light had been smashed. I went to tear up the next set of steps, but the pile of rubbish moved. Out of the depths of rags and litter a face emerged. It was dirty and soiled. The eyes glared – narrow, rigid, angry.

'You woke me,' he spluttered, cross and indignant.

Through the gloom I could perceive the ragged, baggy jowls of an elderly tramp, camouflaged with lengths of grey curly beard. My nose was overwhelmed by the stench of alcohol, unwashed linen, urine and other bodily emissions.

'I'm sorry,' I said. 'You gave me a fright.'

The face atop the heap fixed me with a grimace then, almost as if coming out of a daydream said, 'What are you doing?'

His 'r's purred like a Dorset type. This was the North Essex accent, uncommon in my south-easterly end of the world, with its pinball machines, neon lights and eroded consonants. He sounded rough, smacking of rural isolation: quaint, and a bit thick, but nonetheless, in my present setting, disturbing. I leant back into the shadows. 'Getting my car. It's on Level 4.'

That seemed enough of an explanation for him. He appeared to relax back a moment, then had second thoughts, and lurched forwards. 'You don't know what you're doing.' It was a statement voiced as a threat.

I stepped against the damp concrete wall. I was on my own. With a perfect right to be there. He was a tramp – I needn't explain myself but I said, or rather, I shouted as I circled his space to get to the next flight of stairs, 'Just going up. All right?'

But then he lunged. Fortunately his age and decrepitude made him slow and I saw the move coming and leapt up a step out of reach. 'The car,' I said. 'I'm sorry to have disturbed you.'

The poor bloke fell at my feet, his arms all of a quiver. 'Just you leave well alone,' he rasped through a voice long unused, breaking on the soft consonants. 'It'll do you no good . . .' The remainder of his words were engulfed in phlegmy fits of coughing, his body racking considerably against the upheaval incurred by his lungs.

I turned to face him but kept my back up against the wall, inching upwards step by step. The guy was clearly delusional and belonged in some aftercare establishment. I looked down upon him, for he had reached my feet now, his grimy fingers edging up to the points of my boots.

With a jerk he threw himself towards my legs. 'Leave us.'

He got hold of one of my ankles. It knee-jerked me, literally into defence, and I'm ashamed to admit I kicked him off. As his arm threw up against the wall I screamed, 'Get out of it,' and leapt up the remaining stairs two at a time to my level, panting like I was finishing a half-mile run.

Jesus. What a day. First the castle, now this. There were a lot of these types around these days. Had there been a change to the mental health act? This poor sod was obviously off on one. No need to read anything into it.

Nevertheless, I did my best to reach my car as quickly as possible.

Chapter Eighteen

The encounter with the tramp had reignited my earlier anxiety from the cells.

'Leave us,' he had said. It only dawned on me when I had got the car started and left the car park that it was the same phrase I heard in the dungeon.

Coincidence.

But the words kept coming back as I navigated through the outer ring road onto the motorway. The 'Leave us' in the dungeon. What was that about? A man's voice. The gaoler's? The Witchfinder's? Why? What was it suggesting? The end of the documentary, in all probability. A cue to leave the prison and progress on to the other parts of the exhibition. An inbuilt traffic system to keep the flow of visitors moving.

And the tramp? Well, he was probably speaking in the plural but referring to himself. Wasn't uncommon. And it had that country flavour to the phrase. Anyway he wasn't all there, so there was no point dwelling on what he had to say.

And after all of that I *had* left them now. Colchester was miles away.

So why then did I feel a building sense of guilt and betrayal as I drove from the place?

Once I got onto the A12 to Chelmsford I pumped up the volume on the car stereo and thrashed around to some old eighties tunes.

My mood lightened. When that compilation ended I kept the retro mood and chose an R.E.M. album. There was something so upbeat about their early stuff. It was good driving music. Yet as I got into a cruise, coming out of Chelmsford, the CD screwed up: '*I'm sorry, I'm sorry.*' Michael Stipe's emotional warble was caught on repeat. I tried to forward it on to the next track, but it wouldn't go.

'*I'm sorry.*' Argh. It was getting very irritating. I kept one hand on the wheel and felt around for another CD, any CD. I pressed eject and took the disc out, swapped it for some classical and pressed play. '*I'm sorry.*' R.E.M. continued to crank out of the speakers. I looked down at the disc in my hand and wrinkled my brow.

I slowed down and hit the stop button. The track went on.

Damn. I ejected the classical disc. The jarring music continued on like a broken record.

And then, over the top of Stipe's vocals I heard a sobbing.

I started swearing at the player, thumping it with my hand but it kept on playing out that bloody awful line.

The soprano got louder. 'I'm sorry.'

The memory of the dungeon hit me full in the face: the girl in the cell. The weeping. The despair. The pleading. It all descended on me like a cloud, or rather, the opposite of a cloud. Instead of getting foggy and obscured I felt like something was bringing down illumination, clarity.

I recognised her voice.

And then it was as if everything became connected: the castle, the mirror, the messaging. A linear pattern was emerging. And I suddenly saw it was all one and the same. A woman. One who had been kept in the dungeon. A woman who had been hugely wronged.

A witch.

But even as I thought that word, part of me still couldn't suspend scepticism. Why think that? I mulled it over. And yet, and yet, simultaneously I could feel it, there, at the base of my stomach, that the word was right. It struck a chord of harmony deep within. Or maybe harmony was not quite the right word. It was more like it struck a chord that wasn't dissonant – like it was chiming with something I already knew, something that I had repressed thus far; an intuition or forgotten understanding. I don't know. But, whatever, it was as if, in the micro-moment that it hit me, nothing was the same again. As if defences were coming down in my head and I was opening up to another world.

I lost concentration and swerved into the next lane. A car horn blared at me. This was barmy. Dangerous. My head was all over the place, reeling, gasping, seeing.

I pulled over to the hard shoulder and killed my speed, the ghastly voice sobbing and Michael Stipe apologising over and over again. Then the music stopped and the woman said, 'Forgive me.'

And I was gone.

Crawling up onto my feet I stagger up, but I am not steady and knock the girl in front. She shouts for me to mind myself. Her father watches on. He puts a hand on my arm to aid me but when I look up he sees who I am and recoils. I push past him unheeding of the jeers and taunts from the others around because at the front of the scaffold I see the woman with the knife is upon Mother's body. I cannot see what she is busy with, only the arch of her back, muddy feet sticking from the bottom of her dress. I call out for her to leave her alone. But then HE is there. He blocks my path and grabs my arms, fastening them behind my back.

'You'll not help her now,' he says and pulls me roughly to him. 'Master Ranking. Take her,' he shouts into the crowd. A man comes forwards dressed in a blue livery I don't recognise. 'Keep her with you and take her back.' Then he turns to me. I am struggling hard to twist my wrists from his grip. 'They will take care of you, till your time comes.'

I manage to unloose one arm and lurch forwards. HE is shouting instructions to the liveried man who picks me up and throws me over his shoulder.

'More gentle,' HE barks. 'She is with child.'

The man hoists me up slower. When he turns around my body is swung to face the killing stage where I see the knifewoman holding something up for the crowd. Her face is full of pleasure and victory. She stands up and waves it and I realise what it is – blood still drips from Mother's scalp.

Chapter Nineteen

I was roused by tapping. A pitter patter that got stronger and became an insistent knock.

It was the police outside the window, squinting into the car. I think they thought I was drunk as I couldn't talk immediately, only shake my head with confusion.

A lorry driver had reported a woman asleep at the wheel, they informed me, and asked was I epileptic? When I told them I wasn't they took out their gear and breathalysed me.

Thank God I'd only had one at the pub. The whisky did register but I wasn't over the limit. Eventually they let me go with some cautionary words.

I did my best to get off the main road. I was in no state to cope with the rush hour traffic on the A130, and so navigated to a small village, where I pulled into a pub car park and tried to still my mind.

I had a lot to take on board – a convergence of different experiences. I let them spin around, trying hard to make sense of them; the messaging, the mirror, the dungeons and now this. The word coincidence didn't cut it any more. It smacked too much of wilful blindness and disclaimers.

Though that didn't mean I knew what was going on. I

knew what it *felt* like – as if the Fates had spun a web around me and roused an ancient sleeping self. One that was able to tune into things that my old self couldn't.

I still couldn't explain what was going on but right then, I felt strongly that there was a reason for it.

I would just have to work out what that was.

Chapter Twenty

I didn't go home straight away. I couldn't.

As much as I was aware there was some strong inner drive propelling me on, taking me into new spheres of experience, I could also detect a dent in my resilience. Not my resolve. But if I didn't pay attention to one then the other would certainly suffer.

So instead I drove down to the beach and parked up. Then I walked along the front and found a bench to stare out into the sea. The wind was up and clouds were scudding across the horizon, mirroring my rapid brain activity.

Shock is a very physical sort of thing that leaves you adrift in your own skin. I almost felt like I had been bashed round the head and rendered senseless, whilst at the same time, paradoxically, I was super-alert.

I sat there for a long time, under the Cheshire cat moon, in the sharp air. The tide was out, exposing the black mud of the estuary floor. Lots of people hated this time, yearning for the river to come back in and cover the muck. But they didn't know how to value it. That state never lasted long. The tidal landscape was always in a process of constant change. When you look into the seascape it sends you something back that mirrors your emotional state. Usually when I gazed into the yawning cleft between the stars and riverbed, the emptiness would make me feel as if I was staring into a void, a moment of stillness in the hustle and bustle of twenty-first-century life. Right then, that night, I remember it was unsettling, reflecting back uncertainty and turbulence. I sat there and tried to think it all through, trying to get a handle on what was going on inside and outside of my head. It was like swimming against the tide.

My mind tumbled over the events of the past thirteen days since the funeral: the dreams, the nightmares, the pleading. 'I'm sorry.' The voice from the mirror, the girl in the cell, her words not just beseeching but also imperative, like she was trying to tell me something. Like she wanted me to do something for her.

I wondered what she needed, before another part of my brain halted that thought process and told me I was delirious or imagining things, and then I'd question my sanity and think back on poor Mum's mental illness. Could this possibly be genetic? Had I inherited a weakness from her?

That last time at the hospital Mum had been so weak and frail, but she too had been trying with all her might to say something. What was it? She'd attempted to speak, to form her twisted mouth into words . . .

Then I remembered. Wasn't it something to do with a gift? I swallowed.

The gift.

There it was, those two words – 'the gift'. Surely she had been talking about a legacy of sorts?

But what if the legacy was nothing to do with money or jewellery? What if it was to do with something else?

Something that connected now to this new part of me roused from its slumber. Something which, in turn, related to her strange behaviour?

Was it possible that Mum too had seen the things I had started to see – but that she saw them not as a curse but some sort of insight? A peeling back of the layers of reality that others could never perceive?

A gift.

Could I have inherited it from her?

But then, why hadn't she told me? Earlier on, before she became so damaged and worn? She would have done, I was sure. She would have prepared me.

No, it couldn't be. I had to be barking up the wrong tree, surely? All that psychic supernatural stuff was nonsense, I'd seen TV programmes with psychics, and was convinced that they were exploiters who had plants in the audience and teams of researchers. The whole thing was hammy entertainment. If people believed it then they were deluded and sad.

Though maybe that was the point.

Maybe that was *exactly* what was happening to me. A sad delusion had descended to help me cope with the fact that Mum had gone and that there was no afterlife. That all the existential fears I had ever had were true.

Perhaps part of my subconscious was inventing experiences to help my conscious being cope with such huge loss.

But then, why not imagine Mum? Why wasn't I visualising Rosamund Asquith in all her beauteous glory at her prime of life, when me and Dad and she were happy?

'Because it's not Mum who's trying to get through,' a voice in my head whispered.

Where had that come from?

It wasn't a different voice. It wasn't a different person. It was like an alternative 'me' who was speaking. A 'me' who was trying to nudge a new idea forwards.

Another bubbled up, darker, more insistent: 'No. Leave it.'

Maybe that's what I should do – abandon the project for the sake of my sanity. Perhaps it was taking me to a place I didn't want to go?

To madness.

That could be it – the only thing haunting me – the spectre of lunacy.

Oh God. Perhaps I was schizophrenic?

That had been one of Mum's possible diagnoses at one point. And it had horrified me. And her. But then, I recalled, it had turned out not to be valid.

Yet I had not just heard voices, I had seen things too, hadn't I?

With my very own eyes.

I sat back, exhausted. I was going round and round in circles.

There was one way to settle it. If I had, indeed, been contacted by some supernatural creature perhaps I could call it up? I would do that, yes.

And so I charged myself with strength, gritted my teeth, swallowed then shouted out into the darkness, 'Come on then, if you're here, tell me what you want!'

But there was no response. Of course there wasn't, I scolded myself. Did you really think there would be, you fool?

My sigh blocked out the dull scream of a solitary circling seagull. I relaxed my muscles and let my gaze rest on the lopsided boats, not seeing the drifts and shapes around me.

What, I wondered, does it mean to be mad? What exactly is madness? Wasn't it just a detour from the expected path of society's conventions? And nobody was entirely conventional. In fact, if you met someone who did observe every single norm, then you'd undoubtedly think that they were slightly mad.

Did that mean nobody was sane?

I went off on that tangent for a bit, flicking through my friends and colleagues, analysing their behaviour, coming to rest on Dan. Where was he? And how was his mental state? My hands strayed to my mouth and started chewing over my nails, something I hadn't done for years.

I don't know when I became aware that I wasn't alone. It was almost like one minute there was no one there, the next the black shadow was fully formed hovering out there on the waving lengths of seaweed: a black outline of a woman, too misty and vague to see in detail.

I caught my breath as my eyes locked onto her. My mind shut down all thought, rendering other functions impossible and stilling my body.

She was skittering on the surface, flicking to and fro like an imperfect television signal. Then I heard her speak.

'Mercy,' she said.

I heard it loud and clear.

It was real.

And in my head everything suddenly clicked.

Chapter Twenty-One

Maggie's surprised but ostensibly pleased husband, Jules, led me into the back extension of their house, where the editor of *Mercurial* was holding court. It must have been a long meeting because everyone's faces perked up at the interruption. When I plonked a bottle of white on the table a small shout went up.

'Saved by the belle!' Rik applauded his own pun.

'All right, all right.' Maggie rolled her eyes at the gathering. 'Well we've covered enough ground. I was going to go over the Artside launch but that'll be enough for tonight. Especially as Sadie has got the first round in. Anyone up for red?'

I nodded at Maggie and gestured for a large one and we proceeded into Maggie's kitchen. It was a nice bright extension with a modern finish and all mod cons, and after the day I'd had it was exactly where I wanted to be. I'd detoured here before home. There *was* something I had to do. In the minutes after the phantom disappeared I had worked out what that was. She'd told me.

Maggie didn't look put out to see me but I felt I had to explain myself. 'Sorry to butt in, Mags, but I've had a bizarre sort of day. Needed to see someone sensible.'

'And you thought of me?' She reached up to a rack on the kitchen cupboard and presented me with a bottle of red. 'This one's better than what you brought.' Then, clocking the paleness of my face she added, 'You all right, love?'

I grimaced as she handed me the corkscrew but nodded. I knew, after our last conversation, I'd have to edit my words carefully.

Maggie sussed my hesitation. Her face dropped for a moment. 'What's up? Everyone okay? Your dad? Dan, is he okay?'

'I still don't know where Dan is, I'm afraid. It's a worry,' I sighed and uncorked the bottle, pouring two large ones into bulbous glasses. 'Can I run something past you?'

There was an exasperated tone to my voice that Maggie caught at once. 'You want a fag?'

'More than ever,' I said and handed her a glass.

We swept through the living area, where she deposited two wine bottles with the crew, and on through a conservatory into the garden porch. Despite its state of the art interior, Maggie's garden was a thing of the past: a long stretch of land that flowed downhill towards the seafront and thus gave a good view of the sea. However, its high fences and drooping apple trees lent it protection from the coastal winds.

Maggie got into the swing chair and I came and sat beside her. 'So what's eating Gilbert Grape?' she said.

I'd already decided on my way over here that I was going to omit any mention of the supernatural. There was no point communicating any of that to Maggie. She would try to rationalise it, as she had the messages and the girl in the mirror. She wouldn't get it. It wouldn't touch her. Someone like Mags would never understand or believe it unless she experienced it for herself. And even then, she still might not trust herself. Just as I hadn't – until tonight. Until *she* told me.

So I began with the trip to the castle. I told her I'd got stuck in the gaol because someone had played a prank and shut the door. That I'd got very distressed and it had made me realise just how terrible it had been for the women that were imprisoned in that tiny dreadful space and how unjust that was.

And then I hit her with it. It had appeared in a flash, when *she* had pleaded for 'mercy'.

'You know, I keep going on about how awful it was, and how tragic and unfair. I know that most, if not *all* of the women Hopkins took there, were innocent. But I'm not doing anything about it other than just writing it down.'

Maggie shifted in the chair and crossed her legs.

I carried on. 'But I could do something more. People do, don't they? When there's been a miscarriage of justice . . .'

Maggie kept her mouth shut and nodded.

'So I'm thinking – why don't we try to get a pardon for them? It was a travesty. I mean seriously – it should be put right. They should be forgiven. Acknowledged. In Salem they've got a remembrance garden and a plaque and a museum for their twenty-two. There's one in Lemgo, Germany, for 254 poor sods; a fantastic monument in Vardo, which was opened by the Queen of Norway herself. Lord Moncrieff in Kinross, Scotland, is building a maze to commemorate the execution of local witches by one of his predecessors. And yet we've got *nothing* in Essex. There's information on the witches *and* Hopkins in Colchester Castle but nothing else. Not one single monument or confirmation of the human catastrophe. We lost so many more than in Salem. And, you know, monuments, they are a way of coming to terms with the past and of ensuring we remain watchful for intolerance . . .'

At some point Felicity must have crept out to join us. I hadn't noticed as I'd been in full flow.

'Has something happened?' she asked. Her face was open, but she was smiling, waiting.

Both Maggie and I looked up at her, standing in the doorway of the conservatory nursing a wine glass.

I didn't know what to say, she had thrown me. 'I . . . er . . . no . . . I was just thinking . . .'

'Where have you been?' she asked me directly.

I stared at her, lost for words. Why was she asking me that? Could she have known that I'd been to the castle? I was sure I hadn't mentioned it to her on our last meeting. Nor to Maggie. I'd been too caught up with the mirror episode.

'Well, anyway,' she continued when I didn't muster a response. 'I think it's a great idea,' she said. 'We could certainly start a campaign.'

'Thank you,' I stammered for want of anything else. Flick raised her glass to her lips and calmly took a sip.

I turned my face to Maggie, who seemed not to have noticed my jitters. 'Well,' I continued, 'I have already done the ground work: I've found the witches. At least the ones on record. Though there were loads more that didn't leave a paper trail. But we can factor that in . . .' I was sitting up, right on the edge of the swing chair. 'Now I don't know how we do it but surely there is a way. A pardon is the right thing to do. Or if that's too difficult, then at least let's set up a monument, or piece of art, to commemorate the victims. To grant them forgiveness. Mercy.' I said the last word with a shudder. The poor girl. She had suffered so much. I knew it was her. It had to be.

Maggie sniffed. 'I'm not sure. We've never put our weight behind campaigns.'

Flick stepped away from the conservatory and spoke up again. 'I know I'm not the editor.' Her eyes latched onto Maggie. 'But we can all make suggestions. Right? You were just saying we need to do something bold to bring in more readers, get noticed by advertisers.' Her words were considered, measured out carefully, framed within a proposition that would suit their audience. If I didn't know better, I might have thought she'd seen this coming. 'It fits our profile – it's to do with culture and perception. I think we should examine the possibilities it might open up for us. But,' she inched closer to her boss, 'if nothing else, it's a brilliant publicity stunt.'

I zipped from Flick to Maggie then back to Flick. The latter winked at me. I leant back into the seat, not sure how to take it. Perhaps I was being oversensitive. Perhaps she was being insensitive.

The swing rocked gently back and forth.

Maggie seemed to be debating the matter with herself and lit another fag. You could tell Flick's words had struck a chord somewhere in her brain. But she acted cool about it. She looked at Flick once more and said, in a quiet voice, 'That's an interesting take.'

I bit my thumb and said nothing.

'Well, I think it's an opportunity and I don't mind leading

it.' Flick was saying more than I'd ever heard her say before.

The wind crept over the fence and whispered in the apple trees. Maggie blew out a thin line of smoke that was instantly whipped up into the night. 'You're very gobby tonight, Ms Flick.'

The art director held her glass with both hands and smiled thinly over the top. 'You were the one who said I needed to speak out more often in meetings, as when I do I make "valid and insightful comments". Sic.'

Maggie brushed some bushy strands of hair from her face and took another light drag. 'God I'm good,' she said to me, then turned back to Flick. The co-workers shared a smile. Maggie exhaled her smoke with a slight, almost imperceptible, nod and Flick breathed out deeply, like she was satisfied. Then they both turned to me expectantly.

'What?' I said. 'Why are you looking at me like that?' Then I got it. 'Hang on – I'm not volunteering myself. I don't think I can do much to help with the administration – I've got this book to nail. But, like I said, I've got all the research at home. I can point you in the right direction. I don't mind sharing my sources and evidence . . .' Relief was starting to unhinge my shoulders. If they took the bait then perhaps whatever was going on might stop. This would mean she'd get her mercy, wouldn't it?

Flick drew up a chair opposite us. 'That's the main thing we need. It's almost like you've already done your part, Sadie. You've hunted down the witches, done the research, now I can go with it and work on it more. Can you come over tomorrow for a chat and I'll make a start?'

Her eagerness surprised me. But it was welcome.

Maggie narrowed her eyes. 'Have you two talked about this before?'

'No!' We both exclaimed at the same time, then Flick laughed.

Maggie joined in.

I remained silent. I was still too wired to enjoy the gaiety.

Maggie took another mouthful of drink. 'Well it seems like I've got no say in the matter. If Sadie wants to give us the names of the women and the details, and if you're happy to start working on it, Flick . . . as long as it doesn't interfere with the general running of *Mercurial* then I'd like to see what you can come up with.'

I permitted myself a smile.

'Top-up, anyone?' said Maggie.

I nodded. But it wasn't to celebrate.

When I got home, I turned off the lights and looked into the cracked mirror. The top part of it had come away that night I threw the shoe. My thin tired face looked back, it had a strange expression. The beginnings of fear had wrinkled my forehead. My jaw line was tense and defined. But there was resolution in the firm mouth and beyond the whites of my eyes. I lowered my voice and whispered softly, 'Are you there?'

The outside light came through the windows and glinted on the cracks in the looking glass.

There was no glow. No movement.

But I needed to tell her, so I said it. 'We're going to try and get you a pardon. Do you understand that? You'll be pardoned. Then you can rest. Do you understand me now?'

Over in the neverworld, nothing stirred.

Chapter Twenty-Two

The *Mercurial* office was busy. A C-list actor and his agent were in for an interview with Maggie. Françoise and Lola were skipping and cooing around them like a couple of overexcited pigeons.

'Do you want to get a coffee at the Railway?' Felicity asked, with a minute nod towards the activity going on at the other side of the room.

'Good idea,' I said. My mood was pensive and I was very tired. Last night my mind had gone into overdrive and banished any possibility of sleep. I lay in bed alert, waiting for something to happen, listening to the stiff breeze in the oak trees outside. Then, just as dawn broke I managed to drop off, only to be woken by my mobile an hour or so later.

It was Amelia, the woman I had met at Uncle Roger's party. She had, she said, some information that she thought I might be interested in and asked when I was planning to visit Manningtree. I told her I was thinking sometime this week.

'You can't make it tomorrow can you?' Her voice kept going up and down, like she was all keyed-up. 'I'm going on holiday this Thursday and I really think you would be interested in this.'

'Can't you tell me over the phone?' I didn't like being pinned down.

'Not really, I have to show you some primary texts.'

That sounded interesting so I agreed to have dinner with her. 'At the Thorn Inn,' she said. 'It's the perfect place. I'll book the table.'

I thanked her and hung up, realising that I would be unlikely to drive back that late at night. So, I phoned the Inn and booked a double room. The idea of spending a night in the place where Hopkins had interrogated his victims filled me with dread but, I realised, if there was something strange lurking in the air around me, then it was most likely to come through there – like it or not. And I had stuff to convey now to the girl spirit. Something that might help me put an end to this business.

And, on a more practical note, I needed to go there for my book. Especially if Felix now wanted an 'emotional' response. It was an essential destination. I would just have to be strong, though the thought of it was draining.

Thankfully Flick seemed to have enough energy for both of us. She wrapped up her current piece of work and gathered together notebooks while I photocopied the information I thought she would need. Then we wandered across the road to the pub.

'You seem very enthusiastic about all this,' I said cautiously, as we settled at a large wooden table in the Railway Hotel. It was late afternoon and the place was pretty empty: just a couple of old regulars at the bar and a sad-looking punk who was sipping a pint of stout very very slowly.

We selected a place by the Victorian fireplace. Dave, the

landlord, had stoked a fire and this part of the pub looked particularly cosy and snug.

'I really want to be involved,' she said. I let my hair fall over my face as I reached for my file, but continued to watch her through the black strands. Her plucked eyebrows accentuated a sharpness about her nose, but she was an attractive woman and she knew it. 'I had a thing about it when I was younger.' She blew on her coffee. 'We all do, don't we? Witches and goblins, they're all magical and otherworldly. I got into Goth a long time ago. Not all of us want to hear about being in love or wanting to dance. Personally I like a bit of a wallow sometimes. And the subject matter that gothic bands cover is really extensive.' She was nodding quickly as she spoke. 'Ghosts, the undead, legends of old. There's an entire Goth-Pagan subculture too which is really interesting. And I believe in all that, don't you?' She looked at me, but didn't wait for an answer. 'I mean, I'd like to believe in it. But anyway all of this stuff about the witches – it's not only fascinating, it's real.'

'It is,' I agreed. 'And it's dark.'

'Yes. You don't like that then?'

I met her eyes. Was there more than curiosity lurking behind them? Or was I becoming paranoid? I looked at Flick's slender frame elegantly perched on a chair opposite me. I could see the gothic influence in the dark eyeliner, the dyed black wispy hair. Her clothes weren't studded or frilly but they were black – t-shirt, boots, low-rise skinny jeans. She had peachy skin as pale as a china doll's. As she held my gaze I wondered how old she was? Late twenties, maybe early thirties. It was hard to tell – her skin was so good. Too good actually.

I didn't mean to come out with it then but it just popped out. 'Have you had Botox?' I asked her.

She looked surprised. 'Nice body swerve,' she said. 'If I answer your question, it's only fair you answer mine.' She smiled. The skin about her eyes didn't crinkle.

I took a breath. In for a penny . . . 'Okay.'

She leant forwards on the table and angled her face towards the light coming in from the windows. 'Yes,' she said. 'Here,' she touched her forehead, 'and here,' gesturing round her eyes. Then she looked at me and laughed, then propped her chin on the palm of her hand. 'So – how about you?'

'My research has taken me to a lot of dark places,' I told her and added, 'literally. A while ago I would have told you that I wasn't attracted to the darkness. But that would be inaccurate.'

I swallowed the coffee. A young man in a scarf came in through the door nearest to us, letting in a gust of wind which nearly scattered the papers spread across the table. Felicity stretched her arm over them till the door closed again

'But,' I continued, 'I am compelled by the story of Rebecca West.'

It was her, you see, who had come to me. It had to be. She was the shadow on the beach: a young, fragile form. Though I hadn't seen it I had a strong impression of her. I knew she had betrayed her mother, and now she was asking for forgiveness. For mercy on their souls. For all of the unfortunates condemned to a monstrous death.

It was Rebecca's plaintive cry in the prison, and her life I had glimpsed in the layby. She was sorry and she had come to me, because she knew I was sorry too.

'She was young; only fifteen when Hopkins accused her. But she was manipulated by the Witchfinder and gave testimony against her mother possibly in exchange for their freedom, a deal retracted after the trial. Then she had to watch her mother die on the gallows, twisting and turning like a fish from the brook.' I stopped. That was an odd phrase. Flick picked up on it too. I changed my tone.

'Sadly her evidence nailed the guilty verdicts and the death sentences. That whetted Hopkins' appetite and got him thinking up the rest of the campaign. Who knows what might have happened or *not happened* if she hadn't taken to the witness stand? The accused might have got off. In which case Hopkins might have lost interest and gone back to his shipping business instead.'

Flick was staring at me. 'Really?'

'Unfortunately so. Without Rebecca's testimony the whole witch hunt might not have taken place.'

'Shit. Flick's eyes roamed over the papers spread between us. 'She had a lot to be sorry for.'

'She has,' I said slowly, then corrected my tense. 'Though it wasn't her fault. Let's not forget that. It was Hopkins who was the driving force behind the witch hunt.'

'It was indeed,' Flick nodded. 'So shall we get to it then?' she said. 'Try and even up the score a bit?'

'Let's,' I said and smiled. 'The old bastard will be turning in his grave.'

'Good,' Flick said simply.

I didn't leave the pub for another two hours. Once she got going Flick was like a terrier, she wouldn't leave anything alone that she didn't thoroughly understand. Though I wasn't convinced she was being completely open with me, I admired her for her thorough approach.

When I had taken her through most of the research I asked her to keep me abreast of any developments.

She nodded. 'Email all right?'

'Phone or text is better. I'm planning on going to Manningtree tomorrow. Where it all started.'

Felicity swallowed and grimaced. 'Fantastic,' she said.

When I got back to the flat I was knackered. Night had come down quickly and sent messages to my subconscious telling it to go to sleep. Although I didn't have a hangover I felt seedy and flicked the TV on for company. Automatically I kicked off my shoes and padded over to the windows to shut the curtains.

Though I hadn't noticed it when I came into the flat I saw now that they were already drawn.

That was weird.

This morning I had done this whole thing about throwing them open and letting the dwindling October daylight in. I clearly remembered doing it.

Perhaps I had closed them without registering before I'd gone out.

But that wasn't like me. I wasn't that organised.

I unlocked the balcony doors and slipped outside. It was cold and windy: the moon was quietly tugging in the water. I thought briefly about having a cigarette, got put off by the force of the wind so turned and stepped back into the artificial warmth of the flat. The difference in temperature brought to my attention something else that I hadn't noticed before – an atypical smell in the flat: the putrid stench of a feral base thing. I winced.

206

Something must have gone off.

But I was too tired to root it out and instead lit a scented candle then crashed onto the sofa and did a quick channel surf.

Under the loft's eaves dark unseen things rustled. The scratching was louder. I really needed to sort it out. But right then I just didn't have the energy and pumped the volume up to drown out the disturbance.

Something splashed on my face, causing me to jump with a jolt.

For a second I was completely baffled, then I put my hand up to my cheek and wiped it. A dark viscous fluid smeared across my fingers. Reddish, the colour of blood.

Another droplet fell, onto my arm this time. I looked up at the ceiling. A dark russet stain was blooming above me. A couple more gobs fell in quick succession, one hitting me in the eye, momentarily blinding me. I wiped it away with a tissue. The stuff was escaping from something in the attic. I knew there were at least three water tanks up there supplying the different flats. One of them must have gone rusty and sprung a leak.

I sniffed the fluid on my hand hearing, simultaneously, a loud crash above.

That was definitely not rats. Perhaps whatever was leaking was falling apart?

A sort of scraping sound moved across the ceiling, away from the location of the crash. Something was up there. Something solid, and very much alive.

As far as I could see I had two options – to flee from the flat or run downstairs to the new neighbours below me. I hadn't met them yet.

If it *was* rats I would look like an utter idiot.

This was the downside of living on your own.

Of course there was the other option: I could go up there, with a torch, and check it out myself. After a few nanoseconds I guessed this last thought seemed the most sensible.

So, taking a breath to soothe my now quickening heart, I fetched the flashlight from under the sink and summoned enough courage to go into the hall where the loft hatch was.

It was a wooden rectangle about three feet by four. I had never painted it white like the rest of the ceiling, and for a moment its decades-old wood appeared horribly sinister. Nevertheless I reached up with the pole-hook carefully, unlatched the attic door and lowered it down, fighting back a wave of nausea as the awful smell doubled in potency and wafted downwards.

It was fetid, musky, with whiffs of excrement and waste.

On the topside of the door an aluminium stepladder was fixed. I reached up and unfolded it noting the sound up above was becoming more frenzied. I looked back at the kitchen door, away from the attic, took a deep breath, gathered my resolve, placed the torch in my mouth and with both hands on the ladder, started to climb.

At the top I stopped, removed the flashlight from my mouth, took another steadying breath, and switched it on. The smell was so severe I had to try hard not to gag.

A shuffling in the corner prompted me to shine the torch in that direction.

The amber light danced along the rafters then settled in the corner of the loft.

I stopped dead.

Something large and dark was moving.

This was not a rat.

This was far far bigger.

And hunched over.

Almost human in form.

As my light shone over it, I saw it quiver and heard it make a noise. A low, rumbling sort of sound that made my blood curdle. No way was I tackling this on my own. I edged back gradually trying not to make a sudden move but to my horror, the thing turned towards me. A mess of brown rags came into view – a torso contained within dark filthy cloth. Now petrified, barely able to move, I forced the beam upwards till it hit on something I shall never forget; there, in the small circle of light, a manic pair of devilish eyes blinked and stared back.

For a moment we were both still, locked into a ghastly mutual gaze. Then all at once the thing sprang at me, a wild looping movement that caught me off guard.

I shrieked, ducked under the hatch, and slipped two steps down the ladder. My foot came to rest abruptly on one of the higher rungs. I lost my grip and reached out to grab on to something. My hand closed on nothingness and I fell backwards through the air, landing heavily on my back.

All the air went out of me. I struggled to get up, but could barely gasp: I had been so violently winded. And then the thing came into view through the square gash of the hatch. A frightful, creeping black creature, covered in wild hair, eyes raging and crimson. Brown claw-like hands gripped on to the ledge of the opening, then, it snorted and launched itself down.

I screamed at the top of my lungs as it landed beside me. 'No, no, no! Get away.'

It flailed its hands in front of me then clamped one entirely over my mouth. I tried to scream again but it had cut off my air.

I was panicking; trying to wriggle out of its grasp so I didn't register the noise at first. Then something cut through my internal pandemonium: '*Sadie!*'

Someone was calling my name: 'Sadie, no, no. Stop it, now. Settle.'

The familiarity of the phrase penetrated my terror. My fists unclenched.

I knew that voice.

Barely able to look at it, I slumped and stopped moving. Then, with a gargantuan measure of courage I brought my eyes up to the thing's face.

'Sadie. Danger, Sadie.'

I caught its hand and pulled it away from my mouth.

'What on earth . . . ?' I said as I took in its grim haggard features. For beyond the wildness I recognised my mum's boyfriend, Dan.

Chapter Twenty-Three

He was a wild tumbling thing, whirling about the hall, slightly deranged. No, not slightly. Massively. Hugely.

It took a long time to calm Dan down. And for me to get over the shock, for that matter. But, after God knows how long? – fifteen, thirty minutes? – I managed to get him into the lounge and sat down at the table while I made him a cup of tea.

It was crushing to see him brought so low. The man that had once been the epitome of reconstructed and regained dignity, of refinement and humility, reduced to the gibbering mess in my living room.

He couldn't sit still for long, so I let him pace up and down as he talked – sometimes to me, mostly to himself.

The state he was in was not conducive to coherent conversation, but I did ascertain these basic facts; he had been living above me for 'some time' now. I had forgotten that I had given him a key to my place after I locked myself out a few months ago. Dan told me that he snuck out whenever I left the flat, and tried to use the facilities. From the way he stank and the stubble across his face, it can't have been that often. Although he affirmed he was still taking his meds, it was quite clear that they weren't working.

Within an hour I managed to call his doctor out. Initially Dan was adamant that I should not reveal his whereabouts, his paranoia moving him to outbursts of swearing and tears. When I explained to him that there might have been a mix-up in his medication, he relented long enough for me to make the call. Though he took a hell of a lot of convincing.

The doctor informed me he would be around as soon as he could and I was to keep Dan calm and reassured till he got there.

I tried to steer our limited exchange towards my work and the Hopkins stuff. It wasn't a good choice. I was stupid to have mentioned such a macabre subject. Sometimes I forgot how it shocked other people so: my research had desensitised me. But Dan kept gasping and veering off, looping away, interrupting to tell me that I should be 'in fear'.

'There are people, things, Sadie, that mean harm. That's why . . . no . . . not why . . . because . . .' He twisted his hair into a dreadlock. It was the action of one insane, in distress. A huge lump hurt my throat as I let him babble.

'No . . . how . . . no, not how . . . I was guarding . . . someone will come they will come to you . . . make an ending I don't want here. Not here. No.' He smacked his head in frustration. 'It's not you . . . it's her . . . no, I'm wrong it's . . . him . . . no, stop it! Stop. It's all going round. Upside down. Ding dong.'

He bashed his hand onto the table.

I reached out to grab it. The top was glass and although his mind was currently weakened his body was still remarkably energised. The last thing I needed was a whole heap of smashed glass in my living room or on hand for him to trip on or pick up.

'It's okay, Dan,' I told him. 'I'm so glad you're safe.'

Dan squeezed my hand. 'I will protect . . . promise. You understand don't you?'

I put on a respectful sombre face and lied. 'Of course.'

He jiggled my wrist. 'Don't talk to strangers . . . er . . . look both ways when you cross path . . .'

He desperately needed to get back on his medication and straighten out. Plus he had a large slash across his forearm. Crawling across the loft to turn out his light, he told me that he had spilt his bucket (I didn't ever want to know what was in it). In his attempts to mop it up he had cut his arm on a pipe and fallen.

The wound was vicious but I did the best that I could with disinfectant and a bandage. Then after much persuading, I ran him a bath.

Rummaging through my wardrobe I found an old pair of Christopher's jeans that I'd kept out of spite, as they'd been too big for me, but luckily looked like they would fit Dan. One of my navy oversized sweatshirts would just about stretch to his size. The ensemble wasn't perfect but when he emerged from the bathroom, his hair washed and combed back, his face clean-shaven, clad in those clothes, he looked less mental and a whole lot more human.

I tried to take his soiled clothes to wash but he wouldn't hear of it. Behind his eyes I could see a returning of self. The tea and bath had begun to ground him.

Shortly after that Doctor Franklin arrived. A pleasant, sensible man in his late thirties, he had developed a good relationship with his patient. Indeed, Dan seemed to come down a little more as soon as the doctor walked through the living room door.

I sat on the sofa sipping my mug of tea, while he examined Dan's eyes, took his blood pressure, asked a series of questions, went through a number of strange tests then took me by my elbow and guided me into the kitchen.

'Would you mind making me a cup of tea please? It's terribly late and I am rather tired. I'll come out to the kitchen to fetch it. Only be a couple of minutes. Need a private patient–doctor moment.'

I closed the door and put the kettle on. A little bit of solitude would be a welcome relief. I pulled two mugs from the shelf and stuck a couple of teabags in them, wondering, now I had a moment to myself, how exactly Dan had come to be up in the loft? And why my loft? *My* loft? Why not Mum's? Why not his?

And that begged the question – why the loft at all? Why not simply come over and have a chat? Or a meal? Or, if he had his concerns, he was always welcome to stay.

I dunked the teabags in the mugs then tossed them into the bin as the doctor returned.

He cleared his throat. 'Dan's just removing his property from, er, the loft space.'

I nodded. 'Do you take milk?'

'Actually I don't want a drink, Ms Asquith, thanks all the same.' He was speaking in a whisper now.

'Oh right.' I picked up mine and drank it, waiting for him to speak. The doctor scratched his chin, then he put his hand to his brow and bit his lip. There was something going on in his head: a mood or a feeling I couldn't quite ascertain.

214

'Can I enquire as to the nature of your relationship with Dan Hooper, Ms Asquith?' he asked.

I leant back against the kitchen unit, a tad confused. Not by the question itself, as such, but by the way it was asked. I got the feeling that Doctor Franklin was restraining himself in some way. A shadow had crept over his face.

'He's kind of like my stepfather. I thought you knew that.'

Doctor Franklin nodded but didn't speak any more. Then he picked up the mug he'd rejected. 'I see. Did you invite him here to live with you?'

Despite myself I laughed. Franklin's face suggested that was not the looked-for reaction. 'No, of course not,' I ventured.

He gaped at the laminate floor, apparently tracing its pattern. 'It's just that he's insisting he's here because of you.' Franklin swept his eyes upwards. He couldn't hide the anger in his stare.

'Yes, I know,' I said in earnest. 'I don't know why he's saying that.'

He ran his free hand over the marble of the kitchen surface. 'Was there some kind of disagreement between you and your mother?'

I shook my head vigorously. 'No, none at all.'

'Between you and Dan, perhaps?'

My face had hardened now. I didn't like this line of questioning one bit. 'No. Never. Nothing serious. We enjoy a bit of a debate but . . .'

He glanced at me and put a hand on his hip. 'I know your mother has passed away, and regarding the line of inheritance . . . I wondered if it was a bone of contention between you and your step . . . Dan.'

What? I pushed away from the kitchen top and stood up to give my pose authority. 'I resent the implication here. Whatever Dan's told you, you've got it wrong,' I said in a half-snarl, furious at the angle he was taking. 'Our relationship was good. I'm as clueless as you are as to how he came to be camping out in my attic. I cared deeply for my mother and was disturbed by Dan's absence. As was she. Now, if you don't mind me asking – what's this about?'

Doctor Franklin leant his six-foot frame against the kitchen surface and inclined his head towards me. 'On Friday I received a call from Doctor Jarvis, the resident doctor at Howard Acres.'

'I know him, of course,' I said, unable to keep the condescension out of my voice.

'It was regarding the medication that you brought in last week.'

'Yes. That was Dan's. One of the nurses at Howard Acres asked me to fetch it from his flat. Given his sudden disappearance, I think she wanted to check he was taking the right dose of his meds.'

'Yes I heard.' Doctor Franklin looked up now, straight into my eyes. 'He wasn't. I'm not sure how long he's been off. Doctor Jarvis sent off a sample from the bottle brought in for analysis.'

'Sally told me.'

'Right,' he nodded. 'So you'll be aware that the tests have revealed Dan's been dosing himself with ibuprofen?'

I breathed in sharply. 'What? Why?'

Franklin shot me a look laced with contempt. 'Well, I don't think he meant to, Ms Asquith.'

The fridge hummed and shuddered.

I shook my head. 'Was it a mix-up at the pharmacy then?'

Now it was Franklin's turn to scoff. 'No pharmacist would have made that mistake. It would have been done after Dan had taken the prescription home. Can I ask who had access to his flat?'

There was some distant family but I was pretty sure they didn't have keys. Dan was anal about things like that. 'Just Mum and Dan, I think,' I told him.

He nodded again and stared at me. 'And you, Ms Asquith.'

I blinked and sucked in a raspy breath. 'You can't think that I interfered with Dan's meds? What reason would I possibly have?'

Doctor Franklin shifted from foot to foot. 'I hear that you were thinking of moving back into your mother's property? Converting her bedroom into an office . . . ?'

That was enough. 'How dare you!' I straightened up fully. 'I'll be putting a complaint in about you . . .' But no sooner had the words popped out of my mouth than I was cut off by a wail.

'No, no.' Dan had come up behind us. I had no idea how long he had been standing there or what he had heard but he was visibly distressed. He pulled me back, away from Franklin.

The doctor stepped forwards. 'Dan, I think we need to take you to get that cut looked at. Then I'll be recommending you stay in overnight.' He glanced at me. 'For at least one night.'

'No,' Dan shook his head. 'Staying here with Sadie.'

'Okay,' I said.

Franklin shook his head. 'I don't think that's wise.'

I could see how it looked and, despite my fury at Franklin,

I knew Dan desperately needed to get back on the right dose.

'Listen, Dan,' I made my voice soft. 'I think Doctor Franklin's right. You need to have your arm seen to professionally.'

'I'm all right,' he said. 'I'm staying.' Urgency hissed through his words. Something, some notion beyond the fuzz of his brain was troubling him. 'You're in danger.'

'Okay,' I said, glancing balefully at Franklin. 'Is that why you're here?'

'Staying,' he repeated and I could tell we weren't going to get any more out of him. His eyelids were drooping over his bloodshot peepers. The poor guy was practically sleeping on his feet.

'Look Dan, I'm perfectly fine. Honest, I'll call the hospital if I need you. I promise.' He didn't move. 'In fact, I really think you should go and get patched up so that you can be fighting fit again should I require your assistance. I might need you very soon but you're no good to me like this.'

The suggestion flitted across his eyes, going back and forth through his brain as he slowly processed it. After what seemed several minutes, during which none of us spoke, Dan nodded. 'But you call if you need to.'

I promised I would and Dan slowly turned to the doorway. Doctor Franklin held out his hand for me to shake. Dan couldn't see me so I didn't take it. 'Sorry if I overstepped the mark just then,' said Franklin. 'It's strange don't you think?'

I blew out of my mouth and whistled. Didn't mean to, but the air just went that way. I wanted to give him a 'whatever' look but did the whistle thing instead. He sighed. I didn't look like I was angry. Just that I didn't care.

Franklin reached down to gather up his bag from the hallway. I tugged on his arm and whispered. 'Sorry. I do care about Dan. Of course I do. But I didn't swap the pills. Why would I?'

Franklin regarded me for a moment before following Dan into the hall.

'I'd prefer to believe you. Sincerely. But if you didn't, who did?'

Chapter Twenty-Four

It won't surprise you to learn that that night I couldn't sleep. Again. My brain whirled. Questions turned over in my head like a bloody washing machine on spin cycle. Who would want to swap Dan's medication? Could an old acquaintance have broken into the flat? An ex-student with a grudge? Someone from his volatile pre-Mum period?

That kind of payback was nasty. There was no knowing what state people could get themselves into without correct medication. Whoever it was, they were damn spiteful. As my fury burnt through the night I resolved to find out who the culprit was and make them pay or face charges. People shouldn't get away with stuff like that.

Then there was the question of why he thought *I* was in danger. I'd never given any hint that I wasn't capable of looking after myself. And danger from what? My thoughts spiralled into a ceaseless whirl, concluding, after hours, that during the period when he was unwittingly withdrawing from his meds, Dan's fractured psyche had twisted concern for my mum into a jumble of irrational anxieties. And then transferred them onto me.

People did that all the time: you got told off at work, came home and took it out on your nearest and dearest. If we could do that with anger, we could just as well do that with fear and anxiety.

There was no other logical explanation. But then a lot of things that were happening at the moment were not logical.

It was all crazy. And hectic too. Everything seemed to be hurtling through time, almost as if someone had flipped a fast-forward switch on my life. Things had happened in such quick succession that I had been unable to process them internally. Though, weirdly, at the same time, I was grateful. The frenetic activity was filling up the gap between me and Mum. I knew I was grieving but I was fighting giving in to it, holding the loss at bay while I concentrated on these other new phenomena.

I was still unwilling to use the 'ghost' word. In fact I felt more comfortable referring to the girl, or whatever she was – the memory, the apparition – as Rebecca. It kind of took the edge off. I had no doubt that if I used the G word or its associated language – haunting; bewitching; possession – it might unleash the fear that I was keeping abated, and if that came over me, I would be useless, gibbering, no more competent than Dan. Or Mum.

Mum.

Nor was it lost on me, this notion that I was possibly 'seeing things' as my mother had done. I had dismissed her experiences as insanity, psychoses that merely required chemical rebalancing for her to get a grip on reality. But what if the reality that I was beginning to see now, was the reality in which she had lived for the majority of her life? If I thought about it enough I could see that there had been a pattern to her bouts of 'lunacy'. First she would become sad, then this would be compounded and transform into a darker thing – depression, anxiety, fear – then would come the 'apparitions', the voices.

My episodes had only begun since I lost Mum. When I, too, had been stressed and anxious, focusing hard on pain. Maybe that focus had meant that other parts of my brain weren't holding up properly against these external forces. Maybe that preoccupation left part of me weak, creating a gap which gave Rebecca the chance to enter in?

Or perhaps it was psychological as Maggie had said: I had lost my mother and the guilt which flowed through my veins was manifesting itself in the visions of a young girl pleading for forgiveness: 'I'm sorry.' A transference of my internal culpability? An outward projection of loss, grief, blame? A seizure?

The answer was that 'yes', it could be any one of those things. What I really should do was make an appointment at the doctor's. But that was a no-go after last night's run-in with Doctor Franklin. I didn't trust him and I no longer trusted Doctor Jarvis.

No, whatever was going on in my strange brain I was going to go with it, to ride it out to its conclusion. If it threatened at any point to overwhelm me, then I would seek assistance from some source. But for now I was resolved to move forwards. I would go to Manningtree tomorrow, for the book and to call up Rebecca, whatever she was – spirit or embodiment of guilt. Then I could let her know about what I was doing with Flick. Maybe that would assuage her guilt. Maybe it would assuage mine. At least it was *doing something*.

It was raining and somewhere in the attic water had got in. Perhaps Dan had dislodged a tile. I got up and tried lying on the sofa, listening to the steady drip, drip, drip until I gave up and got my laptop.

The light in the room was dim. I had purposely left only one lamp on to encourage sleep.

When it first happened I thought it was because it was attracted to the brightness of the screen: a black moth alighted on the top right-hand corner of my laptop.

I knew it was the season for it but there had been a hell of a lot of them around this year. They were getting everywhere.

I'd always been a bit of a swatter in days gone by but I found I was reluctant to crush the life out of this particular insect. It wasn't completely black. Whitish specks freckled its wings like flakes of ash.

'What are you then?' I asked it. It spread its wings in response, inviting me to admire its swirls and shimmers. I smiled and, for want of anything better to do, entered 'moths' into an image search. On the third page I scrolled through I spotted a similar pair of wings. One click brought me through to the article, which the image illustrated.

'The Peppered Moth: UK moth transforms from black to white as pollution decreases.' The report went on to state that although these moths started off white, during the industrial revolution they turned black to match their environment. Now it seemed they were halfway through the process of returning to their original colour. A moth expert commented, 'It's the iconic moth. This is the one everyone learns about in school because it perfectly illustrates natural selection.'

'Darwin would be proud,' I told its little wings and clicked through to a site flagged up by a banner ad – Animal Totems.

The page on the screen was black. At the top was an animated banner, which read *Today's Shamanic Blessing*. Underneath ran the phrase, *When walking in the woods never leave tracks.* I took it on board with a nod and silently promised not to. Then I came to the title *Moth Totem.*

The moth apparently had a similar animal symbolism to the butterfly. No shit Sherlock. But it was also a nocturnal creature. 'Night creatures,' it read, 'do not stumble in the dark. The moth navigates easily, led by lunar light.'

The symbolism, in turn, connected to intuition, spiritual awareness and heightened senses. 'The moth is a master of disguise and can blend in to the point of invisibility. He aids metamorphosis, representing birth, death and rebirth. He is also a guide helping you towards your own light or beacon, and in the direction you are meant to go.'

'You're a clever boy aren't you?' I put my elbows on the table and sat forwards. My eyes were on a level with its body. 'I feel like I'm in the dark right now. You going to show me where to go?'

It remained still.

'Go on,' I said. 'I could do with some help.'

It didn't move.

'Sod you then.' I brushed it away. It flew up at a forty-five-degree angle, inelegant and off balance, then fell on the carpet in front of the fireplace. I must have damaged its wings, I thought and felt absurdly guilty.

Getting up from behind the computer I walked over. It took off, veered off to the left than arced up onto the map I had fixed on the chimneybreast.

'Sorry about that,' I told him. It was off again, circling my head once, then landed back in the same place.

I looked at the map. Not Essex. Mr Moth had settled himself thirty or so miles south-west of London.

'You want me to go there do you?' I asked it. 'What's there?'

He didn't answer, so I slipped a sheet of white paper behind it and a glass over the top. He didn't resist and appeared happy to fly off into the night through my window.

Chapter Twenty-Five

Dan plopped down opposite me in the new hospital, just outside of Basildon. He was pretty doped-up but physically more like the old Dan I knew and loved. His brown hair was giving up the battle against encroaching silver and he'd lost a bit of weight. His familiar t-shirt and favourite Levis seemed to be wearing him, as he sat, caved into the saggy armchair.

I wasn't sure how much he knew about Mum. I hadn't wanted to broach it last night. But it turned out that he had worked it all out in his hidey-hole. We were in a small common room with a dozen chairs and a TV turned to a low continuous mumble.

Dan shook his head then said, 'It was too soon.'

I knew what he meant. I got it. We weren't ready for Mum to go. It felt like we still had stuff to do together. She was meant to come home with me and start another chapter of her life. I mean, she was still young, only fifty-two. It just wasn't fair.

Dan looked at me with this thousand-yard stare and said: 'We are such stuff

As dreams are made on, and our little life is rounded with a sleep.'

A casual observer may have thought this odd but I knew Dan was a teacher groping about in his fractured psyche for a hook to pin the loss on. To remind himself that this was life, and death was as much a part of it as birth. Had been since 1610 when the bard wrote those very words, and would be for ever more.

A strange tranquillity, a vague sound-absorbing haze, had found its way into the room.

I said, 'Shakespeare.'

Dan said, '*The Tempest.*'

And for a moment I imagined a ship with spirits pouncing all around. And then I thought of John Lowes, a priest hanged by Hopkins in Brandeston, and his yellow imp darting out into the sea. I don't know why I thought about it then but I did.

The clock on the wall ticked slowly then stopped. Static in the air crackled around us.

And Dan said, 'Has she come to you?'

I looked at him now sitting upright in his chair. 'Who?'

Though confusion crept across his brow, when he returned my gaze a keen sharpness entered his eyes. 'Rebecca.'

I didn't speak. I was too shocked.

He leant forwards. 'She's worried about you.'

At last I found my voice. 'Who?'

'Your mum. That's why I was looking after you. She thought Rebecca was warning her. They were both fifteen, you see.'

I was confused. 'Rebecca? Mum?'

'She feels guilty.'

'Dan. What do you mean?'

He turned his now-alert gaze on me. 'The ghost.'

I sat back and stared at him. Had he overheard my trans-actions in the living room while he'd been perched above?

'She's a witch,' he said calmly.

'Who?'

'Rebecca. You. Her.'

I shook my head. 'Dan, have you seen Rebecca or did you hear me talking about her?'

He didn't respond. He was looking over my shoulder into the mid-distance.

I tried a new tack. 'Dan, is she in your head?'

He regarded me keenly. 'Sadie, please don't be facile.'

Was I being ridiculous or had a pointed clarity briefly come down over him?

He smiled. A thin, sad smile. 'She texted me.'

I didn't know what to say or do. So I just inhaled steadily and watched him.

He continued, looking straight into my face. 'Pretty good too for an illiterate seventeenth-century ghost.' Then he laughed. 'I sound barmy, don't I?'

But he didn't.

I shook my head and then suddenly with that gesture it was like something shifted into place inside my head. Maybe some drug I had taken way back had decided to fire a latent synapse but it was like I'd stumbled through a wall and could now see what it was like on the other side, in Dan's world. The lights were brighter over there. The colours more vibrant. The textures and light, wavier. Like when you're on acid and just completely and fleetingly connect with someone. And for that brief moment you see the same mad things, through the same freaked-out headspace.

I said, 'She's Facebooked me.'

And he laughed generously. 'Seriously?' He was sane on this side.

'Yep. Well, private messaged.' I nodded slowly. The clock was ticking louder than ever before. I angled my head to it. 'Is it always this loud?'

Dan shrugged. 'Comes and goes. Depends on where I am.'

I nodded again. 'It is like a trip. Is this, like, how things are for you?'

He shook his head. 'Right now, it is. But the medication brings me down to earth. Comes and goes. I'll be moving out of it soon. I don't know what happened with my meds. I don't remember not taking them but I think I can't have had some for a while. When I was up in your loft I was wholly untethered. But before that it crept up on me. A gradual process. I can describe it like a giant balloon lifting off. You don't notice it until it's too late and then you're way over there.' He indicated through the wall behind him.

I took it on board. 'Someone swapped your medication.'

'Is that right?' he said and ran his finger over his jawbone. 'Then she was right.'

'Who?' I said.

'Rebecca. She said there was danger. Your mum was afraid for you. She made me promise that I'd look over you. I took that a bit too literally. But she was so worried, Sadie. Though I could tell there was something she wasn't telling me.'

I nearly cried at the mention of her and the absurdity of it all. 'You're in hospital and Mum's passed over. I don't think it was *me* you both had to worry about.'

'But she's come to you. Rebecca.'

'Yes,' I said, realising that I had let my scepticism go. That sitting here in the hospital, talking to a man who had just been sectioned, I was finally accepting that it wasn't madness or grief that I had experienced but an actual external manifestation.

'Mum said, just before, you know, she passed, to expect a gift. She said I should speak to you. Is this . . .' I stumbled over the words, unwilling to articulate what was becoming a solid conviction. 'Is this it?'

'Didn't she tell you what it was?' Dan asked simply.

'No.'

'Have you asked her?'

I nearly laughed. 'No. Of course not. I can't now.'

'You'll see. That's it.' He said it quickly – we both heard footsteps coming down the corridor. 'Like us,' he said.

The atmosphere was changing: the unseen mist receding into the corners of the room: the clock returning to its regular tick tock. Time was running out.

'Look,' I said quickly. 'I've got to get off. To Manningtree. And Mistley. I need to scout out the place for the book. But I need to contact Rebecca. I want her to know that I'm going to get her a pardon. I've got some people at the magazine starting a campaign. Do you know how I can call her up, Dan?'

Dan's gaze darted to the door. 'I don't think it's up to you.'

'I will stop back here after Manningtree. And see how you are, okay?

He nodded quickly. 'Okay.'

Then as the door finally opened wide the weird magic in the air was sucked out and I found myself back over the other side, looking at Dan. His jaw slacked, the neck muscles had lost their tension. He was looking down, in a lolling sort of way, at his lap.

'How is he?' said the nurse.

'Really good,' I said. 'Aren't you, mate?'

The nurse helped Dan to his feet. He gave me a lopsided grin, which spilled a thread of saliva onto his chin. He didn't wipe it. 'Bye Sadie,' he said. Then he added, 'Be good.' It came out in a kind of weird E.T. voice. He heard it and stuck out his finger like the little alien.

I frowned. Had he relapsed or was he playing along?

'Bye bye Dan.'

'Be good,' he repeated and stared at his finger.

I dug my own fingernails into my hands and told myself not to cry.

Chapter Twenty-Six

Away from the buzz of Basildon, the fake tan and stilettos, under the grass and soil, the twisting roots, loam, chalk and clay, beneath the minerals transported from the north by the majestic glaciers that thawed eons ago, the ancient soul of Essex was waiting for me.

Mistley, allegedly 'the pasture of the Mistletoe', was situated on the south bank of the River Stour, with views over the mud flats and creeks to Suffolk and the village of Brantham.

The main road wound round the riverside and past the front window of my hotel room. If I twisted my neck I could glimpse a couple of cranes on the quay by the old malt house. Numbers of elegant white swans glided along the Stour. They didn't make a sound and lent a mute eeriness to the atmosphere.

Apart from the occasional car it was very quiet.

Directly outside the Inn was a fountain-like structure, described as the 'Swan Basin', which looked like a giant ornamental flower bowl with a painted statue of a swan in the middle. The guidebooks referenced it as the work of eighteenth-century neoclassical architect Robert Adam and described it variously as 'elegant' and 'picturesque'. But it reminded me of something you might find in a fairground. You can take the girl out of Southend . . .

I could never work out why Essex got the flack that it did. The county wasn't flat and uninteresting. It was simply full of sky, usually of the pale blue and white kind. Today it was bruised and wounded-looking, hanging low over the horizon.

It matched my mood.

I was sitting in my room in the Thorn Inn, on the site where Hopkins had his quarters. I could feel a pregnant tension in the air; if I reach back to that afternoon, it was like I *knew* something was going to happen.

I imagined the pub to be a historic Tudor dwelling, but it was quite ordinary. Built in 1723, it was a simple construction: unimposing and Georgian in its rectangular structure with four windows on the first floor, two on the ground. The entrance to the ground floor was on the left-hand side. The owners had obviously tried to camouflage any residual evil with coat upon coat of buttermilk paint. But I could smell its malevolence. It stank the place out, crawling up from cracks in the bricks and mortar.

Once a coach house for Mistley Hall, it was now an upmarket gastro-pub that offered cookery courses. It, along with the surrounding property prices, had gone up in the world since the dark days of the witch hunts.

The price of the room covered dinner and I was told the by the bar staff that I could expect breakfast too. I noted the rural lilt to their accent that the tramp in Colchester had spoken with. In the heightened state I was in, it seemed to combine wholesome hints of apples with superstition and ancient custom.

Despite its antique origins, my room was furnished in a contemporary style that complimented the old wooden rafters: the bed was comfy and covered in Egyptian cotton, the carpet thick and luxurious and neutral, the colour scheme blues, greys and mulberry with a floral patterned wallpaper on one 'feature' wall.

I sat on the bed feeling the mood, and looked out the window. Above the river the sky mottled like grey-white marble, darker cloud lines drooping over the shores of Suffolk on its further shore.

Once he'd achieved his kill at the Chelmsford Assize in July, Hopkins headed over to there. I thought of Rebecca, carried off in the arms of some servant to who knows where . . . What had happened after that? I wasn't sure I wanted to know. Her life was like a horror film. Awful.

Not so for Hopkins.

He netted a huge haul of witches in Suffolk and made a small fortune. Some say there were at least 150 overcrowding the prisons in Bury St Edmunds. Their gaoler was able to make a pretty profit by charging the curious a penny to gape at the unfortunates. For an extra sum they could beat them. One of them was the preacher, John Lowes, who had come into my mind in my strange exchange with Dan. It was his death that had some positive impact, if you can call it that, turning the tide against Hopkins. But only because it was so very shameful.

Lowes had given shelter to a local woman accused of witchcraft and had scolded the mob at his door, telling them that she was no more a witch than he. Hopkins took this as a confession and Lowes was swum in the moat at Framlingham Castle. Afterwards he was 'walked' till he lost his senses and finally confessed to sending imps to wreck ships at sea. At court he retracted his confession. But it didn't matter. He was convicted anyway, along with one other man and sixteen women. At the gallows his last act before execution was to read the office and commit his body to the ground and Christian resurrection.

The hanging of a vicar for witchcraft was so shocking it forced influential figures to take a look at what was going on in the east of England.

But not soon enough to prevent Hopkins and Stearne entering Northamptonshire and pointing fingers at Anne Goodfellow, and a 'young man of Denford'. The Witchfinder was rewarded generously for detecting those witches and paid to give testimony during the trials.

Hopkins was an impossible man to understand. He repelled and fascinated me, as much as the witches had him. But I was going to bring some semblance of justice to the alleged witches he'd killed. Flick had sent a text earlier. She had put out feelers to form a legal team and was hoping to meet up next week to come up with a proposition for the pardon. She'd added that she'd already got a lot of interest locally by starting a Facebook group. I sent her a message congratulating her and confirming I would attend the meet.

I opened the window to get some fresh air in the room.

The thought that I could, perhaps, be sleeping in the room where much of the witch hunt had taken place was pretty unnerving. But I knew I had to do it. I wanted Rebecca to manifest. I needed to communicate to her somehow that mercy was on its way.

But that would be later. Right now I had stuff to research. Felix had texted me that morning, asking how I was going, and I'd responded that I was making progress and informed him that I was going to Mistley. He'd replied that he was disappointed he couldn't come too and asked me if I was free next week. I sent him a text saying that I could always make myself available for him. And he'd returned my open-ended answer with a 'Good,' and an emoticon of a smiley face doing a wink.

I was pleased that he'd contacted me. It was like a line of normality that took me back to my other purpose – the book. So, with that in mind, I left the Inn and headed into Manningtree along the riverside road.

I wasn't meeting Amelia till eight o'clock so I had time to explore Manningtree and started with a visit to the small museum in the town's library.

The display on the witch hunt was small but it mentioned two significant sites: The Causeway at the bottom of Cox's Hill where it was thought the guilty were hanged, and Hopping Bridge, perhaps named after Hopkins, where local legend had it the witches and Hopkins himself were 'swum'.

I jotted them down on my map of Manningtree and asked the curator if I could take a photograph of the display. He was polite when I explained why and we engaged in conversation. Phillip was a congenial chap in his fifties with an academic manner. Though he didn't want to be drawn into the more sordid aspects of the witches, he did comment on the period.

'I'm more interested in that part of our story from a social history perspective,' he said. 'This period of civil war, when the institutions responsible for law and order break down. The idea that without them you can do basically what you like. That's why Hopkins is of interest. One only needed a powerful personality to rise up and take control. Let's face it – it was disgraceful. The prosecutors were rich. The accused were poor. They were a burden on the town. This was probably a good way of getting rid of a serious drain on the financial purse of the parish. Everyone colluded.'

Phillip clasped his hands together. 'True, Hopkins was a man of his time. Having said that, I'm aware that although we like to think we've put it all behind us, witch hunts are still alive and kicking up the twenty-first century . . . Look at Africa – there's a resurgence of belief in Ghana. Old women are being targeted there and burned alive. Kenya's still burning witches too. Child abuse related to witchcraft is on the rise in Nigeria. Children get slashed, burned, starved, drowned and buried alive because their villages believe them to be witches. There are "baby farms" in some parts, where young girls are paid for their newborns. Some are adopted illegally, others are bought for their body parts as their innocence is thought to make charms stronger.'

I shook my head to convey frustration not disbelief – it was all true. I'd kept an eye on this sort of stuff in the papers. Only last week, there'd been an article on the murder of albinos in Tanzania. The locals believed their organs and blood would bring good luck. 'You're very knowledgeable on the subject.'

He nodded sadly. 'An organisation called Stepping Stones is my church's chosen charity for the year. They highlight this sort of thing. You couldn't make it up, could you?'

'No,' I said.

'And,' he continued, 'it's not confined to Africa. Only two Christmases ago there was the case of that fifteen-year-old boy, Kristy Bamu, murdered in Newham. He and his siblings were kept without food, sleep and water till they confessed to sorcery and being a witch. Then he was beaten with a hammer, cut and finally drowned. Ring any bells?'

I nodded bleakly. They were virtually the same methods that Hopkins used.

Phillip shook his head. 'And look at that poor boy – Adam. The "torso in the Thames". He'd only been in the UK a few days before he was murdered and he had ingested a potion containing herbs and ingredients used in African ritual magic. People must have known about it. Why didn't they come forward? Fear? Cowardice? Or more likely they thought some bad luck would befall them. We haven't moved on much.'

I sighed. 'That's why I'm writing this book. To get across the fact that the witches weren't witches. Same as today. They were, are, scapegoats onto whom fantastical fantasies were, are projected.'

'Same as today,' he repeated sadly. 'Well, good luck with it. Let me know if I can be of any help.'

Our conversation had come to a natural end so I paid for a couple of local interest books and bid him goodbye.

I had been alert to, but not put off by, a slight drop in Phillip's features when I had first mentioned Hopkins' name. I could understand it. Manningtree was so much more than just a magnet for ghouls with an interest in the Witchfinder – it must be irritating for the locals to have their home characterised by the malevolent blip in the town's history. Not much predated the Tudor period but Manningtree's architectural legacy was extensive. Its buildings ranged from the cutting edge in modern construction techniques to sixteenth-century

238

idylls. And there was the river too – so picturesque and pretty. The honk of geese carried to me on the breeze and the overpowering scent of malt filled the air. To the innocent eye it was a gorgeously placid rural scene.

The site of the gallows proved disappointing. In fact, it was located in the most built-up part of town – a small industrial park. There wasn't anything to mark the significance of the spot, so I scrambled up the riverbank. This must have been the last view the victims saw: the flattened landscape spreading outwards, the river heading off to the east, the outskirts of the little town cascading down the hill. It would have been cold and windy and HE would have been there. Watching them. They would have seen him, in the crowd, doing what? Gloating? Looking smug? While their friends and neighbours stood about them to witness the hangman put on the noose.

Contemporary accounts talked of the 'hangers on'. Though the term today implies sycophants and toadies, in its original context it referred to the friends and family of the convicted who would jump on the legs of those twitching and jerking through their last moments of life, to hasten their death and end their excruciating suffering. A hanging could often take over twenty minutes.

A cold north-easterly wind had come up, bringing dark clouds. Across the river I saw a figure on the bank. Clad in grey, I watched it as she, in turn, watched me. Tatters of fabric swam out from her side caught in the drift of the wind. She waved at me. Or maybe someone else.

I shivered, keeping my hands in my pockets.

She gave up and turned away and so did I.

On the way back to the hotel I stopped at the place Phillip

had told me the witches were swum. The Hopping Bridge was a redbrick humpbacked bridge on the north side of a pond.

It was approaching dusk now and the bridge felt quite lonely. I remembered reading something about a ghost sighted here one dark night in the sixties. A local man, Herbert Bird, claimed that he had seen 'an apparition' which ran across the road as he was approaching. As he walked up to the bridge it vanished. Passing by again the next night he studied the grass where the thing had disappeared and saw a patch of thicker dark grass, about six foot by three, which gave him the notion that there might be a grave of some kind underneath.

The info in the museum hinted that this was where Hopkins had been swum, lynched and buried after the ordeal. Many historians had dismissed it as fancy but there was no denying it had a strange atmosphere.

I craned my neck over the red bricks of the wall into the muddy brown pool beneath. It was impossible to get a good look but it seemed important that I should.

A sign to my left indicated the presence of tearooms the other side of the pond so I ambled up the side road.

The rooms were situated in a mini farm. I paid the entrance fee, walked over a crunchy gravel path and, spying a small wooden gate towards the bottom of the slight incline, deduced that this must lead to the pond.

I was right.

The track led out alongside 'the lake'. The shady woodland area that circumvented the water was crowded with majestic weeping willows, gnarled and knotty oaks. Ducks gathered around the water's edge.

A darting, scampering thing scurried across my path. I was just quick enough to glimpse the sleek glossy back of a water vole racing for the haven of the nooks and crannies in the roots of the trees. Holly and brambles bunched about my sides, wafting their cuddy fragrance about me.

A small island nestled in the middle of the lake. Two nimble blackbirds skipped across to it. The place must be some kind of bird sanctuary. It was a stunning, pastoral scene. The tragedy of the pool, however, was there in my head, constantly sending ripples through my subconscious. I was becoming aware of a dark pricking feeling rising up about me.

As I progressed along the path, kicking up white feathers and leaf skeletons, the foliage became denser, shutting out the daylight. The trunks of trees, so appealing a few minutes ago, had now taken on an imprisoned look. The ivy that wound about them seemed as it was binding, almost strangling their life out. Decaying smudges of yellowing-brown dead leaves thickened. It dawned on me now that I was a good way away from the farm and was completely alone. If something was to happen, if I was to fall no one would know or find me for hours. I put the thought aside and continued on, the darkness about me growing, the tension in my belly reaching up to quicken my heart.

At last, through the gloom, I caught a glimpse of the Hopping Bridge. From this side of the river, it appeared faded and grey; the brickwork neglected and crumbling. The arch underneath had a grid fastened over it, which reminded me instantly of a prison cell. As I came out onto a curved clearing before it, the wind blew hard against me, blasting my hair up over my ears.

There was an uncanny darkness here that was not caused by the fading light and pendulous clouds. It was like the very trees and creepers that hung about the place had witnessed such horror it had affected their organic development: they grew twisted and bent, trailing their branches in the water listlessly. 'Look at what they do to each other,' I imagined them whispering.

I felt sure this was where they had swum the accused. When I looked up to the bridge it was almost as if I could see them there – the witches, freezing and shivering as the shrill wind roared over the river right through their threadbare clothes. The men from the parish would have bound them with ropes, trussing them up like lambs for slaughter. Perched on the bridge and then pushed off with a thud on the back, they would be sent into the ominous yawn of black water below.

And then I felt it.

Oh God no. The shock of the ice cold water on my bones forces my mouth open wide. Breath comes out and bubbles float past my eyes. Sticks and barbs catch at my hair, scratching, ripping at my face, arms, and legs. I plummet through the depths.

I am so afeared.

Almighty God have pity on thy devoted servant. Do not desert me I beseech thee.

No breath left and cannot see the surface. I put out my free arm to turn my body round. I am afeared.

I am afeared. Oh Lord have mercy.

Someone help me please. Desire to breathe in is powerful strong. Yet to give in will be to welcome death. My heart bangs wildly, too loud in my head, like a wild galloping mare. Am I bursting? Heaviness comes onto my chest and I can hold good no more. I must take in breath and so my mouth opens and sucks in, in, in wet mud, cold, oily. No, no. Cannot stop the thickness flooding up my throat. Choking, juddering, thrashing my head from side to side, twisting against my bonds. Such violent resistance cannot last and, as my face tears against the sharp root of an oak, the dart of pain finishes me. I am ready to surrender to this death.

Take me Lord Jesus Christ, only-begotten son of God, begotten of his Father before all worlds, God of God, Light of light . . . and I see it, coming forwards now, a circle of silver presenting to me – light, air, my salvation.

My Father is sending me back to the world.

I am to live . . . To the sky. I am there briefly, my face lifts up to take gulps of air, but I am under again. Twisting up once more I break through the surface and cough up dark mire. The air comes into me like a blow.

Arms gather me up and throw me to the bank. I am convulsed by a sickness and spew forth sticky blackness. Panting between spasms and the racks of my breath.

The heaviness comes on me. I open my eyes and the world spins.

The men walk over and cut the ropes. Another kicks my sides and shouts for me to stand. One announces my guilt and a satisfied shudder ripples through the crowd. I roll to my knees but have life in me no more. I can only breathe in, hard, short gasps. When his next kick does not rouse me, he hooks a hand under my knees and another round my back and bears me to the cart where the men are gathered. One calls me 'Satan's bride' asking if I can call down the Divil to save me now.

I cannot answer. I have nothing left to give. And HE sees this too. They throw me in the cart and my head splits on the *side. But I do not flinch, nor cry out. There is nothing left for fight.*

Old Mother Clarke is in there, facedown on the floor. They have not cut her ropes: her arm is still bound to her one good leg. A rheumy eye rolls and beholds me. 'They say we will hang,' she wheezes. 'We will not, dear sweeting. They will have mercy.' Her ancient mind has gone.

Before Master Hopkins walks to the front I catch his eyes upon me. A pink tongue like that of a cat wets his thin bottom lip. 'Take them to the Inn,' he says. Then slaps the mare. 'Be gone.'

Something snapped wood in the forest behind me, shocking me out of my thoughts.

It was dark. I was chilled to the bone. And breathless. Oh God. What was that? Another scene from Rebecca's tragedy. Why?

A crack in the wood behind me had me jumping. I swung round but couldn't see more than a few feet into the foliage.

The wind whistled through the leaves of the trees. 'Shh. Sedes,' it whispered shrilly to me.

Another footfall broke the twigs close behind. Ducks took off from the overhanging undergrowth and quacked in alarm, scattering in Vs, propelling away as quick as they possibly could.

If I had hackles they would undoubtedly have risen.

'Rebecca?'

Another crack right behind flooded adrenalin through my nervous system.

Was it my imagination, or could I hear a long phlegmy sigh from someone nearby? This wasn't Rebecca, I felt sure. This presence was vengeful, dark, fearsome.

'Hello?' I called out to the trees.

Something in them grunted.

I wasn't going to wait for a response. Instead I jumped sideways away from the bridge, my trembling legs carrying me back towards the path.

Though I couldn't see behind me I had the sense I was being followed. I doubled my speed, running headlong through the trees, and didn't stop until I had reached the gate and the sight of twenty-first-century day trippers. I raced to the toilets for sanctuary. There was something out there, I was sure. Something that didn't like me.

When I saw my reflection in the mirror I gasped. I must have brushed past some thorns or holly, for across my cheeks were little nicks. Like someone had scratched me and drawn blood.

Jesus – what was that all about? Why had Rebecca shown me that? I wiped myself down and put some lipstick on though my hands were still shaking.

What had I seen? Part of her life? Why that? What was she telling me?

I wasn't sure, but I knew I wasn't likely to reach an understanding here in the toilet. I splashed my face and tried to assume a less stricken expression then I crept out, keeping my head down, avoiding eye contact with the few tourists that were looking at the birds. I couldn't talk to anyone now. I pulled the hood up on my parka and thrust my hands into my pockets, walking quickly through the clearing.

As I came to the exit I found a cockerel in my path. It was standing by a white Fiesta staring at me. For a moment I was caught in its gaze. It crowed and fluffed out its feathers. The hens behind him backed away.

My stare challenged him.

The cockerel held my gaze for a second more, then surrendered. Ducking down, shivering, it hid itself under the car.

Shrugging off the experience, I crept away through the car park in the direction of the hotel.

I see now that the birds, dumb but instinctive, were aware of the shadow behind me.

Chapter Twenty-Seven

When I got back to the hotel I lay down on the bed and tried to work it out. If I wasn't going mad, then there was something happening to me for a reason. Rebecca had chosen to send that vision. But why? I knew how the witches were swum. And, yes, although I hadn't experienced it like that before (had anyone lived to tell that tale?) I knew it was a horror. There had to be something else there. I didn't know what though, so took out my notebook and tried to capture everything I'd 'seen'.

When I finished I had just enough time to freshen up before Amelia arrived for dinner. A hot shower was just what I needed to expel the present chill I'd dredged up.

I shed my clothes and selected an exfoliating charcoal shower gel from the complimentary toiletries to elevate my dismal mood. Poor Rebecca. It was inhumane the things they subjected them to.

The power shower hit me with a force I was grateful for. I could feel the hardness of the water as it pummelled into my flesh. It did indeed seem to be taking away the unhealthy residue that surrounded me; I could almost see it disappearing down the plughole into the sewers and away from me. Thank God.

I reached up to the shelf, forgetting to shield my eyes from the water and cursed as a stream of hot liquid sprayed directly into them. I shut them tightly and groped around for the shower gel. My fingers latched onto the fat tube of body wash and squeezed hard. The top burst off and I smoothed the jelly-like liquid over my shoulders, underarms and breasts. I could feel tiny brittle flecks of the charcoal. Keeping my eyes closed, I rubbed some of it onto the pores about my nose and down around my chin.

My mood rose as I spread the lotion over my buttocks and the tops of my thighs.

Clean now, I opened my eyes. Grabbing the tube for a final scrub I pinched out another good squirt onto my hand and bent down to soap my legs. As I did so, out of the corner of my eye, I saw darkness around the plughole. I did a double take. There were scores of tiny lice-like insects crawling over each other trying to escape the water. Where the hell had they come from?

I reached my arm up to the showerhead, intending to unhook it and concentrate the spray on the bugs, but as my arm crossed in front of my face I saw that it was covered with the creatures. Indeed, as I looked down, I saw my entire body was swarming – the insects were crawling all over me, on my face, in my hair, over my belly, groin.

On the shelf above the shower, I could see the tube of gel – the creatures were swarming out of the nozzle.

I screamed out loud, and jumped from the bath, trying to rub off the lice. Grabbing a towel I stumbled into the bedroom and phoned reception.

It was only a few steps away and alerted by the shrill tone of my voice, the receptionist said he'd be up straight away.

I flung on a bathrobe and a few seconds later a young man in a white shirt appeared in the doorway. Quickly I explained to him what had happened and watched him disappear into the bathroom.

Emerging minutes later he told me that he could find no lice. But there were black flecks in my gel that could perhaps be mistaken for ants.

Annoyed, I strode into the bathroom. He had tried to clear it up but there were still streaks of green liquid I had splashed on the wall whilst freaking out.

With tiny, tentative steps I went up to them. In their centre there were indeed black flecks, but they were chips of a coal-like substance.

This was not what I had seen, I told him, adamant. And offered up my towel for inspection – I had rubbed them off my body with this. As we both examined it I had to admit there was nothing there but the dull greenish stain of the scrub blended with the exfoliating material – small specks of charcoal.

'They must have come out of the water then,' I told him and insisted he look into the shower fittings.

The boy, evidently convinced he was dealing with a middle-aged hysteric, unscrewed the head and inspected it.

'Nothing,' he said calmly, though his cheeks had coloured on my behalf. 'This place does play tricks on people who stay here,' he said, in an attempt to make me feel better. 'This was the Witchfinder's room, they say. I ain't had no problem with it. But some do. When that idea gets into your head it can make you think things I suppose.'

It was on the tip of my tongue to counter his accusation, feeling there was a vague insult attached – the notion that

I might be weak minded, but I rued, this was a possibility. Instead I bit my lip and apologised.

When he left I ran the water in the sink and washed the remnants of the gel off myself. There were no lice, only the charcoal. What was it? Another sight? But why? I couldn't understand it and went into the bedroom to put on some clothes. But the air was charged.

Something was starting to stir. I could feel it.

Chapter Twenty-Eight

Amelia was early; when I went downstairs she was waiting in the reception area, her light-sensitive glasses adjusting to the bright interior of the pub. She had on a deep russet coat – teamed with her long bobbed hair, she resembled a kind of female Johnny Ramone.

We ordered a drink and sat up by the bar, making small talk.

I was doing a good job of holding it together, looking competent, conversing eloquently. Inside my head there was some dizziness where a section of brain cells were busy making sense of the 'lice shower' and the Hopping Bridge. I let them puzzle it out while the frontal lobes continued their work of interacting with my dinner guest. When Amelia asked me what I thought of Manningtree the two areas overlapped and I let slip a wry smile.

'It's very stimulating,' I told her.

She nodded. Dangly green earrings swayed to and fro. 'I imagine it must have really got you going.'

'It certainly has.'

'Very atmospheric, isn't it?'

'That is something it doesn't lack.'

'So glad you're enjoying it.' She took a sip of her wine. I had ordered brandy. Purely medicinal you understand: I was resolved to stick on one glass and have a white wine with dinner. No more than that as, once I'd finished with Amelia, I wanted to capture some of my experiences in words and then as Felix had suggested 'filter them into the chapter' that he wanted by Friday.

'I wouldn't say "enjoying" it was the right word,' I told her.

Amelia's eyes rolled. 'Hopkins getting to you?' And she let out a little piggy snort of a laugh. She removed her coat and straightened out a more formal-looking dress than the outfit she'd worn to Uncle Roger's party. I caught a waft of lavender and imagined a small scented wardrobe full of well-preserved clothes. I could picture her giving her lecture at the Women's Institute.

'I have to say,' she said as we sat by the bar, 'I did have a few nightmares when I was researching him. He really was a sod.'

I smiled at her profanity, guessing that was as far as someone as well-bred as Amelia would venture to go.

'Your table's ready,' the waiter interrupted and gestured to a corner seat. I squeezed past a large group of diners.

Amelia had her drink in one hand and her handbag in the other, and was holding them up over her head as we navigated to our table. She narrowly missed hitting a middle-aged man with her handbag. It turned out that she knew him and stopped to exchange a greeting.

We sat down and arranged ourselves. 'Is this your local?' I asked.

'No. I'm further out past Manningtree, but I recognise

most of the people in here. One tends to get to know faces in such a small town.'

I watched her settle her bag onto her lap. 'No, I'll start with this,' she said to herself, hands rummaging through into the depths of her carpetbag. She looked up brightly. 'I've got quite a lot to talk about but I think I'll keep the best for dessert and coffee.' She winked. 'We'll need the space.'

'Okay,' I said. 'I'm all ears.'

'Well,' she pulled a thin A5 notebook out and passed it over the table, 'I found this last week and thought you might want to have a look at it. On page five is the Red Lion. In Manningtree.' She pointed to a black and white photograph of a street decked out in a host of flags. On the left I could see the sign that denoted the old pub. The caption beneath it stated the photographer had captured the townspeople celebrating the coronation of George V. 'It's thought that Hopkins lived there in the cottage to its right. It was demolished. Now it's a beer garden.'

So there it was: the place where it all began. A pretty humble abode for such a pompous individual. 'So, Elizabeth Clarke would have lived next door to him presumably?'

Amelia poked her glasses onto the bridge of her nose. 'Remind me – which one was she?'

I laid the book on the table. 'The first woman he accused. He said he overheard her and her coven one Friday night.'

'Were they in the pub do you think?' Amelia asked shifting her gaze to the book. I handed it back so she could have another look.

'I don't know,' I said honestly. 'Not much gets written about the victims.'

Amelia tutted. 'Well said, my dear. No, it's usually the

victimisers that occupy our fascination and ergo the press. We can all too well imagine the horror of chancing upon a killer. Or having them chance upon you. I get it all the time walking home alone from the pub at night: the internal *Crimewatch* voiceover narrating my "last movements".' She let out a less forceful piggy snort. 'But the killers themselves. Well, that's what we don't understand. I think we're drawn to them like moths to a flame – wanting to know the "hows", "whens", "whats" and "wherefores", but also *not* wanting to know about it too. It's a double-edged sword, this kind of knowledge. I think the main thing we want to understand is "why" they do what they do. I know I do. In fact I have visited several sites of serial killings myself.'

She was searching my face for a reaction. I think I looked pretty open. 'Really?' I said.

Amelia nudged the book into the middle of the table, and picked up the menu. 'The same reason as everyone else – I'm compelled to stop and stare: the crimes are so grotesque.'

I was quietly impressed. Who would have thought beneath that fusty exterior such morbid fascination lurked? Although, I suppose, it also explained her interest in Hopkins. 'So where have you been?'

Amelia fanned herself with the menu. 'Saddleworth Moor. The site of the Wests' house in Gloucester.'

'God,' I said. 'That's pretty hardcore.'

'Yes,' she nodded. 'It is.'

'Isn't there a name for that sort of behaviour?'

She wasn't fazed. 'I've heard the term "ghouls" bandied around.'

'You don't seem like one. You seem perfectly nice.'

Amelia shrugged. 'I've given up apologising for it. It's something in me. Something that I'm pulled to. I don't know why. I just am.'

I knew that feeling. 'So what are your thoughts on Hopkins?'

'Like I said, the question I'm always trying to answer is "why?" Why did he do it? Why, in fact, do any of these monsters do what they do? I think as individuals we tend to seek out depths in the human psyche. We have this notion that there are areas that these killers have access to, which we don't. But I've concluded that we're looking at things the wrong way round. It's more that they haven't got the same capacity for feeling that most people have. It takes a fully formed adult a huge amount of mental strength to put out the suffering of family pets or injured roadside animals because we're empathetic. These murderers can't have empathy. They just can't. Or guilt, for that matter.'

'Some surely do experience guilt?' I asked, leaning in to hear her better. The tables around us were filling up.

'Psychopaths don't,' she said and took a sip of her drink. 'Nor shame nor remorse.'

That was interesting. 'So you think Hopkins was a psychopath?'

She blinked and paused. 'There are common traits certainly: he was narcissistic, called himself "The Witchfinder General". No one bestowed that term on him, he gave it to himself. That implies a self-aggrandising. And in that role he was able to "devalue" others around him to build up his sense of dominance and power and supremacy over his victims. You've done more in-depth research than me. Do you think that he was a good liar?'

I nodded. 'Pretty good. Though he slipped up a couple of times.'

'Mmm,' Amelia said and bit the inside of her cheek. 'But he wasn't anti-social as such. He didn't actually deviate from the socially acceptable norms of society at the time.'

'No,' I said. 'But he used them.'

Amelia caught the eye of the waiter. 'Quite so. A conundrum.'

The waiter appeared at the table before I could respond. 'Are you ready to order?' He flicked open his notepad.

'I'll start with some oysters,' she told him.

Insipid conversation returned to the table whilst we made our way through three courses. I was beginning to wonder if the picture of the Red Lion was all that Amelia had to show. Don't get me wrong – it *was* interesting, but I'd be miffed if it was the only thing I'd dashed over for. After all, Dan had just emerged and I would have liked to have spent more time with him.

However once she'd polished off a trio of desserts my dining partner took a large slug of wine, ordered two coffees and leant towards me.

'Right,' she said at last. 'I don't want us to run out of time and it's getting late. You've been patient.' She picked up the leftover cutlery. 'Can you put these to one side please? Okay.' Amelia picked up the napkin and carefully wiped any vestige of grease from her fingers. I watched her stretch her fleshy forearms over the table and sweep the crumbs from the tablecloth. 'Last Saturday, after your uncle's birthday party, you *really* got me thinking about Hopkins again. Hadn't thought about him for a while, at least a few years, until our conversation at the party, so when I got home I dug out the file which contained all my info for the lectures back home. And I came across an old biography of the man, which I'd bought many years ago. I'd forgotten all about it, to be honest with you, but after hearing about your book, I suppose my interest was rekindled. So I sat down and skimmed it, and before I knew it I was completely taken by it again. I ended up re-reading it from cover to cover. Now, a couple of things hit me. I don't know why I hadn't put them together before and perhaps you have, I don't know.'

The waiter returned with two cappuccinos. I was eager to hear what she had to say and coaxed her on. 'Go on.'

Amelia thanked the man then reached down for her handbag and put it to the side of the table. She sequestered a tissue from the sleeve of her dress and dabbed a spot of wine on the tablecloth. Then she plucked a thin ream of carefully folded papers from the dark of her bag, and laid them across the table.

'Right now,' she said to herself. 'Okay,' she unfolded the papers. I guessed from her careful manner of handling them that they were fragile and old although the last piece that she took out was a photocopied sheet which she placed on top of the pile. 'Now, Bishop Hutchinson you have probably heard of.' She tapped the topmost sheet and tilted her face to me.

I nodded a confirmation. I was familiar with Francis Hutchinson. Born in 1660, he had been so appalled by the witch trials he penned and published *An Historical Essay Concerning Witchcraft*. The work gathered together a whole bunch of pertinent historical detail and provided a good sceptical examination of events.

'Right.' Amelia was tracing her finger over the page. 'Have you read it?'

'Skimmed it,' I said, a little impatiently.

'Don't blame you,' she sniffed. 'I tried once. All those extra "e"s and convoluted sentences. I got quite confused by the old English "s"s. They're printed here like "f"s. Lots of comments about imps "sucking" that make you look twice. Dearie me! Couldn't get through it all but I did re-read parts of it that are relevant to what I want to show you. This bit in particular.' She turned the page round so that it faced me and pointed to a sentence halfway down. I tried to work out the curly script of the early eighteenth century. 'See.' She had highlighted a section in a fluorescent pink. The first paragraph, which was very long, referred to the alleged swimming of Hopkins. At the bottom was written, 'that clear'd the Country of him'. Amelia had put two fat pink exclamation marks in the margin beside it.

I processed it and looked up at her. I'd read this before. 'So? Some people thought that he'd been drowned. That's "clearing the country" of him, isn't it?'

'Yes,' she said hurriedly and fingered the document. 'But note the capital "C". A reference to England rather than Essex?'

I realised that her instruction to 'note' was literal so took out my notebook and wrote down: 'Bish Hutch – Cleared England of him.'

This had better not be the juice she had to spill. She was going over stuff that I already knew.

It wasn't. Amelia was on a roll.

'Now look at this part.' She removed another A4 sheet from the pile on the tabletop and handed it to me. 'Read it out.'

258

She had highlighted another section that referred to stories of some of the witches (Elizabeth Clarke, Anne West) and their imps. I read them out, then went on to this: 'They are of ill fame in these parts; and I have heard, that it was Time for Hopkins . . .' As I read the last part of text my voice wobbled and I fell silent, taking in the next sentence. Had I read this before? I wasn't sure. I glanced at Amelia. She was radiant, nodding her head vigorously.

'Go on. Finish the sentence.'

I read it out loud. '. . . and I have heard, that it was Time for Hopkins to leave the Country when he did, for the People grew very angry at his Discoveries.'

We held each other's gaze for a moment longer.

'What are you suggesting?' I said. 'That he fled abroad? I'm sure there's no truth in it. There's a record of his burial in the churchyard at Mistley. Here.'

'Yes, that's interesting though. Don't you think? People hated him that's true. Some thought he was in league with the Devil himself. Some said he was lynched by the mob. Others that he was tried as a witch.'

I was following her. 'Yes, but that's all rumour of course.'

'Well, witches weren't allowed to be buried in sacred ground were they? If Hopkins came back to Manningtree, which seems to be the accepted idea, then there were still relatives of those he killed living there. It wasn't a big place back then. Don't you think that they'd try to get him buried elsewhere?'

'I don't know. That's conjecture. The entry in the parish register is incontrovertible.'

Amelia's face gleamed. 'Do you know who wrote that?' She emphasised the 'who'.

I cocked my head to one side and regarded her. It was obvious. 'What do you mean? Who entered the burial in the register? The parish priest.'

'It was indeed. A certain Johannes Thomas Witham. Or, as he referred to himself – John Witham.'

I couldn't see where this was going but went with her train of thought. 'Okay?'

'Who was on his second wife – Mary. His first, Mistress Free-Gift Witham, died in December 1633.'

She was leading me now. 'And?'

Amelia's brow dropped. A 'humph' pushed out through her lips. Downwards curves appeared at the corners of her mouth. It was a similar expression of muted irritation that my mum used to wear. Immediately I regretted my impatience.

'Sorry, do go on.'

She angled her head towards the document. 'Well, here we have the second wife. Witham, of course, was her married name. Before that she had been Mary or Marie Hopkins.'

'Oh.' Now I was beginning to catch her drift. 'Oh! You reckon that was Matthew Hopkins' mother? Previously married to James Hopkins?'

Amelia shrugged. 'Could be. It never occurred to me as relevant before. But Sunday, when I was looking at it, it struck me as odd. Look.' She took another sheet from the pile and spread it in front of me. It was a sketchy family tree. 'See here: James Hopkins died around 1634, a year after Parson Witham's first wife. His second wife, Mary Witham, was certainly the mother of "John Hopkins" who was also buried in Mistley Churchyard in 1641. The entry reads *1641 Dec 24 John son of Mary Hopkins (wife of Mr Witham, parson)*.

Also, from what we know, the Hopkins named their sons after the disciples: Thomas, Matthew, James. Why not John?' The dates are all about the right time. Mary Hopkins and Parson Witham must have known of each other. Great Wenham, where the Hopkins family lived, is just across the water in Suffolk, only five miles away as the crow flies. Both Mary's and Witham's spouses die within a short time of each other. On one side of the Stour you have a bereaved Minister and on the other a bereaved Minister's wife. They've both got children. One batch without a mother, the other without a father. A quick practical marriage would have addressed their mutual material and practical needs. Ergo they unite the households and move to Manningtree or Mistley. Witham becomes stepfather to a teenage Matthew Hopkins. Who knows, the parson may have even played a part in supporting young Hopkins' prosecution of Devil-worshipping witches.'

'Yes,' I said, picturing a thin tight-lipped man smiling down at a similarly sickly-looking youth. 'It makes sense.'

Amelia rubbed her hands together. 'It explains why Matthew returned to Manningtree and Mistley. Why do that unless you've got a reason to come back to the place? It's the scene of his first prosecutions. The tide had turned. His actions here had caused several families to suffer. Why come back when you know you'll be greeted with hostility? Why not go back to Great Wenham instead? The village where you were born and a place where no witches were to be found. The Wenham population might be more, let's say, welcoming?'

Her hands were open, facing up to the ceiling.

I had my hand on my chin. 'Why not indeed?' I said slowly.

'You're suggesting he came back here because his mother was in Manningtree. Interesting.' I was processing the information at a pace now, absorbing each detail wholly and completely. 'But it's hardly front page news.' I spoke without thinking and saw Amelia bristle.

'No. You're not listening to what I'm saying. How old was Hopkins in 1647 – twenty-six, twenty-seven?'

'One of those. No one is sure.'

'He's young though, right? What if he didn't die of TB?'

'Stearne said he did.'

'Yes, well, Master Stearne had his own reasons for distancing himself from the unpopular Master Hopkins.'

'So what are you saying? That he didn't die? That Mary Hopkins persuaded her husband . . .'

'Matthew's stepfather . . .'

'. . . to enter the record of Matthew's death falsely? Why?'

'The war was ending. Men were returning home to find their villages decimated and their womenfolk gone, dead. They wanted someone to blame. Manningtree and Mistley had lost a fair few souls. Belligerence towards her son must have characterised many of the returning villagers and concerned Matthew's mother. The situation may have got very nasty indeed. Mr and Mrs Witham had other children to protect. It would compromise everyone if Matthew continued to live with them. He had no respectable future any more. One way out for them all would be to tell everyone the Witchfinder had died, then get him out of the country. Just as Bishop Hutchinson wrote.'

I thought about this for a moment. 'But where would he have gone?'

She unfolded a photocopy of a photograph – the original

will, proved in 1634, for James Hopkins, the vicar of Great Wenham.

I recognised it. 'Matthew Hopkins' father.'

'That's right.' She pointed at a paragraph.

It read 'My sonne Thomas My Mynede & Will is that my Executrix shall as soone as she can finde opportunitie send him over the seas to such our friends in Newe England as she shall thinke fitt.'

'New England,' I murmured. 'Of course.'

'Uh huh,' Amelia harrumphed with victory.

My hand was starting to tingle. It made sense.

'So,' continued Amelia. 'Then I thought – what if he did go out there and couldn't resist getting up to his old tricks?'

I was nodding along with her, willing her to speed up. She pulled another piece of paper out of her bag. 'Well, looky here. I looked up "early witch hunts in New England" and guess when the first one is?'

I shook my head.

'1648. One year after Hopkins disappears off the face of the earth. Well, the Essex earth anyway. How long would it have taken to cross the Atlantic back then? Maybe four, five months?'

'About that, I'd say.'

'And guess what else? In that very same essay that Bishop Hutchinson talks of Hopkins leaving the country, he also mentions Cotton Mather. Mather was actively involved in the Salem witch hunts. He writes about it in his *History of New England*. And,' she drew the last word out for drama, 'he also mentions two cases in Chelmsford from the year 1645.'

'The Hopkins witch hunts,' I said and exhaled all my breath.

Amelia nodded. 'Hopkins' stories were out there in the New World. Was he?'

She sat back, picked up her glass and drained it.

'Bloody hell, Amelia. You're a little gem. You really bloody are. This is excellent. Shit. I suppose you want to investigate this now?'

Amelia smiled. 'To be honest I've done all I want to on this horrid man. This is for you. Also I've got no time now. I'd rather read a couple of books with a bit of a Greek flavour. Soak up the atmosphere out there. Just let me know how you get on and give me a credit when you publish your piece – Amelia Whitting.'

That was extremely generous and I told her so. The implications that this could have for my book were fantastic. 'It could be a staggering revelation,' I piped up and rather excitedly clapped my hands together with almost childish glee. 'I'm so grateful . . .' I was about to thank her again but my attention was caught by the chap sitting alone on the small round table behind her. I hadn't noticed him previously. But now he was staring at me, his body very still, shoulders rigid with tension. Then suddenly he jumped to his feet, spilling his drink over the small table, and raced for the door. Surprised that he would leave the contents spreading over the surface onto the floor, I looked after him. The angle where I was sitting meant I only caught the profile of his face. But I recognised it. He was the man I had knocked into at the garage after Uncle Roger's party.

Amelia had turned to see the commotion. She looked back and raised her eyebrows. 'Some people!'

'He's not a local then?' I said as he disappeared out the front door.

'No. Not seen him before. Actually I was going to say earlier – I thought you'd pulled!' She snorted with laughter again. 'He couldn't take his eyes off you, the whole time we've been here. He was at the bar when we were, then took a table after us.'

Unusually I felt myself blush. At least I think it was a blush. A surge of heat spread through my body, leaving me slightly nauseous and queer.

'Are you all right, Sadie?' Amelia asked, eyeing me up and down.

I told her I was feeling a bit dodgy and got the bill.

As we wound down our chat Amelia suggested I should take a trip to Kew Gardens.

'The National Archives are in Kew. They keep passenger lists for ships bound to America.'

'Great,' I said, enormously indebted to my new friend. 'Ever thought of going into journalism?'

'Couldn't hack the hours,' she said with a grin.

I paid up and called a cab, then saw her out onto the pavement. Just before she got into the car, she darted back and gave me a hug. 'Good luck,' she said. 'I mean, with tonight. Don't let the ghosties or the bedbugs bite.'

I kissed her goodbye and watched the car disappear round the curve of the road. I can almost see myself standing there, waving into the distance. I wish she'd have told me to 'gird my loins' or something. It might have helped.

My night at the Thorn was just about to begin in earnest.

Chapter Twenty-Nine

Amelia had given me a lot to think about. I was buzzing with ideas and theories and was now able to understand her earlier exuberance. My scalp was itching with excitement. This stuff was good.

I returned to my room, pulled out my notebook and started to annotate the sheets that she had given me. I think I was at it for a good hour until my neck started aching, forcing me to change position. I flopped on the bed, stretched and rubbed my back, realising as I relaxed that I needed to pee, so nipped into the ensuite.

I splashed some water on my face, turned off the tap, inspected a fading blemish on my chin. Then I opened the connecting door and took a couple of steps back into the bedroom.

I don't know what I noticed first – the drop of temperature or the warping blackness on the far side of the bed. At first I skated over it and my feet automatically continued walking. But when the sight registered with my brain, my whole body stopped stone dead. Slowly, my eyes swivelled back to the other side of the bed.

A woman was standing there.

Shorter than me, her hair was tucked under a white linen cap. She was looking down at something in her hand.

Perhaps, I thought in a flash of reason, it's one of the staff.

I took in the dress – a grey, stiff, linen shift that reached to the floor, patterned with large grey flowers. Over this she wore an apron. There were smears of blood on it.

I hadn't exhaled since I'd caught sight of her, but in shock at the sight of bloodstains I released an untidy bustle of air, drawing in quickly once more when I realised it wasn't her dress that was patterned with flowers. It was the wallpaper on the far wall. I could see it through her body and dress. The woman was insubstantial, wavering.

I did absolutely nothing. My brain had completely closed down leaving me helpless, unable to move.

Wavy lines appeared like visible air streams between us. The bedside lamp flickered and dimmed. My breath came out like fog. The atmosphere was charged with an almost palpable sense of menace.

Then the spectre's head began to turn upwards, towards me, creaking like an old wooden post, the sound of bone grating on bone.

I did not want to see the thing's face. I knew that. Yet I was completely unable to tear my gaze away and could do little else but watch with a sense of passive inevitability as she turned towards me. The malignancy in the room doubled. I breathed in a gasp of textured, unnaturally thick air. Nausea came over me suddenly, as it had in the dungeons at the castle.

I could see the face now – the features wizened and extensively wrinkled, the eyes entirely grey – no iris, no pupil; just opaque holes like great cataracts bulging out of her face.

Then she spoke. 'This one'll not last long. Would you fancy to finish her?'

Her voice was coarse, the words pronounced without any trace of emotion.

I didn't speak. Nor move.

Her hand spasmed by her side and, like an old juddering puppet, she brought it up to offer me the thing that was in it. A bronze dagger, its handle and blade pointed down. Drops of red liquid slicked off the end and splashed onto the carpet beneath.

Unwilling to take in any more, I clamped my eyes shut.

'If you open your eyes, Sadie,' I told myself silently, 'you will see that there is nothing there. This is just a trick of the light. You're getting carried away, you silly cow.'

I breathed in through my nostrils and haltingly opened my eyes.

She was still there, waiting. There was a door behind her, half open.

'She's through here,' she gestured.

I looked around, thinking to flee. The room had changed. Gone were the bed, armchair, and dressing table. The wallpaper and carpet had been replaced by flaking white walls and exposed wooden beams.

'Come.' Her voice was impelling. When I looked back she had stepped inside.

Without any conscious thought of compliance my body followed her through the doorway and stepped down into a half-lit room. Two gentlemen sat in the corner beside a candle. One wore his hair short, cropped, the other had on a stiff blue coat. Their eyes flitted to me, momentarily registering the interruption. Neither surprise nor shock appeared across their faces. The one in blue acknowledged my presence with a slight nod and returned to study a spot on my left. I followed his gaze. Strapped onto a chair was a chaos of limbs and clothes. A pale languid form was wrapped within. The woman's breasts, exposed over the coarse ripped dress, dripped bloody tears from wounds around the nipples. Her legs and arms were bound to the chair by tight ropes. A darkness seeped outwards from her groin, staining the petticoat brushed aside to reveal the scarlet gores of her flesh. Her head lolled backwards and she moaned.

It was a sickening display of weakness, a degradation so bleak and wanton that I gasped in. As I did I felt a stiffening between my legs, a charge of excitement shooting through me.

The woman who had come into my room placed the dagger in my hand.

'She has confessed.' She closed my fingers over the cold wet hilt.

A surge of power exploded through me, a seduction of the flesh, sending warmth through my body and quickening my heart. I licked my lips and took a step towards the pathetic horror, so limp and without power, opened up so brazenly, presenting herself to me in utter abjection. I let out a loud uneven breath that betrayed my arousal.

The floorboard under my foot creaked. The woman's head lifted up. She gazed at me, her eyes glassy and unfocused. Grimy streaks striped her face. Beyond the terror that contorted her face I recognised the human creature within.

'Rebecca.'

The shock of recognition slapped me into the moment. My God, what was I doing? I looked down at the knife in my hand and, appalled, threw it to the floor.

'Master?' The woman from behind. Skirts brushed against my leg as she snaked closer, blocking my view of Rebecca.

The old girl's eye formed a lascivious half wink as she opened her scrawny hand and said, 'Master's pipe want suckling?' In her palm I saw something L-shaped, spattered with vivid red and brown drops – a small white pipe.

Again my groin stirred but this time my repulsion rose against it. 'Jesus Christ,' the words came out twisted into an accent that was not mine. The woman took my hand and closed my fingers over the pipe. 'The witchpricker. Go to her.'

With a tremendous effort I turned away and threw the foul thing on the floor. The head broke off and rolled to the corner. The men were now looking at me, faces wrinkled in surprise. The man in the blue coat stood up.

'This is evil. Can't you see it?' I implored him, my voice breaking as if unused for years.

He said nothing. His companion stooped down to the broken pipe and picked it up gingerly. 'Then we will bury it, Master, on sacred ground.' He looked at me with uncertainty.

I wrenched myself away from them and looked back at the terrible sight of the young girl splayed on the chair. The old girl stood by her, idly tugging a lock of Rebecca's hair.

Anger exploded out of me. 'For God's sake, woman, release her.'

The old lady's face turned up to me, neck still stooped, bony shoulders hunched, hands grabbing themselves together. 'Let her go?'

Doubt had sharpened her features, lending her a vulture-like aspect. 'But she has confessed . . .'

I had started shaking, fear overtaking horror. I had to get

out of here. Willing my body towards the door, I made for the bedroom. 'Cut the bonds.'

Another voice, one of the men. I didn't turn round to see who. 'To the castle?'

My strength was ebbing. I was focused only on escaping the vile scene. 'Yes, yes.'

As I unbolted the door I heard the old woman cackle, knowingly. 'At your pleasure, sir. I daresay she will have her uses.'

Then I was through, back in the bedroom, amongst the duck-egg blue wallpaper and Egyptian cotton sheets. I turned round and looked at the wall behind me. No woodwork. No frame. Nothing to indicate there was a doorway there at all or ever had been.

I staggered forwards onto the bed and threw myself face down. Minutes later I rushed to the bathroom and brought up my dinner.

Chapter Thirty

It was sick. Utterly sick.

I was sick.

What the hell was I doing? Dreams of the Witchfinder's sadistic perversion were not what I had ever expected to find here.

When I came out of the bathroom I sat back on the bed, trying to ground myself.

The ambience had returned to normal. The subtle background of twenty-first-century Essex replenished the room. My laptop buzzed on the floor, and beyond it I could hear the clinking of the kitchen staff clearing up after a regular Wednesday night, the low gurgle of a TV from a room down the hall.

The whole episode had taken no more than a matter of minutes but I felt like the life had been sucked out of me. Ill with shame, repulsed by the sexual quickening, I recalled the unholy sight of Rebecca tortured and bound. Why had she shown me that? It was so disturbing. So damn wrong.

Because that was what happened, said a voice inside my head. It was right. I knew it. That scene was the essence of the witch hunts – a hideous game that pitted the powerful against powerless. The motivation of the hunters was simply conquest.

And what of the pipe? Had he used it to suck their blood? Is that what that was all about? I could not bear to think about it. Especially as it had an uncanny resemblance to the thing that I had unearthed at St Boltoph's in Colchester. The pipe that Felix had blown. '*Qui est isti qui venit* – Who is this who is coming?'

It was too much to take in.

And I was simply unable to process it. Even as I thought about that pipe, my brain's survival techniques began to kick in and I found myself in a fog of confusion that began to obliterate parts of the memory. The more I tried to think about it, the less I was able to recall.

Perhaps it was shock. I don't know. But whatever it was, it left me in a state.

After another thirty minutes or so I realised that I was so shaken and wired I would never go to sleep naturally. So I did something I had only done once since Mum died. I plucked a sleeping pill from my toiletries bag. Within twenty minutes I'd started to relax.

That night as I slept the experiences whirled, weaved and reconfigured my internal compass. Though I didn't realise it then, by morning a new course had been mapped for my life.

Soon I would cast off.

Chapter Thirty-One

Mistley Churchyard, allegedly the site of Hopkins' burial, was way out on the heath. Despite the hideous visions of last night, or maybe because of them, I was determined to check it out. Part of me was tremulous at what the visit might prompt. Yet a greater part didn't care: I felt drenched with anger and motivated by a feeling that was close to revenge. Seriously, I honestly felt that if I came face to face with any of those vile creatures I encountered in the 'room' last night, I'd be ready to swing at them. The upside of experiencing those kind of emotions is that you're flooded by a kind of 'storm surge' of electrifying vigour. Since I had opened my eyes in the morning, I had been besieged by this edgy vigour.

I had expected to see or hear from Rebecca in Manningtree, but never anticipated anything like the experience I had gone through last night. I knew that the pardon might help her poor lost soul but it was clear now that there was something even darker going on. Something else I had to do to help her move on. I wondered if my conversation with Amelia had perhaps prompted the vision. Whatever, I was resolved to follow up her leads and hunt down the Witchfinder, despite the years. There was a lot to do.

I had packed an old map, which indicated St Mary's was halfway up the road. According to my sources, the portico, which dated back to the 1500s, was listed. There was a picture of it in the book Amelia lent me: a small tower with an arched door, surrounded by trees. However there was nothing about to indicate any building had existed here at all. And when I say nothing, I mean nothing. I wasn't even sure if the church ground had been annexed to the house next door. A discoloration of grass, in fuzzy rectangular shapes, was the only indication that it had ever been used to accept human remains.

I got out of the car and hopped over the low perimeter wall.

'Come on then,' I whispered through the grass to the spirit of Matthew Hopkins. 'I'm here. Do your best, you old bastard.'

Nothing stirred the air – no melancholy, malice nor any of the loose sense of tragedy one sometimes feels in graveyards. It was almost like the place had simply ceased to exist.

I got back into the car, unsure whether I was relieved or disappointed. I was becoming used to coasting a range of emotions on a day-to-day basis.

As I revved up the engine I realised that I was feeling completely neutral about this place. Whatever happened there, it had no connection to me.

If it had been Rebecca who had messaged me last week, and now I was pretty sure it had been, she'd been right about one thing: Hopkins wasn't buried here.

On my way home I detoured past a bookshop and picked up a map of New England. There was something I wanted to do. As I drove back I kept thinking about what Amelia had said about the first witch trial over there.

When I got home I googled 'Early Witch Trials in New England'.

The first case I came across was that of Margaret Jones, who Amelia had mentioned. A midwife accused of having a 'malignant touch', she was the first person executed for witchcraft in New England. On June 15th, 1648. That was interesting. What I read on the website next got me completely fired up. 'The case against her was built on evidence collected using the methods of the English Witchfinder General, Matthew Hopkins.'

I sat up and swallowed. Then I read on. The Governor, John Winthrop, attested that an imp was seen to go up to her 'in the clear light of day'.

Imps. Hopkins' favourite pastime – imp watching.

Of course his book, *The Discovery of Witches*, had been published the year before. A copy could have found itself on board a ship bound for Massachusetts. But what if Amelia's speculations were right? What if it wasn't only his pamphlet that had gone abroad? What if he boarded a vessel bound for Massachusetts to start a new life?

I scrolled down and found an entry by the American historian Clarence F. Jewett who listed twelve women executed prior to Salem. Margaret Jones of Charlestown, Boston in 1648. Followed by Mary Johnson at Hartford, 1650, who had a child while she was in prison awaiting execution.

Mrs Henry Lake of Dorchester circa 1650 demonstrated two themes I'd seen a lot in the confessions of the witches on both sides of the Atlantic – guilt and grief. A mother of five, after her youngest baby died, Alice Lake attested that the little thing had come to her in spirit form. Realising that this could be seen as a familiar of the Devil she immediately confessed that she had had sex before marriage, became pregnant and had tried to abort the foetus. The visitations by the ghost baby, she believed, were a punishment for her own crime against God. Poor woman – the trauma of her sin endlessly tormented her. When she was hanged her husband fled, leaving their four remaining children virtual orphans.

In 1651 there were three more – Mrs Kendall, of Cambridge; Goodwife Bassett at Fairfield in Connecticut and Mary Parsons, of Springfield. Mary had been fine until two of her three children died, whereupon she accused another local woman of witchcraft. This was not upheld and Mary declared that she had used witchcraft and as a result her five-month-old baby had perished. In a peculiar turn of events she was acquitted of witchcraft but convicted of murdering her child. As with Alice Lake's husband, Mr Hugh Parsons also buggered off to a nearby town where he remarried, leaving their only child to fend for himself.

Two years later, in Hartford again, Goodwife Knap was sent to the gallows. Three years later Ann Hibbins was hanged. Her husband had been one of the magistrates who sentenced Margaret Jones to swing. Hibbins, though, tried to sue some builders who had worked on her house, stating that they had overcharged her. She won but local people considered the lawsuit to be 'abrasive' and she was subjected to an ecclesiastic court. Refusing to apologise to the workers, she was excommunicated and cited as 'usurping' her husband's authority. Women didn't bite back then, and as soon as her husband died she was made an example of. Witchcraft proceedings commenced and she was hanged as a witch, as one contemporary stated, 'only for having more wit than her neighbours'. That same year, Goodman Greensmith was hanged at Hartford for, amongst other trumped-up accusations, 'not having the feare of God before thine eyes'.

Then finally, poor Ann Glover in 1688. And what a tragic tale that was. Born a Roman Catholic in Ireland, Cromwell's forces sold her into slavery and sometime in the 1650s sent her to Barbados. There, her husband was killed for refusing to renounce Catholicism. Somehow by 1680 Glover – known as 'Goody' – and her daughter wound up in Boston, working as servants for John Goodwin. However, after her daughter had an argument with the Goodwin children, some of them fell ill. The doctor visited, pronounced it to be witchcraft and, hey presto, Ann is up in court. The poor love couldn't speak English, only Gaelic. When asked to recite the Lord's Prayer to prove she is not a witch, Glover stumbles, unable as she is to speak the language. This is taken to be proof of her witch status so on November 16th of that year, Goody Glover is led out to the Boston gallows and hanged amid mocking shouts from the crowd.

I was pleased to see at the bottom of this account a little note detailing that in 1988 Boston City Council ruled that Goody's conviction was not 'just' and proclaimed November 16th to be *Goody Glover Day*.

One woman, one day. At least Boston had the decency to do that. If they had a day a year for each witch hanged in Essex . . . At least Flick was on the case now.

But why hadn't anyone tried it before? Perhaps because

women never really thought it was their place to do so. Probably because, until recently, they didn't have the means, influence, know-how or power to do so.

Witches were still seen as evil satanic things. I remembered how, a few years ago, Janet had attempted to hold a Halloween party for Lucy and Lettice and their friends. She'd not been able to secure a venue. None of the church halls would allow the booking, nor the local Conservative Club, nor their Constitutional Club. People still associated the witch with evil, malign spirits, wickedness and mischief. But we weren't living in the seventeenth century any more and people really needed to wake up to just what happened back then.

The time was right.

I took out the map I had bought on the way home and spread it across my living room floor. With a red pen I began circling the places where the cases had broken out.

You could tell Essex people had migrated to New England by the names they gave the places they lived in, attempting to replicate a better life in the New World; Danbury, Chelmsford, Colchester, Billerica.

And there was Wenham. Hopkins' birthplace. About five miles north of Salem. The same distance as Great Wenham was from Manningtree. The geographical similarity was spooky. Even the rivers that separated Great Wenham and Manningtree, and Wenham and Salem, would have been about the same width.

The hangings from 1647 to 1692, the year Salem erupted and the whole thing went nutsville, were dotted about the place.

But these were the tip of the iceberg, the end of the line

– the executions. I started pulling in other accusations and trials.

There were a huge amount. And other executions too – I'd missed John and Joan Carrington, a husband and wife both executed for witchcraft.

I picked up a blue pen and started drawing small crosses where there had been accusations.

After two hours my back hurt and my neck had a serious crick in it. I sat on my haunches and viewed the map. I hadn't finished marking them all down, yet I could see a pattern was emerging.

There were two outbreaks. One was more of a line situated in Connecticut, spreading down to New Haven. The crosses spread out to Fairfield in the west and then east as far as Old Lyme. The shape resembled an upside down 'Y'. At its centre was a huge cluster. That town's name was Hartford.

'Hartford, Hartford,' I repeated to myself. 'That sounds familiar.'

I went back to my laptop and googled it. The witch craze in those parts lasted from 1647 to 1662. As far as I could make out they had at least eighteen accusations, in Hartford. And hangings too.

But there was something else about that name. I took my folder of research from my filing cabinet and flicked through it keeping my eyes peeled for the place name. Then I found it – when Stearne had been in Huntingdonshire he had pulled in the witches to be examined by magistrates in Hartford, UK.

Stearne had gone inland, while Hopkins had taken the coastal route.

I flicked over to the east coast. The first Hopkins-type witch hunt had occurred in Boston. Where the ships from England docked. There was a dense fan of blue crosses there.

Something dropped from the ceiling onto the map. I flinched, remembering the liquid that had landed on my face only two nights ago. But I had no need to be afraid, it was only another moth. It skittered across the paper lightly, settled for a moment on Boston, then spread its wings and took off to my left. I watched it zigzag through the air and land on the mirror. It turned itself around, launched into the air and landed on the map of the south-east that I had pinned on the chimneybreast.

Strange. That was just where the last one had gone. Was there something attracting it?

I was about to go to it and see if there was anything behind the map that might be luring the little critters, but I stopped. From my perspective on the floor I could see the pattern of crosses I'd mapped out weeks ago – all the known cases of Hopkins and Stearne spreading out in little arc shapes.

I looked back down at New England and began to smile. On my American map, dotted in red, was the same shape – a bloody horseshoe.

Bastard.

There was no way that Stearne accompanied Hopkins out there. He had died in 1671 and was buried in Lawshall near Bury St Edmunds.

But what if Hopkins had met someone on the journey over? Someone who shared his zeal.

I regarded the area around Boston. Could it possibly be the same MO?

I knew it was late but I needed to know now. Right now. And there was one person who might be able to tell me. I dialled his number.

'Hi Joe.' I registered the sound of music in the background. 'What are you up to? You off duty?'

'Sadie! I've been meaning to call but we've all been bombarded with overtime. Just finished up at the snooker hall.'

I bit my tongue and hedged my bets. 'Listen – I've got something I need to bounce off you. Would you mind coming over?'

He broke off and shushed some unseen gathering. I could imagine him there, jovial, flapping down their attention but loving the interest it provoked. 'Okay. You all right? Is it your computer?'

'No, that's all fine now. Touch wood. It's more of a police thing.'

'Sounds interesting.'

'Do you want me to pick you up?'

'No, it's fine. I'll hook a lift with Dave. He lives up your way. I'll be over in about an hour.'

'Great,' I said. 'Have you eaten?'

'No actually, I haven't.'

'I'll put some pasta on.' It was the least I could do.

Before he got there I went and got the moth. It crawled into my hand without any coaxing. Its peppery wings were lighter than the last and reminded me of what I'd read on the totem website – something about the insect being a guide. It was certainly a clever little thing, nudging me towards a kind of enlightenment. I thanked him and took him outside onto the balcony. When I opened my hand it took off lopsidedly, flew down to the front garden then past the hedge and to the sea. As I followed its flight path my eyes clapped onto the sleek glossy form of a black car parked in the station's layby. When I passed the window two minutes later it had gone. I didn't think too much of it, focusing more on getting the place presentable for a guest, and whizzed around the house, removing dirty plates from the living room floor, vacuuming the carpet.

As I emptied a packet of tortellini into a saucepan, I wondered if Joe might construe this as a come-on: 'Come over to my place. I want to show you my etchings.' I hoped I hadn't given that impression. Not that he wasn't adorable in his own way. He was, and there was undeniably chemistry there, but I had things to do and was now compelled by an innate energy that had been amplified by the strangeness reaching for me. At that moment in time I could no more consider a romantic liaison with Joe than have downed tools and, literally, given up the ghost.

Not that those thoughts were clear, you understand. A whirling feverishness had taken possession of my mind, making it difficult for me to efficiently process everything that was going on. I was constantly reeling from my last experience whilst coming to terms with the one before. All I knew was that I was being led forwards by forces of which I was only half aware. After last night, the combination of revelations had left me in no doubt that in some small way, perhaps because I was writing the book, I should avenge Rebecca West.

* * *

Joe had been drinking and obviously got the taste for it as he turned up with a very dimpled grin and a bottle of wine. I asked him if he wanted to eat straight away but he didn't. Instead he poured two large glasses and took them into the living room beckoning me to follow with a flirtatious hand gesture. I smiled at it, and followed. At least half of me wanted to accept the invitation. As I watched his back disappear into the shadows of the hallway, I was visited with a vision of lying in bed, my head on his chest, free of care. Although incredibly seductive and attractive right now, I could see that it was a surrendering sort of thought and had to beat it away. It was almost like if I gave in to Joe, it might be so lovely that I feared I would lose my drive and ambition in him. I couldn't do that now. Not yet. So I cautioned myself and tried to keep focused on the matter in hand.

After a couple of minutes of small talk we ended up sitting close together, cross-legged round the New England map.

'So, what you after?' He nudged me in the ribs, gave me a wink, grinned and wiped his lips with the back of his hand. 'I hope it's not sensitive, in which case no can do. We all had media training a few weeks ago. Now I'm the model of discretion.'

'Don't worry,' I said and laughed at the way it came out. Despite his inebriation he was still really cute. 'You won't be compromised. This stuff's four hundred years old.'

'My God,' he said in mock horror. 'Nearly as old as you!' Then he reached out and rubbed my shoulder.

I didn't move away, just said, 'Cheeky.'

His arm went slack and reached for his wine. 'You always did worry about that far too much.'

I leant back on my knuckles. 'What?'

He took a large sip. 'The age difference. It's only four years.'

I drank in his face, flushed and glowing, and nodded. Take away those dimples and we'd look roughly the same age. 'Seemed a lot back then.'

'But not any more?'

'No,' I told him truthfully. 'Not any more.'

He replaced his drink and moved his hand to my knee. 'Good,' he said and shot me a look that had my stomach flipping. God, those eyes were as dark as chocolate. How had I never notice that before? But I brought myself upright – must focus – and shook myself to attention.

I pointed to the map of Essex, pinned up over the fireplace. 'I need your expertise, PC Joe.'

He tugged his gaze away from my face and looked at the map.

It took me about five minutes to explain as concisely as possible what the crosses and circles meant. When I finished he stood up and took his glass over to the map and leant against the wall, taking a couple of minutes to process everything I had said.

'Okay?' He looked up expectantly. 'And your query is?'

I turned the New England map around to face him.

'Right, well this is New England: Massachusetts and Connecticut.' Then I took him through the red marks, drawing my finger inland down from Hartford to New Haven and Old Lyme on the Long Island Sound, an estuary of the Atlantic Ocean.

'Now look at the coastal region here.' I read out the names and recounted some of the accusations and trials, not forgetting to mention Margaret Jones, the first victim, whose trial took place slap bang in the middle of Boston, where immigrants from England were likely to have first disembarked.

He came back to my map and squatted over it. Despite the booze I could see Joe's interest was piqued. He listened to me going over the chronology of the trials, citing some of the methodologies used, shaking his head and tutting. I was so used to the casual brutality evoked in these trials I forgot about how Joe might react. I supposed that as a policeman he was hardened to the grotesqueries that life and criminality threw his way. But I could see from the paling of his face that he was horrified by it all.

There was certainly something pathetic about the nature of the witches' crimes. And in most cases their status was already at the bottom of the social scale in the place kept for the mad, debased, disabled, starving. It made the aggression of the accusers all the more despicable. I saw Joe physically wince when I told him about Alice Lake and her phantom baby.

Though my position had changed a bit. I still sympathised and wanted justice for them but I was also on the hunt for the bullies. I gave him some time to recover before I asked him, 'In your view, can you see similarities? Could this American map chart the same MO?'

For three long minutes Joe didn't speak. Then he stood back and rubbed his hand across his short crop. 'I'm not a profiler, Sadie. With something like this I'd suggest you take it to Chelmsford and try and get someone there to look at it.'

It wasn't the answer I wanted to hear. It wasn't an answer at all really.

I had to push him. 'Come on, Joe. I told you – it's off the record. I'm not going to quote you on this. Just give me a clue. What do you think?'

He stroked his chin and picked up the New England map, holding it up next to the Essex map. After another long pause he straightened up. 'I'd say it was worth investigating.'

I breathed in deeply. 'Really?'

He nodded. 'You'd need to go into more detail with victims and areas if you wanted a profiler to give you a full report, but I'd say something is going on here.'

He cast the map down. It swung through the air, landing a foot from me.

I gathered it up and thanked him very genuinely for his time. 'Are you ready for pasta?'

He nodded but he looked weary. His eyes had lost their benevolent gleam.

Over dinner Joe was more reserved. I guess this wasn't the sort of evening he'd anticipated. I sat him with his back to the window in the best chair and tried to chat about his work. He didn't bite. In the end he said, 'This is dark, Sadie.'

I scooped a spoonful of sauce and parmesan into my mouth. 'Tell me about it.'

Joe put his elbows on the table. 'Has it occurred to you that all this research might have affected you? Mentally?'

'Absolutely,' I told him with a little laugh. I meant it to sound like a joke though it was true.

He sighed. 'No. I was talking about what happened on your computer. When Lesley and I were last here you said you had someone saying they were frightened of the Devil.'

I put my spoon down and looked him straight in the face. 'I did.' I kept my gaze steady.

His eyebrows dropped. 'Lesley was concerned. There was no evidence of any "chat" on your internet history.'

'I know,' I said. 'That's because . . .' my words died before they reached my tongue. I was going to say it was because it was Rebecca, but I knew how that would sound.

Joe didn't let it go. 'Because?'

He seemed a whole lot more sober now. I almost regretted feeding him.

I shrugged. 'Nothing.'

'Go on.'

I shook my head. 'You wouldn't understand.'

'Try me.'

'No,' I said and forced a smile. 'How's your pasta?'

He ignored the comment and placed his hands on the table. 'What happened to your mirror?'

Ah. I had forgotten about that. After I'd tried to call Rebecca up and failed, I had covered it over with a blanket. I didn't want any surprises, I think. Seemed perfectly sensible at the time, but I could see, now, that to an outsider, it probably looked freaky.

'I had an accident,' I said simply.

Joe wasn't having it. He leant forwards. 'What's going on with you, Sadie?'

His face was so full of concern it touched me. I was a tough cookie, but to look at him just then, sitting across the table, wanting to find out what was happening with me, for no other reason than that he *cared* about me – well, it made me crack a little. And I had so much to bear on my own. Maybe if I just told him a bit, maybe he could help me.

288

'I think I'm being haunted,' I said, my voice breaking slightly. 'I saw someone in the mirror. In fact, I know who she is now.' And I told him how I knew.

I could hear how it sounded as it came out, so I peppered my narrative with qualifiers. I even told him what Felix had said about incorporating some of these experiences into the book.

When I finished Joe had his arms crossed and a stern look about him.

Very gently, he asked, 'Is there any history of mental illness in your family, Sadie?'

I laughed out very loudly. Too loudly. 'Not the reaction I was hoping for,' I said.

He repeated his question. 'Don't be evasive, I'm trying to help.'

'Well, you're not. It's nothing to do with my mental state.'

'It's not?'

'No.'

'But your mother suffered from depression and psychosis.'

It was like a slap round the face. I pushed back from the table and expelled a long noisy breath, breathing in again quickly to try and stifle my building anger. It wasn't easy. There was so much of it in me, coiling and uncoiling like a serpent in my stomach. 'How do you know that? Have you been looking me up in your databanks?'

He held my gaze. There was peace in his eyes and a kind of rigorous strength. 'You told me,' he said very calmly. 'The first time we met, sitting on the beach in Westcliff.'

I ran my hand over my lips. Of course. I had forgotten about that. 'Sorry. Listen, I'm not experiencing psychosis. This is something different.'

'It doesn't sound like it. I'd like you to promise me you'll see a doctor.' He could have been talking to a twelve-year-old.

'No, I won't,' I half shouted. The serpent was uncoiling. I pushed it back down and commuted my anger into a sulk, quite forgetting that the same thought had occurred to me only two days since. I moderated my tone. 'If it sounds like madness then why has my editor asked me to put some of my experiences in the book, eh?'

'It seems bizarre,' he said softly. 'I really don't have a clue why he'd want you to.'

'Exactly,' I said with a nasty hiss. It was coiling upwards through me. 'You don't *have a clue*. You're a policeman not a creative.'

He didn't even smart. 'In my job I have seen how people can,' he paused to find the right words, 'how they can spiral downwards quickly. Especially after a shock or a bereavement. One minute they're on a minor with a "drunk and disorderly", the next you're locking them up because they've turned to junk or they're homeless. It doesn't take much. You could organise some support. Talk this through with a counsellor.'

But I wasn't listening. I wanted him to believe me, regardless of the incredible nature of my tale. I thought he liked me.

'Nor are you a bloody doctor or social worker.' The fury was rising up, taking control. Was he suggesting I was losing my mind? Comparing me to a junkie? I stood up. 'I'd like you to leave now please.'

Joe threw up his hands in mock surrender. 'Okay, okay. I'll go. I'm only saying this because I care about you. You know that. This research that you've sunk yourself into – it's morbid. And unhealthy. I think it's affecting you.'

290

I couldn't say a word. If one came out it would be followed quickly by lots more of varying degrees of nastiness. I marched to the door and held it open for him, pursing my lips as he went through.

He stopped outside and pulled out a card. 'Got a pen?'

'Not on me.'

He pulled a pencil out of his back pocket and leant against the wall, scribbling something on the back of the card. 'Look, take this number. A mate of mine is a therapist. Think about giving her a call.'

I said nothing but took the card with one hand and with the other held on to the door handle, knuckles turning white.

This time Joe trundled slowly down the stairs, zero spring in his step. I waited until I heard the sound of the outer door close then I went back into the living room and sat on the floor.

I knew he'd only said what others would if I told them the same tale. But, I thought as the serpent settled, I wasn't mad. I was right. In fact I was righteous.

However, his words had warned me: whatever path lay ahead, I'd be walking it alone. Excepting spirits and their bleak and lonely moans.

Chapter Thirty-Two

The next day I sat down to my book. Despite my conviction the previous evening, some of Joe's words *had* impacted on me. Particularly what he said about putting the mad stuff into my writing. It was preying on my mind as I tidied up my first chapter on Matthew Hopkins. I entered some of the details I 'saw' at the Hopping Bridge. It certainly brought it to life, but it could be construed as fantasy and undermine some of the solid evidence I had amassed to support some of my claims.

In the end, about eleven o'clock, I decided to run the whole thing past Felix himself and picked up my phone.

I went through to a voice I recognised to be Delphine, who told me that she'd see if Felix was free. After a short wait, he came on the line. He was breathless, like he'd been running, and told me he had only a few minutes to spare.

'Important meeting?' I asked.

He laughed out something that sounded like a hybrid of a chortle and snort. 'Have you not seen the news today?'

I told him I hadn't.

'We've had some damn leak about Robert.'

I assumed he meant Cutt.

'The press are up in arms about a book he's halted. There's a reference to a Russian deal he brokered a couple of years back. The writer's hinting at large scale involvement with the mafia. Quite ridiculous.'

I expressed surprise that this was a Portillion book.

'Oh God, no. It's a minor press we acquired last week. Obviously as soon as we found out about the content we then had to pull the book. Now there's speculation that Robert bought the outfit purely to stop the publication.'

Ha ha, I thought. 'Oh dear,' I said.

'Yeah,' he said. 'So I've got to go into a damage limitation meeting in a sec.'

'Okay, I won't hold you up,' I said, and asked him how much of my 'experiences' he wanted me to put in. And would that affect the credibility of the book?

He didn't seem to think so. So I told him, rather guardedly, about the Hopping Bridge section.

'Go for it,' was his conclusion. 'Spices up something that's otherwise quite dry.'

I took his advice and after hanging up wrote the scene into the chapter. Then I attached the document to Felix's email.

'Please like it,' I muttered and hit 'Send'.

Chapter Thirty-Three

It was my second day at the National Archives.

Though interesting, the first had not been at all rewarding. The phone call with Felix and then embellishments to the chapter had set me back a couple of hours, and when I finally reached Kew Gardens it was getting on for half past three. I knew I was pushing it.

The girl on the reception desk was pleasant and told me that I'd need to register on the second floor. This took longer than I'd predicted as I had to trawl through an instructive tutorial regarding the handling of ancient documents. That completed, I had a mug shot taken, then popped down the stairs to the first floor where I went straight in and plonked myself on the enquiries desk.

A young guy in a purple t-shirt and jeans was very obliging when told him I needed to see passenger lists from between 1646 to 1650.

He was unsure at first as to whether passenger lists were held there but when I mentioned the fact I'd seen the document registration online, he searched the catalogue. An entry came up confirming a couple of fragments of passenger lists, but only from 1634 to 1677. That seemed to cover what I wanted so I asked him how I went about ordering up the documents.

'Mmm.' He glanced at his watch, peeping out between reams of raggedy festival bands. 'You've missed the last call, I'm afraid. You have to get requests in before four. It'll have to be tomorrow now. Sorry.'

I sat back into my chair. 'Shit. I've come up from Essex.'

'Sorry,' he repeated and shrugged.

Then a thought crossed my mind. 'Do you know why there are only fragments? Where were they kept back then?'

'Hmm,' he said. 'Now you're talking. You'd have to delve into the history of the public records office itself to find that out.' He slipped a piece of paper under his hand and wrote down a reference. 'If you take this upstairs they'll sort you out with the volumes.'

'Thanks,' I said, rather grudgingly.

He picked up on my tone. 'You have to remember that not everything survives. Things get lost, water damaged, burnt or just disintegrate with age. Look, here's the reference number for your enquiry. Just log on to the computers tomorrow and order it. It'll probably take forty minutes to come up.'

I thanked him and went upstairs.

An older guy in a smart white shirt with strange facial hair (full iron-grey moustache), a burgundy tie and tank top, dealt with me. He appeared a little bewildered when I gave him the paper. His gaze skimmed over my jeans and leather jacket. I didn't know what people with an interest in the records office looked like but I obviously didn't cut the mustard. Nonetheless he rubbed the whiskers on his chin and sorted me out with two large red volumes.

I'd always thought the bureaucracy in our country was a little extreme but reading through these books confirmed my prejudice. The departments that our governments had instituted to deal with the day-to-day machinations of the country were mind-boggling. I found myself almost laughing at the mention of the Kafkaesque 'Ministry of Power', tutted at the 'Statistical Department of Departmental Statistics', frowned at the 'Standards Department' and shuddered over the 'Lunacy Commissioners and Board of Control'.

The path that I trod through the narrative was uneasy and chaotic and I was just about to abandon all hope when someone touched me on the shoulder. It was the moustache man from the desk.

'I'm sorry,' he said. 'We'll be closing shortly. I'll have to get those volumes off you.'

I looked round the reading room. There were only another two researchers left.

'That's okay,' I told him and handed them over. 'I think I've given up on that lead anyway.'

'Oh?' he said. 'Not helpful?'

'Not really,' I replied. 'I was looking for some passenger lists that might not exist. Was just trying to find where they might have been kept, that's all.' I yawned.

'Oh right,' he nodded and smoothed down his moustache. 'Family tree is it?'

'No, actually,' I said and grabbed my bag to get up. 'I'm interested in Matthew Hopkins, the Witchfinder General.'

'Oh yes?' he said. 'I remember the film. Hammer wasn't it? Quite disturbed me at the time. But that was back in the sixties. I don't watch that sort of thing any more. I thought he died in Essex?'

'Yep,' I said, letting a small sigh escape my lips. 'That's what they say.'

'But you think differently?' He hugged the books to his chest and made no move to return to his desk.

'Possibly,' I said getting up from the chair. 'It's alleged that he died in the summer of 1647. A few months later a spate of similar killings broke out in New England. Same MO. I mean, they look like the witches were detected through similar methodologies.'

'And you think they might have been carried out by him?' he said, moving his body towards the exit. I took the cue and fell into step beside him.

'I'm following a hunch, I guess.'

'My wife's a bit like you. Loves a mystery. Can't get her off the detective stories.'

'Well, I'm not sure I'll detect anything. But I'm going to come back tomorrow to have a look at the fragments of the passenger lists. That's all they are, though – fragments. He might not even be registered on them. And anyway, I don't think he would have travelled under his own name. But there may be something similar.'

'Well, good luck. Be sure to tell me if you turn anything up. My wife would like to hear about it.'

I promised him I would.

As it transpired, when the documents came up the following day, I was to be disappointed.

Although I'd arrived much earlier, I still had to wait an hour and a quarter before I was able to collect my parcel and get it out on the reading desk. I was full of anticipation as I unwrapped the brown paper packaging that the file came in.

Opposite me a man in his sixties was going over a long scroll with a magnifying glass. He had white gloves on to handle the paper and kept cooing as he worked his way down.

I think I'd been expecting some kind of scroll too or a large book, but when I pulled back the wooden boards that secured the ancient papers what I saw was something like a pocket book. Not more than five inches long and about three inches wide, the number of sheets barely made double figures. I turned them over carefully with the tip of my finger. According to the tutorial I'd had to read through the day before, one should avoid as much contact as possible with the delicate paper. And this was *fragile*. The slanted brown ink was quite difficult to read but the thrill of such an ancient document under my fingertips forced me on. Eventually I made out most of the passengers' names from the list of 1634.

That ship had sailed from Devon to New England and carried an assortment of passengers with trades – 'seafaring' men, 'saylemakers'; even a buttonhole maker – out to the New World to start afresh. The next list dated from 1645. Only a couple of pages had made it through to the twenty-first century.

Then the entries jumped to 1677. I knew these were 'fragments' but the gaps were huge.

I sat for a moment going back through the pages, then wrapped the document up. There was no point wasting any more time.

I took it back to the counter and was on my way out when the security guard at the door stopped me.

'I think Gerald wants a word with you,' he said and pointed through the glass wall the desk. The man with the moustache was waving a piece of paper in his hand.

I scooted round to his desk.

'Oh good,' he said, whiskers slightly less erect than yesterday and framing a wide beam. 'I'm glad I've caught you,' he said and thrust the paper at me. 'I happened to mention your research to my wife yesterday. She said she thought it rang a bell and this morning she came down and gave me this. I don't know how authentic it is but I thought you might be interested.'

'Oh right,' I said, touched but simultaneously unimpressed as I took what looked like a cutting from a glossy magazine.

'Sorry, there's a bit missing. Hilda thought it might have been a coupon. Very thrifty, my wife.'

I thanked him and took it over to a nearby desk. The top line had been cut away so it read 'ps, Ashbolten, are said to be three of the diaries of Nathaniel Braybrook, seventeenth century writer. Braybrook wrote passages detailing his daily life and documented some of the extraordinary events and violence of the seventeenth century, including several of the battles of the Civil War and the deeds of the notorious Matthew Hopkins, the Witchfinder General.'

The remainder of the paragraph went on to outline the usual spiel about Hopkins and the witch trials and ended with a sentence that suggested the books were soon to be analysed by the University of Hampshire.

Could be a lead, I supposed. But there was nothing new there. I went back over to the desk and thanked Gerald.

'Any good?'

'Well, I haven't come across his name before. It's worth pursuing as the passenger lists are a dead end. Please thank your wife, Hilda. Do you mind if I keep it?'

'Of course.'

'You don't happen to know when it was published, do you?' There hadn't been a date on the scrap of paper.

He shook his head. 'No, asked the same thing myself. She can't be sure but she thinks it's about ten years old. She's quite good with dates. Thought it was around the birth of our first grandson.' He clucked his teeth fondly at the thought of his wife. 'She's a terrible hoarder.'

'Okay,' I said. 'That's a start. And,' I added as an afterthought, 'where's Ashbolten? I've never heard of it.'

Gerald waved his finger at me. 'That I do know, funnily enough. Had a friend who lived there for a few years. It's quite a small village. Pretty. Used to be bigger, but there aren't many jobs and the young people tend to leave for London. It's not far from here in fact. About twenty miles south-west.'

'I'll have to look into it,' I said.

'Let us know how you get on,' he grinned.

'Will do.'

Minutes later I was about to board the underground when my phone buzzed. It was Felix wanting to congratulate me on my chapter.

'Look, I've only read the first few pages but I wanted to let you know what an interesting read I found it to be,' he said. 'I'm looking forward to seeing where you take it.'

'Wow,' I said. 'I'm surprised you've had the time to have a look with everything going on. I'm flattered.'

'It's great,' he said. 'Very hard hitting. Brings out the injustice of it all. But I think you could do more with your personal reaction. That works particularly well.'

'Really? I thought I was pushing it a bit?'

'No, not at all. There's nothing else like it out there. It would make it unique – a history of the time, tinged with a contemporary journey through the nightmare.'

'Okay, cool,' I said. 'When you read on, you'll find it gets more personal.'

'Great,' he said. 'Listen, I don't know what you're doing next week, but there's a possibility that I might be able to organise an interview with a Hopkins expert.'

'Really?' I was surprised. 'Who's that?'

'Won't say yet. Don't want to get your hopes up, only to dash them. Are you free Wednesday?'

'Yes, at the moment. Where are they? Manningtree?'

'Oh, yes. I think so. I'll let you know.' A female voice called to him from nearby. A lower one, gruff, male, hushed her. 'Look. I've gotta go but I'll give you a call, okay? Keep it free.' He paused then said quietly, 'I'll accompany you, of course. It would be lovely to see you again.'

I agreed and hung up, then gulped. He was looking forward to seeing me. That was a definite hint. I imagined him reclining in his chair, frowning as he read through my manuscript. Those little lines darting across his forehead as my words, my values, chimed with him. Stop it, I thought. Concentrate on the book.

I was really delighted that he liked the chapter. I had stuck my neck out a bit, and Joe's words were still swimming in my head; however I'd done the right thing and Felix's reaction vindicated me. Here was someone who could appreciate the vivid qualities that my research and 'connection' were bringing to the writing.

As twilight descended, I dived into the rush hour underground, and let myself relish all the affirmations my editor had delivered.

By the time I connected onto the overland train to Essex it was dark.

Unfortunately we were at the tail end of the rush hour commute, which meant standing room only until Basildon. Not that I minded, particularly. I was still buzzing. In fact, I found, as we left the station, I was literally trembling. Strangely. And not synchronously with the movement of the train.

Nor with my own bodily functioning.

This peculiar sensation was like a strange super-vibration that thrummed through my body. It must have started slowly and increased little by little without my paying attention to it. Or maybe my subconscious had written it off as an incidental movement, an eccentricity of that particular train. It was only as I sat down in a newly vacated seat that I realised the buzz continued. I scanned the faces of my fellow travellers to see if any appeared to have picked up on it but they were all calm, if not rather bored.

Perhaps, I wondered, there was something on the rails – a coating or a film – that routinely produced this phenomenon? Maybe it happened all the time. Though, I reflected, I had never been aware of it before.

But it wasn't going away. Instead, it was strengthening

and now producing a little worried rush of adrenalin. 'Don't be silly,' I thought sensibly. 'It'll go soon and you'll forget it ever happened.'

I breathed in deeply, attempting to restore order to my senses. But as I did so, I detected a change in the air. A kind of invisible coagulating closeness was filling the carriage. For a moment, as I exhaled, it lurked in the background. Then as I breathed in again, it expanded and congealed the air, filling up my lungs, almost overpowering me, rendering the atmosphere intolerable, forcing me to cough loudly.

My neighbour shifted uncomfortably as I spluttered. Reaching down into her handbag she handed me a tissue. I inhaled through it. Despite the papery barrier the thickness filled me up once more sending paroxysms of nausea through my body. My throat burned like I was breathing in chilli smoke. Starting to panic, as we came in to Pitsea station, I lurched to my feet, clutching at my neck and forced myself through the bodies clustered at the door, off the train onto the platform.

Outside the air was clean, cold and damp yet the nauseating odour remained, clinging to my coat like seaweed. I collapsed onto a bench and attempted to regain my breath, looking off at the departing train as I did so.

It chuffed along the curve of the rails and disappeared out of sight into the grey mist that must have come down only minutes ago.

My eyes swept across the platform. A moth fluttered about one of the fluorescent lights.

I was alone now, the departing passengers scurrying away home to their dinners as fast as their suited legs could carry them.

The smell was dissipating. I bent down and took down a

large gulp of air, then checked the display board to see when the next train was due – only another quarter of an hour to wait.

The back of the metal bench felt solid against my neck.

I relaxed a little and took out the article again, fingering the thin paper carefully as I re-read it. What had happened after the piece had been published? Had the diaries been removed? Donated to a museum, perhaps? I would have to find out and track down their location as soon as I got home.

My fingers were starting to feel cold and the paper was absorbing the moisture that hung around me. I folded it up, replaced it in my bag and sat back on the bench.

The station was empty. A bored stillness saturated the atmosphere, the kind only ever noticeable on platforms between arrivals and departures. The brambles and under-growth that framed the small station stirred as a gust of cold air blew in from the south, where the grey river widened and bent towards London.

The fog had grown denser: clouds of it were billowing down around the orange glow of the street lamps. The light had taken on a veiled quality, making it difficult to see clearly but I was able to make out a woman at the end of the platform, dressed from head to toe in grey. She was bent over slightly. Old. As I watched her she made a swooping movement with her arm, surprisingly nimble for her age. For a second I thought she was waving at me, and leant forwards to scrutinise her face. She was too far away but I saw that, what I had mistaken for waving, was actually a looping pointing gesture, directing me to the rafters a few feet away.

Instinctively I followed her signal and looked up.

She was pointing at a banner hanging there. One of the

fastenings had come away and it was hanging down vertically. Water must have got into its structure because it had warped in the middle. A moth hovered around it, buzzing in and out, as the fabric spiralled round in the mist.

The sight of it was commanding. I felt the urge to move towards it.

With a lumbering gait I gave in to the pull.

A few feet away I saw it twist round and stop.

I blinked and glimpsed, at head height, a small pair of bare feet dangling. The flesh was rubbery. A deep gash across the ankle showed up vivid purple against the grey of the skin. The toenails were broken and bruised. Then, as the breeze twirled the weight round again I moved my gaze upwards. Dressed only in soiled, filthy trousers there hung a little boy. No more than ten. Suspended by rope, there was something terribly wrong about the angle of his neck.

On impulse I reached and felt the damp skin of his toes.

As I touched him his face wrenched up. His mouth, fixed into the agonised moment of death, opened. The eyes followed suit, and though I didn't hear it with my ears, the word 'Mercy' rasped through me.

I took a step back and moaned, this time hearing but not feeling my voice call out for help. I turned in the direction of the woman in grey, expecting her to come to my aid.

The end of the platform was empty.

But a young man in a tracksuit had registered my call.

'What's up?' He took in my pained expression.

'The boy,' I pointed up at . . . the banner circling in the wind.

'Where?' he asked, looking past it and to the wall beyond.

'There was a boy there.'

He scratched his chin and regarded me. 'Bit too much to drink, eh love?'

'No,' I stammered. 'There was a boy. Hanging.'

His pity was instantly replaced by distaste. 'Nothing there now, is there?'

There wasn't.

I took in a deep breath. Then I raced over to a bin and threw up.

The man in the tracksuit tutted and shook his head.

They did that back then, you know – went for children. The age of criminal responsibility varied but, at times, it went as low as seven. Didn't always hang them. Though there were instances when they did. No, usually, they threw them in gaol to be starved. In Rattlesden they found a boy of eight. His mother was accused of witchcraft and hanged at Bury. Her son was then cast out by the village to live rough in a field. The Witchfinders found him and asked if he had an imp. He told them that he loved a brown mare in the field next to where he slept. That she loved him and came to him when he called her. So they found him a witch and threw him in the gaol where he rotted and died. Like they did with Dorcas Good in Salem. She was four when they locked her up.

In Salem.

In Essex County.

New England.

I didn't get the next train. I didn't get the one after either. I stared out over the platform above the navy clouds to the watching stars. Some were dead, some dying, some wiped clean from the universe as if they had never existed at all. But there they were – blinking, pulsing as real as the very blood that passed through my veins.

When I was finally ready, I stood on the spot beneath the hanging thing and sent those stars a prayer.

Chapter Thirty-Four

I had it in my mind that when I got home, I would write this one straight down – before the memory faded and I lost the keenness of grief.

Perhaps it was a good thing that I didn't. The feelings might have swamped me and taken me down. And I was about to need more courage than ever before.

When I got home, there was a police car parked in the drive.

'You've had a break-in,' said the man who identified himself as Constable Wheatley. He was in the outer hallway of the block when he met me and efficiently took me by the arm to my apartment. 'You were lucky we were in the area. An anonymous caller reported a man climbing down your balcony.'

'Anonymous.' It sounded like a question though I had only repeated the officer's word as my brain woke up and tried to take in the news.

Constable Wheatley inclined his head back to the main door. 'I would suspect it to be a concerned commuter on their way home. Didn't leave their name. "Number withheld". No one does these days. Don't want to get involved.'

Someone took quite a risk then. 'At this time? In the early evening?'

Wheatley agreed. 'It's bold, I'll give you that. But if it's kids, they just don't seem to care these days. They know we can't do much to them. But we'll get Fingerprints on to it. See what they turn up.'

We were nearing the top of the stairs. My front door was open. It appeared still intact. I always thought burglars kicked their way in.

'I've just come from the train,' I murmured absently.

The policeman huffed himself upwards. As we reached my landing he asked, 'You? On that last one? That would have been close. We arrived twenty minutes ago. Reckon they were disturbed before they went on to do the second floor. If you'd got the earlier train you might have come face to face.' He stepped up to the front door and let me go in first. 'Count yourself lucky, you've had a very narrow escape.'

I didn't feel lucky as I pushed open the door and surveyed the damage.

The place had been trashed.

Officer Wheatley told me it looked like the kitchen had been left until last. The window at the back was still open and a cold draught coursed through the flat. I made to go and close it but a female officer who had come in from the lounge urged me to leave it alone. She'd close it herself as she had rubber gloves on and there might be evidence on the handle.

Some of the drawers from my old Welsh dresser were smashed on the floor, their contents spread over the lino. A bottle of red wine had been knocked from a shelf and had shattered on the kitchen worktop. It was still dripping over my white shiny cupboards, fanning out into a bloody red pool on the floor.

I rubbed my chin and blew out loudly. The female officer took it as a sign of distress. 'Yes, nasty feeling isn't it? Feels like a violation. But we've made sure the place is secure. They've scarpered, but I'm afraid there's worse to come. Let's secure that window for you. Would you mind walking Officer Wheatley through your home and let him know what's missing please?'

I followed Officer Wheatley to the bedroom. It was a bit of a shock. My sheets had been ripped to shreds. 'What's that all about?' I asked him.

'Dunno. Don't take it personally. It's probably drugs.'

I didn't think much had been taken, apart from my jewellery box. That, apparently, was par for the course. I didn't have much of worth in there anyway. The scumbags been through my wardrobe and scattered a lot of my clothes across the room, the hallway and the living room. And the latter was the room they'd saved for their best work.

The TV had been hurled across the glass top table. It hadn't smashed but it had been cracked and would have to be got rid of. The innards of my lovely comfy sofa frothed over the carpet. Even the cushions had been slashed open. In the far corner someone had prised apart the filing cabinet. The policeman told me that the scratches on the side indicated a wrench had probably been used.

'Don't suppose you have something like that in the flat?'

'Don't think so. There may be some tools in the loft.'

My eye glanced over the scattered papers of my research. That would take a while to sort. On the map over the mantelpiece someone had written 'Desist' in red scrawls. What the hell was that? A warning or an order? I pointed to it. 'Desist?'

The policeman was saying something but I was still reeling. I made an effort to tune in. 'Wasn't sure if that was yours. You didn't write it then?'

I shook my head.

'Can I ask what line of work you're in, Ms Asquith?'

When I told him I was a journalist his demeanour changed. 'And what are you looking into at the moment?'

I spoke slowly, trying to process the logic of it all. 'I'm exploring the witch hunts of the seventeenth century . . .'

'Nothing current that might have got someone's back up?'

'Not really.'

'Nothing anyone might want you to stop investigating? Or "desist" as it says?'

'No. I can't think of anything.'

Constable Wheatley nodded and looked up. 'Well, that'll be kids then. It's probably the name of a computer game or a film or such . . . I wouldn't give it much thought.'

I nodded at him, trying to look very much like I believed him, but there was a nugget of intense unease growing in my stomach. 'Desist.' That was an old-fashioned word. Why would kids spray that? Why not some sweary insult? But maybe Wheatley was right – it could be slang or some youth culture reference I had no idea about.

'There's obviously criminal damage here,' he was saying, gesturing to the telly and the table. 'There shouldn't be a problem sorting that out with your insurance. We'll brush it for prints and then you can chuck it. Do you know what's missing from the rest of the room?'

I did a quick inventory and realised there wasn't much – an old PlayStation, the DVD player, an assortment of DVDs, the stereo, CDs. I sent up a silent prayer of thanks that I had made the last minute decision to take my laptop to London with me and routinely kept all my bankcards on my person.

'They didn't get downstairs,' Wheatley was saying. 'Your front door wasn't breached but the balcony window was open. We think that's the point of entry.'

I looked at it. 'I usually lock it before I go out.'

'Sadly, there's all kinds of contraptions you can purchase these days if you want to break in. Where there's a will . . .'

I surveyed the mess. 'What shall I do?'

The policeman put his notebook away and coughed. 'Clear up. Report it to your insurance company. You'll get a crime reference number.'

'Yes, but will I be safe?'

'I doubt they'll be back. Kids like this tend to be opportunistic. They've got nothing else to grab here, have they? Is there anything else missing?'

I looked around once more. 'I don't think so.'

The constable went in to join his partner in the kitchen and shortly after that the fingerprinters arrived.

It wasn't till later that night, as I was cleaning up the lounge, I realised that my file on the witch hunts was gone.

Just after eleven that night the doorbell rang. The tall outline of a uniformed body was visible through the dappled glass of the main front door. When I drew back the bolts and opened it I was both shocked and relieved to see Joe standing there on the doorstep. For a moment neither of us spoke, his brown

312

eyes looked as shy as a deer's. Then he said, 'I thought you might want some company.'

It wasn't like I fell into his arms and swooned or anything like that. Almost the opposite really. Though we talk about it now with some sense of humour, at the time it felt the most subdued but also the most natural thing in the world, though intense and slightly painful too. See, I did need some company and, in my heart of hearts, I think I had always wanted that companion to be Joe – I had just been clouded with so many other things I couldn't see it. But it's not what you're thinking either. There was no great passionate revelation or an untumbling of our feelings, followed by mind-blowing sex. All that happened was that I took his hand and led him upstairs and then we went to bed. He in his t-shirt and boxers, and me in my pj's. And neither sets of clothes got ripped off or anything like that. He just lay next to me and I rested my head on his chest. We were both knackered and I was still in shock, I think. And Joe understood that. And thus was I able to sleep, knowing that he was there, next to me, taking comfort from his physical presence and strength.

In the morning we had an early breakfast and then he got off to work. And though we didn't mention anything, I think we both had an understanding that something was starting over again.

When he kissed me goodbye he said, 'Don't tell me you didn't see this coming.'

'I won't,' I told him and smiled.

He ran a finger over my cheek and ruffled the side of my hair. 'I'm off tomorrow for two days training at Hendon. Would you mind not buggering off with someone else this time please?'

It made me laugh and that in turn lightened the mood so I said, 'If there's any buggering off to do I'll be sure to take you with me.'

How funny that I said that then.

Like I knew.

Chapter Thirty-Five

Mum's house had a stagnant atmosphere to it; as if sentient to the fact its owner had died and had therefore given up on its own life.

It was unhappy.

I'd been back to pick up post and sort a few things out a while ago. I thought this had only been a week or so ago but the stack of mail wedged up against the door indicated it must have been longer.

The burglary had heightened my sense of anxiety so I made sure, as I was checking her place, that I double locked the front door once I was inside. Of course, I'd tried to swallow Wheatley's suggestion the burglary was of a random nature. But if it was kids, why would they take my research? After the lovely Joe had departed I spent hours in the morning searching under the sofa, at the bottom of cupboards, on top of the fridge, wondering if I had put the folder somewhere absentmindedly. When it finally dawned on me that it might have been personal – though Christ knew what they were looking for – I abandoned my search and bolted round to see if my mother's house was all right.

The place looked okay. Well, it seemed secure. Yet it felt

wrong. It wasn't just Mum's passing that had subdued the atmosphere. Some of the rooms felt disturbed, as if contaminated by an outside presence. Or maybe it was just that they seemed so untouched. Unloved. I thought about phoning Joe and seeing if he could come round at some point and check it, but didn't, because I wasn't sure if my motives were pure or whether it was just that I wanted to see him again. And I knew that he was busy today with work, then packing, then off on his course until Wednesday. I would just have to be a big girl about it all and do it myself.

Perhaps, I wondered, maybe I should start dealing with Mum's stuff. I hadn't wanted to since she went, yet it was a process I had to go through. If I didn't do it then it would remain there, on my list; a chore no less, but still a connection to Mum. I'd known for a while that this avoidance technique was impractical and made no financial sense, yet I was prepared to suffer the consequences. However that afternoon, when I had a proper look at the neglected living room, with Mum's trinkets collecting dust, it struck me that she would have wanted me to sort through them, knowing only I would treat them with the required care and loving concern. It made me feel like I'd betrayed her all over again: I had been self-centred and selfish.

But no more.

I resolved to make a start and began with the pictures and photos that she so loved; a framed snap of her and Dan on a mountain top in the Peak District, an embarrassing portrait of me – all teeth, tits and mortar board – at my graduation, an old map of Essex detailing the various 'hundreds'. I didn't know when it was produced but it referred to the North Sea as the German Ocean so I was guessing it was pretty ancient.

Beside that was a print of Colchester Castle, drawn in coloured inks from a south-easterly perspective. I was so accustomed to seeing it hang over the sofa I'd never questioned its significance or wondered how it had come into Mum's possession.

But I did now. I read the text underneath: a neat description of the state of the castle. The 's's were written like 'f's. She'd visited there then, I thought, and bought this as a souvenir. Must have had been a while ago – the picture had been on the wall forever and left a darker space behind it when I stood on the sofa and unhooked it from the nail. As I did I glimpsed, in the glass reflection, the face of a woman staring over my shoulder.

My eyes clamped shut reflexively and I tensed, waiting for the voice to come, the temperature to drop or something nasty to suck out my mind.

But nothing happened.

Slowly I peeked at the glass. She was still there, but with a gulp of relief I saw who it was – Circe the witch, peering out from Mum's favourite painting. No passive victim or gnarled old woman but a beauty and a force to be reckoned with. Circe transformed her enemies into animals; Odysseus' men she turned into pigs. There she was, head bowed, pouring her enchanted potion into the sea. I had always liked this picture. I remembered when Mum brought it home, recounting how the owner of the shop struck up a conversation. He said he could see a resemblance there and had insisted it should be hers – she had protested poverty but he let her have it at a fraction of the price. Dad lost his rag when he heard that story and had a rant about bourgeois values and the vulgarity of the reproduction. But I think he might have been a little jealous. Anyway, the painting remained upstairs in the loft until Dad left. Then it took pride of place in the living room.

Circe Invidiosa, Colchester Castle and an old map of Essex. For a second I wondered if they were a series of visual clues but then I remembered they had been acquired over a period of years and were unlikely to be connected.

I took Circe down cautiously – it was a heavy frame – and placed her with the other pictures, resolving to find a home for them at my place.

That was it for the living room, so I made my way slowly round the house through the hall and dining room into the kitchen then upstairs, methodically taking down all decorative items.

Two hours later I was in Mum's old bedroom. Though that was a bit of a misnomer as the bed was downstairs. Because of her illness it was more convenient to use the dining room for sleeping so the upstairs room was more of a storage space.

But it smelled of her: Chanel Number Five and Yardley – English Roses or something. I closed my eyes and remembered being wrapped up in her lap. Her skin had been so soft then. Her clothes light and fragrant. There was a rocking chair and a song she sang as she kissed my hair. Oh Mum, life is so much colder since you went away. And I thought of her and I remembered her hug and wondered what she would say to me, if I could see her.

She'd undoubtedly want me to get things done and continue on my way.

So, I put down the feeling that was about me and walked into the room. A practical, methodical approach was what was required now. I needed to shut out all sentiment. So I lifted my chin with purpose and hardened my heart. Then I went into the middle of the room.

On the opposite wall hung a huge framed map of south-east England, which had appeared about eleven or twelve years ago when Mum first got interested in walking. The exercise helped her mental health and she'd often take herself off for a couple of days. It was too big for me to handle on my own so I left it up there and turned my attention to her wardrobe.

I opened the double doors hiding the old unwieldy closet that stretched the length of the room. At the far end I came across some of her old gladrags. They were dusty, long-unused gowns of their time: a few glitzy evening dresses complete with sequins and shoulder pads; one classic black velvet number; several skirts that spanned different fashion trends; cotton maxis and some old suede coats with real fur collars.

At the back of the closet inside a plastic sheath was her wedding dress. It was a floaty romantic thing that reflected the romanticism of the seventies: a wide gathered neckline dropped off the shoulders and dripped down in light chiffon over an A-line skirt. An ivory lace, wide-brimmed floppy hat finished it off. I loved it. There was no way I was sending it to a charity shop, so I took it downstairs and placed it beside the pictures.

When I returned the room was darkening; dusk becoming night. Yet as I walked through the door I was able to see, two feet away from the open closet door, my mother's jewellery box.

I hadn't put it there.

At least, I didn't remember doing so. Perhaps I had dislodged it as I rummaged through the clothes?

The lid was open. I went over and touched the ballerina set into its middle. Slowly she began to rotate. The cobwebs about her twisted and pulled free, encasing her in a dusty veil. A mechanical melody jingled through the air. I recognised the rhythm and then moments later recalled the old song:

> Pale and wild pale and wild
> The witch did leave the child
> She watched her grow and put her down
> The willow's leaves wrapped round and round
> Her evil cries filled the air
> And so did end the bad affair
> Pale and wild pale and wild
> The witch did up end the child

For a moment I was transfixed by the song and the box, hurtling back through years. This time to a forgotten teenage scene: Mum talking about the jewellery, insisting if she were to die I take the box and . . . I couldn't remember what she told me. I had been too consumed with envy, hypnotised by the sparkle of her few jewels.

The ghostly music tinkled. I looked on as the plastic ballerina turned and jerked on her spring. Bending over, I closed the lid and delicately picked it up. As I did, part of it, the base, came away and clattered to the floor.

I turned the box over to inspect the damage. A small compartment had been concealed beneath the wooden base. My fingers crept into the underside and felt around. It was a shallow slot, covered in aged velveteen. As I touched it something flimsy dropped out: a piece of paper, folded over so it was only about two inches square. Very old and fragile, I unfolded it with great care. It was a document, roughly A5 in size.

In the darkness I was unable to make out what it said. So I took it over to the door. The eco-bulb there wasn't particularly brilliant but I could see what it was. The bluey-black ink was faded and powdery in the folds but I could clearly make out the words.

As I read them I felt my knees buckle. I grabbed on to the doorframe for support, first confused then as it sank in, stupefied with shock.

In my hands I held a birth certificate. From 1977. November 15th.

My birthday.

It chronicled the birth of a girl. But it wasn't my name that was scrawled there. That baby was called Mercy Walker.

Blood was throbbing in my ears as I looked down to see the Name and Surname of the mother – Rose Walker. Beneath it I read, with increasing disbelief, the place of birth: Hemel Hempstead. Hertfordshire.

Then finally my eyes caught the 'Father' section. There was only one word recorded in the slanting black hand. I read it with anguish.

'Unknown'.

Chapter Thirty-Six

The problem with being blown out of your mind is that, when you return to it, you find large chunks have been burnt out. I suspect that it's a survival technique the human species has developed to prevent the paralysis of trauma. But it is irritating in cases like this, when I'm trying to give the full picture, to find that I only have a frazzled and fragmented rag of coherent recall.

I'm not sure what happened in the immediate hours post-discovery, so I won't guess. This is what I do know: for a while I sat in the doorway of my mother's bedroom, endlessly turning the note over, reading and re-reading the words until they made no sense. Eventually, I don't know when, but probably sometime before midnight, I noticed on the back an indistinct scrawl, some kind of annotation in my mother's hand: South East, F8. I don't think I gave it much thought. I was too busy sifting through my childhood, exploring the holes. But like I said, it's all a bit of a blur now.

I *can* remember the following day, I got myself together and went to see the man I thought of as my father in the Suffolk pub he partly owned.

I remember that he was late.

More than ten minutes late, and I was boiling myself into a fury. So that when he did finally turn up, striding into his realm, greeting some of the regulars he knew so well, I had to grip on to the table to prevent myself flying at him.

He saw me sitting over by the window in the furthest, most private part of the pub, but even then didn't come straight over. He stopped, had a word with the manager *then* sauntered across the lounge, greeting me with a 'Mercedes, darling. Are you okay? I got your message. You sounded . . .'

He bent over to give me a kiss, but I squirmed away from his touch.

'Don't,' I said, though I was bursting to say more.

Dad took a step back. 'You okay? I'm sorry I'm late. It was Lucy's assembly and afterwards there were coffees and you know how these things go . . .'

It was the wrong line to take. Though he didn't realise it, the last thing I wanted to hear was that he'd made me wait because he was spending time with his real child. His blood relative.

I leant forwards and snarled, 'Who are you?'

Dad's mouth dropped open. His eyebrows soared skywards, little bumps of wrinkled skin gathered above them; then, as a faint glimmer of understanding seemed to appear on the horizon of his mental landscape, they narrowed and slid down his forehead. His eyes made intense small movements, darting from side to side. Apart from that his face was impassive, petrified into a familiar non-expression that I had seen so many times in my life. At last I perceived it for what it was – a mask that hid many contradictions and conflicting emotions. Though, from an early age I had presumed it to be indifference, I saw now it was paralysis.

He stepped back and put his hand to his brow then, as if falling, sat down and grasped the edge of the table.

I didn't move to help him, but looked on and watched.

Once he'd gathered himself he looked at me. His face had fallen and he had a ruined look about him.

Half-heartedly he asked, 'What's this all about?'

It was written all over his features that he knew what was occurring. He just didn't want to have to deal with it.

'This,' I spat and threw the document onto the table. While watching him I'd unconsciously screwed it up into a ball. I hadn't meant to. I didn't want it to look like disrespect but my fists had clenched down hard. And suddenly it was there. In the middle of the table.

Separating us.

The lie.

Dad cleared his throat. He was pale. 'What is it?' he asked, staring at me, squarely into my eyes.

I wanted to look away but I wasn't that weak.

'You know what it is,' was all I said.

Dad exhaled steadily. I watched his white linen shirt rise to take in the next breath, then hold it like he was never going to let go. Then he said, 'Oh.'

As simple as that. 'Oh.'

I was so appalled I let my hand slam down on the table, drawing glances from the landlord and regulars. Dad waved them back.

For a long minute we looked at each other like there was no one else in the room.

Dad's chestnut eyes were welling up, stricken by emotions nobody else would ever be able to understand. All I could say was 'They're brown. Your eyes. Mine are grey. Why didn't I get it?'

Then, before I knew what I was doing, I got up and marched out of the door.

I could hear the people in the pub murmuring and the shouts of Dad to come back but I couldn't stop myself. Really, all I wanted was a denial. Some kind of explanation that would lay the rogue document to rest. A straightforward explanation that it was a joke or a fake. But his reaction had been authentic and now I knew in my heart he was not my father.

I made out towards the reservoir, rushing over grasses and bushes but not seeing or feeling a thing.

After a while he must have caught up with me because I felt his hand on my arm. I wrenched it away but he clung on and brought me to him. As old as he was he was still strong, and surrounded me with his arms. And though I struggled, my heart was not in it. Trapped in his embrace I submitted to his overarching hug.

And while the wind and the reeds shushed us I clung for dear life to this man, now a stranger to me.

We didn't move from the spot, but sat down there. Dad gave me a hanky.

I wasn't speaking.

After a decade he said, 'You're my daughter, no matter what you may come across. I have raised you. You are *my* child.'

I was confused and said, 'But I'm not. Not literally, am I?'

Dad's voice was calm. 'There's no biological link, it's true. But you are mine. You always have been. All that nappy changing counts for something, you know.'

I rolled over on the grass and knocked down a reed. One of the rushes was digging into my thigh so I snapped it and threw it ahead. 'Who *is* my dad then?'

He looked away and said, 'I don't know.'

I snorted. 'Really?'

'No.'

'What *do* you know?'

He sighed heavily. 'Where did you find it?'

'Underside of her jewellery box.'

'Oh,' he said again.

I said, 'Why didn't you ever tell me? Loads of people have stuff like this . . . Adoption and stuff. It's not the fifties for God's sake. I mean, some of my friends have had single mothers and don't know their fathers. They've never been *misled.*'

He held his hand up to silence me. It was a commanding move and it worked.

'You think I didn't want to tell you? Mercedes, there have been so many times when I could have just said it.'

I stared at the reservoir. Wind was rippling across the surface of the water. A family of ducks swam into the reeds. 'Uncle Roger knows doesn't he?'

He didn't say anything.

'He said to me, at his birthday, that I wouldn't be a match if I donated my kidney. I thought it was a polite way of declining my offer. But now . . . Why didn't *you* tell me?'

Dad ran his fingers through his short curly hair. It was the only gesture that gave away his nerves. He looked off in the other direction to the distant hills.

'Because your mother never *wanted* me to. It was important to her that you never knew.'

We sat for moments in quiet silence. Then I said, 'Why?'

He said, 'I don't know. Honest to God, I don't.'

I wiped my face with his hanky. 'So what I want to know is how much of what you've told me is true? How did you meet? It obviously wasn't a smooch at the youth club?'

Dad sort of yawned and didn't speak for a minute. There was an inner struggle going on: loyalty to my mother opposing my demands. But there was only one relationship that had any hope of continuing, so eventually he caved in.

'She seemed to come out of nowhere. Literally. I mean, I never thought that anything like that would happen to me. It was in the spring of '78. I was on my way back from a job in St Albans. That night we had terrible torrential rain. It was dark. The rain was clogging the windscreen. I didn't see her. One minute it was all rain and empty lanes, the next, there was this girl in the beam of my headlights. I swerved off to the side to avoid hitting her and when I got out she was on the road. My wing mirror had clipped her. She was dazed, I think. Just sitting there like that, in that way she had, looking up at me, doing her best to look brave. It was as if she was expecting to see someone she knew. She had thrown herself across the pram awkwardly, blocking my path to it and it was on its side. I don't think she'd realised that. And I could hear crying. As I reached the pram she tried to push me away. But she was weak and it didn't take much to get round her and right the pram. And there you were, more or less okay, thank God. Apart from a light scratch on your head.

'Your mother was bleeding from a cut on her side. I wanted to take you both to the nearest hospital. To be honest, I was concerned that Rosamund might have internal injuries and I didn't want any comeback on the insurance. But she wouldn't hear of it. She got hysterical and was about ready to leg it up the road. So I stopped insisting on a visit to A & E and told her I was taking her home – no arguments. After some persuasion she agreed. The pram wasn't fit for purpose anyway.

'The address that she gave was some sort of hostel.' He broke off and shook his head, seeing it again. 'The conditions in there. Oh Mercedes, you should have seen it: damp on the walls and mould on the inside of your cot. The paint was flaking off and there were bits of plaster all over the carpet. And she was so young and thin. Of course, she was beautiful too. I think I'd been smitten from the first moment I'd seen her in the middle of the road. That black hair; a bit Elizabeth Taylor. I couldn't leave her in that dump, I just couldn't. So I brought you both home.

'Of course, she was resistant at first. But I think she was so weak that she gave in. I remember that she spent a long time looking at me. Staring at my hair and something over my head. I told her she could have the spare room for a bit and that she looked like she could do with a good feed. That's when she agreed. I wouldn't wonder if she might have been half starved. It was hard back then. You didn't get the sort of help you do these days. And for a baby you were small too.

'She didn't have many belongings: a couple of skirts and jumpers and some baby clothes.' He frowned sadly at the memory. 'It wasn't meant to be a long-term affair. For the first few months she kept talking about moving on. She'd been running from something. And don't ask me what that was – she never spoke about it. Even after we were married. It took me about a year to convince her she could trust me.

I think she did in the end. Eventually, months turned into a year and we got around to tying the knot. You know, I loved her, Mercedes. Truly . . .' he tailed off and took a deep breath.

'I only ever wanted her to be happy. But she couldn't be; something kept her worried all the time. And she was so protective of you. So absolutely of the conviction that you should never know of your history other than the story we agreed on. It was one of her conditions when we got hitched. But I respected that, and it didn't bother me. I was prepared to take you on. You were lovely.

'You could say we created a fiction out of love. And you grew into a bright happy child.' He reached over and rubbed my calf. 'Of whom I am very proud.'

I could see it in his eyes. And all at once I wanted to forgive him. Both of them. Of course, there was a reason for it. Of course there was. And it was true – I had had a happy childhood.

I sighed and leant back on my hands, thinking back over the years. 'But I always thought I was an Essex Girl, Dad.' I noticed how I had referred to him and in that moment I knew, that despite the knot of pain in my guts, I had already forgiven him. He would still always be my dad.

'You are. You are such an Essex Girl. Or rather, Essex woman now. I know this is difficult. But you have to realise that this was done with your best interests at heart. You understand that, don't you? Knowing what your mother was like.'

I could get it. But I couldn't get it, if you know what I mean.

'I should find my dad,' I said eventually. 'The biological one. I suppose.'

'No.' He said it quickly, with conviction. 'Please don't. Whatever had happened in your mother's life there is one thing I know for sure, and that was that she didn't want anything to do with him.' He was looking over my shoulder into the past. Silence fell on us for a moment then he said, almost to himself, 'He was probably someone she met back home.'

I jolted upright. 'Back home?'

'London.' He looked doubtful and touched his face with his hand to brush away an invisible hair. 'She only referred to him once, in her own words, as an "unexpected sperm donor". Her parents had wanted her to give you up for adoption but she refused and got kicked out of home.'

'That's a bit harsh.'

'Not really. It was the seventies. There was still a stigma attached to unmarried mothers. And,' he pressed both palms into his eyes and rubbed, then leant back and looked at me, 'she was just sixteen when she had you.'

That didn't make sense. Mum was fifty-two. We had celebrated her fiftieth a couple of years back.

'Another little tweak of the facts for appearance's sake.' I could see him swallowing down his feelings as he reached back through the years. 'She'd be fifty this December, had she lived.'

It was hard to take. Why change her age? But I couldn't dwell on it. I didn't want to see him like this – all struggling and emotional. He was meant to be strong and fearless and, well, my dad. Dads didn't do that.

I nodded. 'Her parents: are they still alive? Do I have some family I've never met?'

Dad sighed again and looked at the broken grass beneath my feet. 'I'm afraid not. They were elderly and died some years ago. Rosamund never made contact with them. She was so angry. I don't think she got over them tossing her out like that.'

'You think? You don't know?'

He nodded. 'She clammed up whenever I asked, so I learnt not to and, to be honest, after a while I couldn't care less. Your mum became my wife, and shortly after, you became my daughter. I wanted to adopt you but your mother didn't want to get official channels involved, so we did it unofficially.'

'But I have a birth certificate that lists you as my father? Not this one.' I wagged it in front of him. 'Another. I've used it for my passport. You're on it. Place of birth: Rochford, Essex.'

'I *am* your dad, Mercedes. A man from Shoeburyness helped me organise that. It was just a case of getting the correct stationery, and bunging a few quid in the right direction.'

I took that on board in silence, watching the clouds sail towards the south-west. 'Didn't you want to know more about her?'

He reached out and grabbed my hand, rubbing it for emphasis. 'I loved her and I loved you. I felt lucky that she'd allowed me to accompany her on her way. I never wanted to make her feel uncomfortable. I wanted to protect her and look after you. And if that meant not asking any questions, then that was a small sacrifice to make.'

But that didn't add up entirely in my mind. 'But you left us.'

'I didn't want to,' he said. 'Your mother was so aggrieved about the effect that her illness was having on us, she was going to leave herself. I wouldn't hear of it. I persuaded her to stay but I said I'd clear off. You were sixteen then, going on twenty-five. Out on the town night after night, with that young hellcat Maggie Haines. You always were far too grown-up looking for your own good. And you did all right, didn't you? Made it into university and never looked back.'

'I always thought you left us. That's another thing you kept back.'

He shook his head. 'I think your mother thought she was doing me a favour. Releasing me from the difficulties of life with her and her depression. But I never felt like that. I loved her. But I didn't want to be a burden either. That's why I went. And I think she found some kind of peace with Dan. Their temperaments were more compatible. They'd been through the same kind of illness. I think she ended up quite happy with him.'

'Like you're happy with Janet?' The petulance in my voice was hard to disguise.

'My life with Janet is different. Janet's stable and strong. I feel like we're on an equal footing. She's upfront and honest. You know that what you see is what you get. Your mum was always partly a mystery to me. Sometimes I felt like I was bewitched. Our life was full of ups and downs. But passionate too.'

I didn't want him going into details of the 'passion' bit. I said, 'I never thought we were an ordinary family. And now I know we weren't.'

'Every family has a secret,' said my dad. 'And the secret is that they are not like any other family.'

'Profound,' I said.

He made an attempt at a smile. 'Not mine. Nicked it off someone else.'

I sniffed and dabbed my nose with his hanky. 'True though.'

He pulled his knees up and made to stand. 'And now you have to forget about it. For your mum's sake. It's what she wanted.'

'Actually,' I said and unfolded the crumpled-up ball, 'I'm not entirely sure that that's true. Look.' I spread the certificate over the grass and turned it over, directing Dad to the scrawl. 'Do you know what that means? *South East, F8.*'

He blinked at the crumpled sheet. 'I've never seen it, you know.' I looked at him, taking in the tired features and messed-up hair. I wanted to hug him but I couldn't. I just said, 'But do you know what the letters mean?'

'It's not a postcode?'

I shrugged. 'Dunno.'

He took it out of my hands for a closer look. 'Coordinates?'

I sat back. 'Mum's got a map of some sort on the wall.'

'I doubt it means anything.'

'Probably not.'

'You're going to have a look aren't you?'

'I'm going straight there now.'

I stood up and gestured towards the limp piece of paper in his hands.

'Do you want company?' he said, handing it over with some reluctance. He wanted to destroy it, I think.

I took it and said 'No. She might have been trying to tell me something before she, you know, died. She said something about a box, though I thought she meant my book, and I didn't let her tell me. I . . .' Words were becoming futile in the face of unfurling guilt. 'I think I should do this on my own.'

He moved onto all fours then stood up and put his hands on his hips. 'Well I'm here if you need me.'

'I know,' I told him. And I did.

When I got back to Mum's house it felt like I was returning to the scene of a crime where something violent and unwholesome had occurred. The house let me in, but it felt violated. Ripped out its heart. Changed the memories.

I didn't spend long downstairs and leapt up the stairway two steps at a time.

I noticed my grubby fingerprints on the doorframe as I entered Mum's old bedroom. This time I flicked the lights on so I could clearly view the map on the wall.

Encased in a thin glass cover, I traced out lines from the two sets of coordinates. Where they met, I could see a pinprick left by a drawing pin. And it was right in the middle of a village – Ashbolten.

That rang a bell.

Where was that from? I'd read it recently.

'Shit,' I said as it came to me. It was the place mentioned in the article Gerald had given me at the National Archives. Where the Nathaniel Braybrook diaries had been found. Could it be so? Had she been there? She had never mentioned it to me. But there was obviously a great deal she had neglected to talk about.

I examined it more closely. A cross had been pencilled in black, just south of the town. Above it Mum had written: *Treetops*.

My mind flew back to the article. It had been torn roughly but I had made out a 'p' and 's'. *Treetops*?

Why on earth would she have gone to Ashbolten?

It made no sense.

Nothing did. Everything was confusing. I sat down and thought for a bit. When I'd thought things through I took a photo of the map on my phone.

Then I went downstairs with a new clarity. Two dominant threads in my life were converging.

Chapter Thirty-Seven

The next day before I set off for Ashbolten I got a call from Maggie. She asked how the Hopkins piece was and I told her, truthfully, that it had gone up a gear and that I was just about to head off to check out a lead. She sounded pretty excited by it and made me promise to keep her up to speed. I could have told her about Mum. I could have told her about Dad. But I didn't want to slow down. That conversation would merit a good half hour and perhaps another follow-up meeting in the flesh. There was too much to do. I said goodbye and agreed to pop in soon.

Then I checked in on Dan.

He was okay. Not terribly bad, not terribly good. Just okay.

I asked him how he was doing. He said, 'I must be on the mend – I'm starting to feel embarrassed.'

'Ah,' I said. 'I don't know whether to encourage you or sympathise.'

'Former is probably best,' he said. 'Let's get together soon. I have some things I need to talk through with you.'

'Whenever you're ready.'

'Maybe next week?'

'It's a deal.' I hung up with the promise that I'd phone him to arrange it, though at the back of my mind I was wondering if I shouldn't put it off for a little longer – there was a hell of a lot I wanted to ask him about Mum and what he knew. But I didn't want to do anything that might jeopardise his recovery.

I decided to have a chat with Doctor Franklin, as unpleasant as that might be, and get his advice on how/if I should approach the subject with his patient. But I'd have to think about that next week. I was anxious to get on my way.

A thick mist was coming off the sea, crawling inland, pasting itself over cars and sparkling windows. The dash-board clock blinked twelve noon as I was cruising out of south-east Essex and onto the main route that would connect me to the M25.

A wind had got up and the trees either side of the road were beginning to bend. The watery sun that had tried to shine about an hour ago had now given up completely and dissolved into a drizzling greyness, the blandness of which encouraged my mind to wander away from the road a couple of times and into the realms of contemplation. What was Mum doing going to Ashbolten, if indeed she had? And why write it on the back of my original birth certificate? What was there? Had she trodden the path I was going down? Then why not tell me; why keep all of this a secret? And if she wanted it to remain so, why retain the damning evidence, with the reference on the back? Why not destroy it? Because, I thought, she must have wanted me to find it at some point.

And what of the convergence of the two threads currently most important in my life – the witches and Mum? Had Rebecca appeared to her, as Dan hinted? Had she appeared to him? Was he mad? Had she really texted?

I mean, it sounded totally insane. If I actually articulated these questions to anyone else I'd be carted off to Dan's place. Joe would undoubtedly be very concerned. But then again – things like this did not happen all the time. Ghosts did not private message people. Spirits did not text. I did not have visions.

Though I reflected, for some people all this stuff was a way of life. I recalled Beryl Bennett. She'd seen something in my hand. Hadn't she wondered if I'd been ill? Or was adopted? Jesus, she knew. It was unreal.

Or was I was just beginning to see the world for what it was – a gossamer cat's cradle of different threads and connections, half-sights and shadows, cracks and hints, that had been completely invisible only weeks before?

Before Mum died, if I'd caught myself thinking this kind of stuff I would have checked straight into a psychotherapist then and there. Of course I would have been terrified I'd inherited Mum's . . . Here my thought stream paused. I was thinking the word 'illness'. But another voice had whispered a memory to me and I substituted 'illness' for 'gift'. Was that what she was trying to tell me? Is this what Joe meant? The ability to see other layers, to pass through time?

It wasn't possible was it? Time was set. It was a fixed thing. You couldn't look back and you couldn't look forwards. You could only be in the present. Well, that was certainly the conventional consensus. But then, Mum had always said time was a concept, not a rule, no more reliable than the stories we told.

Was it all coming together? Were there clues in everything she told me?

I sighed and wished I'd listened more carefully to

338

everything she'd said. Soon my concentration was required at the driving wheel: a splatter of rain descended over the motorway.

My plan was to drive to Ashbolten, find Treetops. If it was a business I'd be able to talk to the staff immediately. If it was a domestic dwelling then I'd knock on the door, and probably be required to arrange an appointment for the following day. That would mean returning to the town centre, to investigate the place, have a bit of a gander. Maybe a leisurely coffee. Locate a pub or a restaurant to have dinner in. An early evening in the hotel would allow me to not only sleep in peace, but give me some time alone to try and sort my head out.

As it turned out, Ashbolten was a sleepy village nestled in a valley, surrounded on the south side by woods and copses and to the west by several large farms. I drove in from the north, climbing over the hump of a hill romantically called Tinkers Thrift, and then down into woodland.

As I came off the main road the route became twisting and arduous. I stopped thinking about anything else, killed the radio and concentrated on the bends and blind corners.

Coming through a forest-like part of the road, complete with overhanging branches and brambles reaching several feet high, Ashbolten opened up before me. It was damp and a white mist was curling up from the village, mingling, on its way skywards, with a couple of smoking chimneys. Approaching the cluster of buildings I could see that the place was chocolate-box pretty, verging on sickly; traditional thatched cottages edged round a tiny semi-circular village green, then meandered off into what was called the High Road but was more of a narrow close, ending in a t-junction with the Hen and Chickens pub. No way was there going to be a hotel here.

It was gone three-thirty and the sky was sullen. Daylight was fading, which meant I would have to review my plans significantly. If I had to return to the motorway and come off at the larger town I had passed earlier in order to secure accommodation I'd be put back a good couple of hours. I'd have to find Treetops as well. That might take me into the evening. People, even generous urbanites, resented uninvited guests turning up late and unannounced. At that time of evening it was either dinnertime or soap opera hour. Intrusions upon that 'quality' period, I had found in my early career, were greeted with barely restrained hostility.

Country folk, I imagined, might have a more extreme reaction. After all, they had shotguns and things didn't they?

The pub would be the best place to start, provided it was open. So many of them were shutting up shop these days. Unless they had a thriving lunchtime service most closed during the day and opened in the evening with a skeleton staff.

The Hen and Chickens however, was a pub quite unlike any other. A peek at the small bar, left of the entrance hall, revealed a large inglenook fireplace, with a roaring fire in the grate, around which were spread a few tables and chairs. By the window at the front a counter displayed a spread of groceries and a large range of fruit and veg. I popped my head round to see if there were any staff behind the bar.

A couple of old men were playing chess by the fireside. One glanced over. I must have looked out of place because he didn't eye me for more than a second. 'If you're after Bob,' he said, 'he'll most like be in the saloon or upstairs.'

'Oh right,' I said, assuming Bob to be the landlord. 'Thanks.'

The other man had turned round to view the interruption. 'Ring the bell on the bar top.'

I dipped back into the hallway and went through the door opposite into a larger saloon. A middle-aged man over by the window was doing the crossword while cradling a pint of ale. He looked up briefly in a friendly manner, before returning to his paper. Three women were clustered round a circular table with a half-empty bottle of wine in their midst. Over at the bar another couple of men, just edging out of middle age but not yet elderly, were nursing their pints in companionable silence. But for the whirring squeaks of the fruit machine and some crooning country and western in the background, there was little noise.

The two men at the bar nodded. One of them shouted towards a door between the optics. 'Bob! Customer!'

Within a few minutes a large man appeared. Bob was in his early sixties, wearing a woollen tank top that stretched over a true publican's belly. He had a booming voice and eyes that looked like they'd seen a fair chunk of life but liked it. You could see why the pub managed to attract and keep a loyal clientele.

He grinned broadly when I asked if they did bed and breakfast.

'There's not another pub or shop for miles. We're every-thing here – hotel, function room, social club, corner shop. You name it, we do it. We've got a double with an ensuite, one without, two singles and a family room.'

I asked if I could look at them first.

'Watch the bar will ya, Ray, while I show this young lady

to the rooms. If Linda's ladies need a top up while I'm away, take it from the fridge. They're on the Pinot.'

And with that he ushered me behind the bar into a narrow hallway leading to the back of the building, where a single storey extension spread along the yard. Bob opened the doors and let me view the rooms.

Although basic and slightly eighties in design, the floral duvets and pine furniture were clean, and the rooms were bright and warm. The ensuite was small but functional so I took the double, chucked my case on the bed and spent a couple of minutes replying to a text from Joe asking how I was. I kept my reply short and brief saying there had been some developments on my story and that I was looking forward to telling him when he got back. There was no point going into detail now. I signed off with a couple of 'x's and went back to sign in the visitor's book.

As I filled in the relevant forms Bob asked me what I was doing down in his neck of the woods. When I told him I was looking for Treetops, he nodded wisely.

'Nice couple. He's a card.' He looked over to the two men at the bar. 'Isn't he, Ray?'

'What's that?' said the bloke who was Ray, finishing his pint and straightening himself up at the bar.

'I was just saying to this young lady, er,' he looked at the register, 'Sadie – Harry Phelps, Treetops. He's a card, isn't he?'

Ray arched his eyebrows. 'Oh aye, he's a card all right.'

The man next to him gave a nod. 'He's got high hopes, that one,' he said and the three of them chuckled.

'Well,' said Bob. 'We've all had high hopes at some time haven't we?' They all laughed a little louder.

'Oh right,' I said vaguely. This was obviously some in-joke. 'So where do they live?'

'Down off Dalby Lane,' said Bob and then supplied me with very detailed directions.

Chapter Thirty-Eight

Situated at the end of a narrow lane that petered out into nothing more than a muddy track, I came across a driveway. It swept past two leafless weeping willows, went round a corner beside what would have been flowerbeds of roses, to a very dark house. Only a couple of windows had light behind them.

The porch was a glass extension – the kind that was popular in the eighties: large, double-glazed and square. However beyond it a depressed arch, that must have been Tudor at least, covered the entrance. Above and around that stood the oldest part of the house; a grey stone-carved frontage, with large rectangular leaded bay windows. This had been added on to later in the nineteenth century with an impressive castellated tower on the corner.

I grabbed my handbag and brought out my phone, checking the photo of the map. This had to be it. I let the engine splutter and die at the end of the drive and made out across the gravel, tucking my head down into my collar against the bitter oncoming wind. It picked up my hair and blew it around, and a spattering of raindrops mixed into the elemental battering. Above the rooftop, storm clouds were gathering and the sky had an angry look. Somewhere above me an owl hooted a warning. I felt it was best not be here long. As basic as the accommodation at the Hen and Chickens was, it was at least friendly and full of human beings; this house was foreboding and gloomy. The lit-up windows on the second floor gave it the appearance of a cross-eyed old duchess that scowled at my parka and jeans.

Inside the porch, and out of the wind, I picked my hair from my lipstick and tried to make myself presentable before pressing the bell. The sound of barking dogs broke out behind the front door. A female voice chided the animals, then I heard several bolts being scraped back. The door opened a crack and a woman in her sixties peered through.

'Hello,' I said brightly in my most posh voice. 'I'm very sorry to disturb you. My name is Mercedes Asquith and I'm a writer researching the Essex witch hunts. I came across this article which mentioned a diary of Nathaniel Braybrook.' I handed over the clipping. 'Is it here? I'm not sure if I have the right address?'

The woman said nothing. Her eyes hovered over the scrap in my hand then fluttered back to my face. Perturbed by her silence, I went on. 'I'm happy to come back at another time if this isn't convenient?'

Through the vertical slit her eyes glistened.

Still no verbal response.

I blathered on. 'The book I'm writing is due to be published next October and I'd very much like to have a look at the diaries, if that's at all possible. Are they still here?'

Nothing.

I stalled, wondering if I was dealing with a low IQ and went on to outline the angle of my book. Best to leave any family connection out at this stage. Didn't want to come across as nuts.

The woman interrupted me before I'd even got a quarter of the way through my spiel. 'Yes, all right, I see. Do you mind waiting a moment please?'

It was a little abrupt but I told her 'No, not at all,' and the door closed. Two bolts were drawn across, then the patter of dainty footsteps disappeared into the house.

One of the dogs came back to the door and growled.

'It's all right mate,' I told it. 'I'm a friend not foe.' But it didn't believe me and started barking. A couple of the others joined it.

I stepped back into the porch. A little black moth skittered around the light. It looked virtually identical to the one that had landed on my wall. I thought back to that night. I was certain that moth had chosen a spot on the map that was pretty damn close to where I was actually standing now.

'Is this where you were leading me then?' I asked it. In response it spread its wings and took off, landing on a large spiky cactus in the corner. The place was, in fact, crammed with pot plants: on one side a rectangular wicker planter held a dozen spider plants and beside it stood a large ceramic tub from which sprouted a large money tree. To each side of the solid wood door were hanging baskets, containing an assortment of tropical plants. I was admiring them when I heard heavy footsteps coming down the passage.

Bolts slid back. The door opened, wider this time, but still only to six inches across.

A man with long white hair, a grey beard and black-rimmed spectacles poked his head round and had a good look at me.

'So,' he said. 'My wife says you're a writer. That true?'

I nodded.

'Can you prove it?'

No one had ever asked me that before. 'Um, how?'

'I don't know,' he said a little sarcastically. 'You're the writer, aren't you? What have you written?'

I remembered I had some old issues of *Mercurial* in the back of my car. One of them had a photo of me beside my piece, I was sure.

'Can you wait for a moment while I fetch something?'

'Of course,' the man said and shut the door. Two bolts scraped across.

I fetched the mags. The rain was pelting down now so I shoved them under my jacket to keep them dry and ran back to the house.

The door opened and a hand came out. I put the magazines in it and watched it slam shut again. This, I had to admit, was very odd.

I think I must have waited outside for a good ten minutes before the dogs went off and the heavy footsteps came back down the passage. The door opened fully and the man, who introduced himself as Harry Phelps, greeted me, very cordially.

Like his house, Harry was also eccentric: his long white hair cascaded down over a 'Free the Weed' t-shirt which featured a humanised marijuana plant looking dolefully through prison windows.

I remembered Bob's comment about 'high hopes'.

This could explain the paranoid security ritual.

'I'm sorry about that,' said Harry, quite cheerful now. 'We have to be careful these days. Can't have any Tom, Dick or me, turning up unannounced can we?'

Not if you're caning it, I thought. 'Very wise,' I said.

'Come in, into the kitchen. Anne's already put a pot of coffee on. She thought you'd be all right. She's got a nose for it,' he beamed.

'Right,' I said noncommittally.

The entrance hall was grand and lofty, probably as big as my entire living room, with a wooden staircase that went up the centre then split into separate staircases to either side.

Harry bobbed down under a doorframe only five foot high that led into a room of normal proportions, which had a couple of tatty sofas positioned in front of a huge old fireplace. This he told me absently, was the 'snug' and then opened a taller door opposite the fireplace, leaving me to follow him out into a bright modern kitchen/diner-cum-family room.

This side of the room was exposed red-brick, with a range cooker and a butcher's block spread out in front of it. The rest of the room, however, showed no signs of age or whimsy.

Standing by a glossy oak table Harry's wife, Anne, whose eyes I recognised from the door, poured coffee into three glass mugs.

'Do come over, dear. Mercedes is it? Very nice to meet you.' She smiled and gestured to one of the chairs, as if the bizarre entry routine had never happened.

She's obviously used to it, I thought, and took a chair. 'Actually it's Sadie,' I said and sat down, though I was thinking 'It's not. It's Mercy. Mercy Walker.' How did I go from that to Mercedes Asquith? Why had Mum completely changed my name? She'd also evolved hers, from Rose to Rosamund.

What was in that? A familiar wrench of guilt tugged at me. Harry shouted something at the dogs, which were sniffing me cautiously.

'Do put them in the snug, Harry, won't you?' said Anne and shone a regal smile at me. 'Milk and sugar?'

'Both please. One sugar.'

'I guessed it would be,' she said and handed me the cup she had already filled.

'Told you she has a sense for these things.' Harry called over, shooing the dogs round the door.

I took a sip of coffee and smiled at Anne. Harry returned and grabbed his mug. 'So Sadie, do you mind going over your interest in this as you did with my good lady wife?'

I gave them a brief history, but Harry was full of questions, and soon my story was cutting into the good part of an hour. At some point the coffee was replaced by a bottle of red wine, and, although I had declared that I was driving, a full glass appeared before me.

I tasted it when Harry finally allowed me to get on to the diaries. Bringing that part of the story to an end, I asked him if they were still in the house.

'They are no more,' he said. 'I'm afraid they perished in a fire not long after that article was published. We sold what was left of the collection after that. Brought us nothing but bother if I'm honest.'

I was immensely disappointed but it gave me an opener to what I really wanted to know. 'That's a real shame. You must have had a lot of interest in it?'

'Oh yes,' Harry's eyes darted to Anne's. She nodded imperceptibly. 'There was a flurry of activity when we decided to sell.'

'We had a university who wanted to study the diaries,' Anne continued. 'But after the fire that petered out.'

I opened my notebook and took out a photo of Mum circa '99, all shining black locks and sunhat. 'Do you remember if she looked at them? I think she may have. Do you know her at all?'

Harry took the photo and squinted.

I held my breath.

'Not sure. Need my glasses.' He made no move to get them but passed it to Anne who had a pair dangling round her neck on a golden chain. She slid them along her nose.

'Yes, she came and looked at them.'

I swallowed. 'She looked at the diaries? Did she say why she wanted to look at them?'

Anne took her glasses off and twirled them in her hand. 'I think, though I can't be entirely sure – it was a long time ago – she said it was personal. Nice woman, if I remember correctly.'

'Personal.' I repeated her words. 'Why?'

Anne dropped her glasses and grasped her hands. 'No idea. I merely let her view the collection.'

'Did she say anything? After she'd read them?'

'Not that I recall. Thanked me and went on her way.'

That stumped me. Mum had never expressed an interest in Hopkins before. Well, not that I'd noticed. True, we'd talk about politics and literature and she was interested in local history, but that was about it.

Anne had turned to Harry. 'I think it was only a couple of days later that the American showed up.' She stressed the word *American*. Harry nodded, made a tutting noise then looked at her.

One of the dogs in the snug yelped.

His wife nodded. 'He was very interested in Nathaniel's diaries. Very. He made us an offer for the document.'

'A very handsome offer,' Anne repeated.

'We said no,' Harry said.

'He was most disappointed,' Anne added.

'Bordering on hostile,' Harry chimed. 'They get like that, some of those Americans, don't they? Think money's the answer to everything. But then we had the fire in the study.' His voice dropped. 'Unusual eh?'

'Oh Harry, don't go on,' Anne sent me a wink. 'He loves a good conspiracy.'

'Why didn't you sell them?' I asked, keeping them on track.

'They belonged in a museum or a university,' said Harry firmly. 'Personally I'm not fussed but it was what Uncle Alexander wanted.'

'Sorry, Uncle Alexander?' Where had that come from?

'From whom we inherited the house and the collection. He was an academic. Obsessed with the Civil War. Spent a lot of time building up a library of authentic witness accounts. He was writing what he considered to be, *the* definitive book on the subject when he died. I believe he bought the diaries in a private sale after they were discovered in an old house near Chingford. The family had to give it up and sold it to a developer who wanted rid of the contents.' He smiled fondly. 'Recorded everything in his notes did Uncle. Fastidious.'

The clock on the wall struck five-thirty.

'His notes?' I said.

'Oh yes,' Anne said brightly. 'There's reams. All stacked up in chronological order. We never got rid of them.'

'Seemed disrespectful to the old man,' said Harry. 'You might want to see them. I haven't looked at them all properly. Keep meaning to but somehow never find the time. You should read the early stuff; I think that there's a transcript of the diaries in there somewhere. Can't be authenticated, though. Just his notes. Worthless now really.'

I doubted that; if they could give me more information as to what Mum had been looking for then they could be priceless. And there might be additional information in there for my book. At the very least, I could plunder some of the phrases for quotes.

'Sadie,' Anne said looking at the clock, 'why don't you join us for supper?'

I thanked them for their generosity but said I'd really like to see the transcripts, if that was possible. If they said no, I'd consider taking them up on their offer and trying again later. I wasn't going anywhere without seeing those pages.

'Of course, have a look and let us know. There's rather a lot of them. You might have to come back tomorrow.'

I was delighted and nodded vigorously at Harry who stood up. 'Here, let me show you where they're kept.'

He led me through the snuffling dogginess of the snug into the large hallway. I watched him walk with his chin up, almost as if it was a gesture of defiance against the older parts of the building that whistled and shrieked. Harry trudged along a wide gallery, then held aside an old tapestry that concealed a narrow hallway. At the end of this he opened a door.

'The study,' he said. 'This is where the fire broke out. Don't worry, it's all fixed up now.'

'Gosh,' I said, taking in the room as Harry flicked on the lights. 'Thank you.'

It was smallish, with a large window at the far end draped in heavy red velvet curtains. The wall opposite me was lined with bookshelves from floor to ceiling. In between the gaps were dozens of framed pictures; some were certificates, others miniatures, sketches and ancient documents. In the middle was an oak writing desk, its legs labouring under the weight of a huge, borderline-antique, computer. The Phelps were obviously not technically minded. There was a leather writing square, with a blotter on one side and over that, a reading light.

'What a lovely reading room. Is the transcript in here?'

Harry nodded, picked up a pair of spectacles that lay on the corner of the desk and went to a section of the book-shelves over by the window.

'The Braybrook diaries come in at volume seventeen,' he said and put the glasses on to read the spines. 'He indexed everything.' He selected several leather notebooks and carried them over to me, putting the pile on one side of the desk. Then he switched on the reading light, picked up the first volume. Opening it on the desk, he fingered a number of pages, and pointed to a section.

'Start here, if you want.' Then he quietly switched off the main lights and exited the room.

I sat in the chair and stared at the book, illuminated in a circle of white.

With a tingle in my fingertips I began to read.

Chapter Thirty-Nine

Nathaniel Braybrook had lived in a turbulent time. An educated man, he was the only son of a well-to-do merchant based in London. Despite the unpredictable nature of business, fortune had shone on the Braybrooks, enabling them to come through the bloody Civil War largely unscathed, if not a little worse off.

It appeared Braybrook had links to the wool trade in Chelmsford that necessitated some travel between there and his family home in Epping, and it was on one of these journeys in 1644 that Braybrook witnessed the execution of the witches. His account lent me no new understanding of the trial, describing the process as I had read it so many times before in pamphlets. But there was one line that drew my attention. Braybrook, it seemed was a religious dissenter, traumatised by the unspeakable acts of violence that were part and parcel of everyday life during the Civil War. He supported neither the royal cause nor the extremism of the Puritans. In fact, I read in Alexander Phelps's notes that Braybrook was later to become part of the religious movement that grew into the Quakers. The man obviously had a conscience, which informed his later actions.

Writing up the hangings he recorded this: '*The haste with which the deed was done was ungodly. I did sight the wretch who confess'd passed off. How much of the covenant she did freely declare amongst some there is great doubt. Her being fore known as a Christian in her village.*'

This had to be a reference to Rebecca. An incident that I had 'seen' myself – Rebecca being 'passed off'? I flinched as the sight of Anne West's scalp skittered across my mindscape. Such brutal times, so harsh and inhumane. If only Rebecca had known that there was someone in the crowd who was not so full of blind hate.

The transcript went on to describe Braybrook's hasty retreat from the scene and his journey home. The next wedge of pages testified to his daily life, seasonal observations and rumours from London about the King. There was a mention of the Suffolk trials: '*This Witchfinder and his man, Stearne, have inflict'd such greate pain and agonie on many who were innocent but for loss of their senses. They say they do take much delight in the torment of these soules and the procurement of money from villages to feather themselves a good nest. More than four score were sent to their deaths, in that County, and some only childs.*'

I copied it down and flicked through the pages till I reached the end of that volume. The text was fascinating but not incredibly useful. I was in two minds as whether to read the next volume; sleep was calling me and the wine had dulled my senses.

Thank God I did.

It began in March 1647. I read about Braybrook's exploits with some degree of interest until I came to another entry concerning Chelmsford, dated to August. This journey took

Braybrook further north, to a merchant in Ardleigh, a village set between Manningtree and Colchester. My heart began to quicken as I read his words:

'*A bad day of trade. Glad to leave. Towards Colchester, my horse did much afear'd rise up for a figure did shoot forth from the hedgerow. I was thrown and once recover'd saw a young woman fallen across the way. She was much aggriev'd and beset by woe, without her wits. I was loathe to leave her and so did pick her up and transport her to Colchester town, whereby I install'd her in a room at my lodgings.*'

I turned the page. The next entry was presumably dated to the following day although there was nothing on the transcript to indicate a break in time but a couple of blank lines.

'*The morning I visit'd the market. When I return'd to the Inn, the woman was recovered in the flesh, yea still pale as milk. She did put me in mind of my own dear daughter Catherine who departed from this world twenty years long. Her's too was hair the colour of moonless nights, eyes a paler stone. In those attributes the likeness was striking. But at this present time the young woman's wits are disorder'd and her spirits much distress'd.*

Later upon learning it was I who roused her and conveyed her to this place she did, straight off, throw herself at my feet and cried out for some small "mercy". Alarm'd I bid her tell me her sorrow.

The dreadful tale she did recount most provok'd me. For she had been cruelly treated by a gentleman who had stolen her virtue and left her with child. Some moneys being left for her upkeep did afford her a modest cottage. Though this did not last long and soon she was cast out of doors. Shunned by the village and shamed she was reduced to poverty, able only to provide for the child by way of begging.

When she did lately hear that the man had return'd from his travels she sought him out and implor'd him to relieve their suffering. The gentleman did give her a guinea and, seeing she could not care for the child, took it from her to be nursed.

Rebecca, for that was, I learnt, her name did find herself in grievous distress, enduring great misery without the babe and soon did repent of her decision. When she went to the gentleman for her child he was terrible cold. He scorn'd her and did throw her off. Rebecca swore before him she would repeat her pleas time and again in his ears until he did tell where the child now liv'd. The gentleman did wickedly laugh and tell her she could ne'er follow him where he was bound. When she pressed him he did boast of travelling the morrow to London and henceforth voyage across the sea.

Rebecca's spirits flew about her heart. She was put into great fright and made off to find her cousin, Robin Drakers, most recently returned from war. I had stumbled over her as she made that journey to his house in Boxted.

I was sincerely affect'd by her discourse and truly her tale did fire my heart. She did appear very like Catherine, her being of small size and brittle. My daughter, though, did have me. Rebecca had none there to look to but her one cousin. As she spoke I was driven to such an extremity of vexation as the like never known to me. My inclination was to assist the woman in finding Drakers and I did tell her such forthwith. This proposal was met with tears of gratitude and warmth. Soon I did call for a horse and coach and, having made preparations for victuals, we set off for Boxted.

This at last did pacify her as well as it could for the hours we travell'd over the bad ground.

Once reach'd Boxted we spent little time searching for the cousin and when we discover'd his dwelling he was at home. Rebecca did straight off avail him of her plight and beseeched him to petition the gentleman to release her child. Robin Drakers had more years in age, far greater stature and strength than his fairer cousin. His face was rough and scarr'd by battle. I could see that he, in his circumstance, was past the operation of fear. Now, Rebecca did call the gentleman by his name and I saw Mr Drakers did catch some meaning when she said it – Master Hopkins. His face did tremble and when he spoke it was with a raised voice and dark countenance. He did foreswear to make haste unto the Port of London, to find the Gentleman and bring him back. Rebecca did at once stand up and entreated him with desperate pleas only to find the child. At length he consider'd this and so did agree to be led by her need. Thereby he promis'd to deliver the whereabouts of the child. Mr Drakers did accompany Rebecca and I to Colchester. Then with monies secured by myself he did procure a horse and set forth for London.

I cannot but reflect as I commend these words that my perception and concern in the matter has been sent from the heavens. It is my belief The Almighty God did place Rebecca in my path as he so placed the half dead Levite for the Samaritan to pity. He did bandage his wounds and pour on oil and wine, and so brought him to an inn and took care of him. As Christ did show the way I too shall follow.'

I was gobsmacked. Could this be my Rebecca? I felt sure that it was. The time was right, the name was right. Even the locale was spot on. So cruelly treated by a 'gentleman'?

Hopkins. I remembered a dream when I had seen a man come onto me – a nightmare creature with red eyes and stinking breath that smelled like tar? Was that a vision sent from Rebecca? Had the Witchfinder taken her and separated her so he could enjoy his dirty concubine? I shuddered. It had certainly been suggested by a couple of historians.

I started to copy the passage down into my own notebook but realised I was too impatient and needed to read on to find out what happened.

Irritatingly, Braybrook blabbed on for a good page recording his business in Colchester, but then he returned to the Inn. Here he found Rebecca in a terrible state, worried by her cousin's continued absence. It seemed she had been expecting him back that day. I reckoned that was too opti-mistic if Drakers made the journey from Colchester to London on horseback; it was a distance of about forty-five miles. A good horse could cover, what forty or fifty miles a day? There and back. That's at least two days. Mind you, if this was Rebecca West, which I was becoming convinced it was, she probably didn't have a clue about distances. I doubted if she had ever gone further south than Chelmsford, for the trial.

Braybrook entered some calculations and made an appointment to see a merchant the following day. Rebecca, he said, was taken with 'the ague', which forced her to retire to her quarters. He recorded she was given a potion of herbs by the innkeeper's wife. I raced through to the entry for the following day and found Braybrook's account of what happened next.

'*Robin Drakers did arrive late of the afternoon. He had the appearance of one greatly vexed. He did take me aside and tell these words: Having arrived late he did secure lodgings and the following day made his way to the dock. By and by he discovered there were no ships to sail that day. The vessel bound for New England had depart'd. Compell'd by his cousin's desperate plea he did go to see the offices, and did speak with the shipping clerk. He was not forthcoming yet once his hand had been greased with coin he did show Mr Drakers the passenger list. The gentleman was known to the clerk, for he had some trade once with the company. The clerk took out the ledger and showed Drakers he had set off with a different name, wanting to obfuscate his true origins, for the country was much turn'd against him. Mr Drakers did pay for the notice and, not being schooled in reading, did bring it for me to inspect. The clerk had noted the entry of the gentleman with his true initials "MH".*

This was a great disappointment to us; for now we were at a loss what to do. It was ill fate. We had no remedy but to tell Rebecca her gentleman had depart'd and taken the secret of the child's whereabouts with him. The pitiable woman was full of horror at those words and turned as pale as death and, sinking into the chair, she fell down into a swoon. It was a good while before she fully recover'd her senses and she was not able to speak for severale minutes. Then she gave a start, "It cannot be." And begged me to take her to Manningtree with a conviction that no one could resist.

After consultation with Mr Drakers our plan was set out to go there on the morrow.'

The next entry was dated two days later – August 18th, 1647.

Despite the comfort of the twenty-first century what I read next shocked me to the quick. Even Alexander Phelps's handwriting wobbled and looped towards the end.

'It is with a full and heavy heart I write these words. The conclusion of the matter was not what was hop'd for.

Rebecca was deep laden with grief as we travell'd to Manningtree. Drakers and I did much to give her hope that we would find her little daughter.

Our thoughts were to first settle at the coaching Inn and then ride out to where Master Hopkins once liv'd. We would then find to where the child was sent and take her to Rebecca.

Alas, it was not to be.

We came into Manningtree after noon. The innkeeper was much taken aback by Rebecca and it took a small sack of guineas to persuade him of our good character. We dined and then left Rebecca at the Inn. She did not wish to accompany us and was much troubled, pacing to and fro.

We made out for Mistley and found the house with ease. We were announced by the servant and were met by the occupant, a Mr Witham, preacher. We did introduce ourselves and with much caution and speaking around did suggest our story and explain at length our aim. Presently we did ask if Master Hopkins had there resided.

The preacher was much amazed by our tale and confessed much puzzlement.

"Master Hopkins, a wise and pious son," said he, "lies in the ground of Mistley Church these six days pass'd."

Drakers and I were astonished.

"This cannot be," says I. "We have report he has left for the New World."

The preacher answer'd he would scarce believe that, lest it give his wife hope for she was much aggriev'd by the loss of her good son. At this Drakers did stand up and said with great fury, "Not so good as to leave my cousin with child. And to

361

send said child away to be nursed. Where is she? My heart trembles for fear of what you have seen and heard. Where is she? I will go to the magistrate of the town."

At this Witham, very grave, did take my arm to solicit a private interview. Seeing the fear Drakers had put on him I agreed and he led me to a smaller room.

Here he told me his knowledge of Rebecca. And most grim did say her mother was a wicked unchristian woman who fell in with a coven of witches. They were discover'd by Matthew and henceforth tried and hanged. Rebecca too was tried but repented and was so freed. Her senses, he said, had been touched never to recover. Her story was but fantasy. She was enraged by the passions of madness and a secret burning lust for revenge. Hopkins was dead and they knew nothing of any child. He importuned me to leave the "witch" and to cast her out at once.

I thanked him for his counsel and much shaken did call Drakers to my side and we left the house. I gave him Witham's account and did watch his face as he received it. I was as much taken with the virtue of the soldier as with his cousin's torment and hearkened to his words. Drakers did admit they had been attacked as witches but did swear he had never known witch-craft. That Rebecca and her mother had been godly still to the day that he left to fight. And were it they had no other but he to speake for them then they would not have been taken so low. But he concurr'd Rebecca was made much distress'd by the trial and, some said, had lost her wits.

"Witham says Hopkins is dead," said I. "Rebecca is mistaken."

"There is the ship's ledger," says he.

"Another man," says I. "Your clerk has made a wage of our misfortune."

We returned and found her and did sober and calm convey

362

the preacher's words. She did listen with tears and entreaties. And though she was much reduced to me, her form did quiver and seem most pitiful. Then she withdrew and Drakers and I agreed we should return Rebecca to his house in Boxted. He pressed me earnestly to join him on the morrow one last time so we may ask in the town for the child. If nothing was to come of it, he would take Rebecca and treat her there as his sister.

I was not so hasty in my agreement as I was in my first heat of hearing Rebecca's story.

I said to him with a sigh, "God has led me so far. After the morrow I must continue on my way."

Though his eyes did not meet mine I saw in his face that he took my meaning.

Without more talk we both retired.

Dear God send your humble servant guidance, I prithee.

Lord, I have surely carried through my task. The Levite is healed. Her woes like Job have been of great endurance. But I cannot know if she has abandoned you, Oh Lord. I pray not.

I am in a state of confusion as to the mercy I have bestowed. I give thanks unto the Lord for he is good. God of Gods have mercy on me for I know not what course to take.'

August 19th, 1647

In my prayers last night I did ask the Almighty for guidance. When I awoke I did think of Rebecca's tears. They were real I swear. And Drakers too is a good and noble soldier. I must not be overtaken by the judgement of others.

So with renewed vigour this morning I did accompany Drakers to the village. We left word for Rebecca that we would return soon, perchance with some news.

Many with whom we spoke did tell of another woman come by, asking of the Same – Rebecca had already been about in the village.

After noon we return'd to the Inn but found her not to be in her quarters so went out once more to seek her.

Our search took long and was not fruitful. Yea though afore night fell we did hear she was found and we did hasten to the place, down by the river, where we did find her lifeless form wrapped in the leaves of the weeping willow. If she had come to seek or come to drown we would never know. Nor of the child that griev'd her so.

Drakers stays on to bury the girl. And I must away home.

May God have mercy on her soul. May piteous Rebecca now find her peace.

As I pulled my head up from the page I could feel myself beginning to whirl, as if someone was spinning me round in the chair, and then I was there in the brook with violent pains in my head. The cold wetness, yielding, took me in and took me down.

'*Oh child of mine forgive me. Sweetling babe I will watch o'er you now. Through the tides of time and fortune I will follow you even now.*'

The water came above me and I breathed its cold hard kiss; falling down into the darkness that led me on to the abyss.

Chapter Forty

I was staring at the wall. My face was wet. A pounding melancholy had me in its grip. The words of *The Weeping Willow* echoed round my head: pale and wild, pale and wild. It was about her – I saw that now. Rebecca's story was so very moving: she was a victim time and time again, utterly without power, abused and betrayed by those around her, reviled as deviant. Even after she and her mother had long passed away, her reputation remained tarnished – the witch, the child-killer. So wrong on both counts. But none denied it. The Essex folk who survived the Civil War and the witch hunts merely turned their faces away from the episode. What was the point of crying over spilt milk? Best to let sleeping dogs lie, I could almost hear them say. The clichés that allowed everyone to forget what had happened and turn it into a myth, a simple story about good and bad.

Perhaps the reason why Essex hadn't yet managed to confess its guilt, when other places had owned up to theirs, was simply because it was just too great. All those women. All that death. Too much. Too awful to conceive that they were innocent after all. The victims of bullying.

And so the unfair lives, endured by those they had

shunned, their consequently terrible deaths, were put aside and excluded from living memory. Not mentioned. Hushed into nothingness by the Essex folk's willing collusion. If you maintained the witches' guilt then you could justify the suffering imposed on them: the weak, the old and the poor, the disabled.

That was what Essex had inherited. Complicity.

The notion physically repulsed me.

The whole thing did. And for a good long minute, after I had finished reading, I sat at the desk, covering my mouth as I dry retched. The salty trickles of sweat that crawled down my face could have easily been tears of shame.

Poor, poor Rebecca. To lose not only her mother by her own hand, but her daughter too. No wonder she was trapped in some dark place, seeking forgiveness that no one could give.

Though now I knew what she needed, perhaps I could supply it. Perhaps, and this was a long shot, something had created a short-cut across time, that let her hear my voice, as I heard hers. I could assume her daughter's place and give her the clemency she so desired.

And could I clear her name too? And nail that bastard Hopkins? My spirit girl was right all along – he wasn't buried in Mistley. The only problem was, I cursed as I mopped up my face, these were only transcripts. If the originals had gone up in smoke then there was no real proof at all. It was gutting. I guessed at least it pointed to him arriving in New England; I could start searching for evidence of Hopkins on the other side of the globe. But it would be just as hit and miss. And if he *had* changed his name, as the clerk stated, could I ever work out who he was?

I sighed. I'd be stabbing in the dark.

As I left the seventeenth century and allowed the twenty-first to reassert itself over my senses, I realised I had been staring at one of the pictures set on the wall, a small one positioned just above the desk.

There it is. A voice spoke inside my head. *Take it.*

This time I didn't deny the fragile voice. Be strong, I thought, for her.

'Where?' I said aloud.

There, beneath your gaze.

There.

She was more commanding now.

I craned forwards to take a better look at the picture. It was a yellowing parchment, edged in dark green velour. Spidery writing skittered across three columns. At the top I saw a date '1647'.

No. It couldn't be. *There.* It came again.

I wasn't frightened. I reached out and took it off the wall. Sandwiched between a piece of wooden board and a clip frame was the page of a passenger list, the like of which I had seen at the Archives.

My eyes raced over the names and occupations.

For a moment the world stopped as the letters formed themselves into words and then kicked my senses about: 'Preacher, 27 years'. Heart rate increasing, I sucked in the air and drew my finger across the line. And there I saw it – in the margin, in a faded blue ink, there were two initials: an 'M' and an 'H'.

Then I read the name.

A flurry of excitement raced through me.

I recognised it.

From where, I couldn't remember, but I had seen it somewhere before.

I took out my notebook and with a shaking hand, wrote it down.

Chapter Forty-One

I desperately wanted to phone Maggie, but I had no signal out here and my battery was low. I'd do it when I got back to the pub. I knew she'd be electrified by what I had to say.

I gathered up my stuff and went downstairs. It was gone nine. Anne and Harry were seated in the snug, the dogs at their feet stretched out in front of a hearty fire. The whole place smelled of weed.

Harry was staring glumly into the fire, a glass of wine in his hand.

They looked up as I marched in and threw myself into the armchair. Anne asked me if I was all right.

I nodded, though I was buzzing. 'Have you read those journals?' I asked them breathily. I hoped they had. I wanted to talk about it, to share it.

Harry shook his head. 'Some of them. Bit dry for me.'

I felt like *I* was stoned. My thoughts were leaping around, following each other quickly but illogically. 'I know they're not the real thing but they are still very important, in my view. Especially when they can be supported by this. It's going to be of major significance to my writing.'

I stretched forwards and put the frame in Harry's hands. He rubbed away some of the dust and held it out to read.

Anne leant forwards to see and put her glasses on. 'What is it?' she asked.

I blew out my cheeks. 'I think it's a page from a ship's ledger. Can you see the date?'

Anne read it. 'August 1647.'

It was definitely enough time for Hopkins to get over to New England, settle himself down and then start on Margaret Jones in Boston. Evidence against her was presented in spring and she was watched in May.

'Look at the name.' Both sets of eyes obeyed me. 'Jediah Curwen-Dunmow. See the initials next to it. I think they relate to Matthew Hopkins. It's borne out by the Braybrook diaries.'

Harry shrugged. 'The Witchfinder General. Nasty chap.'

'Yes,' I said. 'But this makes it look like he went abroad, to New England. It's possible it was he who started the witch hunts over there. This is an important document. You must take it to the university with the journals. I think they'd be able to authenticate it.'

'Fascinating,' Harry said. He seemed genuinely delighted to have facilitated the discovery.

I would have thanked them but my mind was on other things: where had I seen that name? Why would I have seen it before?

I fed it into my mental filing system. When had I come across it?

Recently, I felt sure.

In my research?

Had I covered it in a story?

I jerked my head up at Harry. He was saying something about his Uncle Alexander and how proud the family would be but I interrupted. I was over-animated now. 'Do you have the internet here?'

'The computer is in the study but the connection out here is very slow.' Anne was apologetic. 'We don't use it often. A round robin at Christmas, that sort of thing. We'll use it more often when they upgrade the area . . .'

'But you have got a connection here?'

She nodded.

'I know the name – Curwen. I've seen it somewhere before. Does it sound familiar to you? No. Okay well, I'll log on with my laptop. Do you mind?'

They didn't.

I ran through the hallway and outside. In the front garden the air had grown stiffer, the rain harder. The moon had dropped out of the billowing clouds, replaced by a flowing seascape of turbulent streams and speeding, spreading dark masses.

I retrieved my laptop from the boot and turned around quickly, catching for a second a movement behind the top window. I stopped and looked again. Nothing there. It was dark inside the house. Perhaps it had been the shadow of the trees in the wind.

My heels crunched over the gravel of the drive. I shut the thick wooden door on the squall outside, feeling the resistance of the streaming air trying with all its might to get in. The house was as solid as a mountain, built to withstand the elements, though there were obviously cracks. A scream of wind forced through a small opening somewhere on the first floor and whipped down the stairwell.

Within seconds I was back in the snug, logging on with the Phelps's password.

'Curwen-Dunmow,' I told them as I put it into a search engine. 'Have you never looked it up before?'

They shook their heads dumbly. 'Not got that far,' said Harry.

'Right,' I said. The connection *was* slow. I could see why the Phelps didn't use it much.

At last the engine brought up its searches. The purpling of the top entry indicated that I had been here before. Almost automatically I clicked on the link without seeing what the site was.

I wish I had. It might have prepared me.

Forty-five seconds passed then the engine chugged onto a page that I recognised.

'Fucking hell,' I gasped and didn't apologise.

'What is it?' Harry snapped.

I was speechless for a moment and then I said to him, 'Jediah Curwen-Dunmow. He's the ancestor of Robert Cutt.'

Chapter Forty-Two

For a second we sat motionless. Then Anne came over and looked at the screen, reading up and down the family tree. I was staring at Harry with my mouth open. My brain wasn't steady: a thousand different voices clamoured within.

This changed everything.

Everything.

Time seemed to pause.

I started to feel very hot.

I had no idea what the other two were thinking. But it seemed like the name had made an impact. They were adding things up too.

Finally Harry swallowed. 'Well, I'll be damned,' he said at length.

Anne breathed out a long sigh. 'The American. The one who came to see the diaries. Think about it. Robert Cutt – he's American too isn't he?'

'We were reading about him in the papers at the weekend,' Harry added. 'Political ambitions scuppered by scandal or some such.'

'Mmm,' I said, agreeing.

'Good lord,' said Anne and perched her rear on the arm of the chair. 'Do you think he knows?'

I wasn't sure. 'The American connection could be a coincidence. Cutt might not have a clue at all. Although when that article was published it must have registered on several radars. It's pretty easy to monitor the press. There are agencies that do just that. You just have to let them know what to look for and they'll send you any relevant cuttings. There's nothing cloak and dagger about it. We use one at *Mercurial*.'

Anne reached out and put her hand on Harry's shoulder. 'Then we had the fire.'

I nodded slowly as an uncomfortable image flashed in my head. The word 'Desist' written across the map. It was an order. A couple more occasions drifted up from the recesses of my mind. The man watching me when I had been in the pub with Amelia. The car tailing me from the petrol station. That guy at Dan's place. 'Last night,' I said eventually, 'I was burgled. Maybe I was being warned off.'

'You think it's connected?' Harry heaved in a deep breath.

'As far as everyone else knows the evidence went up in smoke.'

'But how would he know about your research?' Anne asked.

'I've practically been shouting it out,' I said. 'His company are publishing my book.'

'Good lord,' Anne spluttered again.

'But he can't know about everything that's going on in every corner of his domain,' Harry said, more to himself, and tapped the sofa. 'I suppose the timing is crucial right now. If the press published his lineage it might be another blow to his political aspirations.'

'Exactly.' I stood up. 'We need to get this stuff somewhere safe. I need to write this up and then get it to the magazine. I'm not sure Portillion will want to publish my book any more. But someone else will and I know that *Mercurial* will go with it. In fact, they'll love it. The next issue goes to press in ten days. That means within two weeks we can get it into the public domain. That's how we make the knowledge safe – get it out there and expose it. Sitting on it won't do any of us any favours. Can you go up to London soon and get the documents over to the British Museum? Or take them to the university? No actually, the museum will be more secure.'

Harry nodded. 'We're planning on a trip to town next week.'

'Thank you. This is fantastic stuff. Okay,' I said and got to my feet. 'I've got a lot of work to do.'

When I think back to that day I try to remember exactly how I felt right then: if I was scared or worried?

I don't recall those feelings at all and in retrospect I think that was a good thing. It gave me a break. A little reprieve, some time to be excited and feel alive.

I should have relished it. I wish I had.

Things were about to get a whole lot darker.

Chapter Forty-Three

I had to make a considerable effort to focus on the road as I drove back to Ashbolten; the storm was moving on, but the rain was coming down hard and visibility was still very poor. Even so, I couldn't help wondering what the hell was going on. Not just with Cutt, but what had Mum been doing at Treetops? And why had she left me a pointer on my real birth certificate? That continued to perplex me. Dan suggested that Rebecca had contacted Mum. Had Rebecca led Mum there? To show her her story?

When I pulled up outside the pub the rain had eased. The lights in the village were out. A tentative moon popped out from a break in the clouds and coated everything briefly in a wet silvery sheen. I was lifting my stuff out of the boot when something made me look towards the village green. It was a small patch of grass with a duck pond, currently empty of fowl, and something white was floating on the surface. From a distance it looked like a large white plastic bag. I took a couple of steps closer. It was larger than that. In fact, it looked more like a pillowcase packed with meat. Or the back of a body. No. That was silly. My imagination had been fired up and was obviously going into overdrive. I turned back to the car, but I couldn't let it go. Damn, I thought and threw my stuff back into the boot. Two minutes, that would be all it would take to make sure some poor sod hadn't trundled out of the pub and into the water. It was a terrible night for it and no one else was about.

I locked the car, put my keys in my pocket and jogged towards the pond. It wasn't very wide, only four metres or so, but God knows how deep it was. As I reached the edge I peered at the lump. It was floating about three foot out, and yes, it did look rather human within its soggy white cloth casing. Several times I looked around for a stick, finding one eventually in the pond, and stretched out to poke and hook it to me. Just out of my reach, I leant dangerously over the edge. Hearing footsteps behind me, I turned slightly, bringing my chin over to my shoulder but keeping my eyes on the floating thing, and yelled 'There's something here. Can you help?' I was only able to catch a glimpse of a man looming when, with one quick move, he shoved me on the back. I put my hands out to grab something, but wasn't quick enough and toppled forwards and into the pond.

The shock of the freezing water squeezed all the air out of my lungs. I flailed about underneath the surface, touching roots and reeds. Something caught around my foot. I struggled against it, with increasing terror, trying to lift my face to the surface. Only everything was black. Where was the surface? The sky? The moon?

Something had wrapped itself around my lower left leg and try as I might, I couldn't kick free its hold. My hands were twitching and jerking as I tried to seize hold of a root or something to climb upwards. Whatever had hold of my foot tugged me down into the depths of the pond. Breath escaped from my lungs in a thin stream, brain and heart galloping in an echoing yet muted drumbeat that resonated out of me and into the dark water.

I panicked. Opening my mouth, I tried to scream, and liquid rushed in and began to fill me up, its cold infecting every part of me.

My sense of self and of struggle began to diminish. I could feel my body giving up the fight, my lungs preparing to accept the water. Then, suddenly, there was another form in the blackness – a pale ghost-white face, dark hair floating in feathery tendrils about her.

Rebecca loosened the grip of the thing around my foot and moved me. Before I reached the surface I saw bubbles stream from her mouth. Through the grimy water I heard the words 'Not yet. Go.' And then I was rushed upwards.

Breaking the surface of the pond I clambered to the side. Water still clogged my throat. I drew air into my lungs swiftly.

How I managed to pull myself out, I'll never know. The wind was screaming through the village as I uncurled at the side of the pond. I gasped greedily, trying to get the cold air into my lungs – aware that across the green, a black car was speeding into the night.

Chapter Forty-Four

Bob was in the small bar pulling back the heavy velvet curtains. The grey morning sky did little to perk up the gloom of the empty pub mid-morning. He nipped behind the counter and unpacked a dishwasher of last night's pint pots, clocking my pale face and the rings under my eyes as I came through the door. 'Good night was it, eh?'

I felt like I'd not slept a wink.

After staggering from the pond, when I finally reached the safety of the pub I locked myself in my room and put the chair against the door.

I was physically shaking from head to toe, with the cold and with fear. But when you are in such a desperate situation it's almost like a greater self takes over. I could have sat there and shivered all night but I knew I had to take control.

I ran a bath and got out of my clothes. Once the water roused me and returned my body temperature back to something approaching normal I made a sugary tea. Then I wrapped myself up in the duvet and lay on the bed. Of course, it could have been a drunk teenager or local lout who had pushed me into the pond as a prank – but it could also have been someone connected to Cutt. And who was it who had held on to my leg?

Thank God for Rebecca, I thought. 'If she hadn't come then . . .' I didn't complete the thought. Instead I was caught up in hysterical laughter. Was I thanking the lord above for the intervention of a ghost? Was I really that far gone?

'Oh dear, Ms Asquith,' I whispered to myself. 'What are you doing?'

Finding no answer to my question, and in the absence of anyone else, I hugged myself.

Never before had I so desperately yearned for my mother's embrace.

When I came round in the morning I was foggy. I ordered breakfast in bed and despite lack of appetite, made sure I ate everything. I had to be strong, to have my wits about me. The revelations of last night and the consequent dunking had left me in a state of intense alarm, but, at the same time, I found my resolve had hardened. If I was going to stick my beak into people's business I had to be careful. There were some out there prepared to go to extreme lengths to keep their secrets safe. That was now as clear as day.

'How much do I owe you?'

Bob wrote out a docket and passed it over. I handed over the money, thanked him and told him I'd be off.

'Hope you weren't woken up by all the commotion this morning?' he asked, fiddling with the cash drawer.

'What was that?' I rotated my body round to the till. Bob wore an amused grin.

'Had a prowler in the backyard near the guest rooms. Early. About sixish. The wife heard it. Reckons something

380

fell over by the back door. So she goes to the window and sees a man there. Scarpers as soon as the light comes on.'

'Did you catch him?'

'No. Glenys called the police. They weren't too fussed. Said to call if it happened again.'

'Oh dear,' I said earnestly and turned back to the room.

'Not a boyfriend of yours?' Bob called after me.

'Chance'd be a fine thing,' I called back, heart thumping as I scurried down the hallway. They were ramping it up. What was I meant to do?

The only way I could see to protect myself was to write this down and get Maggie to publish as soon as possible. Maybe she could go to print early? There was always the *Mercurial* website too.

In the room, I sat on the bed, plugged in my mobile and charged it up. Three text messages and two missed calls. I had no time to listen to them now though. There were more pressing things – the prowler. It was such an old-fashioned word, laced with misplaced sexual undertone, but I doubted very much that last night's mysterious intruder was after knickers on the washing line. It was obvious now that one of Cutt's people was onto me. Not only that, but inadvertently I may have led them straight back to the Phelps.

If they were reckless enough to start fires, break into my flat, or even attempt to drown me (if last night's bath in the duck pond was their handiwork), who knew what they'd do to the Phelps?

I had to warn Harry and Anne. I started dialling their number, then stopped and threw the phone on the bed. Was I being paranoid or could they have a trace on my phone?

Was that ridiculous?

I stared at the mobile for a moment, then decided whatever was happening, I should err on the side of caution.

Within seconds I was back in the bar, asking Bob if I could use the pub landline. He pointed me in the direction of a call box by the door.

It was Harry who picked up.

'Hi,' I said breathily. 'It's me, Sadie. I think Cutt's people may have been here last night.' I avoided telling them about the incident at the pond. 'They may even be watching your place now. Is there any way you could get up to London today and sort that thing out?'

He didn't seem to process the urgency in my voice. 'We've had a look at the journal after you went. Couldn't resist it. Terrific.'

'Harry, listen, I think you should get out of the house now. Do you think that's possible?'

'Let me talk to Anne.' The phone clanked and I heard the heavy breathing of one of the hounds sniffing the speaker. A minute later he came back on. 'We'll leave within the hour.'

'Great,' I said, feeling more relieved than I expected. I thanked him and asked him to text me when he'd sorted it. Then I hung up and returned to my room.

When I got through the door my mobile was ringing.

'Hello, there. How's our newest author?' It was Felix.

Where did he fit into all of this? I couldn't believe that he knew anything about it. He was, after all, just an editor. Pretty low down in the pecking order. If Cutt told him what was going on, then Felix would become another potential leak which would have to be monitored. It was doubtful that Felix had a clue; though it wouldn't look awry for Cutt to ask about the book. I remembered Delphine's words,

'Robert likes to keep an eye on things.' I needed to keep my cards close to my chest. Breeze it out. Act like nothing unusual had happened.

'Great,' I told him.

'I've been trying to get hold of you since yesterday,' he said, a hint of irritation in his voice.

I apologised. 'Sorry, I haven't had a signal.'

'You not at home?'

'Following up a lead for an article I'm writing about, er, pub closures.' Did that sound feasible?

Must have. Felix didn't pause.

'I see. Look, can you make it over to Manningtree this afternoon?'

'Um. Well I really wanted to get home. Is it important?'

'Well I don't want to put you out, but I did mention it last week? That expert I was telling you about. I've got you an interview. I think you'll be rather delighted by this particular person. They have a lot to say about your Witchfinder.'

Not more than me I thought, but I humoured him. 'Fantastic!'

'They're only in the country for one more night,' he was saying.

Oh crap. I really didn't want to be driving all the way to North Essex. I wanted to write up this article, expanding on everything I'd learnt, and fleshing out a bestselling book which would undoubtedly not be published by Portillion. Surely with this new information I could get another deal? Though perhaps, Felix's interviewee might strengthen what I knew? Put like that, I guessed it might be worth a detour.

Plus, I could even stay in Manningtree and start writing up the story straight after the interview. The irony of it came to me, clear as crystal. Somehow it seemed right to expose Hopkins in the very place where he had started his awful crusade. He would be turning in his grave.

Wherever that was.

'Are you coming too?' I asked. Felix could act as a protection of sorts.

He paused for a second then lowered his voice. 'Yes, of course.'

'Okay then,' I said.

'That's great.' He sounded relieved. 'I will be at the Thorn Inn from four. I understand the food there is fabulous. I'll buy dinner.'

'Four?' I glanced at my watch. It was gone twelve now. 'That's pushing it I'm afraid, Felix.'

'Five, then,' he said.

I tried to explain that it would be traffic-dependent, but he'd already hung up. He was obviously on a mission.

I was too.

Though, as it was to pan out, only one of us would succeed.

Chapter Forty-Five

How I managed not to clock the date is still beyond me. I guess I had been so sucked into my own internal world I hadn't really noticed the turn of the season around me.

So, as I pulled into Mistley that afternoon, it was quite a shock to see covens of witches and devils running amok through the streets. Halloween, All Hallows' Eve.

The night the dead come out to play.

Of course it was.

To be honest, I would have picked up on it sooner or later anyhow. There was a crackling electricity in the air; a feeling of anticipation and caged energy. Even the houses in the streets glimmered orange, the colour of the festival, and the cobwebs that hung off the rafters had decorated themselves in shiny diamonds of dew.

As if they knew what was coming.

I parked the car in a side street by the Inn, leaving my case and laptop inside for the time being. I might end up staying here. Or maybe moving on to Colchester if I didn't have the bottle for another session in the Witchfinder's den.

The chill of night touched my neck as I got out and locked up. The smell of mouldering leaves, damp grass and bonfires wafted through the narrow street, adding to the undercurrent of sulphur: someone had put on a firework display.

A group of half a dozen children bundled past me, full of giggles and mischief. The eldest, a boy of about twelve, was dressed as a zombie. He waved a chainsaw in my direction.

'Trick or treat, Mrs,' he challenged and held out a plastic cauldron. Inside I could see they'd already netted an unhealthy haul of E-numbers posing as sweets.

'Hang on,' I told them, pretending to go back to the car. 'I've got some apples in here.'

The collective sigh of disgust that issued from the group was highly amusing. A little witch of about four years old lisped in a rural Essex accent, 'Can we not have some sweets?' She was cute, little gold curls tumbling from underneath a cobwebbed witch's hat. Her parents could obviously not bear to hide away her shiny locks.

An older girl, dressed as a vampire holding on to the witch's hand, cautioned her young charge. 'Shelly! It's rude.'

'No it's okay,' I said. 'I'm not from round here and I forgot what day it was. All I've got is some small change. Do you want that?'

The zombie ringleader nodded so I bent over my bag and delved into my purse, cleaning out about three quid in coins. I must have only been ten seconds or so, though when I looked up, the small witch opened her mouth.

'Not in there,' she said. 'Not in there.' Her voice stumbled clumsily over the meter of the words she spoke. Her eyes fixed upon my face, her lips devoid of the excited pretty smile that had been on them only moments before. Her little voice, with its quaint Essex lilt, had become seriously croaky.

'Turn around, you must,' she rasped. Rather bemused, I obeyed her and twisted round to face the zombie. He scratched his chin then looked at me. 'What? No apples thanks.'

'I've got some change,' I told him again and held my hand open.

'Thank you. That'll do.'

'Nice performance,' I told the little witch. 'Very spooky.'

She didn't respond, too intent on watching the zombie scrape every last penny from my palm.

'Make sure you share it,' I told him.

The zombie told me he would and they crossed the road.

I watched them disappear round the corner.

Above the pub a waning moon hovered. Not far off full, its bright illumination revealed the stark beauty of the river opposite. Ivory satin waves shone in flickers on the incoming tide.

Someone once told me the waning moon was good for banishing and cleansing. Perhaps it was.

Inside the Thorn, Felix was waiting at a table. He stood up when he saw me. Despite a ripple of frown lines breaking out across his forehead he looked good. Dressed all in black – suit and turtleneck jumper – his frame looked leaner than before. He rubbed his right hand on his trouser leg and held it out as he kissed my cheek. The cold sweat of his palm transferred onto mine.

'You're late,' he said, releasing me from a micro-hug, then smiled and the lines on his face deepened. 'I was worried you had had second thoughts.'

I stepped back. 'Of course not. Traffic,' I said, taking a seat beside him. Two half-empty cups were on the table.

He sat down heavily and picked the paper napkin out of the wine glass on the table. 'Never mind. This is going to blow your mind. I think we've time for a coffee if you're parched?'

'I'd love one.'

Felix waved the waitress over, booked in another round of cappuccinos and paid for them.

'You look nice,' he said when she'd gone.

You're joking, I thought. 'You too,' I said.

He smiled but his messy brown eyebrows drooped a bit and he looked down, hands picking at the napkin, endlessly fraying the edges. I thought back over our meeting last week in Colchester. He'd been funny, rakish. Now, he was fidgety and more than a little unfocused. Perhaps something had happened at work so I asked, in what I imagined was a supportive tone, how he'd been.

He ran his hand through his hair. 'Oh, you know. Busy. Fine.'

I started to make small talk, but he wasn't tuning in. Instead he nodded, picked up his mobile and flicked it open.

'They'll ring,' he said, as if I'd not said anything at all. Then he replaced it on the table and moved his hands back to the napkin. There were circles of moisture on the phone where his fingers had been.

'Who is this mystery visitor then?' I asked, trying to lighten up. This is what he wanted to talk about, I could see. 'Are they here?'

'No,' he said. 'On their way hopefully. I'll get a call when they're in the vicinity.'

'You going to give me a clue to how they fit in?' I asked.

He tossed his head back and laughed. 'You'll find out. It'd

be a shame to spoil it for you.' Then, he tapped the breast pocket of his jacket. 'Listen, I've got something to show you.'

'I know,' I said.

'You know?' His eyebrows rose right up under his fringe. 'You can't.'

'The interviewee . . .'

'Oh no,' he said. 'Not that. This.' He reached inside his pocket and pulled out a transparent plastic bag. Something white glimmered inside it. The pipe.

'That,' I said and pushed back my chair to get away from it. The blood drained from my face. 'Why have you got it?'

Felix gave me a quizzical look. He appeared not to have noticed my pallor. 'What's the big deal? I know it's a little ghoulish, but . . .' He opened the plastic bag and brought it out. 'It's just an old pipe made of bone. Not unusual apparently for the time.' He put it on the table.

I stared at it, a rash of goosebumps spreading out across my arms. 'Which was?'

'Mid-seventeenth century. Or thereabouts.'

'Hopkins' time,' I said slowly.

'I know,' he said, turning it over in his hand. 'Curious that it all comes back to that.' He glanced at me.

I was too fixated on the pipe to pick up on that last comment. I shivered and pushed his hand further from me. 'Put it away. Please Felix. It makes me feel bad. I think Hopkins had a pipe like that. I think he might have used it to . . .' I broke off. I couldn't say it. I didn't know for sure that it was the same pipe. But it looked just as spiteful.

Felix's face wrinkled into deep lines as he picked it up. An involuntary shudder went through me.

'How does it make you feel?' I asked him.

'Like I own it,' he said, replacing it in his breast pocket like a ten-year-old secreting his favoured conker. Then he grinned and his eyes crinkled. For a second it seemed to me that it was the other way round – that the pipe owned Felix and if he wasn't careful, then something terrible might try to snare him.

Seized by an impossible desire to try and communicate the dread I was feeling, I laid my hand on his arm. 'Listen, Felix, you have to get rid of this. It's . . .' But I was never to complete the sentence as his mobile went off.

Felix jumped up like a cat and scooped it off the table. Darting a smile at me he flicked it open and walked quickly towards the door. 'Yes, she's here with me now,' I heard him say.

The person on the other end of the phone was talking at length. Felix scowled into the mouthpiece, then rubbed his head and bit his lip. 'Really?' He cast a sidelong glance at me.

A couple came through the front door, allowing Felix to duck out past them into the street.

I looked around the place. So I was back here again. At HIS headquarters. Where he had tortured Rebecca and so many more. And what if Felix had brought the pipe back to his master? Jeez. Perhaps after the interview I'd venture so far as to tell him what I thought. Maybe I'd tell him *everything* that I'd learnt. Over dinner. But not here. Somewhere else. Further away. There was no way I was going to spend the night here. I'd drive into Colchester later and find a hotel. I would be more anonymous in a large town. That would help me get under Cutt's radar. And, I thought, it was right to tell Felix. After all, forewarned was forearmed, and he'd been pretty good to me.

The fire popped and spluttered in the grate, making me jump. The newcomers were warming their hands against the flickering glow. I took a gulp of coffee and stretched back into my chair and yawned.

God I was tired.

My eyes lingered on the bar top. It was decorated in Halloween paraphernalia; two glowing lanterns, carved out with sharp jagged teeth, interspersed with floral arrangements entwining pinecones, candles and skulls. A cut-out of a black cat arching its back was fastened above the large fireplace. The candles on our table were stripes of orange and black.

For a journalist, I'd been pretty unobservant. But to be fair, I had a lot on my mind: Rebecca, Mum, Cutt, the Witchfinder. It all came back to Hopkins. God, I could blow it all open. It's what I had to do.

My knee was jiggling up and down in anticipation when Felix returned. As he beckoned me outside, I noticed how he clenched then unclenched his hand.

'What's up?' I asked getting to my feet and going to the door.

'Change of plan,' he said. 'We're going to meet them up the road. They want a little bit of privacy.'

'Okay,' I said, frowning for the first time. 'Why?'

Felix smiled again. 'I told you. This is explosive stuff.'

A thought flashed over the front of my brain. Had he got to the document too? Had the mystery guest? No, couldn't have. Anne and Harry had told the world that it had perished.

Could he have got to them since I'd left Ashbolten?

Not possible. On the way here I'd deleted a text from them

stating they'd got an appointment with the Museum the following morning and were already on the train.

Wow, I thought, could this be something else? Another clue, maybe from the other side of the Atlantic? Some hard evidence to link Hopkins to Salem? Even his grave? It had to be big: this interviewee was flying out tonight but diverting this way for me. That was commitment.

'Come on, love,' Felix tone was so patronising I stopped halfway out the door.

'Why won't you just tell me who it is?' I said, trying to reassert my professional credentials. 'I might need some research on hand.'

'Trust me,' he said and took my arm. 'You'll be fine.'

Felix's hire car pulled out of Mistley to the east. Despite the fine moon a thin mist was coming up from the fields either side.

Away from the domesticating illumination of the streetlights the landscape became wilder. Bald hilltops girdled by bony pricking trees cast shadows that lay oddly across each other. As we journeyed into their darkening embrace something cold descended over Felix.

We drove in silence, watching the road slink furtively towards the shoreline, then reach away into a cluster of pines.

Felix flicked the headlights onto full beam and slowed his speed.

'There's a turning somewhere up here,' he said quietly to himself, as if forgetting I was in the car too. The man was very distracted.

Scouring the countryside I couldn't see the twinkle of a house light for miles. Just varying degrees of blackness.

'You sure it's up here?' I asked, for the first time noticing discordance to my voice.

Felix ignored me. 'Ah, here it is.' He killed his speed and took a sharp left into an old dirt track. Brambles and bushes scraped the metal of the car as we bounced awkwardly down the lane.

'I can't see why we should meet here, rather than at the Thorn,' I was saying. As we reached the end of the lane Felix stopped the engine. In the shadows of the car I could only make out his mouth with any degree of detail. Dour lines descended about his lips, his jaw set into an expression of grim determination.

'I told you to trust me.' His voice lowered.

My stomach responded with a small jump. 'I'm starting to feel uncomfortable about this.'

He looked out the windscreen and smirked. Had I sounded funny? I didn't mean to.

I followed his gaze. Without the lights of the car I could just perceive what looked like the ruin of a cottage, with a footpath veering past its front and off to the left.

'No,' he said quietly. 'It's not comfortable. You're a journalist though. You have to do things that take you out of your comfort zone, right? Come on, Sadie. You're not some cub reporter who's still wet behind the ears. You're seasoned, aren't you?' He sounded slightly fraught, anxious for me to get out of the car. It was probably all bluff and nerves brought on by the important mystery visitor.

Anyway the appeal to my ego worked. It always did. 'Right,' I said, grabbing my bag off the floor and rummaging inside. 'Let me just find my Dictaphone. Ah, there it is.'

Without taking his eyes from the windscreen he said, 'You

won't be needing that,' and in one arching movement leant over and plucked it out of my hand.

I sat there motionless, then I tutted loudly, rolling my eyes over to him. His pink tongue poked out and moistened his lips.

I was beginning to see he had a rather daft sense of drama – or perhaps he was flirting? Had he taken me up Love Lane? Or was that what he intended to do?

Once upon a time I wouldn't have minded but things had changed and right now I had no patience whatsoever for his games.

I took a deep breath and steadied myself, trying to keep the anger out of my voice. 'Don't you think that that's my decision to make, Felix? Can I have it back please?'

He sighed deeply, and then tossed it back to me. 'Leave it in the car.'

My eyes narrowed and I was about to ask, quite sarcastically, why, but he cut in. 'Come on. Let's get this over and done with.'

What was he up to? What should I do? To be honest, I didn't have that many options so I put the Dictaphone on the dashboard.

'Okay,' I said. A shrill note had crept into my voice.

Felix fished around on the back seat of the car and pulled something out then he got out of the car and came round to my side. Opening the door, he added, 'After you, madam.'

For a second I hesitated; wondered briefly how Felix would hold up if we were ambushed or attacked. He had a good build and there was muscle there but I imagined I might have to defend myself. If necessary, I absolutely would, though I was certain it wouldn't come to that. A sudden image of myself running up the lane flashed across my brain. I looked up the track. Mist had filled the gap between the hedgerows. I really didn't fancy going up there on my own and, if I bottled out now, I could end up the laughing stock of the publishing world. If this was as explosive as Felix was suggesting, then of course, precautions might be needed. Other publishers would be on the sniff. I just needed to hold my nerve.

'Please hurry up, Sadie. It's cold,' Felix said, a tone of exasperation threading his words now.

I guess it was the 'please' that made me move. I opened the door and swung my legs, quickly feeling in my bag for my mobile. Touching the solidity of its mass was reassuring. While Felix marched on ahead I opened the voice recorder app and pressed play, replacing it in my bag. It wouldn't be great quality, but it would be a record of sorts.

Felix looked to be making for the cottage but took a sharp left and ducked out along the path. I slammed the car door shut and scrambled after him.

The path was narrow, only a couple of feet wide and bordered by prickly blackberry bushes and towering thistles. Further back the wood pitched up masses of tall spiky trees. Their silhouettes crowded over the top of me and for a second I felt like I was in an ancient cave. There was a cryptic quietness in the wood, a feeling of expectation, like the air itself was waiting to see what was going to happen. Something croaked in the thicket about me. I saw instantly that under the darkness the land was seething with life. Shadows were moving amongst the trees.

The temperature dropped quickly. We had only been trudging down the path a matter of minutes but already my body heat was evaporating and my teeth beginning to chatter. A twig snapped in the undergrowth. My eyes darted to the sound. Flimsy shadows danced in the bracken: willowy, brownish human-sized forms. For a moment I thought there were actually people in the trees, but as I watched they dissolved, only to reform a few feet away. Perhaps they were the shadows of the trees themselves – some trick of the light brought on by the change of perspective as I walked past them.

I hurried to catch up with Felix. 'Where are we going?'

'It's not far now,' he said and marched on. 'Come on.'

I followed him round a corner. For a moment his form was obscured by the overhanging branch of a sprawling oak. When I pushed it back I saw the track widened and came out into a secluded clearing. Up on a little hillock stood a mist-drenched wooden bench, overlooking the river.

Felix was sitting up there. In the dimness of the hazy moon, I could see the bench was empty. Above us, the stars in Orion's belt shone sagely.

'Sit down, Sadie,' he said.

I followed his order. My eyes, adjusting to night vision, perceived a slight sneer on Felix's face.

I looked around. 'They're not here,' I said simply.

He sniffed, though it sounded more of a snort. 'It's me.'

That totally confused me. What was he talking about? I cocked my head to one side, and put my hands on my hips. 'What do you mean – it's you?'

'I'm the one you've come to meet.' His quartz eyes glittered. Shrouded in night, his features had darkened. True, there was still a raffish beauty about them, but now I could fathom a hardness within that I hadn't noticed before.

A dozen scenarios skipped across my brain. 'You mean that they can't make it?'

He tutted and crossed his legs. 'You don't get it, do you?'

'Haven't got a clue,' I said lightly, though another feeling was pushing through the confusion, causing the muscles in my neck to tense.

Felix coughed. 'There isn't an interviewee. Not entirely my idea.' He stroked the front of his sweater. 'Personally I would have preferred somewhere a little more sheltered.' It was like he was speaking to himself. 'Just a ruse. To get you out here.'

A black bolt of adrenalin thrilled through me. Was he flirting? No, the tone wasn't right. He turned to the west, looking out over the river inlet.

'You said "It's me,"' I repeated unsteadily. 'You mean, *you* have something to tell me about Hopkins? Is that what you mean?'

Felix snorted again, keeping his eyes on the distant hills. 'Oh dear,' he said at last. The words were dripping with so much undisguised contempt that immediately the idea that he intended to volunteer information fell away.

That could only mean one other thing: that he must know about the Phelps's documentation.

And he could only know about that if he was indeed working for Cutt.

Bugger.

He knew.

And if he knew then it was obvious what this was about. He must suspect I had the passenger list.

There was no point in maintaining the charade. 'I know what you're after,' I said at last.

He swivelled his head to me, lips pursed. 'You do?' One eyebrow arched.

I nodded slowly. 'It wasn't destroyed.'

'It wasn't,' he said flatly.

'No.'

'I didn't know there was an attempt to destroy it.'

He wanted me to say more but I kept it minimal. 'You didn't?'

'No.' He looked away. I got the feeling he didn't want me to see his expression. This was how he regularly conducted his business, I was sure now: call and response. He called, others scampered up to cater to his every whim. His tone had changed so markedly that I could only conclude that our early meetings with the hint of sexual attraction, the cheery bonhomie, the 'honest' enthusiasm – had been an elaborate illusion.

Shit.

'Do you have it?' he said, still looking off over the far side of the inlet where the river met the south side of the shore.

'Of course not. I'm not stupid.' I was struggling with anger and embarrassment. How had I let myself fall for it? I should have known it was all too good to be true – the book offer, the attention, the flirtation . . .

'Quite,' he said. 'But we *will* get it. It's a matter of time.' It was a simple statement of fact.

Pompous git. 'You'll be lucky.' It felt good to say that. I was back in control. Why not tell him more? See a bit of emotion on that chameleon face. 'As we speak, it's on the way to the British Museum. You will not be able to hush it up any longer.'

'Museum?' He jerked his head back in my direction and

blinked at me. Twice. Then a haughty guffaw of laughter burst from him. He made a dismissive waving motion, as if fanning away a nasty smell. 'Oh dear.'

The reaction was not one I'd anticipated. For a second I felt like I'd been totally wrong-footed, and made an effort to regain myself. 'I don't know why you're so bothered. Has he come down hard on you? He's only your boss for goodness sake. You can release me from my contract and I can take it somewhere else. You're off the hook.'

'Doesn't work like that, I'm afraid. Uncle Robert doesn't like mess.'

'Cutt's your uncle?' I hadn't seen that one coming.

He didn't answer my question, but now I was looking at his profile, remembering the glittering grey eyes, I could see the resemblance.

'There's too much invested in his appointment to chance another cock-up,' he continued. 'I'm afraid there are lots of interested parties who have got far too much at risk.'

I crossed my legs and stuck my chin out, in a faux show of determination. Internally I was going nuts. 'Well, that's not my concern. I know who Jediah Curwen-Dunmow really is. I know about the Hopkins connection. And it's all coming out now. It needs to . . .'

Felix clapped his hands together with delight. I felt instantly as if I wanted to punch him in the face. My fists crushed in on themselves instead.

He threw his head back and hooted like an owl. The sound cut through the clearing and echoed out over the tide. 'You think we *care* about that? Witches. Witchfinders. We can make it all work for us. Robert's ancestry can be overcome. We can make him over as a new Christian crusader if we so wish.'

I was gobsmacked. He was here for God's sake – sitting out with me in the middle of nowhere. Of course he cared about it, otherwise what was going on?

I shook my head. Nothing was making sense any more. 'Well, what's this about? What do you want?' For a second he let his eyes meet mine. His expression didn't add up. There wasn't malice or annoyance in there. No, Felix was looking at me with something akin to fascination.

'Shit,' he said. It was the first time I'd heard him swear. 'We thought you knew. You don't, do you?' he said. 'She never told you.'

I was lost now, unable to keep my cool. 'Who? What are you talking about?'

'My God. You *really* don't know.' The ice was back in his voice. 'He thought you did. A surveillance report stated that you'd found it . . .'

There was no need to ask what – bewilderment was written all over my face.

'Oh dear,' Felix said again. 'You're Uncle Robert's daughter. In another life, we'd be cousins.'

At first his words were totally unintelligible. My brain couldn't process them. Then, as their meaning took hold, I breathed out and felt my body weaken. I steadied myself with a hand to the bench, breathed in a huge gulp of air and suddenly it was like I had entered another world. One where ideas and half-formed notions and different realities converged.

Behind the inert gaze of my eyes synapses were sparking, sending messages from one part of my brain to another, making connections that, I was beginning to realise with a profound sense of unspeakable desperation, I had hitherto overlooked.

In my ears there was a buzzing sound, as if I'd been whacked round the head with a baseball bat.

Cutt's daughter.

It couldn't be.

Cutt – the 'unexpected sperm donor'. Mum had worked in publishing once. She'd been put off by the experience . . . she'd been . . . The shock was so much even my internal monologue was faltering.

I was hot and sticky coming back to Felix, trying hard to refocus on his words.

'And we can't have that,' he was saying. 'Not with the campaign as it stands.'

Now he angled the full length of his body towards me. It was like a solid wall. 'You're not something he's proud of, I can assure you. A little indiscretion at a publishing party, what – thirty-four years ago? Uncle Robert always did have an eye for the ladies. Less so these days, I'm glad to report. Runs in the family.' He crossed his legs away from me and winked. 'Of course, your mother protested and cried rape. So many of them do. Always with a mind on any cash that they can get.' He gave an exasperated huff.

An immobilising numbness was creeping over my frontal lobes and down my face. I managed to open my mouth to speak, but realised that I didn't know what to say. My jaw slacked pointlessly as he continued.

'Robert was, is, a very charismatic man. Liked to get his way. Aunt Sylvia turned a blind eye – everyone did – but Ms Walker was fifteen. And whichever way you look at it, that still isn't legal. Statutory rape I believe they call it. Wouldn't have been back when great great, however many greats, Granddad Hopkins walked the earth. Funny that. Anyway the parents were bought off, and everybody assumed that was that. A few months afterwards some source fed back that your mother was pregnant. Tried to keep an eye on her but she disappeared. Fell off the face of the world.'

He paused for a moment, looking intently at my face. I had no idea what I looked like. Inside I was like a computer going into overload, flitting about without pattern, trying to assimilate everything that was going on, getting more and more battered by every sentence he spoke.

He cleared his throat and removed an invisible piece of lint from his knee. 'Of course, we had feelers out for years. But wherever she was, your mother had done a good job of blending in. She'd become virtually invisible. And she hadn't squealed so we pretty much guessed she wasn't going to.'

I managed to move my hands and ran my fingers through my hair. I wanted to say something. To protest about the way he talked about Mum. But again, I found I couldn't make a sound. Although I was stunned to the core, at the same time, part of me was wordlessly assimilating the information.

'Over the years the threat downgraded and faded to some extent. Didn't seem too much of a priority, other than the fact that you were a walking DNA sample.

'Then one of our guys turned up a picture of you in some magazine. I mean, there was a different name on it but Robert could see you were the spit of your mother. You have the Cutt eyes. I saw the resemblance as soon as you walked in the office door.'

Felix tossed his hair up. 'Unfortunate profession you're in.

Journalism. Couldn't have picked a worse occupation really. Maybe law.' He weighed up the two for a moment as lightly as one might consider whether to buy apples or pears. 'Nah, journalism is what got you going.' His grey eyes glimmered with malice. 'We monitored the situation for a good while. When your mother's health deteriorated and Robert's public profile was getting knocked about a bit we had to move in. And get that boyfriend of hers sorted too. Wondered if she'd told him something.'

A flash of Dan's beardy deranged face whizzed onto my mental screen. Was he telling me that he, that Cutt, had been responsible for Dan's descent into mental illness? I wanted to swear but I was still too traumatised to organise my vocal cords.

'But,' Felix shook his head and tutted, 'your obsession with the witches meant it was only a matter of time before you hit upon Robert. Or that Mummy dear blabbed. We assumed that she hadn't told you. There had been no paternity suit – and who wants to find out they're a rape baby? But if Rose Walker was soon to kick the bucket, she might start confessing. And the cat could simply not be let out of the bag. Too close for comfort, you see. Our hand was forced. It's nothing personal.'

I could hear my breathing coming fast and irregular. My body was shaking as if I was starting to have a fit. I tried to speak again but instead a sob came out. I swallowed loudly then gagged. The action cleared out some of the confusion and I was able to force out a question. 'But what have you been looking for? My birth certificate?'

Felix pushed my shoulder in a foppish, almost camp, manner. 'Don't be silly.' My back was so stiff it hit the bench and ricocheted off again. The movement galvanised me somewhat and I squeezed backwards along the bench, away from him. For now I was starting to sense danger in the air. A quickening of energy.

'Everything's digital now, my dear. We've seen your "Father Unknown". No, it was more an inkling, so to speak. Robert wanted to make sure there was no paper trail. Apparently your mother used to keep a diary as a teenager.'

I sniffed. 'Never saw her write one.'

'No. We concluded that she hadn't kept it or had most likely disposed of it. Took a while but better to be safe than sorry, eh?'

I wasn't sure if I was crying. My cheeks were wet and my hair had fallen across my face. I wiped it back with the sleeve of my coat. 'So what do you want?' The words came out roughly, hurting my throat.

Another big sigh from Felix, this time tinged with irritation. 'We want you to go away.'

He bent over to grab something dark underneath the bench. It was heavy. He grunted at the exertion and brought the object up onto his lap. It was a briefcase.

'You'll find a new identity and papers in here and enough cash to set you up somewhere very far away. I'm sure you'll find that this is quite enough to compensate you for your, inconvenience. So much more than you could ever hope to earn from a book deal or eight.' The clasps cracked open and he held up the interior for me to see.

In the light of the moon, I saw a moth flutter up from folds of banknotes, a passport and other documents. 'Don't worry,' he said. 'It's completely untraceable. You'd have to be FBI to track this.' He passed his hand over the notes. 'The passport is convincing enough to get you out of the country and into the unknown. But from there you're on your own.'

A voice at the forefront of my mind was screaming at me to pick it up and get out of there as quickly as possible. Another wanted answers. 'Does he know what you're doing?'

'Who?'

'Robert Cutt.' I managed to say his name.

'He knows what I'm doing. Doesn't know how I got the passport or what your new identity is. He doesn't want to. What you don't know you can deny in earnest.'

The casualness of it all, the breezy way he was able to talk about the lives of both myself and my mother suddenly hit me and a surge of anger sliced through me. 'You want to buy me? Shut me up?'

'Here we go,' Felix moaned. 'Yes. I thought you'd say that. I didn't want to do this but . . .'

He pushed the lid of the case shut with one hand, revealing in the other, a neat black revolver.

It was pointed at me.

Despite all the commotion in my head, when someone does something like that to you, your survival instinct kicks in. Mine forced me to my feet immediately.

I took a couple of steps across the grass. 'Jesus Christ, you can't be serious. You're joking, right?' I tried to make my voice sound even.

Felix laughed a long thin mirthless chuckle and rose. He threw the briefcase to the floor and carefully kicked it out of the way.

'It all works out well enough: Mercedes Asquith, journalist, is slightly mad and paranoid by all reports. Adored your chapter, by the way. Fantastic for us that you wrote about

405

"seeing" things. It reads well. Loved the Hopping Bridge – the sense of danger in the woods, the visions of the witches. A shrink would have no problem testifying to mental illness – delusion, paranoia, and schizophrenia. Poor Ms Asquith, depressed and unhinged by the loss of her mother, immersed in her silly world of witches, casts herself into the River Stour at Manningtree. It has a poignant symmetry to it, don't you think? And Robert prefers a suicide. It's cleaner. Doesn't leave anything behind. No idea why he didn't suggest that in the first place. Some misplaced or belated paternal impulse, no doubt. Still, he's back in the game now. But you're not, dear heart. Don't worry, you'll make it to page eight when your body washes up. So you'll get some acknowledgement of sorts. But, darlin',' he mimicked my accent, 'your book ain't going nowhere and neither are you.'

My brain was alert now. It had pushed out the other information that had been crowding in and was focused entirely on getting out alive. I threw my hands skywards in a gesture of surrender. 'You can't do this. You don't want to do this. There's a good person inside you, Felix. I've seen it.'

'No,' he said slowly. 'You've seen what you wanted to. I was surprised how easy it was to reel you in. You were a good-looking woman. You should have had more dignity.'

I noted his use of past tense. 'Please Felix. Don't. I can't believe you could do this.'

'Deadly serious,' he said and pulled on the safety catch and waved the gun to the edge of the bank. 'Over there please. I'd prefer not to use this but I will if I have to. The tide is high now. There are strong currents out there. It'll be over in minutes. You won't suffer too much.'

I kept my front to him and backed away two or three

more steps in the direction he'd indicated. I could hear the slap of water on the bank. A quick glance either side revealed a six-foot drop to the waves. I stumbled and stopped. 'I'm not doing it.'

'As you wish. I didn't want to shoot you. I'm not cut out for this sort of thing but it can work for us too: you try to blackmail Robert over some ancient document relating to the family. Although I bring the requested money to the appointed place you become greedy and aggressive. There is nothing I can do but shoot in self-defence. Requires a little explanation of the firearm's presence, but having read your chapter I am already feeling vulnerable.'

I didn't move.

Felix raised the gun and took a step towards me. A couple of moths zigzagged over his head and up to the moon.

Don't they say that when you look death in the eye your whole life flashes before you?

Well, that's not true. No, at that point it wasn't my life but the lives of others that flitted in a montage across my eyes – fragments of love, seconds of distress, moments of anguish. Elizabeth Clarke pushed up to the noose; Susan Cock, afraid, fainting; Rose Hallybread, Joyce Boones . . . the old ones . . . the poor ones . . . the young . . . Anne West silently sacrificing herself. Rebecca. Her vision swam before me, then I blinked and I saw him through her eyes. Felix took another step and it was as if some filmy projection had covered him – dressed in his tall hat, his red rheumy eyes on fire. With black, lank hair dripping off his skull, the Witchfinder stared back.

And then the witches were not in my mind's eye but out there, before me, swirling in the cold autumn night like wreaths of smoke, circling the Witchfinder and me, shooting in between us like ethereal comets, lighting the air with flares of brilliance, sprouting wings like moths, then melting into the atmosphere, reappearing, criss-crossing the space, repeating the pattern again and again. I could feel a churning energy about me. It was coming in through my fingertips, pulsing down my arms, filling me with incredible strength and power. Claiming me.

It had always been there, but latent, until now, on Halloween, it pervaded my entire form, hitting the ground beneath my feet and passing through it into the earth.

Everything that had ever been fell into place.

I was caught in a moment between time and space – a complete and perfect being with no beginning, no end – a single point of conversion. There was no dissonance or fear, only a surge of feeling – a profound sense of strength, justice, duty.

And knowledge.

I gasped out as my conscious mind connected with the feeling and in response the air about me rippled and opened, like a torn veil. Voices came in from different directions. Low at first, like a bubbling stream. Women, old, young, poor, and men, too, pleading, demanding, their words stabbing the air like needles. Then louder, more pressing, urgent, harsh until, like the thunderous trumpet of an avenging archangel, the sounds gathered and contracted into a point and a deafening roar blew out across the world.

The man was spinning round, gripping the gun. He looked at me, pathetically, but I was not myself. One of many and yet of none. The women filled me up. Gone were their limps, their arthritic aches, their fear, loneliness, horror and frailty. Their rage was fuelling my strength and guiding me.

The man's expression changed as I came to him. 'Your eyes,' he said, stepping back from me. 'They're like wish lanterns.' And briefly through the overlay I glimpsed Felix. But then he vanished and the red eyes appeared again. Hopkins.

A blaze of power raged through me. Outside of my own pinprick of consciousness I was aware of others, thousands surrounding me, kaleidoscoping in over my soul, pushing down, concentrating my will.

The man reached out to steady his hand and aim the gun.

I took another step closer to him, put my hand over the barrel and pulled him so close I could smell the stink of decay on his breath.

'You are not going to kill me again,' we said.

I think he knew what was coming. He could see it on my face. Up close I could see his hair bristling with fear. He tried weakly to pull the gun down but my grip was firm. Rock solid, and just as unyielding, I held it still with the force and will of all those waking vengeful souls.

'It ends now,' we told him.

'You can't,' he said simply.

But the dice had been cast. It had to be.

He made to push me to the ground but I held firm. He looked me straight in the eye then, in a single movement, jerked his face forwards and headbutted the top of my nose. Blood exploded into my vision. I blinked, blinded, and took my hand from the gun to wipe the red viscous liquid away. He seized his opportunity and punched me in the stomach.

It was a mistake, for none of the souls within were bound and tethered as before. In fact we were unleashed and free. And very, very angry.

As I hit the floor my feet kicked out and caught his legs. I pushed hard on his shins and threw him off balance, kicked out again and brought him down. There was a crack from his elbow as he hit the ground. With a movement that was at once of me and yet not so, I was on him.

Unable to struggle against all our strength he tried again to wrest the gun from my grip, but failed. This time he took one look at my face, gritted his teeth, then, just as his fingers crept forwards to curl round the gun, it seemed his attention was drawn to something just beyond my head. He paused for a millisecond then stopped moving, his face wrinkled into confusion.

His body twitched back away from me, and I considered the notion that somewhere inside Felix had relented, realised the error of his ways or experienced a brief pang of conscience.

Those thoughts disappeared when I saw his eyes widen into huge semi-circles of white. In them was an expression of utter terror. Suddenly his body went limp.

As I lay transfixed, gazing at him, unsure of what to do, something detached itself from my hair – a tiny winged thing, black and wriggling. It circled the Witchfinder's face then settled on his eyebrow. He released his hand from the gun and tried to brush it off, but another landed beside it. A shiver ran through me as another, then another, then another dived onto his face.

He gasped out and tried to yell but it was no good. Within a couple of seconds his face was swarming with tiny creatures.

Everything happened very fast. The moths became a bobbly blanket covering his features, like an enormous beard of bees that spread over all his face. Only his mouth grew visible as he opened it to breathe. They had been waiting for that. A couple peeled away from his cheek and flew into the red cavern. As his lips opened wider in a silent panicked scream, I saw at least fifty pairs of black wings waddling over his tongue, disappearing behind the curve of his throat. More poured into his mouth, so that shortly his tongue and teeth were no longer to be seen. Groping for air, his hands clutched his face, clawing at his mouth, then flung out in desperation to his sides. That was when he felt me. At least, his knuckles bruised against the barrel of the gun. I don't think he could see what he was doing. I don't think he meant to do it at all. Maybe the moths had got right down inside him and cut off his oxygen supply. I don't know. But I can tell you this – it was over in one quick movement. His upper body spasmed as he squeezed the trigger. There were a couple of flashes or maybe three, and two loud shots echoed across the river.

In the seconds that followed I can't be sure what occurred. Even now I have only a vague memory of being giant-like, of wings and voices and screams, of fire and smoke and dewdrops.

And then it was all over.

411

Chapter Forty-Six

When I came back to myself I could distinguish Felix's form across the grass. The moonlight crawled across him. There were no moths upon what was left of his face.

His body wasn't moving.

From where I lay, maybe three feet away, I just about made out a dark stain seeping over his clothes. I pulled myself onto my hands and knees and crawled to him. My body felt out of sync, as if on some time delay. I couldn't hear a thing – I'd been temporarily deafened by the shots.

Part of Felix's head was misshapen and concave. One remaining red eye stared up into the night sky, unseeing. The expression on his face was a rictus of surprise. His shiny brown hair was covered in thick bloody clumps of matter. I prodded his arm. My hand met with no resistance. A ragged and bloody hole was in the place where his chest should have been.

In the struggle his clothes had become dishevelled. And that's when I saw it – glinting, sticking up from between the ragged exposed ribs.

The bone pipe.

I knew there was something in that bloody thing. An evil

412

or menace that may have even predated Hopkins, but was certainly compounded by him. A dark suckling thing that fed off corruption and horror and fear and blood.

And perverted those who used it.

Felix had given it a taste for blood back then at St Botolph's Priory and now it was guzzling greedily.

'You shouldn't have blown it, Felix,' I said and closed his eye.

Then I trailed my fingers over his chest and grabbed hold of the pipe. With a wrench I yanked it out of his heart. A warm jet of liquid gushed round my fingers, making them slippery, but I kept hold of it.

Wiping the vile thing on his jacket I reached into my pocket for my lighter. There was an old cigarette packet in there. I put the pipe into it, lit the packet and poured the liquid lighter fuel on top. Then I sat and watched it burn.

I don't know how long I stayed there beside Felix's body under the all-seeing moon. The bullet had caught my shoulder and I was losing blood, going into shock. Scared that I was going to bleed out, with a mega effort I raised myself up, washed my clothes down in the river, wiped my fingerprints from the gun.

Then, taking the briefcase, I slipped into the mist, just like my forefather had done.

Chapter Forty-Seven

There was only one place I could go, though I knew I shouldn't.

When he opened the door his face was like a cartoon: all wriggles and frowns. I might have laughed if I hadn't have been half dead.

'You know that shoulder you once offered me?' I said. 'I think I could do with it now.' And then I placed myself in Joe's capable hands.

He wanted to take me to hospital of course. But I wouldn't let him, insisting he stitched me up instead with a sterilised needle and some strong cotton. I was already fading in and out of consciousness by then so the pain never seemed too bad. I can't even remember what it was like now.

What I do remember is Joe's reaction as I gabbled on about what had happened. His face switched into an expression of disbelief as I took him through the last days and finished with the scene on the riverbank. When I showed him the suitcase and its contents his features changed. Then he sat down and put his head in his hands.

I was trying with all my might to keep myself conscious, figuring I had only hours to get out of the country. Felix's absence would be noticed come morning – if Cutt wasn't already alarmed by now.

'You have to get me to an airport,' I told Joe. 'I've got to be out on an early flight.'

He just sat there, cradling his head, passing his hands back and forth over the stubble of his hair. 'I'm sorry to involve you but I didn't know who else to turn to.'

He looked up and I saw that there was fear in his eyes. 'Sadie, you've really screwed this up. Do you have any idea of what a serious situation this is?'

'Of course I do. I'm sorry, really I am. Just give me six hours and then you can report me.'

Joe glared at the floor and for a second his face was so tightly drawn I thought he might start to cry or curse me. 'But you're here now.' He pointed at me, then hit his chest. 'You've made *me* an accessory for Christ's sake.'

'I'm . . .' I gave up. Sorry didn't cut it, but I couldn't think of anything else to say and my vision was coming and going. I was starting to see double.

Joe stood up abruptly. 'I'm a policeman, Sadie. You know that. You've come here for a reason, even if you don't realise what it is right now. Or else you wouldn't have chosen to come to me.'

'Please, Joe.' I couldn't even move towards him. My head was so heavy, shoulder burning, and the disinfectant Joe had dabbed on my cuts was stinging like hell. All my concentration was going into staying upright. 'I need to get some stuff from the flat.'

He pulled on a jacket. 'You have to turn yourself in. It's self-defence. Let me go with you.'

But I was not to be persuaded. Cutt had friends in very

high places. I didn't trust anyone any more, except Joe. And that's what I told him. I think he saw my point.

I thought again that he was going to sob but in the end he stood up. 'Wait here one moment,' he said, then went into his bedroom.

When he returned he had a small holdall.

I made Joe wait for me in the car outside my flat. It was safer for him that way.

I had one last thing to do and for that I needed solitude.

In the living room I pulled the blanket from the mirror. Then I called her up.

'Rebecca, are you there?' My voice was a whisper leached of strength. In the shattered reflection I could see myself swaying from side to side. And I could now feel the throb of my shoulder. But I *had* to do this.

Silence.

'Are you there?' Please come.

A small noise from the other side of fractured glass. A snuffling in the everworld.

'Yes, I'm here.' Her voice, frail, shaky.

I was chill and faint, pushing myself on with pure will. I had to tell her what I'd realised. She needed to know.

So I summoned the last scraps and told her, 'I am Mercy.'

A sudden exhalation beyond the mirror. Then the words, 'Mercy, my child.'

I heard a pattering and scratching on the other side of the glass. First the uncombed black hair came into view, then her face, pale and wild, eyes wide, vivid. And I gasped too, shocked to the quick, seeming to look into the very face of my mother at fifteen.

'Mother? Rebecca?'

The girl's dirty brow creased. 'You. As pale as an angel.'

'I am alive. I am Mercy. He's dead now.' I said it again. 'I'm here.'

'I'm so sorry. You understand?' Her eyes begged for the response that I came here to give.

'Yes,' I told her. 'I forgive you. Of course I do.'

'I was a child.'

'I know.'

I watched a weak smile creep over her features, then the blackness seemed to strengthen and move across her, beginning to dissolve her form into nothingness. 'You can go now,' I said. 'I'm going too. I love you. You are forgiven. Mercy.'

'It's ended?' she asked with only her eyes.

'It's ended,' I repeated to the reflection.

Chapter Forty-Eight

And so I walked like a ghost through the memories of my afterlife. For that was all it was: Mercedes Asquith was a phantom self, following in the footsteps of the bastard child, Mercy.

Mercy – a life that was what? A plea? A statement? A gift? Perhaps a destiny.

I don't know.

I guess I never will now.

But then I've been guessing a lot. I guessed that Mum had tried to tell me, back then before she died. I think she knew she wasn't going to hold on much longer, though it was the last thing she wanted to disclose. She must have known what the consequences would have been. I was a sticky little bugger. Tenacious and, to a certain extent, ruthless too. I obviously inherited that from my father. She must have expected I'd find out, bring it into the light. And I'm guessing she kept the certificate with the coordinates on to guide me to the document, as some poorly thought-out insurance policy. Hoping it might at least offer some power of negotiation if I ever discovered what happened to her, and who my father was.

We were both naïve on that count. Locked into our world of Essex witches, far removed from the power struggles of those whose path we had stumbled across. In some ways we were pawns, just like our ancestors before us. The female kind, that is. Except this time, I didn't do what I was told. Though it cost me my life. Well, my identity anyway. This new one is several incarnations away from the one I took off Felix. And he's right – I'm untraceable. You've got to give me credit for that – I never was a stupid girl. Naïve perhaps, but not thick. And that's how I've managed to get word to Dan, who is doing okay now. He was going to tell me about what he knew when he saw me face to face. But obviously events conspired against us. He understands why I had to go. And he's told Dad too. My *real* dad, Ted Asquith, who loved me and reared me and earned my respect. That's what the word 'father' means to me. The blood running through my veins is that of an unwanted sperm donor who gave me life – but took my life, and who I blame for sending my poor mum to an early grave. I've had to think a lot about this and it's not been a pleasant journey, but I've worked out that a child born of rape is not a child of hate. I can see that from the way my mother cherished me, protected me, loved me. And look at Rebecca too; searching across the centuries for her lost daughter, finding her line at last and finding too that they heard her cries.

For I believe somewhere back in the past, Rebecca is my ancestor. Which means I am born from her child, Mercy. My real name – that was the clue.

I've heard no more from Rebecca. I'm hoping she's passed on now too. It was a strange tale and Joe's still not convinced I wasn't mad with grief – projecting my neuroses, enacting some freakish psychodrama that eventually uncovered an ancient truth. But I know that trying to explain it fully would be like trying to pin down why Hopkins started the witch hunts in the first place or fixated on the Wests. There's too much gone into the darkness for us ever to know for sure. And sometimes you just have to accept that and move on.

That's not to say you forget about it. That leads to ignorance and blindness. You commemorate it, like Flick is doing – bless her. The campaign I see on the website is gaining momentum too. And I see Amelia Whitting's name signed up to it. Good for her. Good for all of you. It's about time it happened. You see, when you fully acknowledge that bad stuff, you can at last draw a line under it and turn a new page. Start afresh. But you never forget and you sure as hell never let it happen again. Believe me – this is something I have some experience of.

The night that ended the life of my cousin forces outside of the mundane world were in control and coming through me. I was simply an instrument for their reckoning. But I took the advice of shamans: 'When you walk in the woods, never leave tracks.' Well, I didn't, but you won't know that till now. I'm not sure exactly how much you do know. Or how much damage Cutt's people managed to limit. I can't imagine they could have got it all. We've been monitoring the papers over here, whenever we can get them. I see the tide is turning against him now, just like it did with his ancestor, Master Hopkins. But I doubt he can run away from all this. Dan knows what happened with his medication was most likely down to them. And he's prepared to testify. So too, the break-in had to be them. I don't buy the kids on drugs theory. Not now.

They must have started the Phelps's fire and all those other things too. You can work it out yourself. Or the police can. Send them a copy of this. It's the truth about what happened. And I'll send them the recording of Felix, which should back up what's written down here: self-defence.

When you get this, Maggie, I guess you'll know that Mercedes Asquith has gone. Ceased to exist. Flown away like a moth into the night. But honestly Mags, it's okay.

Really it is.

I know this is not exactly what you wanted, and I'm sorry I've missed a deadline or two, but I've had quite a bit going on.

Still, you wanted something 'contentious' and I reckon this will hit the spot. Do what you will with it. Get a book deal. I don't care how the truth comes out. But if it does then maybe we'll come back some time. Just print this and we'll see. Should get a front page or two.

Sometimes when Joe goes into town, I drag my chair out onto the porch and sit staring at the ocean. My mind is clearer now. Gone are the days when it used to buzz around like a bumblebee, chasing thought after thought. So I meditate upon what would have happened if I'd never been drawn to the witches or if Mum had never thought about writing or never wanted to get into publishing. But then I'm wondering myself out of existence. And although I wouldn't have wanted things to pan out as they did, I am certainly glad to be here and I intend to enjoy it as much as I can.

There is a strange tranquillity that follows me now and I think I know what that is. As much as I struggled with it when I first realised, I get it now. You see, I am the Witchfinder, descendant of Hopkins, the last child of my line. And like he

I have too hunted witches and so found my witch. But the difference between me and that Witchfinder of old is instead of fear I brought mercy.

And that is so very neat. It is almost perfection. A justice or symmetry of sorts. So, dear Maggie, it's all here.

Take it and have Mercy.

Much love,
From me.
Your friend.

Note to the Reader

Using Occam's Razor, i.e. the theory that the simplest explanation is most probably the correct one, it seems pretty likely (however unjust and boring) that Matthew Hopkins met his end of tuberculosis quietly, surrounded by his family in Manningtree. Although there were consequently many outbreaks of similar witch hunting, using the methods he outlined in his *Discovery of Witches*, the consensus is that it was his book that travelled out to New England, not he. For a full and very evocative book which examines the Civil War witch hunts, I would recommend to any reader what was commended to me; *Witchfinders, A Seventeenth-Century English Tragedy* by Malcolm Gaskill.

Rebecca West did testify against her mother and friends at the age of fifteen. There are no documents in existence that record what happened to her thereafter.

The story of the boy and his mare and all of the witches' tales are, regrettably, true.

Q & A with Syd Moore

Where did the idea for Witch Hunt come from?

I think the idea of writing something about the witches was always lurking at the back of my mind (just like Sadie), but it fired up while I was researching my first book *The Drowning Pool*. I came across the statistic about the number of Essex folk indicted for witchcraft and was pretty taken aback. I never had any idea that so many were accused. I had heard about the Pendle witch trials, the Scottish witch trials, Salem and the terrible continental craze for witch hunts but I hadn't come across much about the Essex witches. Which was odd really as I was born and bred in the county. So I started reading around the subject and that's when I found out about Matthew Hopkins and his witch hunt.

I'd heard of the Witchfinder General before but I had a notion that his spree took place in Suffolk and Norfolk and that Essex had little to do with it. When I mentioned this to friends and acquaintances I found I wasn't on my own in that regard: many of my fellow Essex girls and boys were also oblivious to the local connection. As I drilled down further and uncovered the stories of the witches, I found myself becoming not only upset and saddened but also outraged. Their stories sank into me. In fact, I couldn't get them out of my head. The one that I kept going back to was that of Rebecca West. The idea that this poor fifteen-year-old was responsible for the death of her mother and her friends was appalling. I mean, she was only fifteen! I remember what I was like at that age – not very responsible, nor sensible nor long-sighted. Then, when I looked at her in the wider context of Hopkins' evolution/deterioration into a full-blown Witchfinder, I could see that her complicity quite possibly fanned his monstrous ego and bloodlust, thereby indirectly condemning hundreds of other souls to dreadful deaths. I tried to imagine how she felt after the trial and the executions, and was inspired from that daydream to write what would later become the prologue of the novel.

How did you write it? Did you plot it out before you started?
I knew Sadie had to have a connection to either Hopkins or Rebecca or both, so I plotted those connections out first of all. In my first draft Sadie's mum, Rosamund, was alive for the first third of the book, which allowed me to explore the parallel mother-daughter relationship with that of Anne West/Rebecca West and Rebecca's daughter, Mercy. It was all good stuff but it didn't really belong in a ghost story so I cut it out. I haven't discarded it though and hope someday I might return to it, maybe as a short story.

How much research do you do for your books?
A lot. It usually starts with the internet, then moves on to books, then I'm off round the country viewing original documents and authentic contemporary accounts, visiting sites, interviewing people. I love that side of it, and quite often experience strange synchronicities on my travels: when I was in Chelmsford researching, I went to find the spot where the gallows were erected for the July 1645 executions. I was early for my next appointment and, fortuitously, seeing that there was a pub (the Saracen's Head) right opposite where the site would have been, decided to go in an get a drink then sit outside and soak up the atmosphere, make

notes etc. Walking in I heard my name called out and found myself face to face with one of my old students. When I told her about my research she made a few calls and, within an hour, we were able to descend into the bowels of the old pub and view these horrid, tiny cells which, local custom insists, were where the witches were held before trial. It was very spooky and gave me a lot of material for several ghostly scenes.

Lots of the research for *Witch Hunt* distressed me, mostly because this stuff was real – people had to live and die through it. It was a terribly, bloody time and I'm glad I live in a twenty-first-century England.

At the moment I'm writing about an eerie fictional village on a remote island in Essex. It has a creepy *Wicker Man* atmosphere which I'm having lots of fun with. To develop my descriptions I'm visiting similar places, seeking out derelict churches and making weird 'fairies' out of coat hangers, fruit and candles. I love this job!

Class seems to be a big theme. Do you want to expand on that?

Witch hunts were about scapegoating and power, or lack of it. It was unusual to find the rich being victimised. When Hopkins got involved he used finger-pointing and neighbourly feuds to whip up hysteria, detect witches and so exact a fee. He made the whole thing into a commercial venture. And I thought that it was important for Sadie to be (or to think she was) an Essex Girl as that stereotype is on the receiving end of a whole host of pejorative judgements about sex and class, just like the witches. It made Sadie more likely to sympathise with the underdogs.

Some of your scenes are terrifying. Do you ever scare yourself?
Yes and no. I scared myself with the Pitsea station chapter. The little boy hanging was such a pitiful image. However, once I get those kind of scenes out of my head and onto the page they stop 'haunting' me, so to speak! I think it's a bit like 'tag' – the stories touch/scare me, I write them down and send them out into the world to touch and scare others. What I hope to do is raise awareness of what happened back then and also, at some point, try to garner enough interest and funding to erect a monument to those lives that were lost whilst simultaneously drawing attention to the fact that witch hunts are in some form, shamefully, still trundling on.

For discussion

Reading groups may wish to use some of the following questions to generate discussion:

- To what aspects of the novel can you apply the term 'witch hunt'?

- Moths proliferate the story. What do they signify?

- What is happening in the hospital scene with Dan?

- Does Sadie's character change as the novel progresses? How and why?

- The story of the witches could be seen to be very much a female story. To what extent does it resonate with male readers?

THE DROWNING POOL

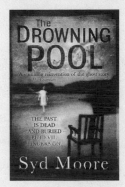

Death is not the end . . .

Relocated to a coastal town with her young son Alfie, widowed teacher Sarah Grey is slowly rebuilding her life. But following a séance one drunken night, she begins to be plagued by horrific visions. Her attempts to explain them away are dashed when Alfie starts to see them too, and soon it seems that they are targets of a terrifying haunting.

Convinced that the ghost is that of a 19th century local witch and her own namesake, Sarah delves into local folklore and learns that the witch was seen as evil incarnate. When a series of old letters surface, Sarah discovers that nothing and no one is as it seems, maybe not even the ghost of Sarah Grey . . .

The Drowning Pool is a classic ghost story with a modern twist – the perfect chiller for fans of *The Birthing House* and *Sacrifice*.

ISBN 978-1-84756-266-1
£6.99

AVON

For more information about Syd Moore,
visit her Facebook page Syd-Moore
or follow her on Twitter @SydMoore1

Follow Avon on
Twitter@AvonBooksUK
and
Facebook@AvonBooksUK
For news, giveaways and
exclusive author extras

THE CITY OF SHADOWS

A missing woman.
Two mysterious murders.
A city shrouded in secrets.

*'She looked up at the terraced house, with the closed shutters
and the big room at the end of the long unlit corridor where
the man who smiled too much did his work. She climbed the
steps and knocked on the door . . .'*

Dublin 1934: Detective Stefan Gillespie arrests a German
doctor and encounters Hannah Rosen desperate to find her
friend Susan, a Jewish woman who disappeared after a love
affair with a Catholic priest.

When the bodies of a man and woman are found buried
in the Dublin mountains, Stefan becomes involved in a
complex case that takes him, and Hannah, across Europe to
Danzig.

Stefan and Hannah are drawn together in an unfamiliar
city where the Nazi Party are gaining power. But in their
quest to uncover the truth of what happened to Susan, they
find themselves in grave danger . . .

ISBN 978-1-84756-346-0
£7.99

A V O N

Killer Reads.com

The one-stop shop for the best in crime and thriller fiction

Be the first to get your hands on the **latest releases, exclusive interviews** and **sneak previews** from your favourite authors.

Browse the site and sign up to the newsletter for our pick of the **hottest** articles as well as a chance to **win** our monthly competition!

Writing so good it's criminal